A sav
shifte

BY DD PRINCE

©COPYRIGHT 2020 – DDPRINCE.COM

All rights reserved. This book is the intellectual property of the author and may not be copied in any way, shape, or form other than brief quotes for review purposes. Please ensure you support the rights of authors by buying or borrowing books from authorized sources. Book piracy is not harmless. It's theft and hurts authors in many ways.

Thank you for respecting an author's hard work.

If you enjoy this book, please consider leaving a review. It truly helps indie authors succeed in bringing you more stories.

Join DD's Chickadees on Facebook for fun, teasers, sales, and freebies as well as giveaways, fun chat about book boyfriends, and most of all… shenanigans.

http://facebook.com/groups/ddprincefangroup

Subscribe to The Scoop, DD Prince's free email newsletter: http://ddprince.com/newsletter-signup/

Dedication:
~To my sister~
Who told me she wanted more paranormal romance.
Who supports my crazy dream.
Who is always there for me.
Who sometimes has trouble reading my sex scenes because she can't help but wonder which parts are derived from my actual sex life. *(Uh... Not nearly as many as I'd like...)*
Kelly, I *fucking* love you like crazy.

Author's Note

SHIFTER ROMANCES DON'T all follow the exact same guidelines. There are different elements in world-building that are common, such as a pack hierarchy (alpha, beta, omega), female heat cycles, fated mates, marking with biting, and in some cases – knotting during intercourse (when the male sex organ grows extra-large while inside the woman, locking it in). My hero doesn't have all the facts about shifter culture due to his upbringing, but learns more about his nature as the story progresses. Shifters and other supernatural beings live in secret in this 'world' and in this world, wolf shifters have the ability to shapeshift between their human and wolf form at will. My shifter wolf has hibernated each winter. I'm aware regular wolves don't.

This story has a very 'alpha' hero with animalistic behaviors. In his world, he's classed as a 'super-alpha' so some of his behaviors are *extreme*.

This is a steamy story with lots of carnal behavior.

This isn't considered a dark romance by me, but does visit some dark subject matter in part of the story. If you're already a DD Prince books reader, you won't find it more graphic than some of my dark romances. If you're new to me, I advise that there are some scenes readers might find upsetting.

1

IVY

"Anybody ever tell you that you look like a real-life Anime girl?" He leans forward, way too close to me, so I rear back.

I should not have come here.

I should not ever have let Megan talk me into this weekend. She just accused me of overreacting, but no. No way. This was not kosher – not remotely.

Why did I ignore my instincts back at that gas station when we met up with this guy? My momma and her sister told me, my whole life: Ivy, never *ever* ignore your gut. And I do. All the bloody time! Why don't I ever learn?

Megan? She's a backstabbing witch and that's why I have no choice but to leave without her. I'm officially done with her completely.

The sales pitch she used: two hundred bucks per person for a luxury waterfront chalet with everything included for the whole weekend. A pool. Hot tub. This place is supposed to have equal numbers guys and girls and be well-stocked with food and booze. Two to a room. We would share a room, she said, unless one of us wanted to spend the night with someone we met, then we'd discuss it. She assured me I wouldn't be turfed out of my room when I told her that *no way* would I let a guy move in on me that quickly.

I have been working my butt off for weeks and have had all sorts of family drama going on between my bridezilla sister's wedding, how my breaking up with a guy who also happens to be in her wedding is me trying to ruin her day, and my parents splitting up with Dad trying to worm his way back in after cheating on Mom, so I convinced myself that I deserved a weekend away. I needed it. I've been working my tail off and I deserve it.

Tired of family drama, I decided I'll ignore them all for the weekend. I'm having a mini family vacation (a vacation *from* my family).

The reality when we arrived? Chalet? Not quite. Stocked? Depends on your definition of stocked. Luxury? Nope. Not even close.

The reality: A two-bedroom single-story cottage. Not quite a dump, but nothing luxurious about it and it could work for two or maybe four people but no more than that. A hot tub, yes you could say that, but it was outside and filled with leaves. Yep, there was a pool, as advertised, but it's a small above-ground pool that is neither filled nor likely fillable as it looks like it's been sitting there empty for a decade. Oh, and it has a giant X on the side made of what looks like several layers of duct tape so filling it would probably not be wise.

I probably wouldn't have minded so much if everything else were as advertised. Not even close. The waterfront references? I guess... if a swampy pond on the property counts. The large living room has two pull-out couches and there's a closet with three more air beds in it. No privacy unless you're lucky enough to get one of the two bedrooms. And they don't have locks on the doors. In fact, neither does the bathroom.

Uh... nope.

The fridge has some cheap off-brand hot dogs, some beer, and there are some bags of chips and boxes of cereal on the counter along with a big bag of marshmallows. All this is complete with two boxes of wine and a bottle of gut-rot whisky.

There aren't an equal number of guys and girls here, though, and that's the biggest problem of them all. I can rough-it for a weekend, sure, but with a bunch of strangers? Worse... a bunch of guys?

There are seven people, but Megan and I are the only girls. The guy who organized this bash scammed us. Or... Megan scammed me. And I'm totally, absolutely done with her. She can stay if she wants to, but I am gone.

I like my creature comforts, sure, but the problem here is less about the cabin and more about the other people here as well as the tone, which is overtly sexual.

She got wasted in less than an hour and talked like a sleazy horndog. Innuendoes up the wazoo! And she is right now in one of the bedrooms with two of the guys. Two! And if that's not bad enough, she's left me alone with the other three guys. They've been eyeing me like I'm prime rib and also eyeing one another likely trying to determine who is going to make a move.

One, I think, wants me for himself. The one who talked about Anime is the guy who met us at the gas station and something about him just completely creeps me out.

The other two, I'm fairly sure, are hoping I'll be like Megan and let them both at me together. They look like they're over in the corner whisper-negotiating.

I am not down for it. None of it. I'm about to find my way out of here. I'm just thinking it over carefully because the guy who wants me for himself? I have a sinking sick feeling that he might be the sort to try to stop me from leaving.

Don't think I'm a jerk for leaving Megan in a cabin with five men. I tried to talk her out of it. I'd pulled her aside three separate times and she gave me the brush-off each time about my concerns. The third time… before she went to the bedroom with two of them? She was adamant that we were staying.

"What are you gonna do, have a threesome?" I rolled my eyes, totally not serious, but she smiled like a cat that got the cream.

She *was* having a threesome. With two strangers we met an hour ago!

"I'm not doing anything with any of those guys," I insisted, keeping my voice low.

"So, don't. That doesn't mean I'm not gonna. This is a bucket list item for me, baby. See you in a few hours, or … at work Monday if you decide you have to leave." She shrugged and turned to go.

"What happened to never leaving a sister behind?"

"You wanna join in?" Her eyebrows rose.

"No. I mean leaving me out here with three men. This whole thing is ridiculous. We don't know these guys. We need to go."

I followed her to the counter where she mixed another alcoholic beverage with a heavy hand. "I'm not going. Feel free to leave this sister behind."

"Don't think I won't," I warned on a whisper.

"Fine." She shrugged. "Boz or Josh will run me back tomorrow. Or Sunday."

She sashayed off, winking at the other guys.

"You're not thinkin' of goin', are ya?" The tall and wide grizzly of a guy asks.

This is the one I think wants me to himself and he is creeping me out to the degree it's difficult to hide that my skin is crawling.

"Naw, I'm good," I say and sit with my cup of Sprite. I've poured it into a glass with ice to make the contents questionable. It's straight Sprite that I brought myself. They don't need to know that.

And I wait exactly seven minutes, dodging dumb questions, encouragement to consume some shots (and a hit off a bong, which I decline) with dark looks from the lone guy, longing looks from another who keeps trying to do some sort of silent communication with his buddy, and that buddy is seeming like he's more interested in his lack of a cell signal than anything else. He seems more agitated than anything and he's suddenly of concern to me as much as the lone guy because the way he's going on about not having a cell signal, he seems capable of snapping and getting violent.

At the seven-minute mark, I jump up and exclaim, "Oh! Speaking of Hentai..." I have no idea what they're talking about but it's a segue that should and does buy their attention, particularly the creepy Anime-loving guy, giving me a minute to scram – "Right back, boys. Got something you have gotta see." I smile brightly as they all look at me with intrigue, even the guy obsessed with his phone.

I don't even take my jacket, hoping it won't arouse suspicion that I am most definitely not coming back. I can sacrifice my $29 jean jacket for the occasion. Thankfully, my purse and overnight bag are still in my car, my cell phone in my skirt pocket.

Megan took her stuff right in; I wanted to assess first. And it's a good thing, too.

I will my body to be casual as I walk out. My knees are jittery and my hands are trembling, but I'm doing my best to not show it because by the look of the one grizzly dude, who is huge and probably three times my weight, he could try and grab me and this will turn icky and maybe even grisly real fast.

I lean into the car casually, without shutting the door because I see that the grizzly one is watching out the window. I rifle through my bag, keeping one eye on him and as soon as I see he's turned his head, looking like he's talking to someone, I climb in, shut the door, click all the locks, then reverse the heck out of there!

I reverse down the tricky, long driveway, past the three other parked vehicles and head out onto the main road. The whole proposition is daunting, because on my left there's a hill going up and, to my right there's a hill going down.

That cabin is a shack of ill-repute. Five guys and just two girls with a threesome happening just an hour into the night?

Screw you, Megan, for putting me in this position. I hope you don't have to bang all five of them, unless, you know... it's what you want. *Grr.* Bucket list? Bucket is right.

Fitting because in my high school, that was the name we had for slutty girls. *Buckets.* Megan? Definite bucket.

About Megan? I only met her two weeks ago. We were having a laugh; she was a fun distraction at work, one of those inappropriately funny girls with absolutely zero filter. She made my days go by faster despite a lot of schlepping and many roadblocks to get things just right for our grand opening. I found it surprising she was in management based on how she acted, but I've had all sorts of drama in my regular life so working with her was a fun distraction. I let myself get charmed into this weekend. And she charmed me all right because I have a car and she doesn't. She insisted it'd be well worth the drive and the $200 and said she'd fill my gas tank, which she did. Megan said her friend organized these parties all the time and I was going to have a blast.

I queried that I thought she said it was her cousin and she waved it off that he's *practically* a cousin. This was my first red flag. Too bad I ignored it. She told me he organized these parties regularly and rented swanky places for them. He's had writeups in the club scene because his parties are *that* legendary. He's had two couples get married in the past year who met at his parties. He usually charges $300 per person or more, she said, but she got me the *friends and family deal.*

She also said we were lucky to get this invite because usually his parties had a long wait list, but this one came up last minute. She said she was done a favor by him – we got to jump a long line.

After working our asses off at the boutique gearing up for the grand opening, which happens in a few days, this getaway was to be our reward.

I just got myself transferred to the new location because it was way closer to my apartment and while I got promoted to assistant manager, Megan got transferred from yet another location where she was already an assistant manager. We'd work different shifts but were on the same rung of the corporate ladder. The busyness and drama of the past few weeks had been exhausting. The getaway I let myself get talked into because I had a bad argument with my family over bullshit to do with my Bridezilla sister's upcoming wedding, being tired of the tug of war between my recently separated parents, and my recent breakup and mostly because I felt like living it up and letting loose for once. I guess my judgement was clouded.

My bad. Because my judgement about Megan was clearly way, *way* off. She manipulated me. She didn't care that we were the only girls and I suspected if she did know, she left that detail out worried she'd lose out on her ride there as well as have me asking for my two hundred bucks back.

Ridiculous. I wasn't usually one to slut shame, but she only just met those guys. And she was being competitive. I knew it three minutes into arriving that she wanted to be the one they looked at. She's attractive, but she's one of those girls who needs to know she's the most desired girl in the room.

Thankfully once the store opened, I wouldn't have to interact with her much.

AND NOW HERE I AM, driving down a long and winding road in a densely forested rural area miles from any semblance of civilization. It's dark. No street lights. These roads are not maintained, and I don't even feel safe on them. Despite lack of streetlights, though, it's already after nine o'clock and while dark, the moon seems exceptionally bright and it's taking up what seems like a whole lot of space in the sky.

I have no signal on my phone and even my GPS won't pick up my location. This was the road I took in, I'm sure I'm backtracking, which would mean I'll get back to the gas station where we met *Grizzly Grisly* any minute now. From there, I can find my way back to the highway and I'm sure to have a cell signal again.

Ten Minutes Later...

Still no sign of that gas station. Or even another road. I'm driving slowly and carefully on this road, but it's like it'll never end. I'm sure I wasn't on it this long on the way in. It makes no sense.

Out of nowhere, I see something large and dark in my headlights coming at me. It's as if my headlights go extra bright for an instant, too bright for my own eyes, and as I squint I catch the flash of reflective eyes, but not on a cat, a big animal and at that same instant, hear the clunk of the animal sailing up my hood. Hard.

Oh no.

I swerve right and the animal slides left while I watch a spiderweb-like crack sprawl across my windshield under the mass of it. The animal falls off to the side and the damage to my windshield glints in the moonlight. The moon sticks out, a massive glowing three-dimensional orb directly ahead of me. I slam on the brakes, strangely feeling like I could actually hit the moon as my car veers way too close to that drop to my right. My gaze hits my rear-view mirror, catching motion. Whatever it is that I hit, it rises slowly like a dark and ominous shadow. It moves, staggering as it does, before it disappears from view. I give my head a shake. Was that a bear? A wolf? Too big to be a wolf but not quite wide enough to be a brown bear, I don't think.

I turn the car off to the sound of nothing but nature – nature that sounds unusually loud in my ears. I hope that whatever it is, I didn't hurt it enough that it'll suffer a slow death. Poor thing.

I look ahead and it dawns I'm on a funny angle, pointing toward the sharp incline. I turn the car back on, but then my belly swoops. It feels like I'm sliding. I brake while I take a breath and then throw the car into reverse. The tires do nothing but spin and then my car lurches forward some more, sliding a good three or four feet, I think, and I squeal in shock.

It feels like I'm sinking.

It's been a cool spring so far, but maybe the ground is finally thawing, because my car is clearly sinking into mud. When Megan and I got to the cabin, the ground was pretty squishy between the cabin and the car, so I tiptoed carefully in, hoping I wouldn't ruin my new purple boots that perfectly match the new chunky streaks in my blonde hair.

I'm stuck. In the muck. How fitting after the evening I've had. I set my forehead against the cool steering wheel as if it'll help.

There's another lurch, then the car rocks, as if something has hit underneath the front and I jerk as my eyes dart ahead into the darkness, but I see nothing.

I see nothing, but I sure feel and hear something. The car slides forward another foot or so and stops.

Fuzz. A big tree is not far ahead of me. If I slide another six feet, I'm guessing my car will hit the tree.

Crunch!

The car doesn't move but the crunch sound is a bad sign and came from the passenger side.

I see nothing, but I hear something hit the car again and my car moves back just a little but then lurches forward and there's all sorts of noise out there as I slide further.

Have I angered a bear because I hit it and now it's trying to enact vengeance on my poor little purple car? It could've been a massive cat like a panther with those reflective eyes, but I don't know. Are there panthers around here? Or mountain lions?

I look at my phone. Still no signal.

Another noise tweaks me, but this time, it's not coming from the front or the back. And it feels like I'm being watched.

Something is looking in the window at me. I gasp, holding my phone in my hand and taking in those reflective eyes, the long line of fur down to a big black nose. A wolf. A massively humungous wolf, bigger than any wolf I've ever seen in a zoo or even on television, is peering through the window. It sniffs and condensation forms on the glass around its face.

Shit! I think it wants to eat me.

I haul air into my lungs. And then... nothing. I'm frozen, in shock, as I see those eyes on me.

I can't breathe.

I finally exhale with a "Shoo".

I wave at it as if to add emphasis.

At least I'm inside the car, but I'm utterly trapped here for the night because no way in Hades am I climbing out if there's the slightest chance a scary dire wolf waits for me. Okay, I know dire wolves are extinct, but that thing was huge. I'll just have to stay put until morning so I can be sure it's gone before I can leg it to look for a phone signal.

It drops back to all fours, I guess, as I no longer see it. I lean forward and then I gasp in shock as I now see a man. A man is unfolding from a bent position and stretching his back as he stares at me now from the same spot.

"What the fuuuck?" I whisper.

He's huge. He has long, curly hair.

He's naked.

He.

Is.

Naked!

I actually hear the shocked blinks I make, which sounds as loud to me as those dolls I had as a kid with the eyes that open and shut.

What in tarnation?

2

TYSON

When I knew her scent was directly in front of me, the urge was fierce. The urge to claim. This is urgency I've never felt.

Now that I've seen her face – I need past all this metal and glass ... to get to her.

Yes, to claim her, but also so I can calm her, so I can then claim her.

I've never had the urge to calm or claim. The sensations in me are foreign.

I search for a way in. It takes a second to remember how these things open. It's been a long time since I've been in this form – man form. Fingers, thumbs. Standing so tall. Feeling the chill of the night air with the absence of my thick black coat.

I pull the handle and it fails to release the door, the door that prevents me from getting to her. Anger bubbles up and I want to use my cock to pierce a hole through it to get to her. My cock aches so much to be inside her it feels like it's a possible solution to my problem. Fuck through anything in my way so I can find my way into that heat, that mouth-watering scent. She's mine. I know it.

Finally.

I slow my reactions to offer myself a chance to think. Think of how to get to her. Think like my man form needs to think.

I lost logic as I tried to breach the machine in wolf form after it struck me. I was raging, I was reacting as wolf, trying to tear through the thing that kept me from what I want. The machine...car... slid and I then tried to halt it, but it took me with it. My feet sank deep into the wet earth before I backed off and came out of that state where I do things that I later decide made no sense. It occasionally happens when something is in front of me that falls outside my natural instincts. It's usually to do with people.

And now I've peered through the glass and laid eyes on her.
She's small, she's frightened, she's beautiful, and she needs me.
She. Is. Mine.

As soon as I knew the sight of my wolf frightened her, a strange sensation hit me, and I shifted spontaneously to man. I haven't been a man in a long time and a spontaneous shift has not happened to me for much longer than that. It's a time that I recall, though it's foggy in my mind, when I couldn't control which form I was in. I hated that loss of control. I don't want it now.

Uncle... it had something to do with him. What?

It hits me. Uncle left. He left me with the supplies because he said he had things to do, errands he had to complete without me because I just couldn't stop shifting. I raged as my body changed from wolf to man to wolf to man for days and days until I found a way to slow it and it kept getting stuck in between. He saw that and told me to practice doing it so I could stop in the middle on command like my father used to do. Before he was killed by his mutinous pack.

Memories wash over me. Memories of dried meat, dry bread, canned fruit and pain and loneliness as my body repeatedly and traitorously shifted without my control. Uncle shouting. Uncle swearing at me. Uncle leaving me for a long time while it continued over and over. Uncle shouting. Uncle and his whisky.

A growl rolls up from deep in me at the memories, but I have no time now for rage because this is her. This is her.

My one. My only. She does exist.

Her eyes have grown larger and the fragrance in the air is fear. She fears something. Me.

She's holding her breath in and behaves like trapped prey. She is trapped, and I'll free her. I'll free her so that I can claim her. She's no one's prey; she's mine. Or she will be when I mount, bite, and knot her.

When I caught her aroma in the air before the sky had completely darkened, I knew. I knew it was why I was here, why I'd felt so aware of everything around me, why I wandered so close to the town. Why my thinking had changed, part way to man.

I've stayed deep in the forest other than during winter when I sleep in the den. I woke just a few nights ago, late waking from hibernation, and for days I've been on the hunt, feasting, gathering strength after my long winter sleep, but staying closer than usual to my den. It was a long winter; I can tell by how weak I felt. And I felt like I woke too early. Yet, it was later than it should be. It made no sense, but I just followed my nose and hunted, feasted, and then today, it hit me.

Energy fizzled in me when I woke, and I couldn't decipher my actions, couldn't know why I remained near the town, why I was feeling so strange, until that scent hit. And I hunted for it like I'd never hunted for anything, but without my typical skills. It's been disorienting. Everything was wrong. The sky, the air, the scents, me...

I was disoriented but I wouldn't stop until I could see the female behind that aroma, could know for sure that she's mine. And now I have, and I do.

I like how she looks. I like the way the sight of her shape makes my cock ache. I don't like how frightened she is. I need to get at her so I can cover her with my body, let her inhale my scent so she'll learn it, so she'll know that when I'm near her she's safe. So she'll know the scent of her mate.

My small female has long and shiny hair the color of sunshine, with a few chunks the shade of blueberries. She has long eyelashes and long legs, though she's not tall. She has pert breasts. She reminds me of how I imagined the sprites in the stories Uncle Cornelius would read me when I was a boy about little shapely fairies that would flit around at dusk. I never saw one, but painted one from my vision of what they might look like. If that painting is still in the house somewhere, I want to see it... see if it resembles her.

I remember that painting and remember wanting to have a sprite of my own but there's a lot I don't yet remember.

It takes time to adjust after not shifting for a year, but I know it's been more than two years, more than four I think. This is why my brain is hazy with confusion.

But there's no time to adjust. I need her. I only hope it doesn't take me so long to adjust that it puts her in peril.

This is what brought me close to the town today. This was why I was thinking halfway between wolf and man. Something changed. *Her.*

I'd woken far too early to hunt, though ravenous and restless until my nose twitched with interest like never before, sending me in aimless circles for what felt like an eternity until I was hit with the onslaught of her scent.

It slammed into me with such physical force that all my fur stood on end as I tried to process the sensations, sensations that were utterly foreign.

As I picked up other aromas with hers, I grew angrier and angrier as I tried to track her because I immediately knew... I knew she was mine. I also knew there was an unpleasant male scent near her. Furthermore, I now knew that any of my previous attempts to find the woman who would be mine was useless because this scent attacked me. I didn't look for it. It found me as if meant to be.

I knew, intuitively what it was. Who she was. The one. My only one.

And the fragrance... the best scent to ever hit my nose, uniquely her was also infused with something wrong. Not quite fear from her but something like fear. I suspected it had to do with the male scent near her. And that made me dizzy with rage.

The moon wasn't right tonight. Too large. Too close. Instinct told me it had been interfered with. Based on the proximity of her scent, it should've taken no time to find her. Uncle once told me that sometimes witches interfered with things. That sometimes they made the road lead to new places. That sometimes they trapped you where they needed you to stay so that they could complete some purpose either for you or in spite of you.

This night felt reminiscent of those things that Uncle talked about sometimes when he would get in one of his dark moods. The dark moods happened often throughout my life and were often fueled by whisky. I would listen, let him speak though his words often didn't make sense, and then leave him be. Most times when I asked questions, his answers were non-answers, or he grew agitated and didn't answer at all.

When her scent moved too far away, I was confused for a time but finally, the haze of confusion lifted enough for me to surmise that she got into a car and left. I hadn't set eyes on her yet at that stage but knew the scent of cars and knew the scent of this particular car, already having had it imprint on me, but tracking that scent isn't as easy as tracking a person or prey. I got dizzy from the onslaught of emotion I was feeling which meant I lost time and the car scent. When the scent got stronger as I scoured while tracking the car, my nose to the ground, finally, the fragrance picked up in intensity and got not only stronger, but the onslaught of the strength of her aroma was so powerful that it disoriented me and because of that, the car struck me.

This was my fault, not hers. If I'd been shifting each year as uncle told me we were meant to do, I'd have more clarity right now. I'd have gotten to her sooner. And now I've shifted to man and the overpowering aroma has me hard, ready, disoriented, and anxious because I need to get to her and yet this car she's in prevents it. And I want her. I want to claim her. And it's in the way. And my head feels...fuzzy.

It has always felt foreign to be in this body. I don't think I've ever enjoyed it, not since that first time I shifted as a child and felt wolf was my true form. But I feel like I will enjoy this form more when I get her under me. The air is cold, and my nails have receded as have my teeth in a scenario that feels like I should be on alert. I feel defenseless out here like this in the chill. How will I adequately protect her if I'm like this?

I will my body to shift back, or attempt it, but it fails and I'm still man. This shift was not a conscious choice, instead a need. And despite how foreign it is, it occurs to me that it's necessary. How can I help her if I'm wolf? Perhaps I'm man right now because my instinct tells me I need to be. For her. I need to listen to my instinct.

In my man form I'm peering in through the glass at my female who is startled and frightened at the sight of me. She was shocked a moment earlier when I was wolf and now she is both frightened and confused. I see it on her face and smell it in the air. Even more than when her car struck me. She fears me even more now, it seems, than when I was wolf. I'll get to her, calm her, and then mount, mark, and claim her.

Uncle directed me to woo them at that bar, but I never felt like I was good at that. Successful always, but never comfortable doing it. I have no need of wooing this time, only claiming, because this one belongs with me.

I know she's not a female of my kind, but that doesn't matter. I know she's mine and feel no disappointment. The opposite. Her fragrance called to me; it woke the dormant man in me.

My wolf waits. Intrigued.

I pound on the window and ponder how to get her out. Can she open the door from inside?

Even though I've shifted annually almost all my life other than this last few years, I speak very rarely. Only if I must. It looks like I must. She fears me; she doesn't know she's mine.

I'd rather show her she's mine than speak the words of it to her. Metal and glass prevent that.

The haziness is dissipating too slowly. I need more clarity.

3

IVY

I'm trying to work this out...

Seconds after the wolf disappears from my view, a man stands in the same place. The exact same place. A muscled, huge, naked man.

My forehead crinkles. Can't be.

Was that this guy's wolf? Where is it? And where did he come from?

The exact same place? No. No. My brain is racing at turbo-speed, trying to make sense of what my eyes have just seen; trying to tell me the explanation – an explanation that just... it

JUST

CAN'T

BE.

He pulls on the door handle and I gasp. It's locked, thank God, so he doesn't gain entry. A long moment passes while he stares at me thoughtfully before he speaks.

"Open this," he demands in a rough, raspy voice.

I hear the sound first and then see rain as it begins to patter on my roof and trail down the windows of the car.

He pulls on the handle again and it doesn't give.

"Open it. Now."

Holy shit. What the heck? I've gone from the frying pan into the fire. I have never been so afraid in my life. The rain is picking up now and this guy is drenched. Where did he come from and where's the wolf? I need to see the wolf, so I'll know my initial reaction is wrong, that this guy isn't – I shake the thought that's circling my brain before it has a chance to fully form.

"Y-you better go." I find my voice. "There's a wolf out there. It was just here!"

"Is this door damaged?" he asks, ignoring my warning.

"What?"

"Can you open from there?"

"I – locked it."

"Open it."

"Wh-why?"

"I need … in." His eyes implore me to open the door. But not in a sweet or kind way, as if it's urgent.

No. No no no. This isn't right.

"There's a wolf out there! You better be careful, or it'll get you. I hit it with my car by accident and I think it's pissed at me. You better go!" I say. "It's huge. Did you see it?"

Maybe I'll see them both now and know it's not true. My eyes try to scan the space behind him.

His expression changes.

God, those eyes are filled with something. Something...

"Let me in," he cuts my thought short. "So I can be safe from the wolf." His mouth twitches as he fights a smirk. His fight fails.

A smirk? What the heck?

I jolt. "Is that wolf yours?" I ask.

"Yes." He jerks his chin at me. "Open."

"I can't." I shake my head vigorously.

This doesn't make sense. He's contradicting himself.

He stares a beat, like he's searching my face for something.

"I'll help," he says.

"Help?" I inquire.

What is he after? I can well imagine. Same thing every other man I've come across tonight wants.

"The car will –" he pauses and looks down the hill. "Will slide down this valley with the soft earth and at the bottom there's a river with..." he stops and considers something, "fast water. You need to open it so I can get you to safety."

He speaks in a stilted and measured way. It's as if English isn't his first language, but he has no accent.

It's got to be freezing out there, it's cold enough in here, and yet he's naked. It's dim, but I can tell that the guy is just massive. He has long and curly hair, hair as long as mine. He has huge shoulders, defined biceps. I halt my measurement before my eyes dart down his torso to where I already know he's got no clothes on.

I shake my head. "Sorry, but I gotta ask you to go. Someone is...um... coming back."

"Back?" He straightens. "Here? A male?"

"Maybe if you wanna help me you can call me a tow truck. My... my boyfriend is gone for help and he should be back any time now. In case, um... he didn't get far maybe you could call a tow truck to haul us out of here."

He has no clothes on, so how can he make a call when he has no pockets? I guess I'm just stalling him.

"Boyfriend?" he snaps. And then he growls.

Yep... growls.

He's just ... growling for a long time, animosity rolling off him.

This guy is not a potential helper. I mean, duh, 'cuz he's naked so that's my first clue, but he looks angry. This feels like it won't end well and shit, I'm unarmed. I'm unarmed with no phone signal in the dark, in the rain and this car is definitely going nowhere without being hauled back up onto the main road unless it's going down toward that fast-moving water.

"Open," he snaps.

I shake my head. "Sorry, but no."

I put my phone to my ear and there's no signal, but I pretend there is anyway.

"Are you almost back? Did you get help? Oh good. Okay!"

"What?" He tilts his head.

"Bye, sweetie." I pretend to hang up. "He's gonna be back any time so you can just go."

"Open the door," the guy demands.

"Sorry, no. I can't do that. I'm not opening the door to a naked man in the woods. Uh uh."

He frowns. "Obey me, female."

I twitch. Female?

His eyes glitter strangely. Light hits them or something and they go a reflective green, like... like a cat. No, like a wolf, the wolf who was likely pissed because I accidentally hit him with my car.

My blood runs cold.

"Name?" he demands.

The pace of the rain picks up and it's more than drenched him now. Why is he naked? The fact he's naked keeps rolling around trying to make me acknowledge the thought in my head that I'm trying to stop from surfacing is correct.

Can't be. Mind tricks. It's dark. I'm stressed out. I didn't really see what I thought I saw. He's probably just a crazy, naked axe murderer who dropped his axe somewhere.

My heartrate spikes and I feel like I can't get any air.

I look around me, looking for something to defend myself with. There's nothing. I mean, I'm in my car, but he could break my window.

He places his forehead against the glass for a moment and breathes deeply, like he's trying to calm himself.

The car feels like it moves just a little. God. I have it in park.

Mudslide. Rain, plus mud plus car nose pointing down a hill toward water (if he's correct) and I am in trouble. Big trouble.

I survey the landscape ahead. Trees everywhere. There is one big one directly in front of me. If my car moves more than a few feet down, it'll crunch into that tree. I won't go down to any fast-moving water, I don't think. It'll stay there. It's a huge tree. But it's gonna cause damage.

"What are you called?" he grinds out, breath fogging up the window.

My heart is galloping in my chest.

He pulls on the driver's door handle, this time looking angry and I see the door handle in his hand.

Oh no. What?

He tosses it, rounds the hood, and goes to the front passenger door and pulls on that handle.

"They're all locked," I tell him.

He breaks the passenger handle, too. He glares at it before tossing it.

"Stop it!" I shout angrily. "Stop breaking my car!"

His eyes hit mine and his nostrils flare. Damn. He looks like he wants to inflict pain on me.

My mouth drops open. A naked man just pulled two of my door handles off. Shit. He's definitely not playing with a full deck.

"D-don't. Please. Just go away," I plead.

He's broken my handles. What kind of strength does someone have to have for that to happen? Why is he naked? God. I'm wishing I was back in that cabin of ill-repute right now. What the heck does my horoscope say today?

"What are you called?" he demands.

"What are you called?" I fire back, snarkily.

Eek. Snark probably won't serve me well right now.

"I'm Tyson." He then jerks up his chin. "Open this door now."

"Sorry, no. Tyson. My boyfriend'll be here any—-"

He slaps the window, making me stop talking, making my body freeze tight before I dive through the two front seats into the back. I catch the sight of back dimples and I try really hard not to look downwards as more of his form comes into view, not wanting to see his bare ass or, god forbid... the front.

"Boyfriend," he repeats through tight teeth and slaps the roof angrily.

He says it almost like it's a dare or like I have audacity to have a boyfriend.

"Oh my God. Did you just dent my roof, too?"

The car begins to slide some more, and I think *oh shit* as it rolls. He gets a furious look on his face as he moves with the car, holding onto the roof, as if he's trying to stop it from moving, but he's only sliding with it. It rests with a crunch sound against that tree that makes me groan. My poor little purple car.

I'm trembling all over. I'm trapped in my car, which is now crunched, with no phone signal and a naked door handle-breaking man. Plus, a wolf is out there somewhere! Unless I've really lost it and he is also that wolf.

Damn it! I chastise myself for letting the thought seep past the lunacy-prevention barrier I've worked so very hard to keep in place my whole life. Too late. Here we go...

My brain unleashes all I've been trying to stop from invading it.

Same green eyes. Wolf goes, man is here. Naked. Nope, nope nope. No. That's crazy. But it's obvious. The naked man is a werewolf. But it's crazy. I've seen too many scary movies. I've listened to Auntie Nelle and her crazy "we are not alone" and "magic is real" hyperbole one too many times. Strangely, today is the one-year anniversary of her death.

I shiver. Wait, what? It is, isn't it?

This whole night feels like a bad, scary movie. There's no such thing as werewolves. But...

I'm still clutching my cell in my hand. I tap the screen and look. I see a bar. A bar! I key in 9-1-1.

The sky darkens and strangely lightens while the rain halts. It goes from pounding hard to just stopping, like someone turned it off with a dial.

The call fails.

"Fuzz!" I snap.

He pushes with his fingertips hard against the top of the driver's window and I hear it protest. He grunts with effort, glaring at me with an angry look on his face.

"No," I whisper.

The sound tells me he's having success. What kind of strength?

I hit the screen to redial 9-1-1. With trembling fingers.

Fail.

No signal.

He pushes the entire window in. It collapses. It falls in on the driver's seat like the little black windows on my little brother's toy dinky cars.

Holy shit. I'm not safe. I'm in big trouble. Even if I got my call through, there's no time for help to get here.

He reaches in, fumbles until he finds the inner handle and opens the door. I scream and grab the button on the door closest to me, lift it, thrust the door open and before realizing I'm leaning into the door, I fall, onto all fours on the wet ground.

I scamper away, trying to run back up the hill to get to the road. I glance back and see the wolf sprint from the car (from the car!) and it's running toward me. Oh shit, shit, fuck! It is a wolf. A wolf! A huge one.

Then he isn't wolf. He's running on two legs again as a guy. A naked running guy. He gets closer, and closer and then I'm hefted up off the ground.

He has me. Of course he caught me. And the minute he does, he makes a roaring sound of triumph. I cry out and go for his face with my nails. He hisses in surprise as my fingers rake across his cheek. The guy looked big through the window but in the flesh, he is absolutely huge. And he's bleeding from where I scratched him.

We fall to the ground and he's wolf again. It's as if an animal has just...kind of... burst from his skin. It's mind-blowing and reminds me of that Michael Jackson music video, when faces just... morphed.

"No, please."

I'm on my back on the ground and the massive black furry animal with the humongous teeth is standing over me. I crab-crawl backwards a few steps and it lets out a loud, deep bark. I scream and flip, then scramble to my feet and run.

I get three feet, max, when I feel something furry land on me and pin me with its body. Oh no. This is it. He's going to rip me to shreds. I hear the deep rumbling voice. "Shh. You're safe."

He's a man again and he's what's pinning me to the ground.

No. No! I'm pinned on the ground and his mouth is at the back of my neck, smelling me. What? He turns me and lifts me up into his arms like I'm a bride and then I'm being carried back to my car. My poor crunched-into-a-tree car.

We approach the side I escaped from and he slides me in through the still open door. He lays me on my back and climbs on top of me.

Oh no. Oh dear God, no.

Pinning me to the seat, his nose moves across my throat to behind my ear. He's so wet from the rain that it's dripping on my face. My face is also wet with tears. Is this how it goes? The end? I can't let this be the end. What a fucking waste. I save the f-word for when it really counts. This feels like it really counts.

"No!" I shout. "Help!" I scream in case by some miracle there's someone that can hear.

My car is little and he's big and he's on me but only half-way in, so the door is open. If I can get out from under him...

I bring my knee up and catch him by surprise as I hit the target. He grunts. But he doesn't roll off. The space is too small; we're just too confined.

He looks away and grits his teeth.

I struggle as he tries to recover from the nut-kneeing; I'm completely pinned and worried because ... am I about to be backhanded for that?

His eyes meet mine. It's dark in here, but they're reflective like a cat's. Or I guess... a wolf's.

Duh. Of course they are.

"What are you called?" he asks, voice husky.

He's obviously recovered from my knee to the groin and he doesn't seem angry. In fact, the way his chest rises and falls while he's looking at me? Like he wants to eat me alive. And not in a wolf for dinner way... in a naked man on top of a woman way.

The sky is bright. It's still night, but through the sunroof I see there are so many stars and such a bright moon that it's as if things the moonlight touches are almost glowing.

I shake my head. It seems important to him to know my name, but I've decided that I won't be telling him.

I do my best to shove and he doesn't budge. I try to go for his face again. He huffs and pins both my wrists down while giving me a look of admonishment. He looks around for a minute and then grabs my bag and fishes through it with one hand, holding my wrists pinned over my head in his other massive hand. I try to kick and squirm but he's so heavy on me. He puts more weight down as he pulls my wallet out of my bag. I see a bunch of other things fall out as he flicks the snap open and the contents of my wallet fall all over me. He lifts a card and drops it. He lifts another one that I assume is my driver's license.

"Ivy Adeline Brennan," he says and then he smiles. "Ivy Adeline Brennan," he repeats, and he says my name as if supremely pleased or something.

It's not bright enough to read something in this dark car interior, even if the moon seems ridiculously bright tonight. I don't even know how he made my name out. But I kind of do. It's very obvious that I'm having a nightmare. A nightmare where a wolf turned into a naked man and a wolf again, then a man again, and he has night vision.

"This is a bad dream," I whisper. "Wake up, Ivy."

Maybe I didn't go to that stupid cabin with Megan. Maybe I'm at home in my bed and just about to wake up from this ridiculous –

"It's not a dream," he tells me as he leans in. "Ivy," he adds in a deep voice that makes funny sensations trill up my spine and across my breasts. His face is only inches from mine. "It's real. You're real. And you're here, finally. From now on, you're mine."

His fingers tangle into my hair and his eyes devour me.

Oh shit.

"Buddy," I whisper, shrinking away, but going nowhere. "Please. Don't. Don't try to do this."

He stares for a long minute and I'm not sure why, then he softly says, "Everything is gonna be good, Ivy Adeline Brennan. You can calm down now. I'm here." His mouth gets closer. His eyes are hooded. My eyes land on his lips. Pillowy, full bottom lip. Nicely formed bow-shaped top lip. A bit more than a five o'clock shadow.

I shake my head and then twist it to the side and his mouth lands behind my ear.

God, I don't want this. I also don't want to die.

I begin to weep with my eyes squeezed shut tight.

"Are you a werewolf?" I ask. Ridiculously. Ridiculously, because I know he is one and also because it sounds utterly bonkers.

"A shifter, yes. Wolf and man," the deep voice answers and with his nose behind my ear, he takes a big breath. And then he exhales very slowly.

"I'm going to put my mouth on yours. I've never wanted to put my mouth on anyone. But I want to taste you while I thrust my cock inside you."

I gasp and try to struggle. It's no use. He's got me pinned.

Oh God. Ohgodohgodohgodohgod.

"Inhale my scent, Ivy Adeline Brennan. Learn it. Let it calm you."

My body is wracked with sobs and tears flow like the rain outside, which is again pounding hard.

"No, no, no, no, please..." I plead.

His thumb traces my lower lip and then his palm cups my jaw.

He frowns and looks me directly in the eyes, his brows knitting together. "You weep. Why?"

"I don't wanna die," I whisper.

"Why would you die?" His voice is gruff. He caresses my cheek with his thumb. "Soft."

"If I do what you say, will you not kill me?" I ask.

He's not putting his weight on me. He's hovering over me, his hair still dripping on me.

The guy is just... massive. His arms are nearly as big around as my waist, I think. It's as if I'm in my tiny little car underneath a guy the size of Jason Momoa. He lets go of my wrists over my head and my fingers go to my eyes to wipe tears away.

"Kill you? Never," he grunts. "Why would I kill my mate?"

"Oh for fuck's sake," I groan without first measuring my words. It's a day for F-words.

Clearly, he's nuts. He's a crazy werewolf. Or I'm having a crazy fever dream.

4

TYSON

She's under me, her pretty hair spread out around her face, and I want to sink inside her immediately. She's frightened and my urges are warring. My hunger for her... it's clawing through me, shredding at my resolve which is telling me to nurture.

The urge to calm her is stronger than the urge to claim her, but barely. Because I need her. But I hate that she's afraid of me. She should be taking in my scent and it should be calming her. I must need to mount her first, for that to happen. Mount her, mark her.

She's looking at me with so much fear. I need to make her face change. That expression... it makes me loathe myself.

Women are never afraid of me. I smell arousal as soon as I lock eyes with them. Then again, I always meet them in that bar, never in the woods. I'm still gathering my man-senses. Even speaking takes effort so far.

I need to try. Use words to calm her.

"I've been smelling you since the moon began to rise tonight on this strange night," I explain slowly, caressing her face. Her skin is soft, but it's cool to the touch. So soft. Too cool. "I finally reach you and you think I'm planning to kill you? I haven't hunted for you for hours for that. I've been looking for you for years, Ivy."

And I am exhausted. Can't remember the last time I was this weary. I have to stay strong, show her she has a strong mate who can care for her.

When she tried to run, my wolf emerged and then man, then wolf, then man. I've lost count. Shifting so many times after going years without doing it must be why I feel so depleted. I can't even stop it part-way. My senses will sharpen. The fog is lifting, but too slowly for my liking.

She looks up at me with her large eyes. They swim with tears. Her chin quivers. And I want to find a way to make it stop.

This is physically painful for me.

I feel a shift trying to come on against my will. I fight my wolf back.

As tired as I am, as much as I'm uncomfortable in this form, my desires won't stop surging. I want to taste that bottom lip that protrudes toward me. She has such a delicate face. Large eyes, beautiful skin. Prickling sensations fill my veins. A fierce need to protect her envelopes me even as blood rushes to my cock because I want to fuck her so much.

I want to hold her close and feel her wrap her limbs around me the way her name suggests she might. Ivy. Ivy wraps around you. It grows as it continues to wrap until you're completely enclosed by it. That's what I want. To completely disappear into this beautiful creature.

"I've hunted you so I can claim you. So, I can make you mine. I can't wait to feel you."

The scent of her has me ravenous. She smells better than any food I've scented or tasted as wolf or as man. She smells like she'd quench my need. Fresh. Sweet. Mouth-watering. Clean. Mine.

Will I finally feel satisfied after having her? Will I find inside her little body that thing I need, that thing I've never found despite the times mounting different females at my uncle's demand?

> *"It will help you get stronger, Tyson. Fuck until you find what you want. It'll teach you how to please your mate when you find her. Mount them, find your pleasure, and watch your senses improve while you get to spill inside them."*

I wish now I'd touched no one but her. I hate that my cock even touched another woman's cunt, seeking strength, seeking release.

A thundering growl rolls up from my gut and I barely resist the urge to thrust inside her body, to make her fit me here and now.

Her eyes fill with even more fear. Horror, even. My words aren't helping.

Her body has been struggling and she's weary, too. If she's mine before we make the journey to the house, it'll comfort her. If I take her quickly it should calm her a little. Won't it?

I reach under her short skirt. Her legs are covered with woolen lined fabric. She has strange boots on as well as a woolen sweater with excess fabric billowing about her throat. It's a brisk night. As the cold flows into the car and I feel the chill along with her struggling and trembling under me, both from fear and from cold, I change my mind.

I can't do this quickly. I'd start and never want to stop. This isn't the place. I want to savor her. And more importantly, I must put her needs first. The temperature is approaching freezing now. That's not good for either of us, especially her.

It'll take time to make the den warm. Not the den. I must alter my thinking... think as man instead of wolf. The house above the den. I haven't been in it for a long time. It's inadequate, but I'll make it warm for tonight, for shelter for us, then tomorrow work to make it better.

She kicks, struggling against the intrusion of my hand under her skirt. I'm craving all of her, but I'll have to be satisfied with just a closer whiff of scent and a small taste of her skin for now. A flick of my tongue along her throat will have to hold me over until I get her to warmth. The sooner we're there the better.

I growl with need at that delicious taste and she startles, looking at me with sheer fear.

Energy crackles in my veins. Need. I need...

"I need to mount you, be inside you. You'll feel better when I've marked you," I assure her.

She stills and this makes me ponder whether I should wait or not. "I want inside you so badly." I take a whiff of her cool skin.

She lets out a cry of distress, her body trembling wildly, I know she'll settle once I've claimed her, but her skin is too chilled.

I'm her mate. It's my job to take care of her. And she'll be mine for always. I've waited this long...

It's decided.

She needs warmth from proper shelter, so for her, I'll wait. Difficult as it'll be, I'll make myself wait.

My cock has not ever ached like this, never been this hard. I groan as I lick her throat and grind against her chilled body. I force myself away from her after putting my lips to her jaw.

I'll take her there, build a fire, then I'll undress and claim her in the warmth. Cover her with my body. Fill her with my fire. Kiss every inch of her until she's keening for me, spread wide. Willing. She'll be warm and claimed soon. And that'll take care of everything.

Pain stretches through my groin at the notion of waiting. I need to get her there, now. Right now.

"We'll go home," I say, taking a deep breath filled with her scent before stepping back and gesturing for her to come with me. I feel the chill of the ground as the wet earth squishes between my toes. "I'll claim you there."

Her eyes dart down to my erect cock and then meet my eyes again. She's afraid to be mounted. She's afraid to come home with me. She doesn't know I'll be a good mate. I will be. I'll always put her first.

She makes a squeak sound as her eyes dart around wildly, calculating, looking for a way to escape. I don't like that she feels this way; it creates sensations in my gut that are foreign and feel terrible.

There's a leather satchel with two looped handles and a longer strap as well as her smaller woman's leather bag with a long loop strap on the floor in the back of the car. I pry the zipper halfway and peer inside the larger one. Clothing and electrical gadgets and cords as well as woman stuff: bottles, jars, tools for her hair, I think. She may want these. I lift things from the seat and floor that fell out of her smaller bag and stuff it in, then zip it up. I throw the straps over my neck and scoop her up as I duck out of the car, immediately breaking into a run.

"No. No! Please!" she protests, trying to squirm out of my arms.

"Behave, Ivy Adeline Brennan."

She doesn't listen, she squirms harder, so I warn, "If you make yourself fall and you get hurt, I'll be angry. I'm already angry enough."

She needs warmth. Her body is far too cool. I won't take the chance of making her ill. I will my body temperature to rise for her, but she's only over my shoulder so it won't do enough.

"Tyson? Right? Tyson, please. Listen... If we can just get to where I can make a call, I can have my car towed out of there and I won't... won't tell anyone about you. You can just go. You can just le-let me go and I won't say a word. Please don't be angry. You haven't done anything *that* wrong yet, only broke my window and stuff and I – I don't care about that. I have insurance. I just... please put me down and we can forget this ever happened."

I pick up my pace. I can cover a lot of ground quickly even if I don't run as fast as a man as I do as wolf, but as I can't carry her and her things as a wolf, this has got to be the way home. I was weary, and then angry at myself because she's cold and frightened, but now I've got renewed strength at the notion that I'm bringing Ivy with me. I've found the person to be mine, fill my bed, to give me sons and daughters. Uncle Cornelius said that not all hybrid shift, but some can, can become nearly as strong as their pure shifter fathers or mothers. It's not unheard of for humans and shifters to mate at all. When they're destined, he said their offspring are strong. I know by her scent and how it makes me feel that she's my destined one.

She's destined to be mine, my finding her happened with a hand from fate and perhaps even a witch, I suspect with the way the sky looks and the way the roads behaved tonight, but no matter... all that matters is that I've got her and we're heading home. I feel like someplace *can* be home.

This. This is what I'm missing. This is what it means to be a man. Having a woman that is all yours. And that she's not wolf means she won't feel that usual urge Uncle told me of, to join a pack like a typical female wolf shifter would. This is right. She'll accept my solo lifestyle. This is how it's supposed to be for me.

I tell myself I must focus as man, find comfort in this form as this is who I'm going to be most of the time. I need to get home in case my body shifts against my will again and gives her an opportunity to run from me. It's because of her fear. Once I claim her, she'll know she's where she's meant to be, and I'll gain more clarity and more control over my form.

She's bouncing in my arms, grunting out with distress as I run, zigzagging down through the woods that will take me back to where I first scented her. From there, it won't take long for me to be home. I smell home and I always know how to get there. Now that I've scented her, I know I'll always know how to find her, too.

I catch the filthy scent of men, one who was with her at the service station where I first noticed her scent. As it comes into focus. I slow, spying a fire burning from near a house. I take a whiff of the night air. The boyfriend?

"Were they who distressed you earlier?" I jerk my chin in that direction as we pass the house with the three cars in front. She whimpers and reaches toward the house as if she wants to go there.

Music plays loudly with voices carrying. Their fire is too large. It's reckless. I smell the whisky my uncle used to drink on some of them, too.

Memories claw their way forward in my mind.

At the busy bar, women offered me their cunts, so I kept taking them, feeling pleasure for a moment and then dissatisfaction. I asked him, if I were in my village, the village he'd taken me from, would it feel different? Better? None of the women in that bar were shifters and none of them smelled like *mine*. None of them smelled like this little sprite. One smelled familiar, though not like she was mine, and I had no idea why until I smelled her on my uncle one day after one of his errands.

> "You smell like you fucked someone familiar. A shifter. I know no shifters but you, why is she familiar?"

> "She was supposed to be mine. She was taken from me."

> "Did you go back and mount her? Why not bring her here to live with us? Take her from them and make her eat the grass. If she's yours, she should be with you."

> "She doesn't want me."

> "Who is she?"

He acted angry then that I kept trying to convince him to take what was his and mount her until she knew she was his. He gorged himself on that disgusting scent-masking grass then, encouraging me to eat more than my usual amount and I knew he was angry at the scent I'd picked up and I suspected he was also hiding something.

He ate it until he spewed it everywhere and got so ill I had to carry him back to his bed over my shoulder as he wept like a child.

The next day, he ordered me to shift early and put his finger in my face telling me to never discuss it or ask about that female again.

Months before my uncle died, he reminded me to eat the grass, to never let *them* know who I was, and to wait until I found my own mate and then keep her safe from them.

Just before he died, he told me that he knew he didn't have long and said after he was gone I should go there to the forbidden village and rip them all apart. Every last one.

The day after he died, right before we were to shift to men again, I shifted early. I went to the house and took the truck to the bar in the village and ordered a beer. That night I took two women who approached me together to a hotel and fucked them both.

One slept while the other talked in sweet voices to me, asking to come home with me. She said she'd give me children. Take care of my house. She wasn't mine and I felt loneliness I knew would ache without having anyone, not even my uncle who was never a good companion but who was all I had.

She wasn't mine and I told her I didn't want her. She screamed in my face and called me bad names, waking the other one, while I dressed to leave.

I drove back to the cabin, locked the garage, and checked the house to ensure I did what we usually did after our month as men before shifting. Although it'd only been a few days as man that year, I was done with it. I shifted and began with a long run, one that took me away for months. Far away, in case I needed to go farther to find my one. I came back and I approached the forbidden village. I smelled no one that was mine.

I got close, something calling to me, an unnamed need. The need for blood like he suggested? Curiosity about that familiar female? I might have wanted revenge. And I realized I hadn't eaten the grass to mask my scent. And I didn't care. In fact, I wanted them to smell me.

When I approached, their smells confused me. They made my head dizzy and I again wanted to mark the entire village with my scent. So I began to do that.

I saw several men step outside a large barn and they froze when they saw me marking. My uncle's voice rang in my wolf's head, his warnings about them. I growled at them, bared my teeth, showed my disdain and strangely, they all shifted and moved to poses of partial submission.

Why would they submit? More importantly, why would it be only a partial submission? Uncle told me my inferiors would submit if they recognized me as their alpha. He told me other alphas would only partly submit to show deference.

Confusion swam through me and I left before I finished marking. With no one to go back to, I didn't go back to the house until winter when I denned underneath it. And the following winter. And the winter after that. I've forgotten how many.

Until today, I haven't even felt the urge to shift back to man form. I've nearly forgotten about this other form I can be. It feels strange, like I need time to adjust after so long. Like my memories are sliding back slowly. Uncle once said if a wolf didn't shift for a long enough period, he'd forget everything he knew as man, forget how to shift. And if he didn't shift from man to wolf, his wolf would become a danger to all. He told me there was a balance to maintain. And when he died, I didn't follow his words. I did what I wanted instead.

I was tired of his words. Of his warnings. Of the times when he made no sense, especially when he smelled like whisky.

Her panic levels are giving me an ache I can't stand.

"Settle down, Ivy." I scoop her against my chest and my temperature rises to provide warmth for her.

Her eyes are wild with fear and the predator in me wants to take her to the ground and devour her body, though with mouth, tongue, fingers, and cock instead of tearing at her with my teeth. The stronger part of me wants to calm and settle her.

"The boyfriend?" I smelled five different males. "Is that who you're calling for?"

I want to rip his throat out. I want to rip all their throats out. I can tell by their scents that they're weak. None are worthy opponents. None are worthy of her. I also smell the female that was with her earlier. Three of the five have the scent of that female on them. One that was with my Ivy. The other woman reeks of all that seed. There's nothing appetizing about her scent underneath it.

Ivy doesn't answer me.

"Forget him," I say.

The fire and those filthy scents shrink off into the distance as we keep moving.

She slumps in defeat in my arms with a whimper.

Will she miss the boyfriend? Does she love him? This makes a funny sensation poke in my chest cavity. I shake it off. It doesn't matter; I'm keeping her. He can find another female. I know I'd win her in a fight if some male was stupid enough to challenge me. I don't smell another male on her, only knew that one was near her when I caught her scent. She hasn't been touched in a while. I smell no male's seed on her at all. This pleases me and tells me even more that the boyfriend doesn't matter. Now that she's mine, she will always smell like she's just been fucked.

5

IVY

I'm in the arms of a naked man who's running with me, taking me to his home.

I squirm harder and manage to slide halfway out of his arms.

"Ivy Brennan," he admonishes and secures me better.

And now I'm back over his shoulder like a flour sack while he runs faster. I'm flopping and seeing nothing but the blurry ground. I scream over and over until I'm hoarse, praying someone will come to my aid and it seems to make him run faster. I grab for his waist, and there are no clothes, so my hands just grasp at wet, hot skin and because it's also naked skin, I let go the minute I touch him.

Blurry ground and bare butt.

God... how does he run this fast in the cold rain like this? Carrying me and my stuff, and... we're running downhill now and he's running even faster. Barefoot! I feel like I'm about to barf at the motion.

I CONTINUE TO WRACK my brain thinking about how I'll get away from this guy and make it back to the cabin of ill-repute (can't even believe that seems like a safe haven right now), but we've gone through dense bush and changed directions several times, not to mention I've stared at moving ground most of the journey so there's no way I'll remember my way back. Finally, he slows and pulls me off his shoulder back into an embrace and I'm dizzy but make out that we're approaching a darkened building. The way the moon shines over it makes it seem like it's spotlighting the place, showing it to me. I'm cold. And I'm shivering at the eeriness of all of this. I also shiver at strange sensations inside me as I look around.

It's got a big front porch and the cabin is covered in a combination of cedar shake tiles and stone. I'm set on my feet while he climbs under the front step and returns a beat later with a key.

It's again raining, though not as hard, and he is turning the key on the door of the single-story cabin that looks like it comes right out of a storybook. Like Hansel and Gretel would've stumbled upon it during their walk in the woods. It doesn't look like it's made of candy, really, but with the stonework, the old-fashioned shape, the high-peaked tiled roof bordered with gingerbread trim, it's almost romantic-looking.

What a strange thought to flit through my head as I stand there on the wide porch behind the naked guy that kidnapped me. The naked werewolf!

He opens the door and catches my hand with his before I get a chance to do anything else... like run.

Duh. Why on earth did I just stand here?

The place is dark. Pitch dark. And then there's light. He's leaning over an oil lamp and my eyes take in the shadows around me. A fireplace. Furniture covered with sheets. He moves toward me with intent, pulling me to his body. His huge, wet, naked body. I look anywhere but his crotch because I already saw it, and it's in proportion to his massive frame, in other words, big. God, he's tall and big. I come to his mid chest. I look up. He caresses my face with callused fingers and leans down like he's about to kiss me. I jerk back.

"Sit and rest. I'll get you warm," he tells me and hauls the sheet off a sofa as he steps back, immediately hunching over the wood stove, stacking it with wood that he lifts from beside it.

I'm shivering, feeling like the cold and damp has run straight through to my bones. It's also dusty in the place and my nose tickles. Beyond physically shivering from the cold, I'm also overcome with not a small amount of apprehension.

I'm inside a building with him and the door is closed. I back up toward it, slowly.

In Hansel and Gretel, the witch wanted to eat them. He's got a different sort of appetite based on what he said to me in my car, based on the erection. And here I am, like Little Red Riding Hood, about to be devoured by the Big Bad Wolf.

He looks over his shoulder at me. And the look in his eyes? Something in my belly twirls and heat floods my face. I don't get a chance to dissect the feeling because my lower back hits the doorknob and my hand slides back to grab it.

"Come. Sit," he commands as he stacks wood and fills it with some bits of paper from a rack beside the wood stove. He strikes a match. "Get warm."

He lights the fire, rises, and stares a moment. I watch that massive cock rise up and my head jerks away. I squeeze my eyes shut tight.

Oh shit. This is it. What's about to happen to me?

"Ivy?"

I open my eyes and see flames flicker as they catch, bouncing off the shadows cast from the oil lamp and my eyes land on him again. I can't help but take note of what an absolutely perfect male specimen he is. Massive in height and wide, though not remotely husky. His body is muscular. His bulk comes entirely from muscles.

His stomach is a series of boxes and ridges. His dark hair curls down past his shoulders... broad shoulders with defined biceps and well-veined forearms that extend to large hands. My eyes travel back up that naked body that he's completely unbashful about having on display to his scruffy razor-cut jawline. His chest rises and falls under my obvious appraisal and then he lets out a sound... a low growling sound that seems to make the room vibrate at the same time as goosebumps erupt on my flesh. My eyes wander over the very prominent length and girth of his –

"Let's get you warm first. It's been hard to wait but you need warmth first."

"First?" I inquire in a whisper.

"First." He nods.

I jolt and then I get into a mini scuffle with the doorknob before I win, managing to get the door open and then I'm running. I'm sprinting off that porch into wet mud that makes a thwacking sound as my poor suede boots pound into it.

I get no more than half a dozen strides before I'm scooped up into the air. I cry out in frustration.

"Ivy Brennan," he says huskily into my ear as he carries me back toward the cabin. "Do you not realize that running will only excite me further? Do you want me more excited? Do you want me to hunt you down and take you in the cold, wet dirt or would you rather it be in front of a warm fire?"

Oh God.

"Help!" I scream.

He stalks back through the door and I'm carried through the main room, past the kitchen area to the left, into a short hall with a door ahead, a door to the left, and a door to the right. He goes right and sets me on something soft. Light glows from a lantern he turns on and I see I'm on a double bed that's against the wall, also covered by a sheet. This rustic-looking room has a small fireplace. He begins stacking wood into it.

I shiver.

From cold. From fear. From deep fear.

6

TYSON

I'm aware of an escalating warming in my blood that began the moment I caught her scent. It went from warm to warmer, and then to hot when I finally laid eyes on her and her scent got even stronger when it was directly under my nose with no barriers between us.

And now that I've made the journey here and brought her into the house, it's so fiery it's bordering on painful as it shunts through my veins.

I need to take her, mark her, mate her. Ahead of that is the need to shelter her well, to make the space warm for her. These nurture urges are holding my appetite at bay. But just barely.

I'm not familiar with these urges to nurture, especially because the urge to mount has never been stronger for me.

Need gnaws, my wolf wanting to chew through everything to sate the hunger.

My body warmed to tell me. My body warmed further to provide warmth for her. As soon as this house is warm, I'll mount her and then while she sleeps, my scent seeping from her pores and my essence leaking from her body, I'll get more wood to the bedroom and the main room so that she's comfortable. And tomorrow, I'll get the dust, webs, and insects out and get food in for her. I think there are things here from when I was last here, and I'll check to see if there's anything usable. There's money to get what I need, all that money Cornelius and I put into the floorboards of the garage, and there's the truck. I'll charge the battery and see if I can make it start.

Uncle said the day would come. One day I would catch scent of the one who was meant to be mine and then I would never want another. I'd want to cover her, sink my teeth into her flesh where her neck meets her shoulder and leave my mark while I take some of her essence into my body, to be there for always. I'd want to take her into my sleeping space, mark her, knot her, and fill her with my seed when she goes into heat. My scent on her would linger, let any male shifter know, know she's mine. When he told me this, his eyes got shimmery and then he left and returned the next day smelling like he'd been inside a female. A familiar female, though I couldn't place the scent. And it made me angry that he wouldn't answer my questions about it. He told me we would shift early that year and go deeper into the forest. He didn't want my questions. He hated questions.

Feeling her eyes on me makes me tingle with awareness even as I try to keep it from clouding my judgement, which wants to simply halt and fuck her raw. Having her run away? It made me harder. It made the wolf in me want to howl, to warn anyone to stay away while I chased her down and took her in the dirt, showed her who I am. That I am hers as much as she is mine.

I quickly build a fire for the second time tonight and glance over my shoulder at her. She's cowering in the bed, her knees pulled against her chest, her eyes wide and on me. I leave the room to check on the other fire as well as slip outside and crawl into my den under the stairs to fuel up and start up the generators and do the other things I need to do to give the house electricity.

On my way back in, I bring her bags in and drop them on the floor before I open the double doors of the vast built-in wall cabinet of shelves and pull out a stack of bedding. I drop it on the edge of the mattress. Her large eyes are on me, tracking my movements. They're filled with fear, but her beauty in the flickering firelight hits me square in the chest. I slip out to the bathroom bringing a towel. I wait as the water comes out brown and eventually runs clear before wetting the towel and wiping the dirt off my feet, thinking on the fact that though much of life as a man is foggy and foreign to me, I've grown up in this house and everything here feels familiar. I decide I'll take a shower after. The water needs time to heat and my cock won't wait another minute to have her.

I drop the dirty towel and turn. My cock stands straight up, pointing at what it wants as I enter the room she's in. Her eyes land on it and the panic spikes in her. I see it. I smell it. Time to put an end to it. I crawl up the bottom of the bed and pin her on her back, her wrists at either side of her head.

She whimpers and turns her head away.

"Please, don't do this," she pleads.

"Don't do this?" I inquire.

"Please don't hurt me."

"I won't hurt you, Ivy. I'm about to make you feel opposite to that. I hurt right now and you're about to end that, too." I run my nose along her jawline and fill my lungs with her. She smells better than any aroma I've ever come across. It's time to undress her. I can't wait to get my mouth on her naked skin.

Her body trembles, and not with cold. The room isn't very big so already the fire is beginning to warm her up.

7

IVY

"I won't hurt you, Ivy," he repeats, leaning in closer while I'm still pinned, nuzzling across my jaw with his nose and breathing me in deep. "I'm about to make you feel good. You're about to make me feel good."

How in the world do I get away from this psychopath? And why do I suddenly feel a little drunk? He smells good. He's naked and on top of me and yet I'm noticing the way he smells. I can't describe it. Like warmth. And citrus. Like... I give my head a shake as the word home crosses my mind.

Okay, so maybe I *can* describe it.

"I'm not a werewolf, too, you know. I'm just a girl. A girl who is very scared right now. Do you like scaring me, Tyson?"

This tactic will either do nothing, or it'll humanize me so that he stops and thinks things through. His face melts into an expression of... smitten.

He caresses my face and moves in, putting his lips to mine.

Whoa. Whoa... I'm pinned under him so there's nowhere to go. I'm about to protest verbally when his lips move over mine and steal my breath away. *Oh shit.* His tongue slips inside and for some strange reason, I go dizzy. The world twirls slowly, as if doing a pirouette and then I have the sensation of falling, toward my doom. Instead of landing, I hear him make a low rumbling sound, thunder-like, and then feel like I'm floating, hovering mere inches over a fiery demise.

Shit. I'm kissing him back.

How has my right hand gone to his shoulder and my left hand gone to his jaw? God, why does his scruffy jaw feel so fucking good?

Oh! How has he gotten his hand under my skirt? He's tugging at my tights. Without realizing what I'm doing, I lift my bottom, and this lets him get them halfway down. He grabs the other side and then my tights are peeled off.

My legs prickle with rising goosebumps and his hot, calloused hand glides up my leg as a low growl comes out of his mouth. His tongue dips in between my lips again and then he has the crotch of my underwear in his fist. He yanks and makes it go impossibly tight around my hips and ass. I hear a noise that first sounds like firecrackers popping and then I realize it's the fabric protesting. It then gives as he shreds the crotch apart.

"Tyson... stop. Please ..."

Too late. He is slamming his huge cock inside me.

I cry out at the breach, at the depth, and the sensation as heat envelopes my entire body.

Lubrication gushes around him. *My* lubrication. And it's hot. This is the strangest sensation I've ever felt.

I *want*, with a weird clarity I've never felt about anything... I want this to go on for forever.

He stares into my eyes and smirks with a gleaming salacious smile.

"Ivy," he whispers and the voice floods directly through me like hot water. "My only."

I swallow.

He pulls halfway out and then slams forward, making muscles bulge in his jaw, making me gasp.

No condom. Oh shit.

His eyes glow briefly, so briefly I wonder if it even happened and then he's hauling my turtleneck sweater up and over my head and tossing it behind him. His hips slam forward again, making me whimper, and then he's pulling at my bra.

"Feel so good, Ivy. Help me get this off before I shred it, too," he rasps.

I do half a sit up as he leans back, then reach behind and unclasp it.

What the heck am I doing right now?

He feasts on me with glowing eyes. *Oh wow*. They *are* glowing. Actually glowing.

"Your tits are perfect. They'll nourish our children beautifully when that time comes. For now, they're all mine."

His mouth closes around my right nipple.

I gasp and arch my back as his tongue does something crazy-good to my nipple and then he suckles. What was that sensation? It actually felt like something leaked out of my boobs at his words.

His hand slides down my hip to where we're joined. He rubs his fingers through my wetness and then slides down my body and buries his face into me, licking me from opening to clit and then slurping hard on my clit, making me cry out.

"Oh. Oh fuck!"

My hands are in his still-damp curls as I hold him there, taking in the vision of him feasting on me with firelight bouncing off those giant shoulders and holding my body with those strong hands. My eyes graze his perfectly athletic ass that I can make out because of the firelight.

My skin is toasty-warm now, thanks to the flickering flames bursting from the crackling wood, and the fact that he's on me with extreme heat seeping from his body into mine. My boots and clothes are in a heap on the floor and I'm spread wide, being given oral sex by a massive, naked man who I've seen shift into a wolf and back again. A man who said he tracked me for hours. A man who carried me for miles through the rain telling me he was going to claim me and make me his.

"Stop squirming. Let me look at you," he commands as his hand trails up my hip to my breast and back down over my pussy. He spreads my labia wide with a stretch of his middle finger and thumb, and he looks down, smiling for a second, before planting another kiss there, on my clit, eyes connecting with mine for a second before his tongue twirls and slides inside me. He puts pressure that hits my g-spot and I gasp.

He smiles, eyes on me while doing it again.

How on Earth did I go from trying to run five minutes ago to spreading wide and holding him by the hair while he tongue-fucks my pussy?

I should run. I should find something heavy to hit him over the head with. I should do something. I should do something but all I can do is feel.

His mouth moves up over my clit and his finger takes over working that spot. That. Spot. That inside spot that has only ever been paid attention to by my rabbit vibe before now. Holy crap. This is so fucking much better.

His giant hands are both holding my bottom and he squeezes as he licks. And then he licks some more. God, his tongue is strong. And then as I'm on the cusp of coming, coming harder than I've ever come, he glides back up my body and rams in deep.

Deep. *So* fucking deep.

I'm moaning and I'm writhing, seeking friction for my clit, which needs just a little more attention to send me over the edge. I reach between my legs but before I get there, he grabs my wrist and pins my hands above my head with one of his hands as his free one slides down there instead.

I grunt in frustration.

"I get to do this," he corrects as he rubs my clit while fucking me and then, as I crest over the edge into bliss, he gives me an insanely sexy smirk before his mouth moves to the place where my neck meets my shoulder, plants a soft kiss there, then he quickly flips me over onto my belly, gets his cock back inside me and his lips are on my shoulder while he continues to rub my clit with his fingers while thrusting hard into me from behind. Seconds later, as I'm crying out the biggest orgasm I've ever had in my life, I hear him say my name.

"Ivy. My only…"

8

TYSON

The minute I'm inside her, I know I'm home.

This. This beautiful creature belongs to me. This fucking is like nothing I've felt. No other woman has felt like this.

My cock feels like it's being ripped, like teeth are cutting through the skin, but then after an excruciating moment of pain, the most exquisite pleasure of my life tears through me and I know what's happening

I'm knotting her.

Mine.

She's mine.

I knew it.

I smelled it.

Now... I feel it.

I feel it in every bit of my being.

And my wolf feels it too.

When Uncle brought me one to mount that first time, the year after the uncontrollable shifting found my boy's body changed to become one of a man, my cock hardened and I mounted her, but after that, I felt nothing. I didn't knot. I didn't bite. I rutted until I was spent and was done. Done and anxious to shift back to wolf and run through the forest to feast. Uncle told me I'd spend empty fluid unless I found my mate. I wouldn't sire pups on any but my mate unless I lost a mate or rejected her because she wasn't fertile. He told me to keep mounting them, see if I liked any to keep, and in the meantime learn to mount well so that I'd be experienced for my own mate, so I'd know how to pleasure her. Take my pleasure now while I sought her out. He said that it'd help me become stronger. Boost my strength and my senses.

I found her. I'll never mount another.

I spot the creamy skin near her clavicle. My mouth waters. My gums pinch before my canines elongate slightly, and it feels like my wolf is close to the surface.

9

IVY

And then my eyes snap open as he bites me. He fucking bites me. That's right. He bit me!

His teeth are on me, they've got me, and I'm frozen, as if paralyzed as it's registering that he's drawing blood. It feels like time slows and a thousand *what the fuck* thoughts stagger through my brain before I'm acutely aware that his dick feels like it's expanded inside of me. He pulls back a little and not much, because it feels like he's stuck. He slams his body forward, sending my face into the pillow as he lets out a long, deep groan that somehow reverberates straight through me. I shiver while the expanded feeling grows even more. He's grown bigger inside me and it's pulsing. Pulsing against... *oh*... my g-spot.

"Oh!" I cry out in ecstasy.

His body stills as he lets out a deep and rasping growl before hot liquid fills me. He's coming inside me. It's hot, and there's a lot of it, so much it leaks out. The growling doesn't sound human, it sounds like an animal and for a second, I wonder if I'm being fucked by a man or a wolf. But then his mouth touches the place he bit me as he sighs out my name softly, sort of... reverently.

"Ivy."

I blink.

What? What just happened?

The full feeling subsides a little and he groans as he slowly pulls out. I feel all sorts of hot liquid come out with him. He flips me to my back and slams inside again and it hurts. A lot. He's huge. It grows bigger yet again as he fills me with more cum.

He sucks on his lip, which has a droplet of blood on it and I watch his Adam's apple bob as his head rolls back. More of that hot liquid leaks out of me.

Thank God he's still a man.

The world squeals to a halt as I'm about to freak out on him. About the bareback fucking, about the coming. About the biting and the blood, but before I can freak, my body goes limp and insanely warm. Sensations of … I think… slow and happy… (euphoric?) thoughts wash through me and I flop. I blink at the fireplace, watching the flames dance, casting shadows everywhere. My eyes flutter closed. I feel high. Yep… euphoric. Toasty.

The best.

"Mine," Tyson says and then he kisses me on the mouth. He's still inside me; my arms are above my head limply, and I feel so… full of him.

10

TYSON

She either passes out or falls asleep before my knot releases for the second time. I slide out and I kiss the spot where I've marked her. She shivers.

She's beautiful. My little Ivy. Beautifully creamy unmarred skin other than my bite marks. My mark takes my breath away as I stare at it on the space between her neck and shoulder, by her collar bone. Soft golden hair. Long, wavy locks. Those purple bits... I know it's cosmetic and it's silly, but somehow I find it's also cute. I don't ever find things cute.

I've finally knotted. It takes fucking to a new level. And my cock still feels good. Like it's still being stroked by the inside of my Ivy's tight undulating inner walls. Ivy takes fucking to a new level. I've gotten a mild sense of accomplishment as I've watched women climax before, but this girl? She looks, feels, and smells beautiful when she comes. And I've never come harder, never felt more than physical pleasure before now. This time I felt physical pleasure better than anything I've felt before plus emotional sensations, too.

She squirms toward me as I sit up and run my fingers through her soft hair at the side of her head, examining the purple silken strands as I rub them between my fingers.

I kiss her little nose and pull blankets on top of her. The sheet that covers the bed should've been changed but I didn't have the self-control to make the bed before taking her. It'll have to do for tonight. I wipe between her legs with a towel and do my best to fix the askew sheet under her so she's not on bare mattress. This bed is old. It's not good enough for her. I'll buy a new one.

I lift her clothing from the floor and drape it over the armchair near the fire, so it'll dry. I feel my mouth tug into a smile at the vision of her sleeping form. She's beautiful. And she's mine. I bask in the way that feels for a long moment before I decide to fetch more wood from the garage to stock both fireplaces for the morning as well as more fuel for the generator. I secure things in the main room and survey the inside of the cabinets in the kitchen. There are some tins of fruit, and only a few pantry staples. I smile as I slip two tins of fruit into the refrigerator. It's noisily working to get cold.

The purpose I feel right now at having someone to care for is a sensation better than any, other than fucking her.

I fetch a quilt from the back of the armoire and pull it over her, noting that more fogginess from going so long without shifting is lifting. I'm still somewhat unaccustomed to my form, still searching my mind for memories of certain things that feel fuzzy, but things are trickling back. Mating my woman helped; I believe that. I'm thinking more like a man now, about the things I need to do to make the house nice for her, the things I'll want to provide for her. Thinking about fucking her again.

She's still asleep and with a peaceful smile on her face as she curls into me to borrow some of my warmth. I'll happily share it with her, all of it, everything I have and all that I am, until my dying day.

This feels different. Something comes over me. Something odd. As I close my eyes it occurs to me that there's a feeling in my chest, a rightness that's deep in the center of it that I've never felt before.

11

IVY

My eyes open and I'm immediately reaching below my waist for the quilt I spot. I'm naked. I'm naked and I've been screwed. I'm in the werewolf's cabin. In his bed.

Screwed.

Screwed like I've never been screwed...

My eyes dart around the space I'm in as I clasp the beautiful nature-inspired patchwork quilt to my chest. The room is warm. Overly warm, actually. The fire isn't crackling like it was when I went to sleep, but there's still all sorts of heat emanating from the glowing embers. This room is dusty, so dusty I could write my name into the dust on the nightstand with my finger.

The sun streams in from a window that's only half covered with a red, green, and white tartan curtain. I'm in a double bed that's against the wall, lying on a rumpled flat sheet that's only over one corner of the bed. My clothes from last night are over an Archie Bunker style upholstered chair beside the fireplace and my boots are on the floor. I see my bag on the floor too, so I shakily reach for it and haul out a pair of black yoga pants, a black jersey hoodie, a purple tank top, a white and black zebra print bra, and black undies. There are pink thong flipflops there too, which is good. I'd brought them thinking they'd work by the pool and hot tub. I glance over at my new purple Uggs; they should be muddier. They look okay, astonishingly. My eyes take in the rest of the room. A tall weathered-looking armoire that takes up a whole wall. The walls are wood paneling, but they've been painted white. The floor is varnished, knotted plank wood. The small corner fireplace has a dusty dome-covered clock and oil lamp on the mantle. A painting hangs over it of a willow tree with a tree swing, seven puppies playing under the tree with seven little boys. Not puppies, wolves. The painting looks amateur, but also kind of good, in an A. A. Milne-like abstract way.

My eyebrows shoot up. Is all this real? The ache between my legs tells me it is. I bite my lip and block the memories from washing through my brain because I don't want those memories right now. That sex was... supernatural. Yeah. Like this entire situation.

I dress quickly before peeking out the door. All is quiet, so I move out of the room into the short hallway where I see two other doors. One is closed. The other is a bathroom. Good, because I need it. My legs and thighs hurt like heck from last night's ... ordeal. Activities. I need to use the bathroom and then I need to make like a tree -—and leave.

It's a dusty, sparse bathroom with a big old white clawfoot tub and pedestal sink as well as toilet and small towel cabinet. The light works. The mirror is a bit fogged up and the air is humid. He's taken a shower recently. This place does have electricity.

I use the facilities, noting basic toiletries on the shelf over the bathtub, which has dust and droplets of water from the recent shower. A green bar of soap. Green shampoo bottle. I catch my reflection in the mirror and my eyes look strange. More purple than blue. I do a double-take, figuring maybe my skin is just pale from my ordeal and that it's the lighting in here, but then I spot the mark on my neck and my eyes are forgotten as my hand flies to the place where it meets my shoulder. I see the mark he made. Teeth imprints. It's pinkish, almost like a branding mark, but it doesn't hurt. He broke the skin last night but there's no scab. When I touch it, I get a very odd sensation. I frown at my reflection as I rub it and goosebumps rise on my body. My mouth drops open. Oh my good gravy... that feels like... I rub it a little more and then I shudder. My nipples are now erect.

Oh my... why does this mark feel like an erogenous zone? It should hurt, not feel like this. It's not quite as tingly as between my legs, but I'd call it more tingly than my nipples. I give my head a shake. I have no time to ponder things; I need to get out of here. Maybe he's turned back into a wolf and has gone somewhere to sleep for the day. I have no idea, can barely wrap my mind around this news that something from the movies, from story books, as well as from my crazy Aunt Nelle is actually real and has happened to me.

To say my mind is blown is an understatement. Aunt Nelle might not have been an absolute cuckoo bird after all.

I hear noise. *Uh oh.*

I carefully step out of the bathroom and get a few paces to where the hall opens up into the main room where I see him standing there at the counter in a pair of faded jeans, tan work boots, and a white with blue striped flannel shirt with only the bottom three buttons done up and the sleeves rolled up to his elbows. The sight of his chest, his corded forearms, and the perfect way those jeans fit? It makes me feel woozy. I get a belly dip and I grasp the doorframe for support. He's holding a bowl with a spoon in it.

"Back to bed," he orders. "I'll feed you breakfast." He advances and I immediately retreat backwards into the bedroom I'd just come out of, feeling my way there with my hands as if I'm reading braille.

His eyes on me look... hungry.

I trip and he moves impossibly fast, catching me by hooking an arm around my waist and pulling me against his body.

Oh wow. He's so warm.

He leans forward and kisses my lips and then my throat at that mark and I shiver.

"Into bed, my Ivy," he says, and his eyes are sparkling with amusement or something.

I blink stupidly at him and sit on the end of the bed. He sits beside me.

Where have all my braincells gone?

I feel stupid. Stupid and blushing and not only hot in the face, but also hot between my legs.

He lifts the spoon and I see canned peaches in the bowl. He brings the spoon to my mouth with a small chunk of peach on it.

"Open," he orders.

I obey.

He slips the spoon into my mouth and I eat a cold piece of canned peach.

"Fruit is my favorite man-food," he says. "Do you like fruit?"

I blink and then I belatedly nod. *Man-food?*

"I eat these when I'm a man. I put them in the fridge last night when I turned the power on. I worried they'd spoiled but they're fine, aren't they? They've been here a while."

I nod again as I chew and swallow.

He feeds me another bite. "Eat all of them. You need your strength, Ivy Savage. I showered and as soon as you're fed, I want inside you again, want your scent back on my body."

I choke.

He rubs my back and his handsome face is etched with concern.

"Careful," he warns.

I recover, and whisper, "Savage? Why are you calling me Ivy Savage?"

"I'm Tyson Savage," he says as if he doesn't understand my confusion.

Does he think we're married? How delusional is he?

He lifts my hand and kisses the top of it and then strokes that mark on my neck, making me shiver. "I'll purchase a wedding ring for you today when we go for supplies if you like. I won't wear one because I'd lose it during shifting."

My mouth drops open.

He lets out a playful-sounding growl against my temple and his lips touch.

"Just one more bite and then I'm having you. I can't wait. You can finish them after."

He saws through a halved peach with the spoon and scoops it up into my mouth. The piece is big, but I chew it and as I'm swallowing, as I'm trying to figure out where to start with all the thoughts rolling around in my brain, he sets the dish on the table beside the bed that holds an oil lamp and a stack of dusty books before he flops onto his back and pulls me on top of him. The piece was so big and with the surprise of being lifted, some peach syrup has trickled out of the corner of my mouth. He sees it and catches it with his tongue.

He groans sexily as he licks his lips.

And now my crotch feels like it's gone to hot mush.

My hands land on his chest as I gasp. God, his body is warm, and this chest is defined. His shoulders are absolutely huge.

I swallow the rest of what's in my mouth, but not without difficulty.

His fingertips whisper across the mark on my neck and his eyes glow just briefly as he kisses me and then smiles. "How do you feel today, Ivy?"

"Uh... can you let me go so we can talk for a minute?"

"No," he denies with a shake of his head. "I need inside you. We'll talk after that." He flips me over and gets to his knees so he can peel my yoga pants and underwear down all at once.

I do nothing to stop him. I just watch.

He gets to his feet, undoes his shirt, shrugs it off and drops it before he goes for his fly and I watch as he drops those jeans.

Commando.

Boing! His cock springs up and it's got a clear droplet on the tip. My eyes move up to meet his and our eyes stay locked as he licks his lips until I can't see him because he's hauling my hoodie and tank top up over my head.

"Remove this garment," he commands and immediately my hands find the front clasp and with a snap of my fingers it flings undone. His eyes fall on my breasts and his nostrils flare.

He grabs my thighs and gives a little yank, making me drop to my back. Instantly, he's lining up and spearing me with that giant beast of a cock without warning. I gasp as my legs wind around his lower back and cross at the ankles. I put my hands to his massive shoulders and a whimper escapes my lips as his fingers slip between us and play between my legs.

"I'm glad you were ready for me. I like that." He puts his mouth to the mark on my neck and sucks on it. I cry out and in just seconds, I am plummeting, nerves sparking, feeling sensations in new cells that I swear couldn't have been there before, and then I'm there. I am *there*.

His cock moves in and out and his fingers play with my clit.

"Holy fuck, Ty-Ty-uh, shit...Ah!" I cry out loudly as I climax. While I cry out, he pistons his hips over and over, staring into my eyes with an expression of absolute dominance.

God, I've lost my mind. I really have. And it's like I think entirely in expletives with the word *fuck* coming out of my mouth and invading my brain on a constant basis. Somebody save me from my insanity here because not only did I not even try to stop him, not only did I bare my breasts on command, but I'm also lying here thinking I could spend my whole life doing nothing but getting dicked by Tyson the man slash werewolf and being completely blissed out.

He flips me to my belly and hauls me up to my knees by my hips and goes harder and faster, grunting.

"This ass. God, this ass, Ivy Savage." He slaps it and I squeal.

He lets out a deep chuckle and then kisses the back of my neck. I feel the heat of his torso against my back. *Whoa.*

He lifts me upright by the throat in a gentle hold and I brace my hands on the wall in front of me. He's on his knees, driving up into me over and over and lifting my knees off the mattress with each thrust. He lets out that rolling thunder sound that sounds a whole lot like a growly purr as he does it and my head rolls back and my eyes drift shut as a warm feeling seeps straight through my body, through my bones from my ears down to my toes.

His left hand goes to my clit again as his mouth goes to that spot on the left side of my neck and I cry out as he's tonguing my neck, rubbing my clit hard, and ramming into me. My body clamps hard around him, making him growl a satisfied sound. It feels as if he expands in size inside me, by a lot, and then there's pulsing against my g-spot and my legs are shaking hard, going weak. I'm stretched to the limit, to where I know I'll feel raw after, and hot liquid fills me. There's so much of it, it trails down my inner thighs, feeling like warm oil. His fingers continue to assault my clit, mixing with the hot liquid that's coming out of me and I come on top of coming, my entire body rattling with the force of it.

I melt back against him and he puts me on my belly and covers my back with sweet kisses. I blow out a long breath. *Whoa.*

He cuddles in, throwing a leg over me and playing with my hair. I feel his hot breath and his mouth against that bite mark. I hear myself let out a happy-sounding sigh. He chuckles and kisses me again. God, him laughing against my skin brings a feeling of bliss I can't describe.

"Rest for a few minutes and then eat the rest of your fruit so we can go out and get some supplies."

I blink, staring at the fireplace, feeling warm and toasty. It feels like I'm glowing.

Shit. What am I doing right now? I can't seem to make myself do anything. I just soak in the warm and strangely amazing feeling of being cuddled by him.

His finger dances down my spine, between my butt cheeks, and then inside me again. He growls once more, and then draws that finger back out, bringing wetness with it, that he trails across my back door and up my crack. I shiver and my nipples tingle.

My inner thighs are wet. And this bed still isn't made properly. The sheet has come completely off its remaining corner. The pillow has an old and dusty, faintly musty odor to it.

I wiggle my nose in distaste.

"What is it?" his deep voice rumbles. "What's wrong?" he prompts, nudging me with his nose at my cheek when I don't immediately answer.

"The pillow smells funny."

Of all the things I can tell him about what's wrong, I say that? Not that he essentially kidnapped me after breaking my car and then dicked me into a coma before feeding me peaches, dicking me again, and not to mention the fact I'm lying here in a puddle of hot sex juice that he's essentially playing in, like a little kid in a bathtub filled with plastic toys.

"The house has been closed up for a long time. Think of whatever you feel we need, and we'll get it today." He squeezes me.

Get it today. We'll get it today? Oh. I'll have an opportunity to get away from him.

"Then we'll come back here and maybe you can work with me to get the den, ah... house to smell nice. I'll get rid of all the dust."

My brain really does feel foggy. He repositions me, getting more comfortable. He stares into my eyes and the expression is kind of puppyish. I get lost in bright green pools. His mouth descends and lips touch mine softly. My hand finds his jaw and I get lost in a kiss. My body breaks out in goosebumps. God, he's gorgeous. I don't even know him. He tastes so good. And the way he smells? Not to mention the way he's looking at me? He's...

His head jerks back and he looks at the window. His nostrils flare and his lip curls in an angry way that has chills trilling up my spine. His body is completely rigid.

A noise outside makes his body lock tighter and he goes even more alert, pulling away from me, standing up and getting his jeans on.

"Stay here," he orders and slips out shirtless and shoeless.

I sit up, pulling the quilt up to cover my nakedness.

At the motion, I feel all sorts of his halfway-to-boiling hot cum leaking out of me, feeling like massage oil.

Shit. I do up my bra and reach for yesterday's ripped panties and use them to wipe between my legs before I slip on my black panties. I get up and look out the window, peering from behind the mostly closed curtains. I see him standing there, chest out, talking to another man (another attractive man, in fact) who looks like he's around the same build and the same age – late twenties, early thirties, maybe. Short dark hair, but there's a resemblance between their profiles. A strong one. Brothers?

Suddenly, a black wolf bursts from Tyson's body, quite literally, he's just gone from man to animal in less than a snap and I see the jeans dropping to pool at his legs. I grip the curtains tight.

As he steps out of them, kicking them back behind him, the other man has a brown wolf burst from his body and the same thing happens to his jeans and boots, fabric of the guy's shirt splitting and falling to the ground.

What a crazy sight. Not as if there's skin being shed, just that the wolf bursts out. The Tyson wolf is showing his teeth. The brown wolf isn't. I throw Tyson's shirt on over my head and get it mostly buttoned before I find myself running outside onto the porch, a poker from beside the living room's fireplace in my hand.

There's a loud, deep bark. Tyson, in wolf form has barked at me and I freeze. That bark's depth felt like it came from the earth beneath me. Iciness sweeps straight through me.

I see that the chocolate brown wolf is standing there, looking almost submissive with his head down in front of Tyson.

Tyson backs away from him, but not in a way that I take as a retreat because he gets directly in front of me and it's obvious he's protecting me.

I stand frozen and in shock. Standing in front of me, he's almost as tall as me on all fours. I've never seen a wolf this large in my life. Obviously, werewolves are bigger than ordinary wolves.

He growls at the other wolf and then lunges threateningly without leaving the space in front of me. I gasp in shock. The other animal runs the other way, stops thirty or forty feet away and then turns and barks at Tyson for about five seconds before walking away calmly rising to two feet as he shifts back, into the woods that surround this place, leaving his clothes and shoes there in a pile on the ground.

I hard-blink at the back of the naked man.

12

TYSON

I shift to man form, many emotions surging through me at once. Relief he's gone, comforted that I seem to have regained control over my form and ability to shift at will. But I also war with the urge to shift back to wolf, chase him down, and then rip his throat out so he cannot come back.

My head is swimming right now with his words, with my urges, and with Ivy's scent. It needs to stop as I have to be mindful of Ivy. She comes first.

I was ready to go for his throat when she stepped outside, and I saw his eyes touch her. I don't know what stopped me. Perhaps his words. His words just before she came out must have stopped me.

I shoot a look of disapproval at her and heft her over my shoulder before heading back inside and slamming and locking the door, filled with anger and other emotions I'm not sure how to decipher.

He hadn't acted as if he had anything but respect for my bond with her, but I was taking no chances. Uncle Cornelius told me of their deceptive nature. This was why we weren't part of that pack. Their nature was what made him flee with me when I was an infant.

They'd killed my father, their top alpha, and then raped and killed my mother before devouring her flesh. They'd planned to kill me, to take me, to devour me so I wouldn't rise to alpha when I grew and so that they could absorb all my unformed abilities. My uncle took me away so I'd be safe. He frequently ranted about how they lived, how the pack had too many alphas, and this meant extreme abuse for betas and omegas. How they lived, thieving from the humans, stealing their women and siring children on them before tearing into their flesh as wolves and devouring them as a pack. Devouring the children who couldn't shift. Enslaving the halfling ones who could. Chasing down lone wolves and mainstreamers to force them into servitude.

The stories I'd heard chilled me as a child, ensuring that when I was young I never got close to their village, then angered me, making me want to destroy them. I knew I'd never want to be part of a pack. And that once, after Uncle died, when I was ready to take vengeance, when I nearly went in and destroyed them, but couldn't because one scent stopped me in my tracks.

And now one of them has approached me here, showing me they know where I am, and he said things that don't fit.

Lies. Deception.

As if I would fall for words from my realized nightmare. I don't want to let a word from his mouth infiltrate my brain, but I can't help but think on it, wonder why he went out of his way to speak to me. His words evidently got to me somewhat because I didn't rip his throat apart.

"Tyson Savage? You know you are Tyson Savage, right?"

I stared. On alert.

"I'm Riley Savage," he informed. "I'm here peacefully. May I speak with you?"

I stood there ready. Teeth bared. Ready to shift and defend myself. Ready for lies. Ready to kill. By the subtle twitch of his nose I knew he smelled my mate. I also sensed he was unafraid of me. I was ready to fight.

"I'm your cousin, Tyson. Our fathers were brothers. Cornelius stole you when you were an infant. You're supposed to be our council's top Alpha. We thought you were dead. You've mated, haven't you? We've known you're alive for a few years, since we saw you at our town hall, but now that you're back, we felt we could try to make our approach. We would like to talk."

"Leave," I grunted, baring my teeth, not liking that he smelled her. "Or you die."

"Just a couple questions, if that's all right. Cornelius. Is he alive somewhere else? We haven't caught his scent in years."

"Why?"

We disguised our scents. Uncle taught me it was necessary from a young age. I'd stopped when he died. Unafraid of them, maybe even daring them to approach.

"Cornelius has crimes to answer for. And Tyson, he is deranged. If he told you who you are and where you came from, he must have lied. He'd have lied or else you'd have killed him and come home. He did heinous things. We'd like you to come see us. To talk. Your mother wants to see you. Let's sit and talk about the truth."

My body went rigid. "My mother is dead."

"She's not."

"Your pack raped and devoured her," I bit off.

His expression was of mortification. "No. Fuck no. She's my aunt. And the lead healer for our pack. I assure you, she's very much alive and wants to see you. You were taken from her, from all of us. Come. I'll show you. You'll know as soon as you catch her scent that she's your mother. He took you young, but that bond was already formed."

My eyes narrowed. Lies. Had to be.

"Where's my father?" I bit off.

"Gone," Riley's head dropped with sadness. "At the hands of Cornelius. They found him dead and you gone. You're our true top alpha. I'm getting ahead of myself. Please. Consider coming. We know you know how to get to us."

Uncle told me they might try to approach if they saw me or caught my scent; might tell their lies to get me there so they can kill me, eliminate me as a threat.

I folded my arms across my chest.

"Leave," I ordered.

"I just wanted to –"

"Leave! Or die."

He bared his teeth at me. "We're your family," he snapped angrily. "You don't have to be alone. It's not right and could harm you. In here." He pointed to his temple. " And here." He thumped his chest with his fist. "Our pack is non-traditional and that's for a reason. Our lines are so strong, we have six alphas, but we're meant to have seven. You're meant to be at the top of the pack."

I bared my teeth at his insolence.

He went on. "We're incomplete without you. We've mourned you for thirty-three years, Tyson. We live a good life and we're a strong family, but we mourn you. You're supposed to be part of us."

I stared, still baring teeth.

"You don't have to live alone," he repeated.

"I choose to live alone," I snapped.

"Because you want that or because it's all you know? Because it's what you need and chose for yourself or what he told you was better?"

I frowned. His words felt like they punched me in the gut.

That was when I caught Ivy's scent becoming stronger and felt a spike of immediate worry. I shifted, ready to go for his throat.

He immediately shifted as well, his wolf eye-level with mine. Uncle was much smaller as man and as wolf and the size of Riley Savage's brown wolf didn't scare me, but it gave me pause. I bared my teeth and he partly submitted, though kept his teeth partly bared, defiantly. This stubborn asshole was determined to make me hear what he had to say. He's alpha to his bones; I instinctively know it. I'm not sure if he's a match for me or not, but he feels very strongly about telling me his tale. And maybe that was why I didn't kill him. Because I had always had doubts about Cornelius and because I wanted to know if there was any truth coming from him at all.

I also realized right then that my Uncle Cornelius was not alpha. Having grown up around only one of my kind, I had no way of knowing. That thought had never before occurred to me. He talked of pack hierarchies when I was a child. I never asked him where he fit in all of that. Why hadn't I? I'd always been of few words and Uncle Cornelius didn't like questions. We would go for long stretches of time where we barely spoke and then he'd occasionally begin spewing facts at me rapid-fire out of nowhere and then just as suddenly, silence would fall again.

He was all I had. He was all I knew. And when words came from him, it was often simple directions, which I followed. When it was more, it was usually spewed at me with the scent of whisky and made little to no sense.

When Riley Savage showed that partial submission, she was there, suddenly, standing on the porch wearing my shirt, her beautiful legs bare, golden and purple hair everywhere, her eyes wild with fear, and my scent all over her. My little Ivy stirred emotion in my gut, standing there and holding the fireplace poker in her hand and pointing it at Riley Savage's wolf form.

To protect me?

I warned her and this made her halt. I got between them, letting him know with my stance that I would not hesitate to rip his throat out if he made a move in her direction.

He left. But not before giving me notice with his eyes that told me we weren't done.

The sensations I felt were so foreign then. Strangeness at how I could feel a sort of connection to him, how I could know the meaning of his expression.

How I knew he was alpha, and the knowledge, that his strength was formidable. Not just from his size. From more.

And there were a lot of other sensations, vibrations coming at me from him, too that I didn't know how to decipher.

I TAKE HER BACK TO bed and set her down.

Her eyes rove over me and I see confusion. Her cheeks are pink as those eyes sweep over my body.

Emotion squeezes my chest like a massive fist. I need her again.

My beautiful little mate, trying to defend me against a massive wolf with nothing but a little stick in her dainty hands. I pounce, pulling my shirt off her body by hauling it over her head, slamming my hips forward, my cock seeking her. She's still wet and swollen from our last fucking, but behind a barrier. She's put panties on. I hook the crotch aside with my finger and push my way inside her.

"Mine. You're mine," I tell her, cradling her jaw in my hand. "No one will take you from me. I protect you; I keep my Ivy safe. You understand?"

My thumb strokes her lips. "Don't put yourself in danger like that again. You should've waited in my bed where I left you. I'd never let anyone hurt you."

I would do anything to keep her safe from them. Anything. That pack that steals women. That hurts them. That lies. Telling me that I'm their alpha so they can lure me there and take her from me, kill me, hurt her. Devour her beautiful body. No. *Fuck no*. Seven alphas? This means there are six threats to me. Riley Savage and five more. I want to kill them all. I won't let them near her.

I fuck her hard, I bury myself in her beautiful body, feasting on her lips, sucking her tongue, digging my fingers into her sweet ass and feeling my body fill with rage at the idea that someone might even try to touch her. I see them in my head, laughing around a fire, palming spent cocks. Pulling beautiful golden and lavender hair from their teeth.

No!

I let out a roar as my cock expands near the base and she cries out an orgasm as my knot pulses against that ethereal inside place that makes her quiver and whimper. I spill with force into her, staring into her eyes, feeling my eyes heat with a glow. I barely manage to beat back the red haze, stopping it from coming through because she's safe, she's here, under me, filled with me.

She looks frightened and I feel immediate remorse.

"No. I won't ever, *ever* harm you. You need never fear me, beautiful Ivy Savage. I've never felt this way about anybody before you, Ivy. My only."

"Only what?" she whispers.

"Only one. You're the only one for me. We're meant to be together."

Her eyes soften as I growl into her mouth and feel yet another stream of essence leave me.

I bury my face in her hair and go limp on top of her, inside of her. Spent with emotion. I roll and take her to lying on me, so I don't crush her under my body.

I scrub my eyes with my palms.

She's trembling on top of me.

I look at her and her eyes are soft, but she shivers. I can see she's overcome with emotion, too, but hers is threaded with confusion where my emotions are sure.

I wrap my arms around her, and my body temperature rises to get her warm. I'll make her sure.

"Talk to me?" she pleads in a soft voice. "We have a lot to talk about. But... I... Fuzz... I don't even know where to start. What happened out there? You're so angry."

I let out a sigh and pull her tighter to me. She feels good. She feels right. She feels like the thing I was missing that I didn't know I was missing until I caught her scent.

She looks up at me with those lavender eyes, her bottom lip in a pout as if she's about to cry.

She wants to talk. She wants my words. I'm not good with words.

I caress my mark on her with my thumb and briefly touch my lips to her little nose. "I've never spoken to another like me except for my uncle, who died."

"You've been alone a long time?" she asks.

I nod. "He, that Riley, he's Riley Savage, of my blood and he said words that felt like a fist thrust into my gut. I had no time to decide what to do about that. I didn't want him near you. I feared he would hurt you or try to attack me so he could take you." I push my anger back at the notion of that. "I don't care what happens to me, but nothing can ever happen to you, Ivy. Nothing. My purpose in life is to shelter and provide for my family. You are my family."

She sinks her teeth into her bottom lip and her eyes rove my face.

I want to fuck her again. This soon. I want to spend my life inside her. Making her whimper. Feeling her body respond to me. My hand grazes the curve of her ass and I feel my cock harden again.

"I need you again," I tell her.

"Tyson, wait. I'm sore."

"What's sore?" I bristle.

Is she hurt? Have I not noticed an injury?

"My..." Her face goes pink. "My princess parts. And my legs. And even my arms. I feel bruised all over."

"What can I do?" I move the blanket away and begin to examine her body, searching for signs of injury.

"Just... don't try to make love to me right now. My body just needs a break."

I frown. I've worn her out with all my... lovemaking. I can't help the grin that comes out, that spreads into a smile.

Smiling is new for me. I like how it feels.

"I've worn you out already? This is going to be a problem."

She blinks in shock.

"Because I plan to love you often. You'll have to toughen up, little mate."

She frowns. And then she shakes her head. "Anyway, what made you talk about a wedding ring and calling me Ivy Savage?"

She's not amused. My smile goes away.

"I've marked you as my mate. You're now mine."

She shakes her head. "Not where I come from. A wedding is part of all that and part of a wedding is me agreeing to it, which I can't do within just hours of meeting somebody. Somebody that abducted me."

"Did you not spread wide for me? Weren't you the vixen who grabbed my head when I licked your little cunt, so that I couldn't stop?"

"That's not..." Her face goes a delicious red color. "That's not the same as a wedding. Fucking isn't marriage."

I graze my mark on her with my fingertips. "No. Fucking isn't marriage. But this mark is. I've fucked women before, but never have I known by their scent that they are mine. Never have I tracked them until I got to them and never have I marked or knotted one. Until you. You are my mate. My only one. This mark means I'll marry no other."

"Knotted? What is that?"

"Part of my cock grows larger inside you so that I can't be dislodged, so that I can fill you with my seed. We'll do that when you're in heat so that you can give me children, but we do that otherwise, for both our pleasure. I've never knotted inside anyone but you. It's never been this good, Ivy. Not even close to this good."

13

IVY

I won't admit to him that it's never been this good for me either. It's going to be tricky enough to get away from him as it is.

It's been about twelve hours and he's fucked me numerous times. And I've let him! He's fucked me raw. He thinks we're married.

I've never been in such a dick daze in my life. If I weren't so sore, I'd let him do me again. He's good at it, better at it than any guy I've been with. There haven't been many, but it also hasn't been that few. I've done it enough to know there are men who are good at it and men who are not so good at it. But Tyson? He's the best at it.

If this is real. If werewolves are real and this isn't just one long, drawn-out multi-chapter fever dream.

This guy has smoldering good looks with his tanned and muscled skin, his sexy long hair, and his piercing green eyes. His large calloused hands won't stay off me. Those full lips won't stop dotting kisses across my skin. The mark he left on my neck is like having a second clitoris and he won't stop touching it. He's calling me by his last name and talking about getting me a wedding ring. Oh, and when he saw my breasts he talked about me nourishing our children. My head spins. Speaking of which, I need to take my birth control pill. I take it every morning and here we are hours since waking up. I haven't a clue what time it is; the clocks in this place are dead and I'm not wearing a watch. My phone is... I don't even know if I have my phone. I need my bag.

God, I hope when he dumped shit out of my bag in my car that he didn't dump my pills and my phone.

I need away from his voodoo sex magic for a minute, so I can think. So I can clear my head and think. Figure out how to get out of here.

Okay, the plan: Take my pill, get outta here, get my car towed out of the valley and get it fixed, and then get to the store in time for its grand opening the day after tomorrow.

Yep. I had a lot to figure out.

"Get dressed, little mate. We're going to town."

"Town?"

"I hadn't shifted in years, so the pantry is practically empty. Only one can of fruit left. And some canned fish. I don't like canned fish."

He taps my bottom and gets out of the bed.

"I need a shower. I have all your..." I make a face. "All over me."

He smiles. "Just down around inside your thighs. I'd like it all over you, though." He looks at me thoughtfully and then turns and puts his knee on the bed, ready to crawl back to me.

"No! Bad." I smack his hand and he startles. "Back up. I'm sore. You can't do me again."

He smiles wide. He has a beautiful smile.

I smile back, my sternness melting away. My belly flipflops.

Gah. No. I scoot to the bottom of the bed to get out of it and head toward the bathroom but then his large hands are on my hips and he brings my back against his front. His mouth touches down on that mark on my neck. My head rolls to the right to give him better access.

God, his mouth on that spot...

"Just a little," he says, spinning me around to face him. "I'll be very sweet to your princess parts."

Oh, swoon.

His green eyes flare with a glow, then I'm turned, hiked up, and put against the wall in the small hallway between the bedroom and bathroom. He pushes his cock inside me again, making my mouth drop open. His eyes sparkle. And then his thumb caresses the spot on my neck and my eyes roll as his lips touch mine.

He rocks ever-so-gently against me, pitching me straight into a pleasure spiral, making a masculine purr sound in his chest. My forehead lands on his shoulder. My eyes drift shut while I inhale the aroma of his skin and revel in sensation. That noise he's making, it makes me... happy. He smells so good.

14

TYSON

"Either we go to town to get the supplies or we can fuck," I tell her. "Decide."

I'm losing patience because we fucked over an hour ago and I can't just stand here waiting all day. I've already waited while she took a shower and fiddled with painting her beautiful face with colors.

I have boots on my feet and truck keys in my hand, but yet she's sitting there on the rug near the wood stove, frantically flipping through her belongings that are spilled on the floor in front of her.

There's a lot of stuff. Face paint supplies. Papers. Electrical cords.

"They must be in the car," she says under her breath. And then she looks at me with her eyes narrowed. "You dumped a bunch of my shit out in the car to figure out my name and my pills and phone must've fallen out."

"What?"

She's annoyed with me.

"My phone and pills. I need my pills, especially!" She's a bit hysterical and waving her hands while she talks.

"Are you ill?" I kneel in front of her. "We'll stop at the car and get them before we go to town. What are they for? Are you hurt?"

She doesn't look ill. Her eyes are clear. Her skin is bright. I put my lips to her forehead. Her temperature isn't too hot or too cool.

The idea she might be ill? It just sickens me. I search her face for answers, my heart racing, my stomach twisting.

I have no experience with pills. Uncle took some before he died, calling them killers of pain. They didn't work very well for him and now he's dead. I've never put pills in my mouth in my life and don't think I want to if they are useless like that.

"My – uh... I just need them. Let's go." She gets into a squat and stuffs her things into the purse. She then reaches for the bag that contains her clothes from the bedroom. Her face is bright red. Not from illness though, something else. She's in a panic. She sidesteps me and heads to the door.

Why won't she tell me what the pills are for?

I take her bag from her and drop it. "We'll look for them. You don't need all those clothes for a trip to town for food." I grab for her hand and her eyes widen in what looks like terror. "But you need a coat," I add.

She's chewing her lip and staring at me with wide eyes and red cheeks. I frown as I assess her face and then she fiddles with the bag.

"I left my jacket at the cabin of ill-repute. I'll be fine." She squats and grabs the strap of her large bag and rises, looping it over her shoulder.

Cabin of what?

"Why would you need that for a trip to town?" I take it from her.

Her face goes redder and she doesn't answer.

I lean in. "Ivy. Answer please."

"I need to go."

"Go?" I ask.

"Home. I need to go home, Ty... Tyson. This is my stuff, so it comes with me because I have to go." She huffs and blows a lock of hair away from her eye.

What?

I take the bag from her once again and this time I toss it out of reach. It lands by the stove.

15

IVY

His expression drops when I tell him I have to leave and for some reason, my heart chooses to drop, too. Why? Maybe because of the way he stares at me, eyes working like he's reading a math question written across my face.

He took my bag and tossed it and now he licks his lips behind his teeth, before saying, "You are home. Your home is with me."

He's gone rigid, like he's decided to dig his heels in on the issue.

Fuzz. I was afraid of this.

"I... have a job. A family. An apartment. A car." I bite my lip briefly. "Well, a car that's got broken door handles, a broken window, broken windshield, and it's smashed into a tree, but it's my car and I –" For some reason, I let that hang. The look on his face is making it difficult to speak.

After an endless moment, he speaks in a scary deep voice, his eyebrows up high. "Have a boyfriend?"

I say nothing. How will I reason with him that this just won't work? He can't just keep me.

He gives me a hard stare and leans forward, aggression rolling off him. "If any man who thinks he's entitled to you comes near you, I'll rip his throat out with my teeth."

I jerk back. Oh my God.

He keeps snapping. "We'll go to town. We'll stop and get your pills from that car, but then we will come back here, and I'll make this home better. For you."

I open my mouth to speak, but something about the look on his face has my heart stampeding in my chest. Not because I'm scared that he'll hurt me. He's angry, it's clear, but more because he looks not just angry but also so... distraught.

I reach for my sad-looking Uggs, which... surprise... I somehow expected to be worse. Thankfully, I sprayed them with protectant spray before I wore them for the first time yesterday.

Yesterday, when things were so different. Yesterday, when I was excited to put on new boots. Yesterday, before I lost $200 to Megan's scammy quasi-cousin. Yesterday, before I had to flee from a cabin figuring I had to leave to avoid sexual assault and then left and found myself in a car sliding down a muddy embankment or something, and being chased by the werewolf I hit with my car.

Werewolf. Still blowing my mind that this is who I'm with right now. Yesterday, when I thought a lot of the stuff Aunt Nelle talked about was nothing more than harmless fantasy.

And then what transpired after that? My face burns with the memories of all the dirty unprotected sex I've been having. In a cabin in the woods. With a stranger. A werewolf stranger!

Aunt Nelle, rest her soul, would be nodding knowingly right now, I think. An "I told you so" all over her face, but smiling instead of being snide about it because she was never snide about anything. She'd be tickled pink, I think.

I always thought she was a little kooky; but wasn't really sure if she told me all her stories as a bunch of parable cautionary tales or if she was romanticizing those stories wishing she lived in a world where she could interact with all those things she talked about. Vampires. Witches. Werewolves. Fae. She looked me right in the eye on my sixth birthday and told me I had a 'fae' look to me.

"You believe in fairies, Ivy?"

"Like Tinkerbell?" I'd asked.

"You have a fae look to you. Sometimes I swear, Ivy girl, that the stork switched you with our Ivy. That you're a little fairy who has been dropped off here for now. Maybe my fortune teller was right when she told me about your future. You're gonna have a magical life, my girl."

"Tinkerbell was really tiny in Peter Pan, Auntie Nelle. I'm not that tiny."

She winked and smirked at me like we had a secret. She was always whispering to me about her fortune teller. I had chalked it up to nonsense.

Now, though, I was wondering about it.

I lose my balance while getting my second boot on, stumble and wind up in Tyson's arms. He's looking down at me with piercing eyes. He looks angry. I find that I hate it. I feel like crying.

"You don't need this." He gestures to my purse that's hanging over my shoulder.

"Of course I do. It's my purse! Can you take me where I can call to get my car towed out of there, please? I need to get home."

He stares at it a moment with skepticism before he grabs my hand and we step outside onto the porch. Looking back at my overnight bag longingly, I trudge behind him.

When I look ahead, I find myself squinting at the eyeful of sun I get. It's a sunny day, but it's brisk. And the surroundings here are rough and gloomy looking as winter ran long this year. It's spring but it looks like most of the vegetation around us is still asleep. The house is pretty, but it's surrounded by overgrowth. This place has been sorely neglected. There's another building set back. He walks us back there through dead-looking tall hay-like grass and unlocks the wide door with keys in his hand and pulls it wide. I see some farm equipment and tools as well as a red Chevy pickup truck in there with the hood open and a battery charger connected to it. It's old. Like around maybe 1940s or 1950s old. And mint. This truck has been loved.

He gets the passenger door open for me, so I climb in, thinking about my overnight bag and all the things I'm going to be leaving behind. Two new bikinis, a pair of jeans that I haven't even worn yet. A super soft robe. The price of those will be coming off my next paycheck at the boutique. Some nice tops. And some high-end loungewear for a chalet weekend, too. Shit. My expensive ceramic curling iron and two bottles of perfume (one of them kind of pricy) will be lost.

Well... can't be helped. This little excursion has to be over, that's all there is to it. He slams the hood and gets in. The truck starts right up, and he pulls out.

He gets out, leaving it running, while he climbs out to double back and shut the garage door. And that's when it hits me. This is my best chance at escape.

Heart thundering, I scoot across the bench seat over to the driver's side, lock the door, and take control of the vehicle. I take off, squealing down the overgrown field, kicking up dirt as I head out. In the rearview mirror, I see him standing there, hand on the still-open garage door, looking at me.

I squeeze my eyes tight a second at the strange sensation that sweeps through me, that image of him burning into my retinas, and then I make myself focus on the road instead.

I HAVEN'T SEEN A HOUSE since his despite driving for at least five minutes. I keep going down this endless country road with no intersections, zero traffic, and nothing but trees to look at.

Feeling a little lost and overwhelmed, I put my elbow to the door and hand to my neck. That's when I feel it. That spot he bit.

Oh.

Suddenly, I'm totally, inexplicably grief-stricken. Tears stream down my cheeks.

What the heck?

Why am I crying?

Because I've been through such a scary twelve hours?

Because I had sex multiple times with a stranger (and liked it)?

Because of that look on his face when I said I had to go?

Because of the likely look on his face now that I've left him there, after I've stolen his truck?

I choke on bitter laughter while the tears continue trailing.

I catch sight of myself in the rearview mirror and my eyes look so freaking purple. It's weird. They were always a blue shade verging on purple, but they look so violet right now.

I keep my hand on my neck and feel those teeth marks under my fingers. I rub the spot briefly and my nipples tingle, my sore vagina aches and not just from overuse, either. It aches with sorrowful need if that's such a thing.

It *is* such a thing; I feel it acutely.

Glowing green eyes flash in my mind and I get a little dizzy. I force myself to focus on the road ahead. It winds some more, and I find myself coming up to a dead end bordered by a wooden fence. And... several people stand there on the other side of a big willow tree. Four men and a woman.

Oh! I can ask for directions. And since I've only been on one road, it'll mean I have to pass back by his place. Ack. But they can help me get back on a road I'll recognize and I'm sure from there I can find out where my car is.

I slow right down before I stop the truck and roll down the window. And that's when I see the guy... the guy that was at the cabin, the one that became the brown wolf. He'd been turned the other way when I slowed but now he's looking straight at me. Damn, but he looks a lot like Tyson. They could definitely be brothers.

Retreat!

I immediately throw it in reverse and back up. Fast.

The guy who was the wolf jerks his chin in my direction and says something to the other people he's with, one woman and three other men (large ones, too), and I do a three-point-turn to go back the way I came.

I dare to look in the mirror to see what's happening behind me and they're all staring.

Through the windshield, I see a huge black wolf. He's barreling straight for the truck. He stops in the center of the road and the truck squeals as I'm hitting the brakes. He shows his teeth and then barks at me, all his fur seeming as if standing on end.

The wolf bursts into Tyson and, naked, he stalks toward me, pointing his finger. The look on his face is terrifying. He's looking at me like he plans to rip me limb from limb.

I'm just sitting there, staring, open-mouthed. I clamp my mouth shut as he grips the driver's side door handle and I hear it ricochet against the car with resistance.

He growls at me. "Remove the lock, Ivy!"

I stare at him, mouth agape.

He sticks his hand inside the already open window and does it himself. I scoot over to the passenger side as he climbs in.

His eyes burn with fiery anger, so I instinctively reach for the handle to get out that side because... scary!

Wait. Why did I just sit there while he got in? I can't make sense of it. He made a demand and I just... did nothing.

I don't get a chance to get out of the truck though, because his massive hand clamps down on my wrist and stops me in my tracks.

"Ow," I whimper. It feels like my bones aren't far from being crushed in his bruising grip.

His eyes change, just marginally, and he releases my wrist.

God, my heart is thumping so hard. My wrist throbs.

"Th-that wolf, that's the brown wolf!" I'm jerking my thumb behind me.

"I know." He shifts the truck into drive, and we speed off.

His chest is rising and falling with his anger. And I'm holding my left wrist in my right hand and staring at his profile, trying not to stare at his nudity, too.

Not a word is spoken and we're driving extremely fast.

We get to his house. He stops and gets out, leaving the door open and reaching to the ground to fetch the clothes and boots that are there in a pile. Obviously, this is where he shifted. He dresses quickly, not taking his angry eyes off me, looking like he's alert in case I plan to dive to the driver's side again. I don't. I'm perfectly still and watching him with all sorts of strange emotions washing through me. He gets back in the truck, saying nothing, with anger still rolling off him.

I see that the other guy's clothes and shoes are still there in the driveway. Tyson drives over them.

He then pulls ahead and instead of going the way we just came in, he takes the other direction, driving toward a big weeping willow tree in the middle of the dirt road. He goes to the left of the massive trunk.

Oh. We're obviously heading to town, in the direction I should've gone. Story of my life... always making the wrong decision. In my defense, it didn't look like this direction was an option.

AFTER TEN OR FIFTEEN minutes of driving in silence (that somehow vibrates with his anger), we're in civilization. It's a small town with a quaint folksy painted sign that welcomes us to Drowsy Hollow, and there are restaurants, we've passed a small hospital, and have just pulled into a strip plaza. The place is bustling with plenty of Saturday shopper types. I'm feeling all sorts of chastised even though he hasn't said a word.

He parks, gets out of the truck, and quickly moves around to the passenger side. He opens the door and grabs my hand as I climb out. I've got to jog to keep up with him as he stalks into the grocery store and roughly yanks a cart out of the cart corral. He lets go of my hand and waves at the aisles ahead.

We've gone down two aisles when finally he huffs, "Ivy Savage?"

I look over my shoulder at him. I'd just been walking slightly ahead, arms folded across my chest, though just loosely because my wrist is killing me.

"Ivy Brennan," I correct.

His face falls. Why does that make my chest feel funny? I unfold my arms and plant my hands on my hips. I stare.

"Choose the food you like," he gestures. "And do it fast."

"Fuck this," I whisper.

Aggression is rolling off him.

He scowls at me and points... at what, I don't know. Food?

My eyes scan the area around me. A little old lady ticks by in a motorized scooter with a front basket filled with food. She's not gonna be much help. I try to make eye contact, but she only gives Tyson a head to toe eye-sweep. She's old, but the eye sweep is appreciative.

I see a man at the end of the aisle, but he's about five foot seven and maybe a hundred and twenty pounds. He breezes past us. I mouth 'help' anyway. Maybe he'll go tell someone. Maybe he'll call the police.

I don't think he caught it.

Tyson leans forward and glares at me, so I return the dirty look and reach out and grab a random bag of cookies from my right and toss them into the cart.

Oh. Milanos. The good ones. I grab another bag and drop them. And then another bag. Oreos. He makes a face at me and grabs my left hand and lifts it. I wince. Audibly. He's looking at the purple bracelet bruise he gave me.

Yep. My wrist is already turning purple from where he grabbed it in the truck. His eyes are filled with horror as his thumb grazes my wrist. His eyes move to meet mine and a swallow works down his throat. His face has fallen and gone is all the anger. All I see is remorse. His mouth touches my wrist and he closes his eyes. His other hand grabs the back of my head and I squeak as he pulls me to his body.

He's sorry. He didn't mean to hurt me.

I'm about to cry. His mouth touches my forehead and I'm trembling, overcome with all sorts of feelings. Weird feelings. *God*. What the heck?

I'm angry, suddenly, and pulling away from him. I look up with accusation in my eyes.

His eyes are soft and just so... filled with remorse.

I turn away and oddly begin filling the shopping cart with food.

Four boxes of cereal. Coffee. Pancake mix. Peanut butter and grape jelly. Marmalade. A bunch of spices. Sugar, flour, and other baking things. Three bags of chocolate chips. Some barbeque sauce and a huge jar of mayo. I move forward and then double back and get strawberry jam and honey too. We're then at the back wall that's full of meat and he's stuffing all sorts of meat in the cart. Giant steaks. Roasts. Pork chops. Chicken.

So. Much. Meat.

Yeah. *Duh*. Carnivore. I continue this throughout the store, angry-shopping and doing it mostly to not have to interact with or look at him.

By the time we get to the last aisle, the cart is full. But I've got a bag of frozen peas across my wrist and it's helping with the pain.

I grab an abandoned empty cart that's off to the side and walk fast, feeling him hot on my heels as I pick four types of ice cream and motor back through the first two lanes again to grab stuff we didn't get. Like fruits and vegetables mostly.

I'm like a shopping maniac or something, because there's enough food to feed a large family for weeks. And I've picked lots of fruit because he said he liked fruit. What the fuck is wrong with my brain?

He's saying nothing. Nothing at all. He's eyeing me warily and his gaze keeps landing on the half-thawed pea bag that's draped over my wrist.

Does he even have the money for all this stuff? He's a werewolf living in a dusty house that looks like no one has set foot in it for years.

We get to the checkout and I begin unloading the food onto the conveyer belt, mostly with my right hand because my left wrist is pretty dang sore.

"I'll do it," he says and starts lifting the rest of the stuff out of the second cart. I'm still holding the peas over my wrist. The cashier glances at them so I flip them over to ensure she can get the bar code. She picks up on the signal and lifts her handheld scanner and scans my wrist.

I feel his eyes on me, so I do my best to simply stare at the cashier's screen, watching the rising total.

I picked everything I'd usually pick doing a full shopping, plus everything I'd pick if I were on my period as well as having a big honkin' party. All he did was drop in some meat.

I'm suddenly embarrassed by the two shopping carts of food.

"My purse is in the truck," I whisper. "I'll get my credit card."

"No," he says. "I have money."

He loads the rest of the stuff onto the belt. The cashier is eyeing him with absolute lust in her eyes.

Yeah. I know. He's massive and gorgeous.

"You scanned that twice," I say, and her eyes bounce to the screen and she does a void, saying nothing.

And it dawns that I was about to go get my card and come back to pay for the groceries he forced me to choose. Not run away.

I've lost it.

I really have.

"Hi," I say to the cashier.

Her eyes bounce to me and then back to him.

"Hi," she squeaks.

I should blurt, "I need help. He's kidnapped me."

I should. But all I'm thinking is, yeah, I know he's ridiculously hot and he likes me. Like... a lot. *Me*. So get your eyes off him.

Yep, I've gone crazy.

A man comes into my vision to start bagging. He reaches for one of our carts, pulling it closer so he can put the bagged-up items in it, and Tyson grabs my non-injured hand and roughly pulls me to him, eyeing the guy. The guy is about five foot six and twenty years older than me. He couldn't help me if Tyson got physical; he'd get hurt.

My back is plastered against Tyson's front and then he caresses the bite marks on my neck while he makes a low growling sound behind me. I twist to look at him, feeling like it's highly inappropriate for him to touch me there. It doesn't feel like he's near my collarbone. It feels illicit. Like he's being dirty in public.

"Tyson," I whisper, looking over my shoulder.

He's eying the man bagging the groceries. He stops growling and stares at me. And it dawns that if I ask for help, someone could get hurt. Right? Is that why I'm not saying anything?

The clerk now looks like he's trying to avoid Tyson's eyes. I mean, I guess most men wouldn't want to get into something with a guy that's about six foot four and built like a professional athlete. Not to mention the growling part. Why is Tyson looking at him like he's worried he's about to steal me from him?

Because he knows I'm thinking about crying out that this guy has kidnapped me?

I should say something. I really should.

Tyson stares at the pile of food still being bagged and then the cashier who is still scanning and has decreased her pace, trying to give the bagger time to catch up. He lets out a huff of impatience.

I'm about to start helping bag the groceries when a late teens or early twenties girl comes over and shoots us a smile as she starts helping.

And now she's eyeing Tyson lustfully.

I stare at the screen and the rising dollar value.

Finally, it's at the end.

"Three hundred and seventy-seven dollars and sixty-three cents," our cashier says.

Tyson pulls a wad of cash from his jeans and drops bills on the conveyor belt. He drops too many of them and looks confused for a second, but then shoves the stack of bills at her. She gives him some change and he pockets it.

I'm biting my lip, pondering my next move. His eyes hit mine and he's looking at me with an intensity that makes me tremble.

The spell is broken when the cashier holds out the long receipt. Tyson doesn't take it, so I do. I stuff it into one of the bags.

"Thank you," I say to her, but she's busy staring at Tyson and doesn't notice. "And thank you," I add, to the clerks who are bagging up our last bag. The man acknowledges me with a nod as he sets the final bag into cart number two and he's studiously avoiding making eye contact. The girl has flipped her hair and sashayed away, obviously looking to get Tyson's attention. She looks back at him and deflates that he's not looking at her.

I grab one cart. Tyson grabs the other and shoots the man a dirty look as he passes. I follow him back to his truck and heft some bags into the bed of the pickup truck.

"Into the truck, Ivy," he orders and opens the door.

"I'll –" I gesture to the cart.

"Now," he snaps.

I climb in.

He slams the door.

And then I think, wait... what? Am I going along with this? Why did I listen to him? Why didn't I ask for help in there? Why didn't I scream my head off?

I get back out. He's got half the bags in and he stops and looks at me and he points at the spot I just vacated.

"Pff," is the sound I make.

I grab my handbag and sling it over my shoulder while I walk away from him, still holding the bag of peas.

Screw this. Why did I even let him get me into his truck? I should've kept going. I should've – *oof*! He's lifted me over his shoulder and he's carrying me back to his truck. People are driving by and ignoring us. How come? How can they ignore this? A man pushes a cart while talking on his phone and glances at us but with what looks like irritation and keeps going.

"I'm crazy. But you're crazier if you think I'm cuckoo enough to keep going along with this. I'm out of here."

"Out of here? We're out of here. We're going home."

"I'm leaving."

"Not alone, you're not," he retorts.

"I'll scream my head off," I warn. "You made me lose my peas!"

"Do it," he dares. "It makes no difference."

"You go to your home and I'll go to mine," I snap.

"My home is wherever you are," he announces and deposits me into the truck seat before leaning close to me. "Move again," he warns, "and I'll make you submit to me right here in this parking lot. You want that?"

I don't know what 'that' means but I shake my head.

His voice goes lower. "I'm sorry I hurt your wrist, Ivy. I am more sorry than I can say. I didn't realize… but if you think you're running away from me, I'll do what I must do to make you submit. Understand?"

"What does that mean?" I ask, voice barely a whisper.

"Misbehave again and you'll find out," he warns me.

He quickly lifts the rest of the bags in one scooping motion and dumps them all into the back of the truck, uncaring. Something shatters back there.

My eyes track his movements until he's back in the driver's seat and pulling out. He hands me the half-thawed bag of peas that he must've fetched from the pavement.

"You didn't even put the carts back," I mutter.

One rolls into the side of an old minivan. I doubt it damaged it, but still…

He grinds his teeth and I actually hear them squeak.

He then grabs my face and glares in my eyes.

I'm suddenly terrified.

I reach for the handle, not caring that the vehicle is moving, and his hand hooks around the back of my neck and holds on a second as he accelerates.

"Behave or I'll stop the truck and make you submit," he tells me, eyes moving to the road.

"You're scaring me, Tyson."

"If that makes you behave, good. You've been very naughty, my little mate."

I blink.

"And when I get you home…" His eyes bounce to me briefly and he shakes his head.

Oh my God. What? What does that mean? I'm trembling all over.

He speeds up.

I swallow hard and hold the peas over my wrist.

ABRUPTLY, HE STOPS the truck. I look around. We've been riding in silence up until now. We can't be far from his place judging by all the trees and little else around.

"Stay here, Ivy," he demands.

"Huh?"

"If you make me hunt you down in these woods, I'll fuck you in the dirt." His eyes then rove over me and he looks, for a second, like that's precisely what he'd like to do. Fuck me. In the dirt.

Why is that spot on my neck tingling?

He leaves the vehicle, taking the keys with him (shooting me a dirty look as he pockets them as if he just thwarted my plan) and then he rounds the front and heads down the hill. Oh. That hill.

I roll the window down and stretch my neck to look out. I see my car down there. My poor little car! It looks small and damaged and… sad.

I've only had this car six months. I love my little car.

A minute later, he's back with my packet of birth control pills, my very old Blockbuster membership (why did I even have that in my wallet still?), three random business cards that'd been stuffed in my wallet, my coffee club card (with all the stamps needed to get my freebie except two), and a lip gloss. He passes them through the window to me before he rounds the truck hood and climbs back in.

16

TYSON

I don't like that she's frightened of me. At all. The scent of her fear sickens me, especially knowing she's afraid of me, but I'm having trouble keeping myself calm. She's trying to leave me! I can't allow it. I won't.

And that I hurt her? I'm disgusted with myself for it. The mark on her wrist makes me want to rip my own innards out.

She should be settling; she should know she's mine. I've mounted her and knotted inside her. I've given her my mark. Why is she trying to leave me?

And she came in contact with *him*. A wolf shifter who could be a real threat. *And* those he was with. I ran after her, unable to keep up with the speed of the truck, but knew she'd come back around because that road led to nothing and then when I caught the scent of Riley Savage with others that I knew were shifters, one scent that I recognized with a sickness inside me that I haven't been able to shake, dots have been connecting in my brain ever since. It doesn't feel good.

I found speed I've never had and got to her as soon as she was fleeing from them. And then this ridiculous game in the food store and the parking lot and I'm infuriated with my little Ivy.

More than infuriated, I'm confused. Why isn't she settling? Am I doing something wrong?

She's going to learn that she's not to leave me, ever, and I've decided she's going to begin learning that through submission.

Now that we have supplies, I can give her my full attention. I want to bond with her. I want her sweet and cooing under me. If it takes some lessons and punishments to get there first, so be it.

When I think of what could have happened if they'd captured her?

I'm seeing blood in my mind, their blood. If they try to come near her again I should rip them all to ribbons. But there's also this uncertainty about them that has me way off kilter.

She pops a pill out of the packet I'd fetched for her into her mouth and swallows. I want to ask her what the pills are for. I don't like that she has to take them. It makes something sick bubble and rise in the very back of my throat.

I swallow it down, thinking it's best to ask my questions later. Right now, I'm anxious to get her home.

17

IVY

Far too soon, we're back on his property. I've paid attention to the route, too, so that even if I'm on foot, I'm semi-confident I know which way to go to get to my car. It's not close and there were a few twists and turns on top of the fact that Tyson's road isn't marked, but I've done my best to commit some landmarks to memory.

He's stopped and is out of the truck quickly, slamming the door angrily. I hesitate before I take my seatbelt off, watching him round the front to come to my side.

The look of sheer anger on his face is frightening. I engage the lock just as he gets his hand to the handle. His eyes go fiery.

"Open it!" he demands.

I'm terrified of the look on his face.

"Ivy!" He shouts.

I shake my head.

He looks at me with astonishment.

His keys are in the ignition, still. *His bad.* I bite my lip.

"Do not even think about trying to leave me again," he warns, but his eyes suddenly look afraid and that does something to me.

I look away. If I don't look at him, I don't have to feel whatever this feeling is.

He steps around to go to the driver's side, and I scoot over and lock the door before he gets there.

He sighs and closes his eyes.

"Come out."

I shake my head.

"Ivy."

I shake it some more and close my eyes as I turn the ignition.

I feel the vehicle bounce a little. He's jumped into the back of the pickup, with the groceries.

Fuzz. If I leave, he's coming with me.

Damnit.

The ice cream we got is gonna melt.

What a stupid thought.

What a stupid, stupid thought.

I look back and he's got his face in the back window. He lifts an eyebrow and my adrenalin spikes.

"Come out. Now," he commands in a deep and menacing voice.

I'm frozen, locked in a fiery green gaze, and it's as if my mouth is suddenly filled with cotton. I turn the truck off and unlock the door with a sigh. I'll have to figure something out later.

He's already hopped over the side of the truck bed and is catching me as I'm exiting the truck by scooping me into his arms.

"You don't need to carry me," I protest but my words are ignored as he marches to the house, evidently not wanting to take chances. He opens the door and storms directly to that bedroom I'd been in before, dropping me on the bed.

"Wait here. Don't move."

I spring to my feet and in an instant, he's pushed me back down, flipped me to my belly, and is pinning me with a hand in the center of my back.

"Tyson," I protest.

His teeth are then on the back of my neck, not biting hard, but I feel them. He's growling at me. His torso is warm, bordering on hot, over my back.

Holy fuck. He's holding me down. With. His. Teeth.

I squirm.

He growls and his teeth tighten ever so slightly, so I stop squirming.

After an eternity, he releases.

"Stay. Here," he bites off and then he's gone.

I hear the creak of the door followed by slams three times as he's obviously bringing the food in. I hear the refrigerator open and the rustling of bags. At least the beast has the sense to put the perishable food away.

I'm still on my belly on the unmade bed.

All sorts of questions float through me about him and his existence.

What the heck is gonna happen to me?

I need to go. Like soon. I have to get back to my car, find a way to get it towed, and get back home. It's Saturday afternoon now and the boutique's grand opening is Monday, so ideally Sunday morning would be a good time to get home. I told Megan we would need to leave the cabin of ill repute at the crack of dawn Sunday (before, when I thought it was a swanky chalet) and she agreed that'd work for her. I wonder, idly, if she's staying the whole weekend and who she's going to get a ride back with.

My car is too far down that embankment to be spotted. She won't be looking for me as she leaves.

I'll see her each day this week for an hour as we crisscross shifts just for that hour to ensure everything is smooth. After that, we'll be ships passing in the night with a five to ten-minute crossover to hand over responsibilities. Our boss doesn't want any hiccups during opening week that would taint our reputation. I'm going to be all business with her. It'll be like this weekend didn't even happen and it'll certainly be like the friendship we'd cultivated didn't happen. I'm not risking my job or the respect I have from my boss for her. Her true colors were revealed to me this weekend and it won't take long for Becks to see her nature, too.

My thoughts of work and how Megan got me into this mess I'm in are interrupted when I feel the bed move as he climbs back on. He's got a knee between my legs and the other beside my hip. He lifts my hand and I draw in a sharp hiss of breath.

"I'm sorry about your wrist, Ivy," he says softly.

I roll my eyes. The brute doesn't know his own strength. I know he didn't mean it. I also wonder why I didn't just drive, despite him being in the back of the truck. I could've driven until I got to a police station and laid on the horn. Why didn't I?

"I'll be careful in future, Ivy," he vows.

I'm thinking *whatever* but he leans over and puts his mouth to my wrist and for some reason this makes hot tears prick my eyes. I feel those soft, warm lips tenderly pucker as he drops a kiss there.

After releasing my hand, he grips my waist and gently turns me over onto my back. Our eyes meet as his fingers caress my jaw. He stares deep and time seems to be of no consequence because I have no idea how long our eyes stay locked before his fingers slide down my face, then down my arm to my hip, which he squeezes briefly and then his hand slides under my bottom and into my yoga pants as his mouth descends toward mine.

"Saying that, I also need to say... you," he says against my mouth, "don't," he drops a kiss there, "leave me." His fingers slide further down the back of my pants and find my slipperiness.

I'm suddenly aware I'm panting, unable to tear my eyes away.

"You're mine," he tells me, sliding fingers inside me.

I swallow and grab his shoulders.

There's no hesitation in his touch. None. He touches me like he has the right to do so. I don't want to find it so arousing, but I do.

He leans sideways to kiss the inside of my wrist again.

God, his skin is hot. It's burning hot through the flannel of his shirt.

"I claimed you, Ivy, because I knew it was the only thing I could do the second I caught your scent. I've never claimed anyone else the way I've claimed you. I never will. It's my job to protect you. To provide for you. To fill you with me."

I draw in air until my lungs are full.

"To punish you, when you need correction," he adds, and then his fingers are gone and I'm quickly flipped to my belly, which has bottomed out.

"Tyson..." I breathe out, trying to protest, but my pants are being yanked down and he bites my bottom. Hard.

I squeal.

"Ow! Fucking ouch!" I exclaim.

I hear his zipper and then feel the tip of his cock glide through my crack down to my center.

He slams inside.

I should've been dry. I should've been bone-dry. I wasn't. He got zero resistance from my body.

I cry out into the crook of my arm, smushed into the pillow.

I feel it immediately grow inside me and begin to pulse against my g-spot, first slowly, and then faster. Holy shit. I'm trembling and crying out a climax in about the count of twenty.

His hand slips under me and then strong, hot fingers play with my clit at the same time, and I come on top of coming with a cacophony of sensations thrumming through me, pulsing inside me. Heat envelopes me and it feels like sparks must be bursting from my clit, scorching the sheets underneath me.

"Holy fucking shit," I groan as hot liquid fills me.

Just when I think I'm about to pass out from climaxing so hard, he's rubbing that spot on my neck. This makes me cry out harder. The sensations just go on and on and on. Higher and higher. My body is shaking. It should be ebbing now, but he's grinding against my body with that throbbing cock inside me and he can't pull out because it grew inside me.

With the grinding motion, he just keeps pulsing against that spot inside and to top it all off, he's making the sexiest purring sound in between grunts.

"Ty...Ty... Tyson, too much. Too much," I squeak out.

"No. Take more," he demands and then he's twisted sideways to reach those bitemarks with his mouth and sucking on that spot. It's too much. Too, too much. I'm crying while I'm coming because it's just insanely intense.

He needs to stop.

He comes even more. More of that hot liquid spills from me and finally the fullness subsides just a little bit and I'm feeling relieved that I can come back down to earth. But I'm feeling that way too soon because instead of him rolling over after he pulls out, instead he flips me to my back, and then he rams inside again, eyes ablaze and jaw ticking.

Holy shit. This has to stop.

He's not gonna stop.

How is he still hard?

Sensation tears through me like an inferno.

"Stop," I breathe.

He pulls out, hauls my legs up so the backs of my ankles are resting on his pecks, and he's slamming inside again, spearing me with that heavy, hard cock.

"Please. St-top. Ty-Tyson, please. Stop." My whole body is buzzing and I'm having convulsion-like tremors as my vagina spasms, spilling out hot liquid while he continues to hammer it into me.

"No," he snarls. "You're gonna learn, Ivy."

He knots inside me again. A-fucking gain.

Learn what? Learn what it means to be fucked to death?

18

TYSON

She feels so tight, so right. Her little pussy is hugging my cock so hard, squeezing around me with intention, telling me I should never be outside of her despite what her mouth says. This pussy is the boss. It wants all I want to give it and I'm going to keep giving it. This perfect creature is mine. Her beautiful tits are bouncing, the tips like ripe raspberries pointing at me, begging me to taste them. I'm too busy knotting inside her and groaning as the sensation of warmth floods me and makes my balls empty inside her again. I stare at her tits as they bounce, listening to her whimpers and her pleading with my name, and with a short version of my name that she seems to use when she's either coming hard or pleading with me to stop. She shortens my name to Ty. I like it when she does that. When she does that, she feels me inside her, feels me owning her.

Finally, my knot subsides and I'm again moving both in and out as she flops listlessly, tears spilling from her beautiful bluebell-colored irises.

I lick one ripe raspberry nipple, then the other and caress where I've put my mark on her and this makes her whimper some more.

"Please, please," she whispers, eyes closed and her body shaking.

The sun is setting and my stomach needs food. I'll have to stop fucking her long enough to get food into my little mate as well as into myself.

I kiss her.

"Please stop. I can't take anymore," she cries out and her body is limp. She's exhausted.

I've brought her to climax more than half a dozen times.

"You're mine, Ivy. Your body is mine and your heart will be, too. You don't leave me," I remind her.

Her eyelashes flutter and she winces as I pull out, my cock ready to take a break if it must. Finally, the muscles inside her pussy are no longer tightening around me. She needs a break.

I want more, but she's eaten so little today and it's approaching night. There's also a chill in the air since I hadn't rebuilt the fires when we got back from town. The kitchen is filled with the food we bought. I only put the meat and the other cold items in the fridge; everything else is in bags on the floor and on the countertop and table.

I rise and stretch out my back muscles and she whimpers again and pulls her legs together but her eyes on me are appreciative. My little Ivy likes my body. I like hers, too.

"Ow," she whispers, eyes closing, and then she shivers.

I lift the blanket over her and caress her face while I give her a low purr, which makes a smile spread across her face. She likes when I make that sound. I've never made it in my life before. I only make it for her.

It's a sound that I somehow know comes from my wolf, my wolf who would normally, in spring times when I've had to shift to man form, be whining and pining to come out and run. At night, I ran when I wasn't mounting a female. My wolf wants to run and leap with jubilation at the fact that I have her. It also wants to celebrate by hunting and feasting, then returning so I can mount her again.

I know I can't run and feast as wolf until I know that she's not going to try to leave me and that no one will attempt to harm her. That Riley Savage was here today and that he with others from that forbidden village congregated on the end of my road doesn't sit well. This is miles away from their village and there's no reason they should be here other than to interfere with my life. It makes me want to hunt them all down, destroy every single heartbeat in that village. But what stops me from raining blood on all of them is likely the niggle that weighs on me about the female that was there today when I caught up with Ivy. She was there with them, the tone of an accord, not under duress. Her scent calls to me in a foreign way. And her scent invades my mind because it's as if memories are trying to surface.

I didn't allow myself to look at her, but I knew she was there, and I felt something from her that I shook off, that I shake off again now.

Memories of my infancy are too far away to know for sure if that's her. I left that village too young to remember anything or anyone, but maybe scents from the past did imprint on me. Perhaps they imprint on all shifters. I never asked my uncle about it. I asked no questions when I got to the village and they submitted, when I remembered when I'd scented one of their females before. I push the thoughts away. I can't give them any time now, or my mind will spin, and the red haze of anger could l strike like lightning down my spine. When that happens it takes over and I become nothing but the urge to hunt and kill. It can't be allowed to spin when I have Ivy to think of first.

I find this odd. The wolf in me has always been dominant over the man in me until now. Now, I feel that something is shifting. Instead of that wolf being angry that it'll take second place in my priorities because Ivy is first, it's happy that I have her and content to wait until it's safe to come out. Unless it needs out to protect her, then I know it'll thrust its way forward as it has been doing.

I pull jeans on, remembering that uncle told me clothing on a man was something females preferred outside fucking, and make my way to the kitchen.

I look through all the food she chose and half of it I don't even recognize, though I notice she bought all sorts of fresh fruit as well as frozen fruit and fruit in cans like the fruit I've bought before.

I bite into a long yellow fruit or vegetable and the inside is squishy and pleasant. The outside isn't. I spit the rind into the sink and dig the rest of the inside out. I like it.

I wonder if she wants one.

19

IVY

I dozed for a few minutes, I guess, and when I open my eyes, it's because I smell food. As that registers I also become aware of all the leftover cum between my legs. The bed is wet and it's gonna get gross, or grosser, if I don't clean it. I need another shower.

Tyson's coming toward me with a plate in his hand, and the sight of him bare-chested, jeans sitting low on his hips, and eyes on me in that way of his has my belly doing a flip-flop.

I sit up and bite my lip. My stomach rumbles.

He sits on the edge of the bed and I see what's on the plate. A giant T-bone steak, cut into cubes, the bone on the side. Steam rises from it.

He picks up a cube with his fingers and puts it into my mouth.

He cooked this over fire, obviously as it's smoky, looks rather charred, and it's bland. I don't think he's used any spices.

It's tender, though. I chew and swallow.

"Good?" he asks.

I wrinkle up my nose.

"Not good?" He frowns and takes a bite.

He shrugs and takes another bite and then puts another cube to my lips. "You need to eat."

"It's not very..." I scrunch up my face again.

He leaves with the plate.

I'm gathering the quilt around me and am about to get up, when he's back with a banana in his hand.

"You need to try *this*! This is delicious." He bites the end off and lets it fall out of his mouth onto his hand.

I double-blink at the craziness of it.

Instead of peeling it, he digs two fingers into the opening in the top of the banana and scoops some of the fruit out of the peel before he brings his fingers to my mouth.

I accept. How crazy am I for accepting food from his fingers? I give my head a shake at the ridiculousness. He's so... disarming.

He smiles and licks his lips. "It's good, right?"

I swallow. "It's a banana," I state.

"And it's good." He squeezes an inch or two down to make some more ooze out.

"Here." I take it and show him how the peel comes down, one petal at a time, and he gives me a giant smile and breaks a piece off and shoves it in between my lips, making me startle before sticking the rest of it in his mouth.

"That's so good," he says around a whole mouthful of banana.

I can't help it; this makes me giggle.

He smiles and looks at me with questions in his eyes as he chews.

"I need a shower," I tell him, sobering.

He swallows and shakes his head. "First, you need to eat."

"I'll eat. I'll take a shower and then I'll cook us something. Something with flavor."

He stares at the banana peel in his hand.

"I like bananas, too, Tyson, but not for dinner."

What's his story? How does he know how to drive a truck but not how to peel a banana? He paid for groceries. He can build a fire and he obviously has basic survival skills.

He shrugs. "I'll take a shower, too."

He drops the banana peel and then drops his jeans, steps out of them, and grabs my hand, pulling me out of the bed. I scramble to reach for the quilt so I can cover myself, but he doesn't seem the least bit worried about us both being naked. Of course not.

I'm tugged into the bathroom where I'm feeling very bashful. I'm naked and I need to pee.

"Wait until I finish," I tell him and try to nudge him out of the bathroom.

"I'll take a shower with you," he's decided.

"Okay, but wait until I use the bathroom."

He tilts his head, confused.

"I need to use the toilet," I clarify.

"Okay, use it." He moves to the shower and turns it on and then gets inside and pulls the curtain over.

I stare at the white curtain with the faded purple flowers for a minute and then realize that there's something of a cultural barrier here. I sit on the toilet and go about my business.

His head pokes out and he looks at me.

Oh shit, I want to shrivel up and die right now.

"Don't try to leave!" He points and then he's behind the curtain again.

I say nothing.

"Or I'll need to teach you some more," he adds loudly.

I glare at the curtain and after wiping with toilet tissue from the dusty-looking toilet paper roll, I flush.

"Oh! Brrrr" This comes from behind the shower curtain and I grin. The water turned cold. Serves him right.

I pull the curtain aside and he's shivering, holding his biceps with his hands, and standing back from the water stream.

He looks at me with alarm and holds his hand out to halt me. "Wait, Ivy. It's gone cold. It shouldn't. The hot water might be broken. Oh. That's better. Come." He grabs my hand and I climb into the tub. He's immediately washing me with the striped green bar of soap that he slides over me, everywhere, including between my legs. It falls from his hand and he keeps going with soapy palms, rubbing up and down and up and down between my legs. I squeak and try to cross them, but he's adamant and focused on his task. He then reaches for the shampoo bottle and squirts some standard green 2-in-1 shampoo into my hair and lathers it up, smiling at me.

He starts purring happily as he's playing with the bubbles in my hair.

I close my eyes and soak in the feeling of his fingers on my scalp. Then those fingers are on my breasts, so I take over pushing water back down the length of my hair under the stream but then I feel a hot mouth close around my nipple. His fingers walk their way between my legs.

"No, I'd like to stay clean for a bit," I tell him. I squeeze my thighs in an effort to deny him access while I also squeeze the excess water from my hair. I move past him to get him in front of the flowing water and grab the shampoo and squirt it into his hair.

"Your turn," I say, deciding on a distraction.

It works, I guess, because he smiles. He's too tall for me to reach his scalp properly.

He slides a little on the slippery soap he dropped, and he catches himself by grabbing the shower curtain, tearing half of it off the shower rod. His look of panic vanishes, and he stares down at the offending bar of soap and lifts it. "Slippery," he says and tosses it over into the sink.

"One sec," I say, seeing way too much water escape the confines of the tub because the shower curtain is hanging by just three rings now, and I squat to twist the steel plug in to block the drain. I flip the shower knob so that water begins filling the tub before the entire floor gets flooded.

"Here," I say and nudge at his shoulders until he understands my gesture and sits down. I get behind him, legs on either side of his thighs and he shifts down a little as I begin lathering up his fabulous long, dark, curly hair. He leans back against my chest and makes a happy sound while caressing my legs. I soap up his shoulders and his chest with the excess shampoo on my hands. He grabs his cock and strokes it as I do this and holy moly... it's the hottest thing I think I've ever witnessed.

I stare at the sexy, muscled, wet body in front of me, nestled between my thighs. Every water droplet is fascinating. The big soaker tub is a tight fit for the two of us, but he's not complaining. His knees are cocked and he's soapy everywhere. The way he pumps his dick, it looks so normal. I mean, huge, but normal, not like it could be the same thing he used inside me that transformed into a vibrating g-spot stimulator that was locked in place. I reach sideways as far as I can and am able to grab it. It feels normal.

Suddenly, I'm mortified at my actions. I can't believe I just grabbed it. I let it go and stew in my indignity.

What's wrong with me? I need a brain transplant. Or maybe I got one when I wasn't looking, because after everything, I'm here giggling and giving banana-peeling tutorials, then washing the hair of the guy that hauled me to his wolf lair and has been dicking me half to death.

He twists sideways to look over his shoulder at me.

"Why is your face like that?" His eyes are so soft on me, so concerned.

"The way it moved inside me. It got bigger and... vibrated. Is that... is that normal?"

"It?" he asks.

"Your..." I gesture toward his cock, which is right there in all its thick, veined, glory.

"Ah. For me it feels like the most natural thing. Others? I have no idea. I know all wolf shifters knot their mates. Rinse the soap from my hair or I'm going to have to fuck you in this tub, Ivy Savage, and I intended to give you until after we eat dinner for that but then you grabbed my cock and I've decided that after we eat, I want to climax with my cock in your little hand."

"Uh... oh."

He smiles. "It'll give your princess parts a break. My... parts don't want a break."

"You don't know if others like you have the same thing happen? The pulsing action?"

"I don't make it a habit to ask other men about their cocks. I only know what I was told. That I'd only be able to knot inside my mate. I've never knotted inside anyone else."

"Oh. But..."

"I spent no significant time with any man but my uncle and he was the only shifter I ever met before this morning. My uncle told me things but was a man of few words, so I don't think he told me all the things. And now I don't know if all he told me was truth or not. My conversation with Riley Savage today has my mind jumbled. But you're my focus. I'll figure all the other stuff out later when you're finally settled."

"Finally settled?" I ask.

The tub is filled deep enough with water and shampoo bubbles now that his cock is now hiding under the water level.

"When you stop trying to leave me."

I fight to swallow, but it doesn't happen.

"My whole life I was told they're the enemy. Part of me wants to hunt them and erase them from this world. Part of me wonders if my uncle told only lies. My mind is ... considering a lot of events growing up."

He goes quiet and I think he probably feels like the weight of the world is on his shoulders.

I put my hands to those massive shoulders and squeeze them. I feel his body relax a little.

"What things did he say to you today?" I dash bubbles that are about to slide down his forehead into his eyes back into his hairline.

"I don't want to think on that or talk about it. I want to eat. And then fuck you." Tyson stretches, wanting my mouth. I grant it. He kisses me sweetly and his voice drops an octave. "I need this shampoo out. You're very sweet to protect my eyes. I've gotten it in there before and it isn't nice."

"It's small in here with both of us. I'll get out and you tip your head back under that running water before it gets too deep."

"Stay," he says and spins around so that he gets his head under water and his feet are tucked on either side of my hips. This gives me a direct view of everything going on between his legs briefly before the water and bubbles slosh over his body and cover him.

"Tyson... we need to talk about you fucking me," My eyes fly to the ceiling. I realize it's likely he can't hear me as his head is under the running water. He finally rises to sitting and squeezes his hair of excess water. "We need to talk about you fucking me. About you not fucking me, I mean," I feel my face go red. "I need to go home. I'm not trying to hurt your feelings, you seem very... sweet, but..."

He lunges forward and water spills over the side. He puts his mouth to mine, cupping my jaw. My eyes drift shut as I let him steal the words from my mouth. He kisses sweetly at first, and then he's kissing with tongue and making that vibrating purr sound again and my nipples are tingling. I'm clutching both sides of the tub and then he's licking my throat.

"Please don't try to fuck me again," I plead. "I can't."

"Then don't talk about having to go," he threatens and backs away.

I have a full body shudder.

He climbs out of the tub and shakes his head rapidly from side to side.

Water is flying everywhere.

I squeal and squint.

Holy shit, he's shaking the water off like a dog.

"Towels are a lot more effective, Ty," I suggest, blinking, laughing.

He laughs hard. "I forgot." He fetches a towel from the rod and rubs his body, still laughing.

I twist the taps off and pull the plug.

"I never laughed before. I like it," he says. "It's fun. It feels good in here." He points to his stomach. "and here." He points to his chest and leaves.

My expression drops.

Never laughed before?

He comes back with another towel and reaches out to take my hand. As I stand, feeling bashful about the way his eyes devour my naked body, his muscles are bulging in his jaw and he's examining my face, trying to read my expression, I think.

I try to take the towel as I step over the tub onto the sopping wet bathmat, but he doesn't let go of it. Instead, he moves closer and dries me, staring into my eyes as he does.

I stand there while he gently dries me. He grabs my waist with one hand and lifts one foot in the other. "Hold on so you don't fall." I grab his shoulder and he dries even the bottoms of my feet. I'm watching him and thinking *holy shit... Some girl some day is going to be very, very lucky to be your wife.* And then it dawns.

I could be that girl.

I could be.

He wants me to be.

He thinks I *am* that girl.

I swallow down a lump in my throat. My chest feels strange.

He looks up. "What's the matter? Is your wrist still hurting?" He looks at it. It's a fairly ugly purple. Regret washes across his features again and it hits me in the chest as he kisses it.

"It's okay," I say, and he rises and begins drying my hair with the towel.

I'm biting my lip.

"What are you cooking for me?"

"Um, how about bacon and eggs? I'm starved and that won't take long." I reach for, then hang the wet bathmat over the side of the tub.

He shrugs. "Bacon and eggs. I'll try it."

"Try it? Haven't you had it before?" I'm wondering if this is going to be as foreign to him as a banana.

"Well..." He looks like he's sifting through his mind. "I'm not sure. I've done my eating as wolf except when I was very young and couldn't shift yet and one other time when I was having a problem with shifting for several days. So, maybe. I don't know."

"You ate canned peaches as a wolf?" I ask, laughing as I wrap the towel around myself and head back to his bedroom. He follows. I reach for my bag, for a change of clothes. My iPad is there, too. I have no idea if my phone was in the car and he left it or if it's outside the car somewhere. I chew my cheek thoughtfully and sift through for the cord.

"No, I ate canned peaches when I shifted. I shifted about a month each year until he died. I'd be man during the day and shift to wolf and run and hunt at night. After efforts to find a mate."

He reaches into the armoire and pulls out a pair of trackpants and puts them on. He slicks his wet hair back with his fingers.

"My uncle bought this cabin for us when I was an infant and purchased some items to care for me until I was old enough to shift. I don't know what I ate as an infant or a small child. My memories are hazy because it's been so long since I was man. But, when I hit puberty I remember problems shifting for a time, so he provided some man-food to me. Canned fruit was something I ate a lot of. I didn't grow tired of it." He shrugs.

"You were only a man a month per year?" I ask.

"Yes, except when I was a small child."

"And during those times..." His words about looking for a mate are rolling around in my head.

"I'd shift at night and hunt. Sleep and read during much of the day."

"So, you mostly ate other animals?"

"Yes."

I make a face. "Have you ever eaten a person?"

He considers my question a minute and flexes his jaw. "I remember once. Some of him. More than once, maybe, but once is vivid."

I gag. He frowns.

"I disgust you?"

"You can't help what you are any more than I can." I shrug and slide my panties up my legs and try to get them on without dropping my towel. He watches with interest.

"You eat, what? Deer? Bunnies?"

"Yes."

"You kill them and eat them?" My face heats.

"I don't find dead ones and eat those. I'm not a buzzard shifter."

"Bleck."

"It's natural, Ivy."

"Let's not talk about that stuff. Let's just say you do 'wolf' things."

"Okay," he agrees.

"So you can read?" I ask.

"My uncle taught me, yes. He purchased textbooks and taught me from them until I could read well enough to take over and teach myself. He grew frustrated with the teaching and I was anxious for more learning, so I took over. I haven't been a man for some time, Ivy. Some of the things I know are still coming back to me. Like the bananas. After you peeled it I remembered a book about a monkey who ate a lot of them and remember him opening the fruit to get the inside parts." He gets a light in his eyes and then he's gone.

He calls my name a few seconds later. I finish pulling a sweatshirt over my head and slide on a pair of loose short drawstring linen shorts I have in my bag.

I head out and see the door that was on the other end of the hall is open and a light is on. I step inside and this is a chilly room with a small bookshelf and a desk. There's a twin mattress on the floor and everything in here is coated with dust. It smells like it hasn't been opened up and cleaned in ages.

"This was my room, where I slept and did my studies as a child. The other room was his until I grew, and he gave it to me for bedding women and took this one."

I lift my eyebrows and feel heat rise in my face. What's that ugly feeling I have inside me?

"How many women have you brought here?" I ask, feeling my cheeks flame.

He ponders a moment. "Maybe six or eight, I think. Ten. Ten, yes."

"You've had sex with ten women?"

"No, more than that. Many more than that. That's just the ones I brought here. I often brought them to the motel or would go to their home." He tilts his head. "Does this anger you?"

"No!" I answer too quickly. "Why would it? You bring me here; you bring plenty of women here. Were they here against their will, too?" I've got my arms across my chest and I fight my brows from knitting together.

He looks amused.

The asshole.

"They weren't my mate, Ivy. I didn't know it until now that I should've known the minute I was in their presence."

I say nothing but heat continues rising in my face.

He chuckles and then hands me a dusty yellow book. "I loved this little monkey," he says. "For a long time, this was my only book. I read it over and over."

I feel a smile tug my grimace away. "I loved him, too."

"You read this?"

I nod. "I think my mom still has it and all my other books. Boxes upon boxes of them in the attic. She's saving them for some day when I have a baby."

Tyson smiles wide. "Then our baby will have two of these books. Or one for our sons and another for our girls. We'll have many boys so if shifter boys don't like to share, they'll have to learn."

My heart skips a beat.

His expression drops and I realize it's mirroring my expression.

"Or maybe we'll need more copies of this book. I wanted siblings and didn't have any, but I would not have wanted to share my books."

"I should... uh... cook," I say and make my exit.

20

TYSON

Her cheeks burned with jealousy as she asked how many women I'd brought here and tried to guess the number I'd had sex with.

This is good news.

The nurturing nature of my little one, her carefully shampooing my hair, protecting my eyes from soap, wanting to cook for me, it's further proof she's a gift to me.

More and more from books and lessons as well as experiences are sliding back into place in my mind. Uncle struggled to teach me the basics of reading and comprehension and I'm sure I learned later than I would have, but after I had the basics down he was relieved and told me the books would do the rest.

They did.

I devoured books throughout my childhood and even after puberty I had a thirst for knowledge during the month each year that I was a man. I'd study until night fell and then I'd shift, run, and hunt until bone-weary and then I'd fall back into bed until the next day when I could devour a new book. Textbooks. Novels. Atlases. Encyclopedias. Each year he insisted I mount multiple females so I could seek out a mate. I read a lot in between those times, in between errands he had us run. He took me to a book shop sometimes and would ask the owner for books to teach a child all they'd learn in school.

A conversation from early manhood comes over me.

"What if she's not at that bar, uncle? What if my destined only one is in the forbidden village? Or in another city, another country across the ocean?"

I'd been reading of foreign lands. I'd run out of the books we had and on a trip out of town for supplies as well as one of his errands, I found a different bookstore and there were thousands of books that had already been read by others so were inexpensive. I had two twenty-dollar bills in my pocket and purchased as many as I could carry.

"Shifters find their mate in their territory. It's basic, Tyson. A shifter's born territory is meant for them. They rarely stray far from it. If we weren't to find our mates close, we wouldn't stay in the same zone all our lives."

But we left our zone often for his errands and came back soon after. He didn't like being away from our property and would grow agitated easily whenever we had one of those errands.

And in one of his dark times he muttered about taking me, as an infant, to a place far away because I couldn't eat the herb to disguise my scent, but said as soon as he could feed it to me, we came back. He needed to come back because if shifters left their territory it was bad for their minds. He didn't explain that.

When I asked him about finding a mate for himself, he went sullen and told me,

> "Not all stories have the happy ending, Tyson. Our pack decided to control my destiny instead of letting me be in charge. I showed them."

Instead, he directed me to keep mounting women from the other village where the witch lived, telling me it was too dangerous to go to the forbidden village where they hated us, would kill us if we let them scent us. But yet I was drawn to the village.

"Is she there? Is that why I'm drawn?"

"Maybe," he told me and one year, we moved along the fringe of it after taking extra efforts in masking our scent so we wouldn't be discovered.

I wanted to mark the perimeter.

"I need to mark it here."

I'd never felt the urge to mark a territory as mine. The urge was strong.

"You can't do that, Tyson, we'll be discovered. This was your birthright, that's why you feel this, but you can't take it. Things have changed."

"Why? If it's mine, I should take it."

"Trust your uncle. There are things you don't know."

"Then tell me. I'm not a boy anymore. I'm a man now so fucking tell me."

He went on to remind me of all he'd sacrificed to save me and told me 'later, when it's safe, I'll tell you.'

I didn't smell my mate there, so we left.

"Ivy," I ask, "where do you come from?"

She's pulling cooking things out of the kitchen cupboards and surveying them with distaste before setting them in the sink. Everything is dusty from not being used or cleaned in many years. Some items in the cupboards have been there as long as we've had the place. The house came partly furnished and outfitted with most of that kitchen gear. She finds an unopened package of sponges and a large yellow container that I recall contains soap, so she begins washing. I decide we need a fire. Her legs are bare and she's wearing rubber footwear that consists of a v across her foot, plugging into the rubber sole between her first two toes. She must be chilled. Her hair is still wet, too. I pull a log out of the basket and shove it into the wood stove.

"I live a few hours away. But I was born in a little town not far from here, as a matter of fact. My parents moved when I was about... three or four I think."

I smile as I work on the fire and she furiously scrubs at the surface of the electric stove with a sudsy sponge. This makes my chest feel warm.

Her attention moves to the food we got today, and she begins stashing items in cupboards, moving the few items in those cupboards around first. She opens the refrigerator with a jar of something in her hand and gasps.

"The ice cream doesn't belong in the fridge, Tyson. It belongs in the freezer!" She opens a lid and breathes relief. "It's only partly melted. Phew."

She opens the top door of the fridge and sticks that container in. She moves some other cartons and bags up there with it and some of the meat, too.

"The meat too?" I check, remembering that section of the refrigerator will turn the meat to blocks of ice meat.

"There's too much meat in the fridge. It'll spoil before you get a chance to eat it all."

"And when I'm ready to eat it, I'll break a tooth?" I ask.

She smiles. "You can take it out the morning of the day you plan to eat it and it'll thaw by supper time."

Oh. This makes sense. Meat only lasts so long before it no longer tastes good. I don't know from experience, I've always eaten whatever I've hunted immediately, but my uncle explained that as a child during his first nighttime solo shift and hunt, he came upon rabbit and tasted it, figuring he didn't have to hunt to eat after all, but it was old and filled with larvae and tasted bad, made him very sick. He nearly died. This was how it was determined he had problems with his sense of smell. He made use of my scenting abilities from an early age.

This recollection makes me feel strange, suddenly. I hadn't thought about this lately, how much he relied on me for such things. Some tasks he'd have me complete for him. We had a rhythm to the way we did things. I led and he followed. I hunted or took down prey and we both feasted.

He made use of my senses many times while I grew. And then by the time I was a man, his major focus was coaxing me into finding my mate, though my biggest concern was always running, hunting, feasting. I particularly enjoyed hunting evasive animals that were good at dodging me. I thrived on challenges. And I always shared with him the fruits of my labor, often letting him eat first.

Memories sweep over me of me hunting a man and ripping his throat out before devouring a bunch of his flesh in a rage and I don't recall why. What did the man do? Why did I do that?

The haze. The haze of anger. Uncle was there afterwards. There, leashing me, trying to calm me. I almost destroyed him too, but he injected something into my flank that made me sleep so that the haze would leave.

Bumps rise on the back of my neck and I feel a chill. An angry one as I start to remember some of the errands we had. Errands that filled the space under the garage floorboards with money.

I watch as she moves things around and puts away more things. I'm in the chair beside the wood stove and I like the view of watching her move around the kitchen, her short pants hugging the curves of her ass. My thoughts of my uncle fade away as she lifts her arms up and takes her hair up into her fist and winds the end around and tucks it so that it stays up in a ball on the back of her head. My eyes travel her torso to the swell of her tits.

She comes to me and for a moment I think she's about to straddle me, but I'm disappointed when she instead bends and reaches into the bag of hers on the floor near me, lifting a black circle out and wrapping it around the ball of hair to hold it in place.

She moves back to the kitchen and uses a knife to slice open a plastic package of striped meat then places the strips in a pan before washing some more dishes. Smells fill the house. Nice smells. Food smells. The yellow soap in the kitchen. The fragrance of that meat has me salivating.

She cracks an egg over the rim of a dish and drops the insides in and then repeats it before stirring it furiously, putting the shell from the egg into a different dish. She moves to the fridge to fetch a paper container and pours white liquid into the bowl of stirred eggs. Milk. I remember milk. I smile as the kitchen smells and sizzling sounds coupled with the warmth of the wood stove and the sight of my mate makes me happy.

She begins running a knife through food of different colors and dumps small chunks all into a pan with a brown sandy-looking substance. A third pan goes onto the stove (I wasn't aware I had three pans) and she drops a glob of something yellow into that pan as well as the pan with the food bits before dipping bread slices into the egg bowl and flips it before dropping it into one of the pans. If I weren't so captivated I'd have her on the floor, thrusting inside her. My cock aches at the sight of my beautiful woman with her long bare legs moving around the kitchen, using it in a way it's never been used.

She takes a fourth pan and puts more yellow stuff into it. All four stove burners are bright orange and now there are sweet and savory smells in the air. It makes me happy. I find myself purring softly as I watch her.

She cracks eggs into another bowl and stirs the contents and then drops the egg liquid into the fourth pan while flipping meat with a fork in one pan and then stirring the fruit pan and flipping a piece of bread over, then another.

My woman has kitchen skills. This makes me happy.

I look back to the fire and stoke it as I watch her alternately dance between the four burners and the soapy sink. She's washing things and putting other things away in between tending the food.

She wipes her hands on a towel and looks at me.

"Can you wash the table and set it instead of just sitting there looking pretty?"

I tilt my head to the side as she says, "Here." She holds out a soaped-up sponge.

I move to the simple table that was always here and begin to scrub it. The yellow sponge's surface quickly blackens. She catches me staring at it and brings me a new soaped-up sponge, taking that one away.

A moment later, she's marched to the bedroom and before I've blinked twice, she's approaching the table with a sheet. She dries the surface with a towel and then passes the wet sponge and towel to me.

"Put those down over there, please? Food will be cold if we wait until that table is clean. Let's just eat. You can finish de-grossifying it later." She flips the sheet so that it unfolds and spreads it across the table, covering the rest of the dirt.

"Sit," she tells me as she drops off two forks and two knives and then twirls to go back to the counter. I watch the light catch her hair and purr some more. She returns with two plates.

"We didn't get anything to drink. I don't want milk. Is the water from the tap any good?"

"Any... good?" I ask.

"Has the water been tested for safety?" she asks.

"It's... water," I answer.

She shakes her head. "Never mind. I'll boil some just in case." She gets up and lifts a pot from the counter where it sits drying with other dishes she's washed and fills it before putting it on the stove. "I saw teabags here. And there's no coffee machine, so we'll have tea."

My eyes follow my nose and I look at my plate.

There's crispy strips of meat on one end, a pile of yellow fluffy substance, and two slices of bread covered in a brown sauce filled with colorful chunks.

I taste some. There's banana and something that looks a bit like a seedling, but it's white and familiar-scented, and there are berries like the ones I've eaten from the ground shrubbery as wolf sometimes. The sauce is sweet. The brown sand and fruit together sauce is the best food taste that has ever touched my tongue. I look up at her in astonishment.

She smiles. "Eat some with the French toast."

I look down at my plate, lift the bread, and chomp down on it.

She giggles. "Use your cutlery and your manners, Tyson."

She sits and takes her knife and fork and saws her French toast into several cubes like I did with the steak. I knew she'd need the little cubes with her small teeth. She forks up a piece and then dunks it into the fruit sauce and puts it in my mouth.

I chew. And she watches.

"Is that the best thing you've ever tasted or what?" The excitement in her eyes is contagious. I want to fuck her.

I need to fuck her.

I drop the toast onto the plate, suck the sweetness off my fingers and then I lunge for her, lift her up out of her chair and wrap her legs around my hips while putting her against the humming refrigerator. My mouth is on hers while she gasps in surprise.

"Almost," I say. "You're the best thing I've ever tasted." I suck on my mark on her and she shivers.

"Ty-Ty-Tyson, we have to eat."

"I like when you call me that."

She moans as I lick her throat and then nibble my way up to her ear and suckle on the lobe, which has a tiny white shiny ear jewel in the center. It clicks against my teeth. I lick the ridge of her ear.

"Huh? Call you what?"

"When you call me Ty. When you say Ty, I know you're pleased."

"Let's eat, Ty," she whispers, her warm hand stroking the side of my neck.

I smile, carry her back to her chair, and set her down. Immediately, I reach for the crispy meat on my plate and put it in my mouth.

My mouth feels wonderful. I stare wide-eyed at her.

"Bacon," she announces with big eyes. Happy eyes.

Before I've finished it, I've shoved another piece in my mouth. It's delicious. There are only two pieces left on my plate. I want an entire plate of this crispy meat.

I taste the fluffy bits. They're good. Not as good as the bacon, the fruit sauce, but as nice as the fried bread. I've eaten bread. Bread was something I ran out of quickly when Uncle left me during that time of uncontrollable shifting.

The bread was raw then, dry and bland, not savory and textured like this.

I catch her smiling when I look up. She's barely made a dent in her food, but I'm nearly done. I guess I was ravenous. And it's delicious.

"What sand tastes this good?"

She frowns. "Sand?"

"That sand." I rise and move to the counter and see the label. Oh. Brown sugar. "Never mind. Brown sugar. I thought it was sand you were cooking with the colorful bits of food."

She giggles as she lifts the pot from the stove and pours water into two brown cups that have been around since, always, but that I've never used. If I've been thirsty as man, I've turned the water on and stuck my mouth under it.

She adds something from a small jar shaped like a bear with a spout on his head and brings the cups to the table.

"The tea just needs to steep a bit."

"What did you put in it?" I ask.

"Honey."

I take another bite of the eggs. She pours milk into each cup on top of the steaming water.

"Why is the jar shaped like a bear? Shouldn't it be shaped like a bee?"

She laughs.

I like that sound.

I smile. Uncle used to drink the water with those little sacks in it. Tea. He drank a lot of it. He often put whisky into it, too.

"Bears like honey. There's a brand with a honeybee on the jar, too."

She eats another forkful of the fluffy food and then her face changes.

"So, you live alone and that's why you stayed in wolf form?"

"Yes. My uncle died a few years ago. It was just us two since I was a baby. He told me he rescued me when the pack we were in went mutinous and killed my parents."

She gasps. "That's so horrible!"

"Riley Savage came today and said he's in my blood family and that my mother isn't dead. That Cornelius lied and stole me. That he was responsible for my father's death."

"Oh. Oh my God."

I watch her use a spoon to squeeze the tea sacks against the side of each cup, before lifting them out and putting them on the side of her plate.

"Riley said I'm their top alpha, that I belong there," I add.

Her mouth opens into an adorable o as she listens raptly to me.

"He could be lying. Uncle told me they're liars." I take another bite of egg bread.

"What does your instinct tell you?" she asks.

I stare.

"Listen to your instinct. It usually knows."

A wolf's instinct was all he had. It drove him to eat when hungry, to rest when weary. To protect himself from the elements, from enemies. As a wolf, I'd fought off a bear twice. I'd killed poisonous snakes three times, once to save the life of Cornelius who slept as an old wolf that would've perished several years before he did if not for that instinct I always lent to him. His wolf aged much faster than his man form did.

What if that instinct had failed me where he was concerned? What if all this time, he'd been the enemy?

What could he have gained from taking me from my family and living alone with me? Teaching me to be wolf, to be man? I couldn't comprehend it.

Except... he regularly used my senses and some childhood memories were surfacing about things he gained from them on the errands we took. The money in the garage. The man he had me rip apart. How he couldn't hunt well and continually found himself in peril where I'd get him out of it.

I didn't want to think about it. Not now. I wanted to focus on her. On Ivy. My Ivy.

"Gonna help me with the dishes?" She stands. She's only eaten half her food.

"You're not done your food."

"I'm done. Can't eat another bite." She puts her hand on her flat belly and inhales deep then blows out a long breath with force that makes her cheeks go fat for a moment.

"I'll eat it," I reach for her plate.

"Go for it," she says and rises.

I watch her put away the dishes she'd already cleaned and then she begins to wash the pans. I finish everything but the tea and bring my empty plate to her as well as my knife and fork. She smiles and passes me a towel.

"Start dryin'."

I dry the dishes carefully and put them away. When we're done, she cleans all the countertops and scrubs the stovetop. She grabs our cups of milk and honey tea and takes them to the sitting area by the wood stove. She sets them down on the table and sits.

I lift the cup closest to me, take a sip as I sit, and I decide I like the sweet, warm drink.

She pulls her feet up to the seat and curls into a ball, resting her head on the arm of the sofa. I sit close, rubbing her hip with my free hand as we stare into the flames and I sip more of the drink. The warm feeling in my body comes from not just the fire and the tea but from something else. From happiness.

"You're purring again," she says with a smile.

"I'm happy," I tell her and set the mug down so I can pull her to my lap and hold her close. "I've found you. I want to know everything about you."

Her smile slides off her face and she looks conflicted. Little lines form over her nose as she seems to ponder a problem.

Me. I'm a problem to her.

"I have a job and responsibilities. My car is in a valley all squished and I have no way to pay for it if I'm here getting sexed to death by you. It's like my mind keeps blocking my responsibilities and I just get lost... in this." She gestures toward me. "My parents, my friends are gonna worry about me."

I feel something ugly crawling through my veins at her words, at the distress in her voice. She's still trying to figure out how to leave me. She says get lost in 'this' like it's not something she should get lost in. Like being happy to be with me would be wrong.

She made me food. She washed my hair. She said my name with sweetness. She laughed for me. She's making the kitchen clean. Even when she's in my arms, warm and cuddled into me, at the same time she's thinking about needing to go.

How do I make her not want to leave me?

"What am I doing wrong, Ivy?" I can't help but ask. My chest hurts. She climbs off my lap and puts her face in her hands, her nearly dry golden and blueberry locks falling over her face as she lets out a big breath.

"Maybe you think I won't be a good mate, but I will. I'll keep you safe, I'll provide for you, and I'll do whatever it takes to show you that your happiness is linked to me."

"Tyson," she says, her voice sad.

She doesn't believe me. She's not the same as me, so of course she doesn't. She's not wired the way I am. I just need to show her.

I grab her hips and pull her short pants down, snatching her underwear to yank them down too as I quickly haul her onto me.

Now she's straddling me.

"Ty, don't," she orders, with her eyes all angry.

I growl at her. She's called me Ty, like she does when I'm inside her. That's where I need to be now. She rears back as if frightened.

I grab the back of her neck and use my other hand to free my cock from my soft pants without the button and zipper. This is much easier than fussing with the typical man jeans I wear.

I slam into her heat and she cries out. I've still got her by the back of the neck and her neck is so small that my thumb can graze my mark on her while I continue to hold her where I want her. I ram my hips up as I glare at her with anger and frustration. I only want to make her happy, make her know she's mine, make her feel like no one and nothing is more right than this, than us.

She looks both horrified and aroused. I growl into her ear. "You're mine. I'm yours. You'll learn this. Forget everything but this. This is all that matters."

She cries out as I feel my knot swell inside and I begin climaxing inside her.

I can't wait until she goes into heat and I can fill her with my children, bind her to me in that way so she will know it's real, that we're a family.

A family. I wanted that as a child. I wanted it with a fierceness I took out on the environment around me. It washes over me, the memories. I remember wailing at the sky for the lost family I didn't have, though I didn't know what I was howling for until my uncle told me. He was in one of those dark moods where his words jumbled, and he smelled like whisky. He talked about loss, about having things taken away by evil. He looked me in the eyes and told me that evil took the things you wanted, that being alone was difficult, but better than seeing what others had that should be yours.

Alone isn't better.

I wondered if I should be lone wolf or should be with a pack. He told me lone was better, that our former pack was too corrupt.

"Why don't we find a pack that isn't corrupt? What about other packs, Uncle?"

"There are no others for us."

As I grew, I felt like it was a lie. I felt like it had to be.

If our pack was bad, why didn't we seek out another? I craved companionship, wolves to run with that were my size. Boys to play with and talk to when I was in my man form. Uncle didn't like talking unless he drank the whisky and then his words were always confusing.

I don't know what age I began shifting but I know he used my wolf senses and my size to his advantage both when I was a small wolf and when I was a large one. I remember rules about when we could and could not show our nature and the grass we had to eat to hide our smell, and I fucking hated that grass. Then things changed and we were wolves more often than we were people and we continued to eat the stupid grass.

I remember being much smaller than him and then being much larger a few seasons later. I remember him being a man of few words except when he needed something done or when he'd have one of his dark times and then he would talk words that made no sense until my ears grew tired of hearing him. He hated my questions. He only liked me to do what he told me to do. He liked to remind me that he saved my life, that without him I'd have been killed like my father.

I'm still spilling into my Ivy and she's crying into my shoulder as her body trembles with her pleasure. I groan mine into her soft hair. She goes limp on me as my knot releases and my pants are soaked with my essence.

"I can't have any more sex right now, Ty. Please, please no more." Her face is buried in my neck.

"Okay, sweet Ivy," I whisper into her hair. I kiss her purple wrist and feel terrible. I've hurt her wrist, made her cry, taken her more times than she wanted. I won't feel bad for stopping her from leaving me.

Doesn't she understand that I do this because I have no choice? She's not angry at me. She seems sad and that's confusing. Some of the women I tried from the bar got angry when they knew I was finished, when their attempts to get me to take more from them failed. Ivy doesn't get angry at me. She gets sad. And it hurts my chest and my stomach and now I want to go hunting and rip things apart, make them bleed. I'm angry. It makes my innards feel foul.

She's gotten a little angry a few times, but her face isn't ugly when she's angry. In fact, when she gets angry, it makes me want to take her to the ground and mount her as much as I want to do it when she's smiling or laughing.

I carry her toward the bed so I can lay her down, but then my left foot slides and my body goes airborne. All I can think of as I land hard on my back is of keeping her from being hurt, so I manage to hold her high up enough that she feels no impact. I hear her gasp as my body protests at the pain.

She's on me. I'm on the floor.

"Are you okay?"

She's moving off me and I'm wincing in pain. This was like the soap incident in the bathroom, but worse. I fell and I nearly allowed her to get hurt.

"Are you okay?" she asks again.

"Yeah," I grunt and sit up and stretch my back.

"Oh, Ty." She giggles. "You slipped on a banana peel."

She lifts it from the floor and then she laughs. "I'm sorry for laughing, but it's a classic slapstick comedy we've got going on here." She's laughing so hard, she's rocking to and fro.

I'm still holding my back, feeling a little disappointed that she laughs.

She suddenly sobers and swallows. "You protected me as you fell."

I did. I always will. "I'll always protect you."

She leans over and no longer laughing, she puts her hand to my face. Her eyes fill with moisture. "You're so fucking sweet." She has a big smile on her face.

"But you still want to leave me. Wolves mate for life, Ivy. And I've mated you to me."

Her face loses its joy and looks haunted as she stares at me for a long moment. Finally, I see a swallow work down her throat.

"But I'm not a wolf," she says, and then she blinks rapidly, shaking off her emotions. "And I only just met you. I can't know something like that instantly, especially when meeting them in the woods and they're naked and breaking my car and then they steal me away to their remote cabin and refuse to let me go."

My chest hurts at her words, at her expression.

She looks away and then gets to her feet, taking the peel out of the room. I follow her and see a dish of food waste in the kitchen. She deposits the banana peel there on top of broken eggshells.

"Now you know better than to throw banana peels on the floor. Do you have a compost pile outside?" she asks.

I frown. "A compost pile?"

"Where should we put this? If you have a place to put it and you turn it over once a week or so, eventually it'll break down into nice soil for a vegetable garden."

"Do you like to grow food?" I ask.

She nods. "I do. I always grow some herbs in my window and lettuce, cucumbers, and tomatoes on our little patio. We don't have much of a yard, we have a tiny piece of a yard because there are two other apartments, but the stuff I grow is the best tasting stuff ever."

"I'll do this compost pile for you," I say.

She gives me a sad smile, one that tells me it doesn't matter if I do things for her because she won't be here to enjoy them.

She's wrong.

"I'm kind of tired. I think I'm going to go to bed." She goes to her larger satchel and pulls out a white computer screen. I've seen devices like these in town before. She pulls a white cord from her bag and plugs it into the electricity outlet over the kitchen counter.

"Goodnight," she says and then she goes to the bathroom with a small pink velvet bag she's pulled from her larger bag.

Women I'd spent the night with would take bags into the bathroom to remove cosmetics. Brush their teeth. I lick my teeth and decide I'll use her toothbrush after she sleeps. Mine is old. I stare at the closed door and listen to the water running, thinking on what I'll do the rest of the evening while she sleeps.

I'll refill the generators and chop more wood. Clean that table better and then … I can't shift yet and run. When she's more settled and safer, I'll shift and go for a run. Hunt. I'll mark the perimeter around the property so any animal will know to stay away. Will Riley Savage and his family heed that warning?

I don't know if they will. And I don't like not knowing. No. I can't run. I can't hunt. Not until I know they're not a threat, even if that means eliminating them. Or moving Ivy far away. But, what if I lose my mind away from my territory?

Uncle's mind wasn't right. Maybe he was wrong about the territory issue.

Inside, I don't feel like I want to eliminate them. I feel like I should find out more about them.

WHEN SHE EXITS THE bathroom, I lift her into my arms.

"Tyson."

She's protesting something but I'm simply carrying her to bed like I intended to earlier. I set her down and pull the covers over her body.

The room is warm. It's not as cold outside tonight so with the door open the bedroom should be warm enough with a fire in the sitting room.

"Rest, my only one." I kiss her lips softly.

Her chin trembles and she stares at me briefly before turning over. When she does, she lifts her arm as if she hurt it before holding it to her chest with her right hand. Guilt sits in the middle of my chest like a stone. I can't hurt her again. I need to be careful not to.

I want to hunt, I ache to run, I want to tear into flesh and feast, but I can't. I glance at the painting over the mantle of me and the friends I wished I had when I was a boy. That sits in my chest, too. I think of Riley and those other shifters and that woman by the fence for a minute before I gather up from the chair the pile of clothes and towels as well as sheets she pulled off the bed at some stage. I put them in the machine in the garage and start it up, then wash that table she wanted me to clean until it no longer makes the water dirty when I squeeze the sponge, and then I chop wood until I grow tired.

When I climb into the bed, she's asleep, but she curls into me and makes a cute sound. I take her mouth with mine and then I peel her clothing off. She doesn't protest. She whimpers for me. She sleepily kisses me also. And then she whispers, "Ty".

When I run my tongue over that sweet spot between her legs, she pleads with me to not stop. It makes me happy. I carefully slide my cock into her, and I feel her stiffen and see the grimace on her face despite the dark. I know I've given her no time to recover, but then I purr for her and her body relaxes. She rocks into me. I knot and try to be as gentle as I can, moving just a little inside her, feeling her inside walls squeeze around me until I come and come and come. The more she whimpers the thicker the stream of fluids leaving me. Finally spent, I reach for the shirt I had worn and dab between her legs after pulling out, then she climbs on top of my body and tucks her head into the place between my chin and my shoulder. Her arm with the uninjured wrist wraps around my neck and she falls asleep with the other palm on my cheek.

I want this little beauty to sleep on top of me every night just like this until it's time for me to turn to dust.

21

IVY

Tyson fucked me when he came to the bed. It was late, I think; I felt like I'd been sleeping for hours, and I woke to hot hands roaming me, a skilled mouth nipping, licking, and kissing me all over. He fucked me gently, in multiple positions, including from a spooning position with his fingers on my clit and his mouth on that bitemark. It was slow, gentle, and so very good.

I fell asleep afterwards on top of him, which is sort of embarrassing, but he was very comfortable. Until I woke again, feeling gooey between my legs while it was still dark. I tried to get out of bed, and he grabbed me by the waist.

"You can't leave, Ivy."

"I just wanna clean between my legs. It's all messy."

"Stay here," he ordered and got out of bed.

It sounded like he left the building and I was about to go looking for him when he was back and cleaning between my legs with a warm towel.

"How is this so warm?" I asked. "Is there a fire in the other room?"

"All the towels were dirty, so I washed and dried them. I did wipe between your thighs after I fucked you."

"Well... there was a lot of -—you, I guess." I shrugged. I saw the reflection of his eyes and the white of his teeth in the dark room as he smiled with pride or something, and I looked away, shyly. "Where's there a washer and dryer?" I didn't see a basement door. Maybe it was outside?

"The garage," he said, kissing my nose. "I'm tired. Talk to me after I sleep." He rolled half over me.

"Your leg is heavy on me," I whispered.

"I need to hold you here, so you don't leave me while I sleep," he reasoned.

My throat clogged up at that.

"Just hold my hand," I suggested.

He pulled his leg back and reached over my head, so I reached up and grabbed his hand and squeezed. He squeezed back. The warmth, the feel of it, it made me choke up. I tried to shake those emotions off.

I've been a bundle of nonsensical emotions since meeting this man.

And if I was honest, I kind of missed the weight of that leg. I said nothing about that, though.

"I notice you don't try to convince me you won't leave," he whispered.

I shrugged.

His mouth touched the back of my head and his big, warm hand over my right palm, which was above my head on the pillow, squeezed again.

"You know how to do laundry and drive a car but not how to peel a banana. So odd." I saw through the window that the sun was beginning to rise. I yawned.

He chuckled and put his free hand to my hip and gave it a squeeze. "My head was foggy. The fog is clearing. Mostly. I haven't spent time in this form for years. Things are coming back. I suppose some things are just things I never forgot. Some things, like things in this house, I remembered. I never bought bananas before."

"Oh."

"If I'd gone many more seasons without shifting, I might never have come back to this form. Even to catch your scent."

"Whoa."

I thought on it. On how different his life is to mine. He's here in the middle of nowhere and said other than hunting for a wife occasionally, he spent all his time with an uncle who he said was a man of few words.

He's not very worldly. He's quite savage in many ways, in fact, like his last name suggests. I wonder, idly, about the people who he talked about. Maybe he did belong with those people. The idea of leaving him alone, with nobody, in such a state of lonesomeness that he'd opt to live as a wolf all the time? It bothered me.

Wouldn't it be better, more gratifying to spend your life with others? And I supposed it would be freeing to be an animal with few worries, but would being a human be preferable? To have conversations. To have more choices about where to go, what to do, who to be? I didn't know what it was like to be an animal, of course, so how could I know which was preferable?

I fell back under, into a blissfully cuddly sleep before the sun completely rose and I was warm, comfy, and snuggled by a man slash werewolf. As I slipped under, I did it thinking that something about this felt right, deep in my gut. My momma and her sister told me, my whole life, Ivy-—never ever ignore your gut. But I always veered toward not trusting my instinct. Why was that?

IT'S MORNING. BRIGHT and sunny. Birds are chirping and heat beats through the drapes, against my skin. I'm awake first. He's still holding my right hand over our heads and his body spoons mine.

I slip my hand away and turn over to watch him.

He continues to sleep, so I carefully inch my way down to the bottom of the bed and off. It doesn't rouse him.

Maybe I should go now. Get out of here and drive to town. Leave his truck there so it's not like I've taken it too far. Call a tow truck. Get my car. Pay for the tow truck to bring his truck back, maybe. Get home.

The idea of the loneliness of this place without another person would drive me absolutely bonkers. How can he be alone like that? Isn't it sad? Of course it is, for me, but he knows nothing else, except for companionship of one person, a person that died and someone that doesn't sound like he was great company.

Should I encourage him to go meet that guy that says he's family? If I do that, it doesn't mean he's not going to try to stop me from going again. But the way he stops me? Visions of yesterday assault my senses in a delicious way that makes my belly swoop.

It's just gotta be because of how lonely he's gonna be that I feel bad right now at the idea of leaving him alone.

Maybe he ought to try to live in society, where there's the opportunity to meet people.

I understand, being supernatural that being away from prying eyes is probably better. I'm guessing it's a rule that they don't reveal themselves to the general population or something.

He's on his side, lashes resting against his face, mouth full and pouty looking. The lines and angles of his face... he should be replicated in bronze and put into a museum. Perfect Male Specimen.

His face is shadowed by a few days of not shaving, though not really because he wouldn't have shaved for a lot longer than that if he'd been living as a wolf for years. A completely different form. An animal.

Reconciling it isn't easy. I've always been pragmatic, amused by Aunt Nelle's anecdotes and her eccentricities, but my feet remained firmly planted in healthy skepticism.

Here was fantasy as reality. This meant magic was real. Maybe aliens, too. Vampires? Ghosts? The skeptic part of me now ceased to exist because Ty is flesh, bone, and emotion. He's excitement and wonder. He's passionate and protective. He's also nurturing and enjoys being amused.

He is a multifaceted person that I find myself fascinated by.

I now feel like anything is possible, like magic is real, just like my aunt told me.

I gaze at his massive frame, all those muscles, that sexy tanned skin. He's the epitome of masculine. And yet he's tender. He treats me with reverence, but with a caveat that I really like.

I'm a waif of a girl and this often instills protectiveness of me by men. As if I'm too easily breakable. With Ty, he touches me like he means it. No feather-light caresses when he's in the throes of passion. When he touches me, I know it. He touches me like I'm his. And fuck, but I like it.

Holy moly am I ever using a lot of F-words these days. Sometimes they're the only word with enough oomph to describe a situation, I guess.

He stirs and sniffs at the air like he smells something. And then he makes that purring sound as he rolls to his back. I round the bed and get back in with him, without thinking on it, just simply lifting the blanket and crawling in, plastering myself against his warmth. He pulls the blanket up over my shoulders and puts his hands on my ass. I smile against his chest and close my eyes, feeling the gentle vibration of the purrs coming from his chest.

"Good morning," I say.

"Good morning," he parrots and then his hands caress my backside. "I smell you."

"What do I smell like?" I ask.

"Like you want me. Like you're mine."

What a way to wake up. Enveloped in warmth by someone who wants me. Someone good with their hands (and mouth and other parts besides...). Someone who, on sight, decided I was destined to be his.

How bonkers is that?

It's not like I'm the only female he's ever seen. If that were the case, I'd be my usual skeptical self. He makes it sound like he caught my scent on the wind and hunted until he found me.

So, not on sight, really, more like he decided on scent that I was his.

He's had women before, so this isn't just a case of a wild man seeing a female for the first time and getting hooked on me for that reason. He has had others and didn't want to keep them.

He made a mark on my neck that feels like an erogenous zone. He's said he's given nobody else that mark.

He can burst into a wolf in a snap.

He does that magical thing inside me with his penis. His magical, no, supernatural penis.

I'm suddenly wishing I didn't have to be at work tomorrow for the opening of the boutique. If only I had a few more days. I could use the extra time to... what?

Convince him to move to my city and date me?

Ha. Funny.

Convince him to go meet those people who say he's their family so I can go, conscience clean, because he wouldn't be out here with nobody to keep him company?

Say forget the job, screw my responsibilities, and just stay?

I was at the edge of the bed, ready to flee, but then what did I do? I climbed in with him, climbed onto him.

My thoughts are cut off as I'm rolled to my back and kisses are dotted down my body. My mouth drops open as he mouths my boobs over my shirt and then finds his way to between my legs. My panties are peeled down and then his mouth is there. There.

He'd yanked my shorts off when he came into bed last night so they're somewhere in the mess of bedding.

It's Sunday, and I have got to get home. I really need to be at work tomorrow. There's no plausible excuse other than death for missing work tomorrow.

Certainly, I can't stroll in a few days later and tell them I was abducted and forced into mating with a half man / half wolf.

I bite my lip. His head rises and his eyes meet mine. God, how they slice me open and see right inside. He knows. He knows I'm pondering my exit.

He's not half man. He's *all* man. 100% pure male. God, he's gorgeous. And possessive. And normally, I find possessiveness in a man off-putting, but with Ty, I don't. Something about the way he wants me, the way he looks at me... it's not off-putting at all.

His jaw muscles flex and he moves up my body and spears into me in one solid thrust, making me gasp. His large hands frame my face as he uses his elbows to take his weight.

"Forget it," he orders, thrusting deep, as deep as he can possibly go.

My lips part and my eyes roll back as my body accommodates his girth. A whimper escapes my mouth before I ask, "Forget it?"

He flexes his jaw muscles again.

"Forget what?" I ask breathily in a failed attempt at being haughty.

"Forget everything but me."

"Aren't you full of yourself?" I state.

"Who's full of me?" He notches one eyebrow and slams his hips forward again.

I whimper in reply and then find some words. "It's not so easy," I tell him, feeling the wind come out of my sails a little. "I have to be at work tomorrow."

His eyes narrow and he slams his hips forward again. This time with a swivel.

"Whoa."

He looks at me like *Damn right*.

I decide to lay it all on the line.

"They're relying on me, Ty. The store needs me there. It's the first day."

"Who's they?" he demands, body going still but his cock still in me and hard as steel.

"My bosses. My coworkers. The store is opening. This weekend was a break for me after some grueling weeks of getting ready. Tomorrow is important."

His lips touch mine and he rotates his hips, sending beautiful sensations through me. His fingers slide between my legs. Oh, he's trying to distract me. Not happening.

I tighten my legs in a futile attempt to stop him from moving and grab his jaw so that he's forced to stop and listen.

Or, that's how it's supposed to go, but he keeps moving and lets out a sexy groan as my heels dig into his ass cheeks.

"What do you do at this store?" he asks.

"I'm the assistant manager. It's a women's fashion boutique. I handle supervising the staff, cash management, inventory, employee training, opening and closing, customer escalations, that kind of thing."

"You're very distressed about this store. What else is bothering you?"

Another hip flex from him.

A small whimper from me, that I try to ignore.

"Isn't that enough?"

"Is that all there is?"

"No. My family expects me home this morning. In a few weeks, my sister is getting married so on top of my new job, there's a whole lot goin' on in my life."

"What about that boyfriend you mentioned?" His expression darkens and he swivels his hips then caresses my throat, caresses that spot as if to remind me that he put it there, to remind me what it means in his mind.

I grab his wrist to stop him from doing that.

"Ty... if I had an actual boyfriend, do you really think I would let you do this to me?"

His body seizes for a second and then he puts his mouth to my ear and his voice vibrates through me. "I've decided you're mine. Do you really think I'd let anyone stop me, you included?"

My blood turns instantly to ice.

Wow. That's ugly. So ugly I unwrap my legs from him and put the heels of my hands against his shoulders and shove.

"Get. Off me."

He doesn't budge.

"Tyson!"

His tongue moves along the bitemark, sending buzzing threads of heat through my frozen blood.

"You have no boyfriend," he breathes. "This makes me happy, Ivy."

"I broke up with someone just a few weeks ago," I whisper, trying to ignore the sensations in my body, how they work in tandem with his cock slowly, lazily sliding in and out and in and out. "But that you would even suggest you'd touch me anyway? You're a filthy fucking animal."

His body goes completely taut and his eyes hit mine.

A long moment of silence passes where his eyes burn into mine and I do my best to mirror that expression.

I growl at him and try to shove him off me.

He pins my arms above my head. "What a cute little growl you've got, my little mate. Mine is bigger. Let me show you what a fucking animal I am." He growls against the skin behind my ear and I do my best to pull away but there's no denying how that sound reverberates through all my erogenous zones.

"You act angry, but your tight little cunt just fastened harder around me."

He's right. There's something primal about him growling while he fucks me that serves something carnal, sending my body into a wanton frenzy.

"I am angry." I am also wetter and about three notches away from orgasming.

"And you lied about the boyfriend. You're lucky we hadn't mated yet when you told that lie or I'd be angry about that. Never lie to your husband, only one, or you'll be severely punished." He slams his hips forward and puts his lips to mine.

I struggle, but I can't get out from under him.

"I don't have a husband. And you better get off me," I snap.

"No, I won't get off you." He glares into my eyes. "I'm glad you don't have a boyfriend. I'd hate to have to disembowel someone you care about. But I would do it. No one claims a right to you, but me. No one."

"Get off," I shout. "You're really making me mad!"

He pulls his cock out and flips me to my belly effortlessly and then smacks my ass.

"Hey!" I shout.

"You *are* angry, aren't you? I'm gonna have to fix that."

I try to crawl out from under him, but he grabs a fistful of my hair and is slamming forward, spearing me. His cock swells inside me, doing that 'knot' thing and I take fistfuls of sheets into my hands and cry out as throbbing against my g-spot begins.

God, when that happens...

I'm angry, but coming. I'm angrily coming and it's a whole new thing because it feels like I'm being electrocuted between the legs, from the inside out, and it feels freaking great. My whole body throbs with that sensation. It's like a dance. A sexy as fuck dance between us with his body rocking, my body responding, and the sexiest sounding panting coming from his lips while he growls low.

He's growling and my vagina is buzzing while he has a handful of my hair and it doesn't hurt, it feels good. Great, actually.

He takes one of my breasts into his free hand and massages it, me impaled on him completely. And then I'm not touching the mattress; my ankles are hooked back around his thighs. His mouth suckles that spot in the crook of my neck and...

It.

Is.

Torture.

Beautiful torture. I can no longer think, only feel. His growl shifts to a purr as he assaults my body with his mouth, his cock, his hands. My hair is released so he can glide his hand down to cup between my legs, fingers pressing hard against my clit.

"Oh! Holy fuck. Oh God," I cry as my orgasm unfurls and triples in intensity.

He groans loudly, then the pulsing inside me stops as fluid leaks out even as more comes out of him. We both fall forward, and Ty buries his mouth behind my ear, so I get to listen to him grunting and purring alternating because he's spilling hot cum into me.

I'm so stuffed with him and after my body having that huge reaction while I'm so angry, my mind is racing. I'm so filled with fury right now; I could spit nails.

But he's dotting kisses down my spine, caging me in with his arms and then he kisses his way back up and his mouth is against my ear. "You're mine, Ivy. Nobody's but mine. I'm glad you're not wishing for someone else; I'm very glad. We don't have to mention this again. But do not ever lie to me again. I love you, little soulmate, but I'm very angry with you right now."

He kisses my shoulder and gets off the bed.

He loves me? Loves me? How can he say that to me? I spin over and emotions just burst from me. They erupt from my pores the way a wolf bursts from Ty when he shifts and I go at him with a feral cry, slapping his face.

This catches him by surprise.

"Do not ever fucking put your hands on me without my permission again. Ever again. In fact, you have no permission to touch me, you fucking monster." I get up on my tiptoes to get as close to his face as I can get and scream, "Ever again. I'm going home!"

His cum is leaking down my leg so I angrily storm to the bathroom and slam the door.

"You're already home," he shouts, voice like thunder. "You succeed at leaving me, Ivy, I will hunt you down and when I find you, you'll be sorry."

Alone in the bathroom, I burst into tears.

"Very sorry!" he vows in a guttural voice that makes my chest bloom with pain.

22

TYSON

Uncle told me we had to keep our nature a secret because the non-shifters would fear us, exploit us, think of us as nothing but animals that were beneath them. He told me it was a vital rule, most important, because they would lock us up like animals and make us live in our own filth.

When she called me a filthy fucking animal, it cut deep. And then a monster? I'm angry with her.

I'm even more angry with myself because she's upset with me. Truly furious. And that she thinks that of me? That I'm filthy and monstrous. And I must be, because I would rip apart any man or monster like me who thought she was his.

I would stop her from leaving me by any means.

Even if someone thought they claimed her first.

And if she did accomplish escape, I would hunt her down and bring her back. I won't live without her.

I don't like how I feel, staring at the closed bathroom door that's between us. First, I hear things falling or being thrown more likely, and then the water running, the toilet flushing, followed by the sounds of my Ivy crying. I hear her whimpering. Not the whimpers I give her that make her tremble and writhe with ecstasy; these whimpers are not like that. Her breath hitches and she's sad. I not only feel but smell the sadness and it's immense.

And I wanna hold her, comfort her, take the sad away.

My chest feels heavy at those sounds and I don't like it.

I don't like it.

I'm angry. I'm an angry filthy monster and I want to rip something apart.

I wanna rip the door down and pull her into my arms even more.

I want her laughing and sweet, holding me, running her fingers through my hair.

She makes a choking sound and I can't take it anymore.

I rip the door wide and find her sitting on the floor beside the bathtub, her knees up against her chest and her face buried in them. She jerks up and looks at me with red eyes and a swollen face. She dashes tears away with the back of her hand and I see her purple wrist. I put that purple there. I put those tears there.

I feel sick. So sick.

I drop to my knees and gather her toward me, but she pulls away. Of course she does. She wants nothing to do with me.

"Ivy..."

She slaps at my face and I'm shocked. She slaps it again and then she's pounding on my chest with both fists, tears streaming down her cheeks. She's wild with her anger, smacking me and crying, her breath stuttering with her sobs.

I lift her off the floor and take her to the bed. I want her to stop hurting, stop being angry and sad.

I don't know what to do, how to make it better, so I try purring. She likes it when I purr.

She stops punching and buries her face in my chest, puts her arms around my neck and sobs harder.

"Ivy," I pull her close and pull the covers over us.

Those arms around me feel like everything I want.

Now she's trying to escape again.

I hold tight despite that she's trying to pull away from me.

She's so very angry at me and she doesn't know whether she wants me or hates me. I hate it.

"Lemme go, lemme go, lemme go." She punches me with her little fists. One catches my jaw. The other pounds on my chest.

I let her go. She turns away and buries her face into the mattress, her body shaking with her distress.

"Leave me alone!" she demands in a voice that sounds wet and hoarse.

I back away, grabbing yesterday's jeans and reaching into the cabinet for a shirt. I step outside and stare at the sky.

I feel lost.

I feel hopeless.

I hurt.

I prowl back and forth across the porch, dragging my hands through my hair, wanting to rip my own innards out.

I have no choice but to find a way to get this aggression out. I know this rage inside me can be deadly and it needs out and needs out nowhere near her. If she runs, I'll just have to hunt her down. I let my muscles flex; I allow the beast in me to thrust its way forward. He comes hard. I shift. I shift and then I prowl off the wood porch, across the grass, to the edge where it turns to dirt and rocks, by the willow tree. I begin to mark a perimeter around the house. All the way around, so that no animal, no bird, not even an insect would dare approach.

I snarl while I do it, chest rising and falling fast with the pending haze.

Will it work to keep her safe? I hope so. I glance over my shoulder at the building, knowing that by going for a run there's a chance she'll leave. The truck keys are in my jeans on the ground, so if she goes without figuring this out, it'll have to be on foot, and she'll be covered in my scent if she does

I have no choice but to go. I need this fury out of me nowhere near her.

IT'S A THIRTY-MINUTE drive to the forbidden village, a hamlet nestled in rolling hills and dense forests.

This means it's a much longer run than that and I don't know how long it has taken; I only know I've run fast, trying to run out my aggression, hunting down and devouring a deer and a rabbit on my way. I've run, my feet taking me in this direction, and I don't know why. I'm just drawn here, much like I was directly after Cornelius died.

It's not often anyone would happen upon the intersection where the forbidden village begins by chance since there is no common roadway in. It's accessible through a long country road, longer than the road leading away from my house, outside the Indian reservation property, which is sprawling, beyond private property signs, and detour signage designed to make you believe you should turn around and go back the way you came.

I get the sense that this place is designed with the idea that there's no reason for outsiders to linger here. A gas station with a small store attached, plus a non-descript large wooden barn-like building are all anyone passing through would see other than a few homes. The chance of someone even coming in this far would be small. I don't know what else is here, don't know how many are part of this pack, but before I've stopped at the intersection, I've been assaulted by many odors. Aromas that are familiar, that tug threads inside me, making the things I thought were real feel as if they unravel, making nothing make sense but yet fusing things together that feel like they could make sense.

I strive to flip through the scents that last time confused me, to untangle and name them. Some of them I feel like I know. Some, I don't. I know some are young, some are older, some are men and some females. I also know some are more like me than others. Relatives? Alphas in the pack?

A door creaks open at the gas station and a woman near my age stands there, staring. She then drops her chin to her chest and she's weeping.

She's weeping while holding the doorknob.

I don't know her. Why does she weep at the sight of my wolf? Fear? She's a shifter. I don't sense fear from her.

Motion catches my attention from the edge of my periphery. Two men are beside the large barn-like building, a door open. They, too, stare at me in my wolf form with something emanating from them that I don't know how to translate.

They aren't a threat.

They're not feeling threatened.

There's something else coming from them and I don't understand what it is.

I hear car sounds; a car moves fast toward this intersection from the left and when I see it, I spot two men and a woman inside. They exit. Riley Savage. He gives me a nod and his eyes have a gentleness in them that I haven't yet seen from a man and I can't wrap understanding around it.

He holds up a fist and thumps it against his chest before he drops his chin to rest on his chest.

Another man who I know is alpha by his stance, by his scent, he stands there with eyes on me, too. He thumps his chest and drops his head, a similar facial expression.

The woman between them? She smells like… her. The one I smelled before. The one I feel an odd familiarity about. She was at that fence. I also caught her scent last time I was here.

Is she my mother?

My wolf's eyes meet her woman ones. She has eyes like mine. Dark hair that falls to mid-back with curls. Hair like mine, but a touch of silver threads through it. She's trim, athletic, and has little lines around her eyes but doesn't look old. Her scent… her scent wraps around me like something warm. Something familiar. Another woman runs in my direction and I straighten to give her a warning, but I don't need to, because she stops at the side of the woman I am now sure is my mother and puts her arm around her. This woman smells like her, but different. Family to her. This means… family to me. The second woman weeps openly, looking at me with affection before she says something to my mother and my ears would hear it if I were focused on it but I'm not. I'm taking everything in and trying to comprehend what I'm seeing. My mother takes a step forward. I make no moves. She shifts into a black and grey wolf with mostly grey over her face and moves in my direction. I lift my chin and watch her slow approach. She's as small as a non-shifting wolf, and her wolf is stunningly beautiful. So beautiful it hurts.

A foot away, her eyes stare into mine and the pain in them grabs me by the chest and seizes that thing that beats in me. It stops beating for a moment and then returns with a tempo that spills anguish. I see in those green eyes the loss she's experienced, the pain. I feel that sorrow. My anguish transforms to anger.

Cornelius smelled like he'd been inside her. I smelled her fear. I smelled what he took from her and brought back. He stole into this village and he took her against her will.

And before that, he took me.

Why? Why did he take me and raise me and lie to me? Why?

I miss when she moves closer until her nose strokes my muzzle and I tremble with anger when I see the sorrow and loss in her eyes from this close. I want to shred things. I want to shred him. But he's already dead. He's already decayed, turned to dust and earth other than some bones that are bleached white from the sun.

No, not all that's left. He left something else. Me, like this. Filled with this emotion.

There are people surrounding me, people who look at me with what feels like respect. Most of them have moved closer. I've never had respect before and if what Riley Savage told me is correct, respect is what I'm due, what I would have had growing up here, being one of them, contributing to their society.

I can't do this. I can't bear it. If I didn't feel so much loss, the anger would take over and send the lightning bolt through my spine.

I take a step back away from her, from them, and my eyes trace an arc across my perimeter to see all of them.

Almost all of them are now in wolf form; more have joined, around two dozen of them. Four more cars are coming to this intersection and I see others moving in on foot, too. Shifting, one after another. Men, women, older children. Several women with babies in their arms stay in person form. Every single one is in a pose of submission and respect and they watch as I stretch my neck and feel the emotions cleave through the center of me, through the man and the wolf, both.

I release a cry of undiluted grief, a lament to the sky of absolute emotion.

I turn and I run the other way, back the way I came, without looking back.

23

IVY

It's been quiet for a long time, and I'm hungry.

I get out of bed and find myself alone in the house, so I boil some water for tea and eat a banana. I wash down my birth control pill with tea and then I pace. I pace the cabin as I climb the walls in my mind, thinking about all the things I have going on in my life that I don't like. And then I decide to tally up all the things I *do* like.

I'm excited about my new job.

Um...

That's it. That's all. Is it really all?

Yep.

I'm not excited about my sister's upcoming wedding. In fact, these final weeks leading up to it will be fraught with stress because Amelia Brennan is a bridezilla of the tallest order. She doesn't want Dad walking her down the aisle and got mad at me for trying to make her make up with him. I worried she'd regret it later if they eventually made up, but she didn't have him at her wedding.

I fought with Amelia about breaking up with Ben and how that affected her wedding. Mom fought with me about how me and Amelia were fighting. Dad whined and complained to me about Mom and Amelia.

See, Dad cheated with his assistant and broke up with Mom and then his younger girlfriend dumped him, and he tried to sweet-talk his way back in with Mom. Thankfully, she told him to take a flying leap.

This weekend was supposed to be an escape from all of it. And boy, has it been because now I'm faced with a whole new set of things to stress about.

I've stewed in my anger at Tyson's comments for long enough without it getting me anywhere, so I decide to put my pacing to good use by cleaning this grimy house. I clean up the bedroom, first, dusting the surfaces with a damp cloth and then I clean the bathroom, washing everything with dish soap as that's the only cleaning product I can find. It does a pretty good job considering how long it'd likely been since this place saw any elbow grease.

I find a broom in the space between the fridge and counter and it looks like it's been in there for a decade or longer. It's coated in dirt. I have to wipe down the broom handle before I can even get started. There's no dustpan, so I sweep the bedroom, kitchen, living room, and bathroom (deciding the other room will wait as the door is closed) and push the mammoth pile of dust, dirt, dead bugs, and hair to the front door. I open the door and ceremoniously sweep it outside.

I can't find a mop, so that's the best I can do unless I want to get on my hands and knees and wash the floor that way, and nope, I do not.

Seeing no movement outside I keep sweeping the wide porch and several things strike me all at once.

The garage is closed, and I don't think he's in there. Where is he?

The other thing, the really weird thing... a strange haze hangs in the air. A dark mist, like chem trails but not in the sky, in front of me. The air has a fragrance, a musky and wood-infused aroma. I step off the porch and survey the perimeter. It's not just in front of me, it goes all the way around the house, surrounding me like a smoky crop circle, but suspended at around my chest-level. It wraps from behind the garage over to the weeping willow, and coming around to wrap around the back of the house. A perfect circle.

I take a step off the porch and stumble in confusion as I head toward the big willow tree, eyes darting back and forth across the space. I reach the tree and the muskiness is stronger. This smells like Tyson. I feel my brows knit together in confusion. Where is he?

If he's not here, I should go. Why, though, is his scent surrounding me? I should go to town and get a tow truck to pull my car out. Get driven home, or to the nearest bus station. I'll call Tamara, my roommate. No. She leaves today for Jamaica with her guy. She's probably already gone.

Or... stay here forever and forget everything else.

I shake that thought off. Hard. It's neither practical nor responsible to think that way.

I begin picking some pretty flowers that have bloomed around the dead-looking grass behind the house while pondering things.

I'll find my way to town and call Mom. She's kind of pissed at me since I ended things with Benjamin, because I can't "play nice" like Amelia wants me to.

'You couldn't have hung on until after Amelia's wedding?'

Sorry, Mom. Just because you stayed with dad twenty years longer than you've been happy...

I didn't say that, of course. Amelia went off on me and I had been planning to play nice, but the way she went off, I fought back, saying that maybe her groom should pick a new usher since Ben was only in the wedding because of me. Amelia argued that Ben and Rick had bonded, and I'd just have to suck it up and play nice for the day. It's not even like things with Ben and I are hostile. It's more that Amelia simply lost her shit when she found up we broke up worrying more about how it'd impact her wedding day than me.

Mom is pissed that me and my sister are on the outs, but she'd drop everything to come to me if I call, even though it's over three hours away.

I'll get questioned and lectured all the way home because where is my car? Why didn't I come back with Megan? Why did I spend my money on something with that much risk? Why did I go with Megan in the first place if I wasn't one hundred per cent certain about her character? Did I trust my instinct this time and if I did, is my instinct broken? Yada yada yada.

Truthfully, I do get along with my mom, I'm just feeling salty.

I'm definitely salty. At Tyson. At my situation. Sour at myself for going to that cabin with Megan and getting myself into this mess. But I love my family and I feel guilty for my negative thoughts. That's me. I get angry and immediately feel remorse for any thoughts associated with the anger.

Like me and Tyson. I feel bad for calling him names, even though he might have needed something harsh to give him a wake-up call. Maybe.

Ben and I weren't compatible, but the idea that Tyson would physically harm him? That's just... awful. And that he insists I'm staying when I tell him I need to go... that's just bonkers. As if I'm going to stay with someone against my will!

Ben and me had a bit of a strange relationship, so I wasn't expecting it to go anywhere serious. It wasn't even a 'given' that we'd spend every weekend together. He had a busy job, lots of hobbies, and was sort of emotionally unavailable. But that was okay, because it wasn't like I was head over heels either.

My sister took it upon herself to ask her guy, Rick, to ask him to be in the wedding without discussing it with me. She wanted nice pictures and matched up couples and because of that, she's got a wedding party with eighteen people in it and they're all couples. Even my little brother and his girlfriend, who he told me he's sick of being in a long-distance relationship with. I'm fairly sure their breakup will happen after Amelia's wedding, because Leo doesn't wanna rock the boat and court our big sister's ire.

Why didn't she ask me if Ben and I were solid first? I'd have told her that the relationship wasn't going anywhere and that, in fact, I was looking for an opening to end it and that's what I did, after he'd been away for three weeks on business and I realized I didn't miss him while he was gone.

Why would she want someone in her wedding pictures that she'd later struggle to remember the name of?

Amelia would pick me up, too, if I called, but I'm not about to call her because all she is about is her wedding. I think her wedding is more important to her than her actual marriage. Seriously. She's going to be depressed when it's over, because then what will she do with herself?

And as much as I know I need to go and get back to my life, I'm not going to be in the mood for any trivial conversations on the way back to regular life because I already know it's going to emotionally wring me out to go back to life and contemplate this time I've spent here, this man I've spent time with.

I go back inside and tidy up a bit more, then decide I should really go. He could be back any minute.

I stand there for what feels like too long, biting my lip, pondering it all.

Finally, I grab my iPad from the kitchen counter where I've been charging it and stuff it into my bag with the rest of my things. I charged it so that if I get to town, I can try to hop on someone's Wi-fi and use one of my apps to get ahold of somebody to come get me.

I have all my stuff and I'm holding the doorknob. I take in the space one more time.

Time to go. Time to go before he's back. I know it'll be a long walk and there's a chance he'll see me, but I have a half-baked plan for dealing with it.

And then images assault my mind. Images of us together, me and Tyson. Memories play on a reel in my mind of us and there are so many more that will stay with me in the span of this short time with him than there were of me and Ben after a few months.

My heart is in my throat. I feel so conflicted.

But, I have to go. That's all there is to it.

I reach into my bag and grab my little notepad and a pink gel pen to leave him a note.

Five minutes later, I pass by his heap of clothing and shoes near the other side of the big willow tree. He's out there somewhere as a wolf. I have no idea what the strange Tyson-scented mist is, but I'm able to walk through it with no apparent ill-effects, so that's something.

I stumble after a few steps feeling a bit of strange vertigo and then I set off on my journey to Drowsy Hollow, which will likely take a couple hours. Maybe I should've eaten more than a banana. Whatever. Onwards...

I don't let myself look back over my shoulder at that pretty little Hansel and Gretel house. I just... can't. Because if I do, I might turn around and go right back.

24

TYSON

I'm coming up toward the top of the ridge, only now feeling the haze beginning to lift, though just minimally now that I've towered over his bones, shifting uncontrollably for at least ten rotations from man to wolf and back, pissing on those bones. In both forms.

I had to get away from them, all of them, and mostly from my emotions. Emotions I haven't been able to unravel. All I know is I'm angry.

I'll need another run so I can get it out, then I need to get back to her.

I stood over Cornelius's remains and felt my lip curl, my fists clench, and then the world vibrated with my anger as I stared at his bones.

If only he was alive so I could kill him, if only I could take back so many moments where I provided for him, where I saved his ass. I stood and in my rage, relived many events throughout my lifetime that I hadn't thought of before.

How weak he was, how much of an opportunist, as well as the fact that he was obsessed with my mother.

So many little things are clicking into place from things he said, actions of his, memories that flood my mind from my very early childhood. I feel so much fury, so much I don't know what to do with it.

I need to go back to her. If this were yesterday, I'd say I need to go home and bury myself in her warmth, but I don't know that it's an accurate description because I'm angry at my mate, for her wanting to leave, for her words of loathing.

I see a brown wolf standing at the top of that ridge and I halt.

Riley Savage.

He shifts to man form.

I do as well.

"Not interested in talking to you." I walk past him, ready to shift back so I can run.

"Tyson," he says. "I'm here for you. What you just set off will summon any of us on the team."

I stop, turn around and glare at him. "I don't know what that means, I just know I can't do this right now." I move past him and hope he won't try to follow.

Another wolf, a black and white one runs toward us and stops suddenly, and stares at me. He shifts to man. He's large, dark-haired, and bearded. He straightens up and thumps his chest when he looks at me.

I turn back to Riley and sigh. "What is he doing?"

"That's Lincoln. We heard your call. The others will be on their way as well. Well, all but two as they're too far right now to hear it."

I didn't call for anyone. I suspect he knows I didn't intend to do this.

"I'm guessin' you have a lot to process," he says, "but that... whatever happened in that gorge down there, resulted in you summoning us, your team. When you're ready to learn more, we're ready. Our home is your home. Our pack is your pack. We want you there with us. Just come. Test things out. There's a home there for you and your mate. A community for her to be part of, and so she learns our ways. The house we got ready was your father's house, where you were born. Your mother ordered it be prepared for your return years ago when you came to the village. She told us she knew in her soul that the day would come, and that woman is never wrong. She moved into an apartment above her clinic. She lives there with Stan, a non-shifter she's now with. He's a good man. She..."

"Stop. I won't do this right now."

"Fine." He gives me a look that is filled with wisdom. "When you're ready, we're waiting."

"And if I'll never be ready? If I want you to leave me be?"

He considers this a minute before responding.

"Your destiny was stolen from you. When you're ready to take it back, we're there. And just saying, Tyson, we need you. I need you." His eyes change briefly and then he straightens. I frown. An odd emotion comes at me and it's from him. Before I get a chance to attempt to translate it, it's gone. "Get to know us before you decide. Our uncle that took you from us, that also took us from you..." He gives me a meaningful look. "It was wrong. The longer it goes on, the more all of us lose. That includes the rest of the team. There are aspects of their lives that are on hold."

He waits and when I make no reply, ask no questions about what that means because my mind is just overflowing already. He shifts back to wolf, turns tail, and leaves me standing there as he heads down into the valley where Cornelius died.

I shift back to wolf and pass the other man standing there, paying no attention but feeling his presence with a strangeness I can't decipher as I resume my journey home.

I may have pissed on Cornelius's bones in both forms, but it's as if he pissed on me. Repeatedly. For my whole life.

I CATCH HER SCENT ON the breeze not fifty paces away and every hair on my coat rises. Why does she smell so close? She's not okay. I pick up pace and follow the scent until I see her, in a trench beside the road, curled into a ball, rocking back and forth, and crying.

The path she took here was strange and erratic. One look at her and it hits me, the path she took through the grass rather than on the gravel road.

I shift to man form when I see the top of her golden head.

"Ivy!"

She twists to look over her shoulder at me and her eyes are filled with wet. Her cheeks are red and swollen and her chin trembles.

"It... it bit me."

"What bit you?"

"The snake. Maybe both of them, I don't know. There was a... tussle and they were all tangled up. They slithered away." She gestures with her hand.

"Fuck."

They were mating. She obviously happened upon a mating. This was the time of year for it and if she wandered through the trench along the road a long way, it's not a surprise she happened upon that. She smells like me, but that clearly didn't matter stepping into a mating between snakes.

Her tight jeans are bulging around her ankle and it's obvious that she's swelling where she was bit.

"I should've worn my Uggs."

"Your what?"

"My purple boots." She gestures to the canvas ankle shoes she has on. Her circulation is being cut off, so I grab the cuff of her jeans and rip upwards to give her leg some room. I see the bitemark just below her ankle, above the shoe. I pull her shoe off.

"Oh no! My Lucky jeans. Shit, Tyson..."

"Getting bit by a snake isn't very lucky, Ivy," I inform her.

Her brows furrow and then she shakes her head. "Not that kind of luck – never mind." Her face goes panicked and she forces a swallow. "Am I gonna die?" she whispers, "because it feels like –"

"No!" I interrupt and then wrap my mouth around the wound and suck.

"What are you doing? That's poison!" She tries to pull back, but I don't allow it.

I hold her calf firmly and I suck and spit and suck and spit.

Her heart is beating very fast. Too fast.

I taste her blood belatedly and taste something vile within it. The venom.

I smell Riley Savage in the air. And the one he called Lincoln.

My attention snaps over my left shoulder.

They're both shifting to man. "Tyson. What's happened?" Riley demands.

"Back the fuck up!"

"What's wrong? Let us help."

"A snake bit me," Ivy says, and I see she's got her hands over her eyes.

I sift fingers through her silky hair.

"Ivy? Look at me. You won't die. I won't allow it. Understand?"

"I can't look at you, Ty. They're naked."

"What kind of snake?" Riley asks, leaning over and looking at her ankle. "Stop, with the suction, it won't work. She needs antivenom. Let's take her to Aunt Cat. Don't carry her prone, keep her head above her legs."

"Aunt Cat?" Ivy asks, eyes still covered. "Who's she?"

"She's a healer. And Tyson's mother," Riley tells her.

"Come! Fast!" Lincoln demands, leaning in to look at Ivy's ankle, too close; I growl at him.

He rears back and says, "Come! Cat'll help! Hurry."

I lift her up and we run.

I run for my life. For hers.

BY THE TIME I GET TO that village, Ivy's skin feels hot and her body trembles in my arms.

They've beat me there as they shifted to wolves, but I'm not far behind, even as man and even with her in my arms because I run faster as man than I've ever run in my life. I feel her distress, I smell the sickness as that venom courses through her veins, and I feel her fear, knowing she's running a fever and it's climbing and climbing.

From there, things happen quickly. A man and the woman who I saw earlier come out the same door at the gas station, with a now-shifted to man, Riley who is talking on a phone.

"Come with us," the woman calls.

"I need a healer. Now!"

She's already looking at Ivy's ankle, which is even more swollen.

"I'll take you," she says, then ushers me to a truck that's parked at the back of the gas station.

Riley nods at me, communicating I should go with her.

I climb into the back seat, holding her in my arms and as the man with her starts the truck for her, Riley calls out. "I'll meet you at the clinic. They're getting ready for you."

Ivy trembles in my arms despite her skin feeling hot to the touch. I grind my teeth together and hear a motorcycle start up. That's Riley, behind us.

"This is Riley's truck. He keeps a few sets of clothes in the back, Tyson, if you want them," the man in the passenger seat says.

As if I care if I'm clothed. I care only about Ivy, in my arms, who no longer smells right, who smells like snake venom, like me, and only vaguely like she used to smell. She's pale and trembling so hard with her ankle swollen to larger than my own ankle. I see purple marks forming on her calf. Those marks are from my fingers, from when I held her still and tried to suck the poison out. *Fuck.* I keep hurting her!

"Tyson? There are clothes –" he repeats.

I grunt to make him shut up.

"Ty?" she whimpers.

"Almost there, Only One. Almost there." I press my lips to her forehead. Her burning hot forehead. Fuck.

I don't know if we're almost there. I don't know if Cat will have medicine for Ivy and will be able to help her or not. I don't know if these people mean me harm. I don't think they do, but I spent my life with someone who I now know lied to me nearly every time he opened his fucking mouth.

I hate questioning my instinct. My instinct is what drives me. How do I proceed if I don't know if I can trust it?

"Drive faster!" I demand.

The driver complies.

I shouldn't have left her. I shouldn't have gone. My scent warned any animal or shifter approaching the property and I assumed she'd cross the scent if she dared leave (which I'd hoped she wouldn't) and it'd keep all from her, but I never counted on her wandering until she came upon mating venomous snakes who evidently bit before taking note of my warning scent. Perhaps my scent on her could've even been provocation.

My gut churns and acid bubbles up in my throat. We're stopping at a grey concrete building beside a creek. Across the iron bridge over the creek is an entrance to an establishment with a small sign outside that reads Roxy's. Several houses dot the creekside on both sides.

"We're here," the woman in the driver's seat says and pushes the door open and then opens the back door. I slide out carefully cradling Ivy, whose ankle is even more swollen, whose skin is now verging on scorching hot.

I catch the scent of Cat before I'm done climbing out and she's rushing toward the car with gloves on, two men flanking her with a cot between them. I step out with Ivy in my arms and head toward the door, ignoring the men with the cot. One gets too close, so I lunge and bare my teeth at him, resulting in his immediate submission. He cowers, showing me his throat.

"Follow me," Cat says and leads us through a big room with several chairs and a desk. She crosses it into another room dominated by a bed with pendant lights overtop. Cabinets and countertops take up the perimeter of the room.

"Honey, I'm Catrina Savage. You can call me Cat if you like. What's your name?" She's leaned over my Ivy. "Set her down, Tyson, but let me elevate the end. We don't want her prone right now."

Ivy's eyelashes flutter and her mouth moves but no sounds come out.

"What's her name, Tyson?"

"Ivy Adeline Savage."

Her eyes are gentle. "Tell me everything you know about what happened."

She puts an instrument to Ivy's forehead, which beeps. She looks at it and sets it down.

"She happened upon snakes mating. She was bit. I attempted to remove the poison with my mouth. Riley Savage said you could help. Her ankle is swelling more and more by the minute, she's been trembling, and her body grows hotter by the second."

Ivy's eyelashes flutter and she reaches for Cat's hand.

"Hi," Ivy says.

Cat squeezes it. "Hi Sweetie. We're gonna take care of you. Don't fret. Do you know what color the snake that bit you was?"

"Gray and brownish gr-gray," she mumbles. "And brown. And shaky sounds, rattly."

Her body trembles again and I want to lash out and make Cat do something.

"Do you have allergies?"

Ivy doesn't answer. Her lips part, but she just winces.

"Any allergies, Tyson?"

"I don't know. Snake bites? Do something."

"Ivy?" She jiggles Ivy's cheek with her hand.

Ivy groans and her eyelashes flutter some more.

"Do something!" I bark.

"I'm about to," she says calmly.

She has a voice that I might find soothing if I wasn't feeling like something had to happen immediately to save my woman.

I pace back and forth in the room. The couple that brought me are in the other room that we entered into and they sit there, with eyes on me. I hear a door open and more voices assault my ears. They all smell like shifters, every one of them, though one, a female, has only a mild shifter aroma, as if a halfling. I don't linger on that thought; I thrust my hands through my hair and a low growl rises from down deep in my bowels until it breaks past my lips. She has to survive this. She has to.

If she doesn't, I'll join her wherever she's going. I'll rip my own heart out and join her.

"Fix her!" I shout.

Cat's eyes dart to me. "I will, darling," she says with strength in her voice that surprises me. "I'd tell you to sit down or take a walk while I do that, but I can tell you're a stubborn alpha so instead you'll pace and growl and boss me around. And that's okay. But just do it from five feet back so you don't get in my way." She opens a cabinet, fetches a bottle and a bag, and fiddles with things on a tray beside Ivy. Just a moment later, she's sticking a needle into Ivy's hand. It's attached to a clear hose and that hose is attached to a metal contraption that holds a bag.

It's a good thing the person caring for Ivy is who she is to me and that I know this because I now know I don't like anybody touching my woman and seeing someone poke something sharp into her would otherwise send me into a haze of rage. I trust this woman. Everything inside me tells me she's my mother and that she is trustworthy.

"Fix her," I whisper, and her eyes hit mine.

"I will, son."

Riley steps in with a bundle of fabric in his arm.

My eyes track his movements as he comes in and I step in front of Ivy, blocking her from him.

"Here. Clothing." He sets the bundle on a counter dropping a pair of boots on the floor beside me. His gaze is filled with something. Knowing, maybe. Knowing not to bother me with words. Right now, what I need is to see her improve. He grabs the doorknob on his way out. I've already seen more people out there; the room is filled with at least a dozen and many sets of eyes are trained on me as the door closes.

"How long will it take?" I demand, seeing the liquid from the bag moving into the hose where it'll deliver the medicine to my Ivy. I hope it works. I stare at it, demanding it to work.

"A few hours at least," she says. "It was too late for a venom extraction kit, and it penetrated the muscle anyway, so we're doing slow IV administration of the antivenom. I'm going to give her antibiotics as well."

I get the jeans on and pull a white t-shirt over my head. I pull socks on, then note the boots are too tight on my feet, so I pull the socks back off, kick them aside, and resume pacing.

Later, after I've watched Cat come in and out and clean everything she used and check Ivy's heart and pulse, a young shifter woman knocks on the door and opens it. She drops a pair of shoes and gives me a quick smile before she quickly backs away.

She's dropped shoes similar to the shoes Ivy wore in the house with the rubber soles, though these don't have a plug between the toes. Instead they have a black and white striped band across the top.

"Thank you, Leona," Cat says.

The woman sits down, but the door remains open.

I slip my feet into them. They fit. Not more than a moment later, I'm kicking them off, not liking the noise they make or the way they clap my soles when I pace.

It's shoes like these that leave men and women vulnerable to being bit by a snake.

And any sign of vulnerabilities increases the chance of others taking advantage. I loathe even the slightest notion of feeling vulnerable, never mind looking that way.

I'm not wired to show a vulnerability. A vulnerability would lead to opportunity from other predators. Vulnerability in prey did the equivalent of making me hard as a wolf. I'm the predator. And those around me are also predators. I won't forget it.

I sit on a small sofa, resting my forearms on my thighs as I stare at Ivy.

Her eyes are on me. She's awake. I jump up and go to her.

I see that the swelling has already decreased some. Color is returning in her face. She's definitely improved. Relief nearly knocks me over.

My hand goes to her face and she stares at me with her large violet eyes. Her skin still feels warm though maybe slightly less warm.

"Will she survive?" I demand of Cat, eyes still on Ivy.

"Definitely," Cat replies.

My eyes move back to my mate's face.

"You left me," I accuse.

Ivy swallows and looks away from me.

The silence feels like it has a noise to it. A noise I don't like. My hand slides away from her face and I try to get a read on her expression.

She moistens her lips and looks to Cat. "Looks like mother nature didn't want me to go, either. Um, Doctor?"

Cat's head rises from her task at the counter, where she's writing something down. She looks expectantly at her and Ivy startles. Ivy's eyes bounce to me and back to Cat and then to me again and she gives her head a shake.

She sees the resemblance.

"Yes, dear?" Cat asks.

"Can I... use a phone?"

"Of course. You're feeling a bit better?"

"Definitely. Not a hundred per cent, but way better than when Ty found me in that ditch. Thank you. Thank you so much. I'll get better, for sure?"

"For sure. And my pleasure. We need to see where things are at when that bag is empty, but don't worry, just rest. Be right back."

Cat leaves.

"You look like her," Ivy whispers.

"I know. She's my mother."

"Yeah," Ivy breathes. "Thank you for pulling me out of that ditch."

"You should not have been there," I hiss.

She bites her lip. "But..."

Cat's back and Ivy stops speaking. She's passed a phone and she immediately punches on the keys. I watch from her bedside listening to the noises coming from the thing. I'm familiar with the gadgets but I've never used one. I don't know who she's calling.

"Becks? It's Ivy. Yeah, hi. I have a little problem. You're not gonna believe this. I got bit by a poisonous snake and... no, I lost my phone and haven't had a chance to check my email either, what's up?"

Ivy listens and her face goes shocked, concerned and then her eyes land on me and I see something I can't measure.

Ivy's eyes go wide and then she swallows. "Oh. Wow. That's just... wild. No one got hurt, right?" She pauses, looking concerned and as relief spreads across her face, I feel it inside my belly. I'm growing more and more connected with her by the day, it seems.

She continues to talk. "Good. Good. Thank goodness. Well, yeah, I'm in a kind of rural clinic right now, hooked up to an IV and I have no idea what happens from here, so how about if I just call you in, say... two or three days and we talk then? I'll shoot you an e-mail as soon as I'm connected again."

She waits patiently as the person on the other end is obviously talking before wrapping up her call with a smile in her voice. "Yeah, no, it's fine. The doctor says I'll be good. No idea what kind but a rattler of some sort. Yeah... Oh, lonnnng story. We got separated and I had a car problem, phone problem too, but, oh... gotta go. The doc needs to, um, do something here. Okay then... will do. Thanks so much. Bye."

She punches buttons on the phone and with her free hand she crosses her middle and pointer fingers and whispers, "Don't answer, don't answer, don't answer..."

I frown as I notice her face has paled again.

She blows out a long breath and shifts her body a bit in the bed. I look at her ankle and it appears as if the swelling has receded some more. Progress, but my Ivy isn't fully recovered yet.

"Hi Mom?" Ivy says cheerily, "It's me. I'm still out of town. I got bit by a snake; can you believe it? I was, um, hiking and I ..., I did say by a snake, but I'm fine. I'm gonna be good, but I lost my phone and I'm guessing I'm gonna be here in this, um hospital overnight, so I will call you soon. I'm totally fine. I had a problem with my car, but I'll figure all that out and... yeah. I love you and I'll talk to you later. Don't worry, okay? Even if it takes me a few days to get back to you. Things are, um.." she looks at me. "Complicated for a few reasons, but I have the work thing covered, and I'm guessing you already know about that since you watch the news every night, so not a problem there for me to be off for a bit. I'll call you as soon as I can."

She punches a button on the phone, lets out a big breath and then she lifts the phone again and looks at it before she puts it down on the bed beside her and closes her eyes. She swallows.

There were no pauses among all those words. She waited for no replies so unlike her first call, that second one wasn't a two-way conversation. The amount of 'um' uses says a lot about the conversation and her relationship with her mother. She said 'um' to me when she lied about the boyfriend when we first met. I stare at her, waiting for an explanation. I don't get one. She's making an effort to avoid my face right now. It's pissing me off and I don't need to be angrier than I already am.

Cat returns and uses medical instruments to check Ivy's forehead, her wrist, and wraps something around her bicep and it tightens and registers numbers on a machine.

Cat writes down some things and then pulls a wheeled stool over beside the bed and begins to ask questions. I learn Ivy's twenty-seven, learn her date of birth, her blood type, that she has no known allergies, and that she's had her appendix and tonsils removed. Cat asks about her last tetanus shot and then tells her she'll need to administer one. I don't know what a tetanus shot is, but I know what an appendix is, and I know what tonsils are.

When Ivy answers what medications she's taking, she says just one name under her breath and I don't quite catch it, so I have no idea, still, what those pills I fetched from her car are for, but Cat's eyes move to me just briefly before she writes something down on the paper and purses her lips. "How long have you been mated?"

"It's a couple days since he... caught me and bit me." She says this with ambivalence in her voice and it angers me to hear the tone she uses as well as the words that make it clear to Catrina Savage that she's with me against her will. I know this is the truth, but it won't change a thing. She's mine. And as soon as she's out of this clinic, well enough, she's getting mounted, knotted, and again taught who she belongs to. Maybe the lessons will stick this time.

My chest hurts as I have this thought, because I don't know if my lessons will make her submit in a way that I lose the Ivy I've been growing to love, the one who forgets she wants to go away and does sweet things and looks at me with smiles in her eyes.

I don't want to put bruises on her. I wanna make her smile with her mouth and with her eyes. I want excitement like when she was anxious for me to taste that sandy fruit sauce she made for me. I want her to look at me like she did this morning and then climb onto me and wrap her arms around me. I don't want her crying in a ball on the bathroom floor and punching me when I try to hold her.

I clamp my teeth together and level her with a dark gaze. She looks away from me. Again.

"Right. I'll talk to Tyson for a minute. Try to rest. How's your pain?" Catrina asks.

"It's not too bad," she says. "It's there but better than it was, for sure."

"I gave you some pain medication and I gave you a small dose since you're such a small girl but if the pain gets worse, you let me know and I'll get you some more."

A greying bearded man, not a shifter, not even half shifter, pokes his head in, then he looks at me with a startled expression. "Catrina. A minute, please?"

There are more people in that other room now and I don't like it.

Lincoln sits there and catches my eyes. I gaze at his feet, seeing Ivy's two bags there. He didn't have them when he ran as wolf. He must have gone back to the site and retrieved them. He signals Catrina also, and hands her a dead snake. He fetched that, too.

"Good. Now we know precisely what we are dealing with," she says, looking over at me.

I nod at Lincoln. He thumps his chest.

I don't like the feeling I have right now, which is similar to when I had to go to the bar to meet women and there were people everywhere. I'm even more uneasy now because these people are the people Uncle warned me about. They are closing in and I have to wonder if they do have any ill intentions. These people seem more than aware of who I am, almost as aware as I am of them. It's as if there's static in the air, the way it feels when there's a pending storm.

I sense none are threats, but I don't trust that feeling because it's contradicting everything I've been taught. I'm at war with what to feel because of all the lies.

I wait for Cat's return. Ivy's eyes are closed and she's either trying to sleep or pretending to sleep. Despite her eyes being closed, I know she's awake. I know by the pace of her breathing, of her heart, that she's warring with emotions and filled with stress.

As for me, I'm staying alert because if any of those people make a move toward us that gives me any feelings of threat, I'll be ready to either rip them to shreds or bolt with my woman.

I now know for certain Cornelius hurt Catrina Savage at least once, likely a lot more than once if he's the source of her spending these years without her son, without her husband. I know that was her scent. I knew it earlier when she had that woman beside her with a similar scent but not close enough that I could be mistaken about who Cornelius was with.

I know little to nothing else but what I've pieced together and barely given myself an opportunity to process, as Riley would say, because of Ivy and because of me. The way I process now might be different from how I'd process if I hadn't neglected to shift for so long. I hate this feeling I have, the *no-control* feeling, over protecting my mate, over the people around me; I hate the way my mind keeps shuffling through all I know, or all I thought I knew.

Cat slips back in and shuts the door behind her. This time she locks it.

"Tyson, can I take your vitals please? And do a blood test?"

"Why? Nothing bit me, I'm not injured."

"For my own peace of mind. I have some concerns about the hormone levels I'm sensing from you, and..."

"Not now." I rise and pace the floor some more.

"Maybe soon?" she tries.

"Maybe. What's with all of them?" I gesture to the door that leads to that waiting area. "Why do they wait here?"

"They're merely concerned. They're here to show you that they're here for you and your mate. There was a lot of buzz today after your visit so now that you're here again and your mate was in jeopardy, they just... well, it's very normal pack behavior, Tyson. Can I get you anything? I'm going to get Ivy some water. Would you like anything?"

I shake my head.

She leaves.

My eyes move to Ivy who was watching the exchange.

"Your mom," she says, "is awesome."

I make a non-committal sound and approach to look at her ankle. Definitely better. Even better than earlier. That swelling is coming down quickly but not quickly enough to put my mind at ease. Ivy's scent is still wrong. And I hate the sight of the small bruises on her leg from my grip as I tried to get the poison out.

When I think about what could have happened... I could've found her dead. If I hadn't stopped to piss on Cornelius's bones and had that episode of rage, I could've stopped her from walking where she did. I could've had her in my arms, carrying her back home before this even happened.

That angry haze that came over me wants to come over me now.

It crackles at the base of my spine and I shove it back. I roar out my anger and she jerks in fear. I get directly in front of her face so that she can't look away from me. I can't say any words. I just breathe in and out and in and out. Her eyes are filled with fear. I don't want fear, but I have no words to show her how my emotions war right now. If she weren't in a bed hooked up to medicine to save her life, I'd have her on the floor under me, rutting her for as long as it took to get her to understand.

25

IVY

His eyes are wild with fury. I watch, unable to tear my gaze away, as a blood vessel pops directly in front of me. It just bursts in the white of his right eye and he bares his teeth. He's so angry.

Tears stream down my face and at the vision of his eye, a sob bursts from my throat. His face is only inches from mine. He leans over me, a fist on either side of my hips and his chest is rapidly filling with air and then depressing as he glares. This goes on for probably less than a minute, but it feels eternal before he snaps away and roars out another snarl, fists clenched, veins bulging in his muscled arms, and then Cat is in the room with us with two bottles of water.

She looks at him and then me and hands him the water, her brows knitting together only a bit. "Drink. Calm yourself, Tyson. You're frightening your little mate. She doesn't know much about you yet, about our kind, does she?" She says this with so much authority in her voice, I'm sure he's going to listen. She doesn't know him and yet seems unaffected by the scary way he's acting. This is baffling for a minute until it dawns that she likely knows many others like him. Other werewolves. I can't imagine this behavior being typical in my life. Then again, I wasn't born around this, so I have no comparison.

My dad and brother get grouchy sometimes and I've had occasion to accuse them of being alpha males, but it's glaringly obvious that I knew nothing of the term until now. They were nothing like this. If I dated a guy remotely acting like this, it'd be game over for us.

Date. *Ha.* This guy thinks we're the equivalent of married.

He yanks the bottle from her hand and twists the cap off before tipping it back and drinking it so fast that it vanishes in four or five swallows.

He doesn't answer her, so she looks to me.

"Is his eye okay?" I ask.

"He'll be fine. I'll give him some eyedrops when you go. Remind him to put them in. He'll probably be stubborn about it but try." She shrugs. "If he shifts, it might correct on its own. I'm not sure. Do you heal when you shift?"

"Yeah," he tells her. "Usually. She's ripped my face open twice with her nails and it's healed after a shift."

I blink. He's right. I didn't even realize.

"I'm not a violent person,' I defend. "We just met two days ago. I know next to nothing about your kind. He… he's been alone a long time, so I don't know how much he even knows about his own nature. He wasn't in person-form for a long time, until he … uh… smelled me. Things got physical when he…"

"Took you?" Cat fills in.

I nod. "He said things are foggy because he hasn't been a man for a long time but they're coming back to him. He knew how to drive a car and do laundry but not how to peel a banana."

Tyson stares at her, ignoring the fact that I'm talking. He's so angry right now, yet shows no change in reaction after I share that information.

"What can I do for you right now to put you at ease?" she asks him.

"Tell me my Ivy's gonna be fine," he barks, then adds, "If it's the truth."

The way he says *my Ivy* even though we're obviously in a fight… it does something to me. My belly flip-flops.

"She's gonna be just fine. I will only ever tell you the truth, Tyson. About anything you ask me. Do you have other things to ask me?" She gives him a look loaded with longing.

"Are those pain medicines working, or is she in pain?"

"The pain medicine is helping, Ty," I throw in.

His eyes dart to me briefly and burn into me for a second before they go back to Cat.

"I didn't mean about Ivy," Cat says. "I'm sure you can ask her those questions."

Yeah…if he were speaking to me.

He shakes his head. "The other thing you can do is make all of them go." He gestures toward the door.

"Done," she says and then she slips out and shuts the door behind herself.

I drink half my bottle of water and close my eyes. I'm feeling really drowsy.

Cat comes back in.

"I'll have things to say to you, my son, things I need to know, but not right now," she says and her voice cracks on the word son.

I pull my lips tight, feeling emotional for her, for them both.

"You and I have a lot of catching up to do and I hope you'll be open to that when Ivy is feeling better," Cat adds.

He says nothing in reply, but his eyes lose a fraction of their anger.

She turns away to check on my IV bag and I catch a swallow move down his throat as he stares at her back with a softer expression. She misses this and tells me it won't be much longer until she's ready to check my vitals again and then do some bloodwork. She suggests I rest and then she leaves, telling Tyson, "I'll either be outside the door or you can find me upstairs. My apartment door is beside the back exit. I'll be back in twenty or thirty minutes. Feel free to lock the door if it makes you more comfortable. You can also reach me upstairs on the intercom with the phone. She needs rest," Cat says, giving him a stern look.

"Thank you for everything, Cat," I say.

Her eyes warm. "I'm very glad to meet you, Ivy. I hope to get the opportunity to get to know you."

I smile in a non-committal way and Tyson scoffs. Both of us look at him. Animosity rolls off him. And it's aimed at me. Because I was leaving when I got bit.

She slips out and Tyson looks out after her and then shuts the door and locks it. He turns to look at me and his eyes narrow.

I stare directly into his eyes. I don't know what he's about to do right now. I brace for more roaring.

It doesn't happen.

He moves in and examines my ankle. His hand traces the mark and then runs up my calf briefly.

"More than one set of bitemarks on me now, huh? At least the snake won't try to claim ownership, I guess."

He glares at me with shock.

"I'm joking. It's a joke."

"The snake is dead. The one called Lincoln fetched it to show Catrina, so she'd know which type of snake bit you."

"Oh," I whisper.

"You could have died, and you talk with jokes?" he asks, his voice laced with accusation, as if I've committed a crime.

"That's just me. Um... thanks for getting me to your mom. She seems very nice. I wish the snake didn't have to die, though. It's not his fault I tripped over him and likely scared him. My sister is terrified of snakes, but my brother just calls them licky noodles. It makes them less scary; I think. That is... until you scare one and it bites you."

His eyes glitter with anger and his jaw clenches and unclenches. He sits down on the couch and lets out a long breath.

"The building of the boutique I work for caught fire last night," I say quietly. "I called Becks to tell her why I'd miss the grand opening but there won't be one, not yet. I don't have to be at work tomorrow. My boos thinks the fire was bad enough that it could be a while before we get to open. I'm gonna call her back in a couple days and she should know more then about how much damage there is, and... uh... all that. At least no one got hurt."

His eyes are pointed at his feet now, but his jaw keeps flexing.

I don't continue talking, because he's not being very receptive. And I find that it's making me angry.

I mean, I was the one bit by a venomous snake, not him. Why is he so angry? Yeah, I guess it's because I tried to leave.

My bladder nudges at me, but the IV bag is nearly empty, so I decide to sit tight and wait for Cat to come back in.

We sit in silence for... forever before she does. First, I inspect my nails. Then, I count the tiles on the drop ceiling. And then, I decide to look at him. No, I decide to watch him. I decide to stare at him with my best evil eye possible so that when he looks at me, he'll see that I'm angry, too.

He sits a while, staring at his feet. Then, his eyes are trained at the ceiling. I'm on the precipice of feeling invisible when our eyes meet and his lips twitch, as if he's about to finally speak to me when there's a knock at the door.

He unlocks and opens it, letting Cat in.

"Is that bag empty? We can go then, yes?"

"Not so fast."

"We need to go."

"I think she should stay overnight so I can keep an eye on things."

"You said she's gonna be fine." He steps forward and is about to lift me.

She puts her hand on his arm and his eyes go strange. She steps back as if she didn't mean to do it.

"Tyson, listen, please. I need to keep an eye on her blood pressure, the wound site, her temperature. I'll get her a blanket and you can sleep on the sofa. Ivy can stay in that bed so I can check on her a few times and make sure there's no complications. If all goes well overnight, take her home in the morning, but I'll then need to see her the following day so will want you to either bring her here or have me to your place."

Ty glares at her for a minute with his lip slightly curled. She stares directly into his eyes and her no-nonsense attitude is not only impressive, but evidently effective.

"We need food," he says.

"That was going to be my next offer. I'll get something sent over. I'll wheel in the television from the waiting room and you two can watch. I'll be back with food in a bit and then I'll be in every two hours to check on Ivy."

He grunts at her in acknowledgement and then sits back down.

"Um," I start.

Both sets of green eyes swing to me.

I close my mouth and straighten up.

"I have to pee. Where can I do that? And my ankle really hurts like it'll kill if I step on it, so I don't know if that's because I twisted it when I fell after the bite or if it's because of the bite."

"It's best you don't walk on that foot. Let me get you a wheelchair. I have one in the storage room. I've got rails in the bathroom, and—-"

"I'll carry her." Tyson erases the space between us and is lifting me before she gets a chance to finish.

"Oh. Okay," she says belatedly and wheels the IV along beside him, gesturing to the waiting room, which has a big reception desk, several chairs and sofas, a television, and two doors, one marked as the restroom.

Tyson carries me in.

"Don't put any weight on it. Come, Tyson."

"I'm not leaving her." He looks at his mother like she's insane.

"I have to go pee," I tell him.

He frowns. "So, do it."

"I need privacy for that."

"Why?" he asks.

Cat's eyes go round and she gives her head a shake. "Just wait outside the door for her. Women don't like to do that in front of men."

Tyson's eyes bounce between us and then he sets me down carefully and I hold the metal rail on the wall so I can keep my weight off my foot. He steps out of the bathroom and I shoot Cat a relieved look that gets me a half a smile from her before she shuts the door.

"Don't pull those jeans back up, Ivy," Cat calls from outside the door. "I'll zip upstairs and bring you back a pair of shorts."

"That'd be great, thank you."

"I'll let you know when I'm back and you can let me in to help you change."

"Okay, Cat. Thanks."

"RILEY, JOEL, JASON, and Lincoln want a meeting with you. You can use the waiting room while I go upstairs."

He shakes his head at his mother. "I don't want a meeting. I need to stay with Ivy."

We're back in the room with the hospital bed, I'm on the bed and I'm wearing a pair of grey jersey shorts which are much more comfortable than jeans. The sight of my now torn Lucky jeans that were brand new and not bought on sale is sad. I could cut the other leg and turn them into boyfriend cuffs, or maybe just capris. *Boo.*

The TV from the waiting room has been wheeled in and a 24-hour news station is on.

"She'll be absolutely fine in here while you use the waiting room. Or, you could have the meeting in here so that you don't have to leave her alone."

He looks at her like she's nuts.

"You think I'm stupid enough to be in a small room with four men and my woman in the midst of that?"

"Stupid enough? What about that scenario is stupid? This is your pack, Tyson. We're your family."

"I don't know any of you."

Her expression falls. There's a long moment before she says, "I see you don't trust us. What lies did that man's poison tongue and demented mind poison you with? What did he say about where you came from?"

The room goes dead silent.

"Riley Savage didn't tell you?" Tyson asks.

"Tell me what?" Cat's eyes look haunted.

Absolutely haunted. Goosebumps rise on my arms watching the exchange.

Tyson leans toward her and his voice takes on a sinister tone. "He told me you were dead and that the pack raped and devoured you after killing my father. He told me this when I was a small child. He said he's my father's brother and that he took me to save me from the pack that would have me dead as well."

I swallow.

She straightens her back and says, "Cornelius is one of your father's brothers, all right, but other than that, the rest is a pack of lies. You believe that I'm your mother, don't you?"

"I recognize your scent."

Her face changes, it half-crumples, but she composes herself.

"Tyson, six years ago, I caught your scent on the breeze and it made no sense. I couldn't figure it out. I thought I was going crazy. The grief of losing you both has never left me, never... but I was living life at that point and then I could smell you. And then you showed up. You showed up and I didn't see you with my own eyes, but I caught your scent in the air and knew that what they said was fact. A great black wolf was our Tyson, the alpha, son of Tiberius and Catrina Savage, prophesied to be the pack's top alpha of this generation and they knew not only your scent, but they knew by your bearing that you had to be him. Larger than any alpha in our pack and an air of authority that could not be mistaken. Not to mention pure black like Tiberius. Just like him, except with my green eyes instead of his amber ones. We hadn't lost you. Just before this, Cornelius's scent was caught on the wind. In fact he'd been caught a few times but never physically, because his scent would simply vanish. I don't know when you came to spend time at that home Riley visited you at but..."

"Cat grass," Tyson says.

She jerks and her back goes rod-straight.

"We ate it daily," Tyson said. "Disgusting as it was. I've lived there my entire life. He couldn't bring himself to leave the region, saying a shifter couldn't leave his territory for more than a few days or else go mad. We ate it and we lived on the fringe. I lived in that house until he died. We denned underneath, hibernated there each winter as he couldn't stand winters and each spring lived as men for a month before returning to wolf. When he died, I stayed in the bush, denned at the house in winters, but stayed in the forest otherwise.

"Almost under my nose." Cat shook her head. "Cat grass." She dashes a tear off her cheek and then reaches her hand out and cups his jaw. He leans into it just a little and his eyes drift shut. A lump forms in my throat. "And hibernating? That's insane. We don't do that unless we need to due to food shortages. And we haven't needed to for centuries. Why would he make you hibernate every year?"

"I don't know. He told me we had to. He despised the cold. Couldn't regulate his body temperature the way I can. I think he hated himself, could barely stand to look in the mirror more than necessary."

"It's not true about the territory. Shifters can go where they like."

Tyson's lip curls in anger.

"Where is he now?" she asks.

"The bottom of a gorge halfway between this village and my house. If you knew he took your child, why didn't your pack go after him?"

She blows out a breath and then looks at me before looking back to Tyson.

"We couldn't find him. We didn't think you were alive before six years ago or I'd have moved mountains to find you. We knew we couldn't approach you. Rye said you were feral and thought of us as enemies, would destroy us on sight. Then, you came back, and we could tell by the surge in certain facets of your scent that you'd found your mate. We decided to make an approach. We hoped it would mean you would calm down and be open to the truth. We didn't know what lies were told, we didn't know what he'd done, we didn't know why his scent would show up occasionally, but we never caught yours until six years ago and since then, we've never smelled him again. And yours came up often, but we suspected you didn't know you were ours. Didn't know we were yours. If you did, you'd come h-home."

Tyson leans forward.

"I stopped eating the disgusting grass. He wasn't there to insist, and I didn't give a fuck whether any of your alphas ran into me or not. In fact, I wanted them to. I wanted to run into them in the forest or even to come here and destroy all of them, for what they did to my father and you. But something stopped me."

"What?" she asks.

"I don't know," he growls and thumps his chest. "Something in here."

"Feeling like you know, deep down, there's more to the story?"

"That and mostly... your scent. Something about it was familiar. And I smelled it on him once... when he..."

Her eyes close and she raises a hand. He stops speaking.

"If I knew he had you with him all this time?" Her eyes open and they are filled with wrath. "If only I could deal with him now. He knew something about a habit of mine to collect a healing mushroom and he found me in the spot I'd usually go that year. He wouldn't have found me otherwise because he had a poor sense of smell."

"He had no sense of smell. None. He made use of mine to survive. He made use of me for many things." He crosses his arms over his chest. "Food for Ivy, please." She freezes and stares at him a moment, then seeing he's done talking, I suppose, she nods and turns on her heel and leaves the room.

He sits back down and completely ignoring me, props his elbow on his knee and puts his chin to his palm.

I tilt my head to the side. "Wow," I say. "I'm sorry, Tyson."

His eyes sweep over me and then they drop back to the rug.

Fine. Silent treatment. I'll close my eyes. I'm feeling like crap anyways.

"IVY?"

Cat is jiggling my arm.

"Sorry, sweetie, I have to check your vitals."

Tyson is sleeping on the couch, sitting up, head back. The television is still on, still playing the news station.

She catches me looking.

"If anyone else were here, he would've woken as soon as I entered. It's nice that something inside him knows me, knows I'm no risk to you."

"It's a lot for him to digest, I bet. After thinking one thing his whole life and then finding out it wasn't true."

"Yeah," she says softly. "You slept for six hours; your swelling is way down. How do you feel?"

"Sleepy."

"That's the pain meds. I've got more fluids here since you slept, and I didn't want you woken. Talk about coercion to convince him not to wake you up to force-feed you a tomato and bacon sandwich." She smiles. "He likes bacon. He ate your sandwich. Though he tossed the lettuce."

I smile. And then my smile falters. "I'm so sorry for what you've been through," I whisper. "I just can't imagine."

"Tyson is a lot like his father from what I've seen so far. I've heard you call him Ty. I called my Tiberius Ty as well. That's why we named our boy Tyson. It's astounding to see him all grown up when I hadn't seen him since he was eight months old. It hurts but it feels good at the same time. Because he met you, we might have a chance at a real relationship."

Tyson straightens up, eyes open. He's awake and it's obvious he's heard what she said. I grab her hand and give it a squeeze. "I'm so sorry for all you've lost. Words just aren't enough."

"No, but hope is everything. I'll let you get some more sleep. I've given you more pain meds. How's the pain?"

"It's there, but it's pretty dull."

"Good. I'll send you home with some more. You're gonna be fine."

"Thank you. Thank you for everything."

"I'm gonna get back to bed but here." She lifts the phone I used earlier from the table where it must've been moved to at some point. She puts the phone beside me on the bed. "If you need anything, anything whatsoever, please just hit the intercom button. It'll ring on the phone in my apartment at my bedside. I've put some ice water, some apple juice, and a few pieces of fruit there if you get hungry before morning, but I have a feeling you'll just sleep."

"Thank you," I whisper.

She squeezes my hand. "We have lots to talk about, you and me. I look forward to some girl time. I can help you navigate this strange new world you're in. My niece, Leona, as well as some other of our younger community members will be even more help as there will be things, I'm sure, that you won't want to talk to me about." She winks.

I feel my cheeks flush. "Goodnight, Cat. Thanks again. Sleep well."

She stops in front of Tyson. "Do you need anything?"

"I need to leave," he grumbles. "But as you've said we need to wait until morning, we'll do that." He folds his arms across his chest stubbornly.

She leans over and drops a kiss on his forehead and then slips out.

He looks sort of shell-shocked.

The door clicks shut.

I close my eyes, feeling like I should give him privacy for whatever emotions he's having right now. I can see emotion all over his face and it looks just too personal for me to 'eavesdrop' on.

I really am tired from the pain medication, so I drift under again in no time.

26

TYSON

I watch her sleep, filled with urges. I long to wrap her up in my arms, to take her home. The need to punish her is still there, but it's simmering under a layer of other emotions, specifically the need to nurture her.

It still hurts that she was put in harm's way because I allowed it.

It still hurts that she was hurt while trying to leave me.

The fact that my efforts with her so far haven't convinced her that what we can have would be worth walking away from her old life feels terrible.

There's also all that's being revealed around me to contend with. And the feelings I have about these people. I'm confused about it.

I feel affection for Catrina Savage. I feel connected to her. I've felt no affection for anyone other than Ivy and I'm conflicted about all of it because I don't know what this means. I know very little about this pack's culture and history. My culture. My history.

I've been told lies. I've done reading but I don't know if what I've read are myths or not because the ones who wrote those stories and those facts have either written it as fiction or under the guise of fiction. As for what Cornelius told me, are they only lies or is some of it true?

And despite my efforts to remain distanced from the alphas in this pack, I feel a strange sense of connection to them, too. I don't know how that works, but I am curious about the fact that two of them showed up when I was in that gorge under the haze of anger about Cornelius because I somehow summoned them.

I slip out of the room to empty my bladder and sense other shifters close, and I know Riley's scent already but there are others with him, close. I see out the window that Riley is there with two other men, talking near this building's entrance. I don't know either of them but by their scent and stature, I'm certain they're other alphas in this pack. Their heads all swing to the window simultaneously, sensing me.

Riley gestures for me to come out. I shake my head and open the window instead. No chance I'd leave Ivy in a building while I'm outside it this soon, certainly not when there are three alpha shifters outside, even if one of them is supposed to be a member of my blood family.

"Tyson, this is Jason, and this is Joel." Riley gestures.

My eyes meet the eyes of Jason, light brown hair, light brown eyes, and built like Riley, which is to say like I am, though like Riley he is an inch or two shorter than me. Next, my gaze connects with Joel who is even taller, as tall as I am, possibly taller, and not as heavily built though definitely muscled. Joel has dark hair and vivid blue eyes. Both men look at me with what I think feels like affection and respect.

"How is Ivy?" Riley asks.

"Better. And thank you for yesterday." My words can't possibly convey how grateful I am. And that's another thing that angers me. That I needed help to save her, that I didn't have the capability to save her myself. I feel like I should've been able to. I despise that helpless feeling and never want to experience it again.

"Anything for you. We wanna talk with you. We understand that your mate is your focus right now but need to talk about a few things."

"Talk."

"While Linc tracked her scent to find the snake that bit her, he found a car that was also filled with her scent. He had it towed out of the valley. It's at Larry's Auto Repair in Drowsy Hollow. He wanted you to know he's having it fixed for her. There was a damaged windshield and damage to two door handles as well as some bumper and hood damage."

He stops speaking and I wait to see what else he wants to say. I know there's more, but I'm unable to fight the urge to narrow my eyes at the notion of Lincoln filling his attention with the scent of my woman.

"Lincoln has above average tracking capabilities. He did it to help."

How does Riley so easily read my thoughts? I stiffen.

"Rye thinks the way you think, Tyson. We all do," Joel says and then he folds his arms across his chest and waits for me to reply, I think. I say nothing.

Riley breaks the silence. "I know you'll be taking her home today, according to Aunt Cat, but also that Cat will be coming out tomorrow to see her unless you're coming back here…" He lets that hang.

"I won't be coming back here tomorrow," I answer. "My woman needs to rest."

"Then, if it's acceptable to you, we'd like to come out with her and bring the car. Talk to you. Most of the team. This is Ivy's phone." He hands me a device he's pulled from his pocket. "Linc said it was under the car."

I look at it. It's a flat square panel with a red sparkled back.

"It's dead. I grabbed you a cord in case she didn't have one. I figure she might have calls she needs to make or return." Riley reaches into his pocket and passes me a power cord attached to a block-shaped square with electrical prongs protruding from it.

"No to a meeting, but yes to you bringing the car," I say. "Just you."

The other two men don't look bothered.

"It's a start," Riley says. "And I appreciate that. See you then. I'd invite you to come with us for a morning run tomorrow, we're just back from that, but I'm sure that's not something you're ready for. So you know, we meet behind the barn at the four corners of the village every morning at five. Whoever wants to come meets us."

"Good to meet you finally," the one called Jason says, extending his hand.

I reach out the window and grasp his hand. Something crackles between us. I flinch. He sees it.

I don't know how he reads it from me but there's nothing but respect in his eyes and emanating from him.

The one called Joel steps up and reaches to shake my hand. I get the same sensation.

He steps back; Riley steps up, and so I hold my hand out and instead of shaking it, the man embraces me with both arms around me. The window area isn't big so it's awkward, but he slaps my back and gruffly says, "Means a lot to me to have you in my life. It really does. See you tomorrow, cousin."

I slap his back once in reply and he promptly releases me.

They turn and go.

I stare after them for a long moment before I hear my name being called from behind me.

It's Cat. I turn to look at her.

"She's awake. Everything looks good and she's hungry. I'll make you both some breakfast and then I'll drive you home."

"I'll take her now," I say.

"Oh." She looks disappointed. "She's hungry."

"You can drive us," I tell her. "I'll feed her at home."

She smiles, but it doesn't reach her eyes. "Oh. Give me two minutes to get my keys and tell Stanley."

27

IVY

Tyson carries me in through the front door of his house. He has my bags, which I'm relieved about; I hadn't even thought about them in the clinic because I was sort of reeling from everything.

I don't know how he got them since he didn't leave my side but suspect someone from the clinic helped.

Cat drove us in her SUV and Tyson carried me into the back seat and held me the same way he did when I was injured even though he didn't need to.

"I should – " I tried to scoot off his lap.

His grip around me tightened and his eyes were like green fire, warning me to stay put. On him.

"I can't put on my seat belt from your lap, Ty."

"Are you a good driver, Catrina Savage?" Ty called out.

"Only the very best," she said with a smile in her voice.

He grunted and stayed put. Okay, then.

"Especially with precious cargo," she tacked on.

I caught a smile in her eyes in the rearview mirror. I smiled at her.

The ride back was silent and broody, just like the mood in the room before we left. One minute she's giving me the okay that I can go and offering to make eggs benedict and introduce me to Stan, who I guess she lives with, but the next moment, she's coming back with Tyson on her heels and he's gathering me up to take me back to his lair.

I can't help but feel nervous about being alone with him. The way he's been with me has been frying my nerves to a crisp.

We get back and he has to fetch his keys from his jeans by the tree before we can go in.

"Eyedrops three times a day unless you shift and it gets better on its own," she reminds him.

He grunts in response.

HE KICKS THE DOOR SHUT behind us and my body jerks in response to the slam. He's barefoot, and his face scruff is now officially a bit more than scruff, and it's yummy. Though, I'm trying to not ogle it too much because we're obviously in a fight.

He goes still and my hands fiddle with one another from their position in my lap. He sets me down on the sofa and looks around with surprise on his face.

The atmosphere has changed and it's not subtle. He looks around with big eyes and then his eyes land on me.

The house still smells like lemon dish soap, cinnamon, and wildflowers from my cleaning spree yesterday that used almost the whole bottle of soap. I also sprinkled cinnamon into the fireplaces and on the kitchen burners. It's evident that it's much cleaner at a glance even if I only got the floors swept instead of mopped.

He's eyeing me with that 'math question' face again. I say nothing.

Before we got out of the truck, his mother said, "Make her some breakfast and some tea when you get in. She needs to rest today so nothing that requires anything... strenuous. Understand?"

He flexed his jaw muscles in reply.

"Nothing too strenuous," she repeated. Then winked.

He gave her a subtle nod and that seemed to satisfy her.

"See you tomorrow," she replied. "I'll be here around this time. Here's my phone number if you have any questions or problems. And I gave him two dressing changes for the wound site, Ivy. Change it tonight and again in the morning. Pain pills every four hours. I'll bring more first aid supplies tomorrow." She held a card out and I took it.

"Thanks, Cat, but there's no phone here."

"I have your phone," Tyson informed, and this shocked me.

I told her there were some of Riley's clothes and a pair of boots near the tree and she said she'd grab them and take them back with her. "Our kind tend to leave our clothes absolutely everywhere." She winked at me and then left.

And now that he's put me down, he's walking to the kitchen counter and emptying his pockets of all the things she gave him at the clinic. Pills, bandages and gauze, eyedrops, and my phone plus a cord and charging block.

He lifts a pot out of the cupboard, fills it with water, and sets it on the stove. He turns the stove on, likely to make tea per her orders. After that, he opens the fridge and surveys the ingredients. The fridge is jam-packed from the shopping spree of two days ago.

The table wasn't dirty yesterday as he'd obviously cleaned it the night before after I went to bed because I noticed it no longer had the sticky-grimy film on it, but I found an actual lace tablecloth deeper in that stuffed armoire in the bedroom and had put it on as well as a pretty (once I washed a decade or two of grime off it) turquoise crackled glass vase I'd found in the back of a cupboard with some flowers I'd picked from the jungle of fragrant wildflowers behind the house.

He leans over and lifts the note I'd put down. His eyes go wide, and I feel self-conscious as he stares at it.

It flutters toward the floor and then he's erasing the space between us, to get to me and before the paper even lands, he has my jaw in both hands and his mouth is on mine.

His teeth nip my bottom lip, making me gasp and this grants him access with his tongue, which licks at mine. He is devouring me. Devouring me with his mouth and there's all sorts of heat rising in me along with crazy emotions coming at me from him. From me. Sort of swirling around us both, I think.

Oh. My. God.

What's happening here?

I'm pulling away, trying to get some air because I can barely breathe. I search his face and the anger that I've been looking at since yesterday is just... gone.

"Ivy," he breathes and then he's kissing me again.

And now he's purring.

And I'm melting.

He's kissing me again and I suddenly don't care about oxygen. It feels like everything I need... I can get from him.

I'm kissing him. He's kissing me. My hands are on his shoulders, then in his hair and he's groaning, liking the way it feels.

Wait.

Wait a freaking minute.

"Wh-what are you doing?" I pull back, ready to show how hurt my feelings are, though I'm relieved that he's suddenly all about showing affection instead of roaring in my face like an angry monster. "Two seconds ago you were fuming. Now you're... what?"

"Your note. You weren't just... you didn't just want to forget what we shared. I'm ..." He stops and licks his lips.

"Sorry?" I ask, haughtily. "Are you about to say you're sorry for the way you've been behaving? Because what if I'm not ready to hear a sorry and accept your apology? What if I'm still upset about you growling in my face so much in the past twenty-four hours?"

He pulls me against him, squishing me to his chest. Then he's maneuvered me over and into his lap, his arms around me, his nose in the crook of my neck, where his teeth prints are. He drags his nose up and down the crook, purring louder, and....boom... my panties are drenched. Completely.

"Damn it," I whisper and then his lips find mine and his fingers tangle in my hair once again.

"I *am* sorry, my beautiful Ivy. You shouldn't have left, do not leave again, please, please never. But that you left me your telephone number for your house line, whatever that means and the phone number for your store fills me with so much joy. Coming home to this house made nicer and now seeing you didn't want to just forget me..." He lets that hang.

Yeah. I felt bad. I wrote that I had to go, that I was sorry if it hurt his feelings, but that my job was counting on me and that I couldn't let them down. I told him to please phone me, that I'd really like to talk to him again. I underlined the word 'really' three times.

I almost crumpled up the note and started over, but it seems that the few lines on a piece of paper were enough to make his anger at me disintegrate.

That's why he's been so growly. He thought I left him without a backward glance.

"I left because I had to, Tyson. I had to," I whisper. "I didn't wanna hurt you. I kept trying to tell you that I had responsibilities and people would be worrying about me and you just wouldn't listen…"

"I know. It still hurts, but it doesn't hurt as much."

Oh, my heart.

I snuggle into him, realizing how much I've missed him putting his hands on me affectionately in such a short time.

"I have, in a few days, had my life changed," he whispers into my hair. "I'm not good with words, Ivy, but I'll try to explain."

"Okay," I whisper against his shoulder.

He squeezes again. "I found you. You, who are already and always will be the most important being in the world to me."

I bite my lip. He keeps going.

"I found out about family that I didn't know I had. I found out a pack I thought was against me has instead mourned me. The man who raised me, who told me he did it to save me? Lied. He lied my whole life. And I'm piecing together many other things about my life with him that I hadn't taken the time to think about, not really. I'm in a different mind state now. And all those people who want to know me. And Cat…"

"Your mom. Your mom that you thought was killed."

"But she was raped, Ivy. By my uncle. I knew he went to the forbidden village and took a female against her will. I smelled the sex and fear on him when he came back. And when I was faced with the scent and the eyes of Catrina Savage I knew that she was that woman he did that to and that she is my mother. My mother who he said was dead. He told me he saved me. He threw that in my face many times over the years that I was alive because of him. No, Ivy. I was alone because of him."

"Oh, Ty." I put my hand to his jaw, and he stares into my eyes with a wondrous expression.

"She is nothing like I expected. None of them are. There are so many things happening, my Ivy. And you tried to leave me and you were nearly killed by a venomous snake and I had to take you to them, not knowing if they'd save you or if they'd try to harm us and doing that while worrying about you…"

"I get it. Into a den of wolves. Or what you thought was one."

"They are wolves. Wolf shifters," he says, confused. He leans back and looks at my face searchingly.

"I know," I explain. "It's an expression for stepping into a dangerous place where… where everyone will betray you," I say.

He jerks.

"That's what people think of wolves? And yesterday you called me a filthy fucking animal and a monster then left me. And now you speak of dens of wolves as if it's a bad thing." He shakes his head.

"And you're upset at your uncle for taking your mother against her will and that's what you've been doing to me," I return.

He jerks back like I've slapped him. "It's… we're mated. You're mine, Ivy."

He doesn't understand.

I sigh. "You don't get it."

"You're right, I don't. I'm caught between a world of shifters and your world where I understand very little of either, Ivy. And you spoke vilely of me and then left me. And nearly died. Nearly died while I was running off anger so you wouldn't have to see it and then came face to face with the woman that birthed me, a woman who had her husband and child taken. She's in a pack where they mourn me, where they want me to be their leader. I don't know how to be one of them or don't know how to be with someone like you who doesn't understand me or them." He runs his hands through his hair. "And I don't show vulnerability to anyone and yet here I am showing it to you."

"Because you trust me," I whisper.

He looks into my eyes.

"You thought I was the one for you and—"

"You are! I tell you this, but you continue to try to leave me."

"I explained that," I defend.

He huffs.

"I get it, baby. You feel like everyone betrays you." I caress his face again. He leans into my touch and his eyes go so liquid with heat; they glow. "I was angry because you talked about hurting someone merely because I had a history with them. Just because I used to date someone doesn't mean they deserve to die. Would you actually kill him just because he used to date me?"

His lip curls. He still can't hack the thought of me dating somebody. How can he feel so possessive this soon?

"We have a major culture divide between us, Ty. We'd have had that if you were a shifter growing up like a typical shifter, but you didn't grow up in a way that's typical for... anyone."

"No, I didn't."

"And I don't even know a whole lot about how you grew up. But I do know that if you and I are gonna work, we're gonna have to take the time to try to understand one another. Be patient with each other."

"If we're gonna work?" he asks. "Does that mean you won't try to leave me again?"

I sigh and give my head a shake. "It means I wanna try and see what this thing is..."

"You won't leave me," he orders. "Ever."

I roll my eyes. "God, you're bossy. Go make me some tea and breakfast. I'm injured over here." I shake my head and fold my arms across my chest.

He looks into my eyes searchingly for a moment and I point exaggeratedly at the stove. "And I could use a blanket over here. My legs are cold."

Cat let me hang onto her shorts so I wouldn't have to try to get my jeans over my ankle again.

"Who's bossy?" He cocks an eyebrow and then his sexy mouth splits into a breathtaking smile. "I'll make you tea. And food, little boss. What food do you want?"

"A deli sandwich and soup," I say. "And for you to promise not to kill any of my exes."

He frowns. "I don't know how to make that. I can cook meat over fire. I could try to..."

"Sandwiches."

"Yes?"

He doesn't know how to make sandwiches. I can tell by his face.

"You slap deli meat between two pieces of bread and put mayo and mustard and cheese and lettuce and tomato if you have it."

"Okay..." He doesn't sound sure.

"Soup, you heat up in a pot on the stove. The can will say if you have to add water or not."

He blinks at me.

I'll make it," I tell him. "Just put a chair by the counter and I can rest a knee on it so I don't have to put my weight on my foot, and you can help. Or stand there and look pretty. Whatever. Let's go."

"I need to mount you first," he informs, looking like he's getting ready to devour me.

Mount?

I put a hand up.

"You need to wait," I correct, "until I eat, get some caffeine into me, and take a shower. I'll have to cover my foot with something so I don't get it wet but...your mom said I can't do anything strenuous. And we need to work on your seduction skills there, baby."

"Are you telling me I'm not allowed to fuck you?" he stares into my eyes.

"That's exactly what I'm telling you."

"You don't get to tell me that," he denies, pointing at himself. "I'm the man."

I laugh.

He looks affronted. And confused.

"And I'm a woman with a voice. And besides... your mom said so," I add.

His eyes track my face and he looks like he's trying to figure something out.

I raise my eyebrows. "You gonna listen to your momma?"

He gives me a 'what the fuck' face.

"Okay, how about this then..." I try instead. "Do you want to have another fight with me before we even get a chance to have make-up sex?"

He tilts his head and eyes me sexily. "Make-up sex? That sounds interesting."

"Oh, it is. Don't blow it or you won't be getting it. C'mon. Carry me to the counter. Your mom doesn't want me putting weight on my foot at all today. Not only did I get bit, but I also twisted my ankle trying to get away from the snake, so it hurts."

"More pills?" He asks.

"I can't have any for at least three hours. Gotta follow the schedule with pills or you can get sick from taking too many. You know that right?"

"I guess." He doesn't look so sure.

"You guess?"

"I've never had pills."

I shake my head in surprise. This guy is just... fascinating. "I don't need pills right now, but I wouldn't be able to take them if I did feel like I need them, I'd call your mom and tell her that they're not strong enough. Anyway, I'm fine though. I'll rest after we eat."

That reminds me, I need to take my birth control pill. And he needs his eyedrops.

"Let's get that plugged in." I gesture to my phone, not recognizing the cord.

He plugs my phone in and then starts working on a fire, so I take that minute to grab my birth control pills from my bag, which is at my feet. I pop one in and swallow it down dry. He's rubbing his eye like it's irritated.

"Ty, put your eyedrops in," I say. "It'll help with the irritation."

He gets just one in and acts like a big baby about it, scowling and rubbing his eye.

"Another one. You have to put two in."

"I've got a better idea," he says, and he shifts, shifts back, and steps up.

"Better?" he asks.

My head shakes in astonishment. I can still barely wrap my head around his ability to do that.

The white of his eye is still red.

"No. Put the rest of them in."

"I don't like how it feels," he says.

"Then I'll do it."

"Later. You need food."

"Ty..."

"Later."

I decide not to push it.

He puts his clothes back on and helps me make lunch. Tea, deli turkey and swiss cheese sandwiches and I realize there's no soup, so I make myself one sandwich and I make him two. He devours them and then looks at me like he wants to devour me.

"I liked that," he tells me, and then he eats a banana and a bunch of strawberries, which he groans over like they're the best thing he's ever eaten.

"Try this," I say, sticking a Milano mint chocolate cookie between his fabulous lips.

His eyebrows furrow and then he takes the cookie out of his mouth and looks at it before taking a bite.

His eyes pop a little.

"Right?" I ask, nodding.

He eats three more immediately after that one.

I'm barely finished my last bite of one cookie when he abruptly lifts me and marches to the bedroom. He halts inside the doorway, looking around in surprise when he sees I'd cleaned it, too.

"You need more cleaning supplies. I did my best with what I had but it's by no means spic and span. You need some all-purpose heavy duty cleaner and a mop and a dustpan, and—-"

"Whatever you need to make this feel like home, I'll get it for you."

"How about a big screen TV, a hot tub, and a bunch of modern appliances?" I joke. "Oh, and the internet. And a furnace and air conditioner"

"Okay." He kisses my nose and I'm set on the bed. He immediately reaches for his fly.

"I was kinda joking."

Besides, I didn't say I'd stay here forever, I certainly don't want another fight with him though, so I don't bother to point that out.

He unbuttons his shirt and tosses it and then drops the jeans and... boing. He's naked.

Naked and ready.

"How?" I ask, staring at his cock. "How would you get all that stuff here?" I drag my eyes back up to his face.

"However I need to go about doing it." He puts a knee to the bed and I scoot over toward the wall. "I have a truck. I'm sure we can buy those things and drive them here."

"Tyson, I was kidding. All that stuff costs a whack of money. And you're pretty far out in the boonies here so I'm not even sure if there'd be decent internet, and..."

"I have money."

"Okay," I mutter, deciding I really should remind him that I'm not sure how long I can stay here, that we have to play this thing by ear, but then he starts talking again.

"Ivy..." He pulls me against his body. "I have a lot of money. My uncle... he used me to help him gain wealth. He did some devious things. And had me help when I was very young as well as an adolescent. We have enough money for anything we might need. I don't quite remember how much is there, but I counted it before he died and researched the costs of things. I can buy us things to make this house better. That's the least that money can do."

I tilt my head. This has my attention. He cocks his elbow and rests his jaw on his palm. I put my head to the pillow and listen.

"When I first began shifting, I was a small child, I don't know how old, but I was quite young. He'd have me shift to attract attention, looking like a small, cute pup. He put a collar on me and a leash and left it dangling."

My hand flies to my mouth.

"People would take me into their homes, into their shops, thinking I was a lost pet. He told me the things to look for like car keys, jewelry, money, wallets, and then I would take the opportunity to shift back when they went to bed or weren't looking. I'd leave with their belongings. With wallets. With jewelry. Later, in my young teen years, after the period where I lost control of shifting and got it back, I ran into two banks and a few jewelry stores in two different towns near here in one week. It caused a commotion and people ran out, afraid of the wild animal. That wild animal changed to a man when no one looked and used a bag planted under a bench to dress in clothes, steal money, and hide in the bathroom or out of sight until it was safe to leave."

"Oh God. I think I remember reading something in the newspaper about that. Holy shit. It was a feature about some old unsolved mysteries talking about people using a rabid dog or wolf to distract and do some smash and grabs."

"That was us. There's a lot of money in the floorboards of the garage. He had me fight in dog fights several times, too, for money, when I was young and my wolf wasn't so large. Then when I was older, he used me in other ways for large sums of money. I don't... I'm not proud of any of it."

"Of course you're not. He was treating you like a puppet. What a creep!"

"He didn't have the means to provide for me otherwise, justified it as doing what he had to for provisions. Every year, he sold some of the things he took in different towns so he wouldn't draw attention, often waiting a year or two after a crime before selling something. He said the money or things were insured and people wouldn't lose out on their wealth. I didn't think they deserved it, most of them, but Uncle said most times only greedy insurance companies would lose money. The man didn't even have any senses to care for himself as a wolf but couldn't tolerate being man for long periods of time. He rarely spent any of that money but couldn't seem to stop looking for ways to collect more."

"Oh my God, Ty."

"He was deranged half the time he was a man, making no sense, but he had devious bones in his body, obviously. When he was wolf, he said he felt like he could live. But he couldn't hunt or protect himself without me without the senses he needed. I know now he'd have been in the bottom of the pack. Considered helpless. He told me they treated him like a worthless slave because of his disability. He said it was their fault he had the disability, but he never did explain what that meant. When I asked questions he would change topics or not answer. I lived in quiet. I never learned to use my words very well because he rarely spoke to me. I read a lot of books. Books were helpful. Things are still coming back about books I read. I'd like more books. I have many in the garage.. Do you like books?"

"Who doesn't? And you're doing just fine with your words, Tyson."

A big exhale comes from him. "I need you, Ivy. I need your body wrapped around me. I need inside you. Are you too ill for my cock? I need you but if you really need me to wait, I'll wait."

Gulp. I want to say I need him to wait. I should say that. I should slow this down a little, with how addicted he's getting to this thing we have, but I don't want to. I want him. I don't know what the heck I'm doing here, but right now, I want him, too.

"Be gentle, Tyson."

"I will. Nothing too strenuous, my Ivy. I'll listen to my mother." He winks. Just like she did when she gave the orders. I laugh.

28

TYSON

My body feels so much lighter. Walking in, thinking of punishing her but not wanting to do it, though feeling like I should do it… it felt like a weight on me. And now, it's lifted. I'm relieved instead. And astonished.

The state of the house – a shock. Her note to me was a bigger one. And talking to her about what I've been feeling and some of what I've endured makes me feel strange. In a good way.

I like the lunch we had and the talk we had and when I take her into the bedroom and see it's also much cleaner but looks shabby, I want to rip everything out of this place from my old life and give her things that are better. Much better.

I want a better house for her with nicer things, all the things that will make her happy to stay, that will make her miss nothing from her old life.

It never sat right, that Uncle had us steal all those things. Some of the people who thought I was a dog when I was young were kind, had nice homes and children who wanted to play with me, and it made me feel longing, longing for what I was missing – a family. It didn't feel like those people deserved to be deceived and stolen from. Even some in the stores and banks didn't seem like terrible people. And the fights. I hated the fights. He'd do things to send me into the haze, remind me my father was murdered, my mother was devoured, and use his twisted words to his advantage. Deny me sleep and food until I was in a certain state, then whisper things in my ear to push, send the bolt up my spine and make me see red. I know I've killed men and he got paid for it. It now sickens me.

It's in the past, I can't change it. But, to have that money to provide for Ivy? If it provides things that make her want to stay, I'll use all of it.

Maybe I'll use the money to buy a fashion store in the village for her, so she can do the job she loves.

As her back touches the bed, I notice her eyes are filled with emotion. She's looking at me like she wants me. I'd know it from looking at her if I couldn't smell her arousal. But I do smell it. And it makes me happy.

"I'll be gentle," I assure.

"Okay, baby," she whispers, and her eyes are sweet.

I close my eyes and sensations wash through me.

I think I like when she calls me *baby* even more than when she calls me Ty. She says it now with a rasp to her voice, a rasp filled with wanting me. I smell it. I feel it.

I touch her mouth with mine and carefully undress her, taking my time to touch her, taking the time to watch how her body reacts to every touch. The arch of her back, the way she moistens her lips with the tip of her tongue. How her thick fringe of lashes lower just a little and her chest rises and falls with deep breaths because she's filled with anticipation.

I kiss my mark on her and watch little bumps rise on her arm. She likes that. I lick the spot and then suck it briefly and groan out a pleasure sound as her fingers weave into my hair. She rakes through my hair with them and then nips at my jaw with her little teeth, thrusting her pussy toward me.

My Ivy doesn't wanna wait anymore. She wants me to fuck her now.

I kiss a path down her body, careful to avoid putting any weight near her sore ankle, and find my way between her legs.

She's got a small thatch of blonde curls in a triangle over her mound and she's smooth everywhere else. I like it. I've been with women with no hair as well as with women with a lot of hair between their legs and never had a preference. I like that her scent clings to the little bit of curls and I also like that I can see the peach shade between her lips peeking at me, inviting my tongue to have a taste. I do.

"Open your legs a little, Ivy," I instruct and my beautiful girl obliges.

I look up at her face while I taste her and she's panting, staring at me while skimming her bottom lip with her front teeth, and I reach for her breast, gently twisting her puckered nipple while I suckle her clit.

"Oh yeah, Ty, yeah, baby..." Her mouth opens as her legs tremble on either side of my head.

I suck again and she's writhing against my face, and crying out her soft little whimpers quickly with a low 'ah, ah, ah' and then a long 'ahhhhh' before her body shudders and goes limp.

My cock wants inside, but she needs me to be gentle today so instead I roll to my back and pull her close to my side, grabbing her hand and placing it on my shaft.

She immediately squeezes and now it's my turn to make sounds.

She's got a much smaller hand than me but with a good grip. She arcs her thumb repeatedly over my tip as she squeezes and I close my eyes, focusing only on the sensation, feeling good, feeling happy that we're not in a battle right now. I like make-up sex.

Wet heat wraps around my cock and my eyes jerk wide open.

She's crawled backwards down to get her beautiful mouth around me.

Fuck, yes.

"Don't hurt your ankle," I order, and my voice comes out hoarse.

She releases my cock to say, "I'm fine" and then she's taking me deeper.

My fingers weave into her beautiful wavy blonde and purple locks. She gags, trying to go too deep and then changes strategy, using her lips and both of her hands to lavish attention over my cock and my balls, which are heavy, getting ready to spill my essence down her throat this quickly. Fuck, but I love the feel of her hot mouth around me.

I hold back, wanting to enjoy watching my mate between my legs, her sexy ass up in the air. No way I'll close my eyes now. I wanna see her like this, looking beautiful like this. I'll never forget this moment for the rest of my days.

She's propped on her knees so both ankles are in the air and the sight of the wrapped injured one makes me bare my teeth for an instant because I still hate that she got hurt, but then it dawns that the path taken has brought us to this minute where she's voluntarily in my bed, not trying to leave, where instead of me taking her and rutting her to dominate her, she's giving me my pleasure instead.

Fuck, but I like this.

I love this. Her beautiful silky locks along my thighs, her mouth moving up and down my cock with little licks, sucking, and her squeezing with her hands.

She's keen about it, too, looking like she's enjoying what she's doing. Now she's running her hands across my hips, up my stomach muscles, and then she squeezes one of my nipples between her thumb and index finger and it feels great.

I'm ready to come. I groan as sensation bursts through my body and heat snakes through my groin before I'm spilling my essence down her throat. She chokes and then it's spilling out of her mouth, coating my inner thighs.

My woman gets enthusiastic about cleaning it up and she's licking and sucking harder with the mess of me all over her face, which is still spilling out of me. She shoves her hand down and then I realize she's playing with her cunt while I'm still spilling cum all over both of us, and that won't do. I flip her gently to her back and put my fingers between her legs to finish her off. In no time, she's trembling again.

My greedy girl got her orgasm and wants another.

I decide to give her a third. She's earned it.

Immediately after she's stopped trembling from number two, my mouth descends again and she's pleading with me to stop while her legs are pointed at the ceiling, jerking, toes flexing.

"Too stre-strenuous. Your mom said nothing too—-"

"No mentioning anyone's mom while I'm licking between your legs Ivy," I whisper, and she giggles. Loud.

It's a beautiful sound.

She's earned many more climaxes by being so eager, but I know she needs to rest, so I carry her to the tub afterwards, setting her in it and keeping her foot high over the side of the tub while I run her a bath and wash her body from head to toes. She smiles the entire time, shy with me but affectionate and enjoying it. I'm on my knees beside the tub, running the soaped-up cloth over her body and she's glowing with her smile, a playful but sleepy look in her eyes.

I very nearly decide to give her a fourth orgasm, since keeping her ankle dry means having one of her shapely legs over the side of the tub, giving me a beautiful view, but she yawns as I rinse her hair of all the shampoo, protecting her eyes as I do, and so instead I lift her out, set her on the sink, and squat to dry her body. She pleads with me to set her on the toilet and leave so she can "water the flowers" in peace and privacy and I laugh heartily at the comparison. She looks at me with what seems like affection as I laugh.

I don't recall doing much laughing, any. Maybe a chuckle here and there but never laughter like this. I've seen it around town when we've gone for supplies, I've read about characters in books I've read feeling joy or humor and letting it all out with laughter, but it's not something I've had occasion to do in my life. I told Ivy already that I like how it feels. I haven't told her that I love her more each time she makes me do it. Not only does it feel good to do it, I love watching the joy on her face when she watches me laugh.

I wait outside the bathroom door and upon her calling my name, I return and take her to bed. I cover her naked body with the blanket and then take a shower myself before returning and joining her for a rest.

29

IVY

Getting bit by a snake was the scariest moment of my life. Well, the second scariest, the first being faced with a naked man in the woods who I was pretty sure was the wolf who'd just been staring at me.

Having Tyson come to my rescue was a huge relief. It was as if the minute I saw him, I somehow knew I'd be okay. But, then he looked scared, actually scared, and that scared me to death.

The rest of the day following the snake bite was blissful. Who'd have thought a little note and a tidy cabin would make him so happy?

I get it. He thought I was gone, that I didn't care a lick about the fact that he didn't want me to go. And knowing that although I did go, I didn't do it without a backward glance meant something to him.

Seeing what it meant to him meant something to me. Something profound that surprised me. I haven't quite got my feelings figured out yet.

I'm not gonna try to figure it out yet. Because of the fire at the boutique, I actually have time to just relax and enjoy time with him. There's no rush. And it's all very complicated. I had a brush with death, and I've decided to enjoy the now and figure the rest out later.

We had lunch, we had sex, he bathed me, caring for me in a gentle and nurturing way that was swoon-worthy. We napped until early evening before I woke up to him spreading out all sorts of food on the bed and we had a bed picnic of cheeses, crackers, fruit, pretzels, and nuts until I was stuffed. I really had shopped like I was having a party and it was fun to watch Ty explore new flavors. He tasted everything with a wondrous look on his face.

I've never been so comfortable with someone where we just sat and did nothing. It's like I just keep getting lost in him. Not only can the man sex me like nobody else, but just being in bed with him, snacking and hanging out ... watching him smile, trying to make him laugh wherever I could... I was just so ... happy.

IT'S NIGHTTIME AND it's a little bit chilly so he's gone outside to fetch some wood for the fireplace, so I take the time to sift through my bags, which are on the floor of the bedroom, looking for my lotion to smooth on my heels, which feel a little dry.

When he comes back into the bedroom with an armful of wood, he puts them beside the fireplace and then curls up beside me, lifting my tablet.

"What do you use this for?"

I press the button and bring the screen to life.

"Banking app, movie streaming apps, music, reading app, this one tells you what the weather will be like, this one is my cell plan, here's my Amazon app for online shopping, and my social media sites, pictures, and my um... girl time tracking app. Some of my apps work now but others need Wi-fi or a hot spot."

"Pictures?"

"Yeah." I touch the icon.

I see several icons in the picture gallery app, so I touch 'recent' and there are 1600 pictures to scroll through.

"Show me," he says, getting comfy.

"Okay," I say. "That's my sister, and her fiancé."

"She doesn't look like you."

"She actually does," I start to tell him. "She's one year older than me, to the day, and—-"

"You're much more beautiful," Tyson says.

I feel my cheeks heat up.

Truthfully, my sister is gorgeous. Movie starlet glamorous. And she knows it. She's the Serena witch and I'm the Samantha witch. She's dark haired and I'm blonde. But she's also voluptuous and confident. She has assets and knows how to flaunt them. I wouldn't say I'm the polar opposite, I'm not exactly a wallflower, but she's just so much more out there with her personality. She's definitely a Type A personality who knows what she wants and makes that crystal clear to everybody around her. "Here's my brother and my parents and I at their engagement party."

"Who's that?"

"Ben." Ben is on the other side of me, arm around me.

"The boyfriend you just broke up with?"

"Yeah. Don't hunt him down and kill him." I swipe to the next photo and it's Ben and me in a snuggle at the table, so I swipe past it again, feeling Tyson tense.

"Forget this. Let's do something else."

"I wanna know more about you," he says, and his voice has taken a more dangerous tone. He takes the tablet from me and swipes through some of the pictures, looking at mostly family Christmas pictures, which thankfully predate Ben.

"Okay, I'll show you more later after I get rid of the pics of any men who aren't blood related or completely platonic. You should put your eye drops in by now, shouldn't you?"

He tilts his head. "How many men are in there?"

"Probably just a few. I haven't been serious about anyone the last couple years." Or ever, but I don't want to reveal that much about myself.

"How many men have had you, Ivy?" His eyes are now bigger, and I swear his pupils look blown.

"Why?"

"Answer my question."

"Are we about to have another fight?" I ask.

He clenches his jaw.

"Because I'm not down for that. I'm all happy and sleepy and have enjoyed most of the day in bed with a wild werewolf man and I'm not lookin' to fight about something stupid."

"Something stupid?"

"Yeah stupid, like men I no longer have relationships with."

"How many?" he pushes.

"How many for you?" I return.

"No more than seventy," he shrugs. "I've lost count."

"Seventy?" I choke. "You've fucked seventy women?"

"There; I've told you. Now it's your turn."

How is that possible? He's only a man a month per year and hasn't been a man in years.

I stare in shock. "Fifteen. Well, fourteen, since that one barely counts. We drank too much, and he lost his erection two seconds after he was, you know, in there. I think it might not have counted so much because I found out later he was gay. I think he was trying to play hetero and it backfired, but whatever."

Tyson's nostrils are flaring.

I touch his hand. "Sorry, baby, too bad you didn't catch me and abduct me when I was a virgin."

He squeezes mine tight. "Too bad your parents moved out of the area or I'd have smelled you as soon as you were ripe to be plucked."

My jaw drops. "That sounds so wrong."

He shrugs. "I can't stop my wish that no one but me has touched you."

"You're moving awful fast here with me, Ty, but I'm not blowin' smoke when I tell you that you blow all of 'em out of the water."

"Meaning?" He looks genuinely perplexed.

"Meaning..." I lean forward and put my mouth to his ear. "You are so much better at sex than any of them were. Half those guys were terrible. A couple were okay. Only a few were what I'd consider good and even the best of them has nothing on you."

He smiles big. Huge, even. He's happy about that. I mean, what guy wouldn't be? But I'm being honest here. He's amazing at it.

He kisses the back of my hand. "Was the last boyfriend bad at it?" Tyson asks.

Sex was one of the things Ben had going for him.

"Well, he wasn't bad, but he wasn't as good as you are."

"I wish he was bad at it."

"I mean, nobody has a penis that does that magical throbbing thing inside me that yours does."

He smiles.

"Besides," I add, "It doesn't matter. I ended it with him. I don't want him."

"You want me?"

"Well, I'm here, aren't I?"

"Because I won't let you walk away or because you want to be?"

"Because I'm here. I'm here and I'm enjoying this time together with you. Let's just focus on now, how about that?" I decide not to focus on his chosen words because otherwise his 'let you walk away' phrasing will piss me off.

"We have a future, too, Ivy. I'm not letting you go."

I smile. "You're so fucking sweet."

"I'm very serious," he warns.

I wave at him dismissively as I stuff the iPad back into the bag.

"Why did you end things with him?" he asks, pulling me close.

"I didn't miss him when he was gone." I shrugged. "There just wasn't that... spark."

He stares at me a moment.

"You said you didn't feel anything until me. I guess..." I stop. Wait. Is that it for me, too?

"You've felt nothing until me?" he tries.

Whoa. It's way too soon for a declaration like that.

I say nothing. I'm like a deer caught in headlights.

His eyes bounce back to the bag. "I'd like to see more pictures," he says.

"I'll show you some more later. Can you take me to the bathroom so I can pee and then get me some ice cream?"

"You said you were full."

"I've always got room for a little ice cream."

WE AVOID ANY FURTHER heaviness the rest of the evening. And I loved the night we spent talking. I talked about my job, about my family, about my roommate and her boyfriend and how they were in Jamaica right now and that I would bet money he was going to propose to her while they were gone. I then filled him in on the nightmare of the cabin of ill repute with Megan and her bucket list and told him I didn't like the vibe in there with those guys, that some of them reeked of 'sexual predator'.

He told me that when we passed by the cabin the night he caught me, she smelled like three of the men had fucked her, not just two. I wondered if she'd been through all five of them by now. I wondered if she was gone home and whether or not she gave two shits about the fact that she'd fucked me over. I wondered if she knew about the fire at the boutique.

"Then again, if she hadn't screwed me over, I wouldn't know werewolves exist."

"Yes you would've. I would've taken you from that cabin. I was hunting for you, little one."

I smile.

"Do you think of me as a sexual predator?" he asks.

"No," I say without hesitation.

He looks relieved about that and that says something. I mean, the way things happened didn't feel like that. I know they were far from conventional, but based on who he is, based on how he's been since then, it's just not the same.

"What happened with us, I now know it was instinct, Tyson. I don't blame you for being what you are."

He stares thoughtfully at me. "Anyone else who I was with was with me willingly, Ivy. I never took someone with me against their will before."

"I believe you."

He looks concerned, like the fact that I might think of him as my kidnapper is upsetting. It kind of is that way, but it's also not. He believes I'm his perfect mate for some reason and I can't say I understand it, but I do believe that's what he thinks and I also have some pretty gripping emotions developing for him, too, though I don't know what it means so far. I decide to change the subject. I don't like the look of concern in his eyes. "Too bad about my car, then. If I'd just stayed put, you would've found me and taken me to your lair without my car gettin' trashed."

"Your car was pulled out of the valley and is being fixed at a repair shop in the closest town. They did that while we were at the clinic."

"Your pack did?"

He makes a face.

"What?"

"My pack."

I smile. "That's the right term, isn't it?"

He nods. "It would be if I were part of that pack, yes."

"They could be, you know. Your pack. Your family."

He shrugs. "We'll see."

He looks like the weight of the world is on his big shoulders suddenly as he stares into the fire.

My hand finds his. "If it's meant to be, it'll be," I tell him.

"Like us. We're meant to be," he says, eyes bouncing from my face to our fingers. He stares at our joined hands a moment.

"Are we?" I ask with a smile.

His hand tightens.

I really wanna keep things light tonight. I'm enjoying my time with him and I don't want to do what I tend to do -—overthink things.

He nods and then his lips find mine. "I'm happy, Ivy. For the first time in my life, I'm happy. And it's only the beginning with you. I feel like it might be too much to ask that I also have a family, a pack. And you."

"You don't wanna be alone anymore," I tell him.

"I don't know how to not be alone."

"You'll figure it out."

He squeezes my hand and then reclines on the bed, pulling me to his chest.

"I also know in my gut that I'm supposed to be with you."

I say nothing.

"How's your ankle feeling?" he asks.

"It's not bad. But it's time for my medicine. Maybe I'll take it. It'll make me sleepy again, but sleep is good for healing."

"I'll get it."

"Can you get me my phone, too?" I ask. "And bring your eyedrops, I'll put them in for you."

I watch him, appreciating every inch of his sexy body as he walks out.

I hadn't checked my phone at all. Hadn't thought about reconnecting with civilization even though it's been charging for seven or eight hours. Surely by now my family got my message about the snake bite. There are probably texts and phone calls to return.

Tyson brings it to me and it's off, but I see the screen show the notification of 100% charged before the screen goes dark. I put it on the table beside the bed and decide that civilization can wait another day.

He comes back with all four tubs of ice cream and two spoons.
I laugh as he sets them up between us.
"What about your eyedrops?" I ask.
He wrinkles his nose.
I laugh. "Don't be such a baby. Go get them or no ice cream for you!"

30

TYSON

I hate having eyedrops put in, but I like ice cream. Especially the brown one with the darker brown bits and soft and spongy white things in it. I liked the food we ate today, most of it, except the dry brown sticks with all the salt. They didn't do much for me until she showed me that I could dip them into the cheese container with all the herbs in it. I loved when she fed green grapes to me from her fingers while half her body was sprawled across my torso and she told me funny stories about her family. I'm full and happy with her here in the bed, sleeping on my shoulder.

"Someday, we'll have funny stories to tell about our family," I said, and she laughed and said, "We already have one... you slipping on that banana peel!" And then her face changed, and she looked remorseful for something.

She doesn't want to admit we have a future. She's trying to be casual with me.

I'll make her want to stay. I'll make it so she can't imagine being happy anywhere but with me.

I love her so much.

Tomorrow, I want to start making this place better for her and then maybe she'll feel like it's her home. I'll ask her to choose things she likes. The few pictures I saw on her screen showed she spends time in much nicer places than this.

I'M AWAKE, THINKING about all I've seen and experienced in the few days since I've shifted back to man form when I have the urge to check on things. I carefully slip away from her and check on the house, feeling like something isn't right.

No sooner than I have that thought, I catch the scent of a shifter, a shifter I do not know. I smell another person. I know that smell but can't place it. I've smelled so many individuals in the past day without being told which names go with which scents.

I quickly move outdoors to find out who the fuck this is and what they want.

When I step off the porch, I see a male and female approaching from near the willow tree where they've parked.

They stop when they see me and wait there, so I make my approach.

He's tall and dark-haired with dark eyes. She's short and curvy, with long light brown striped with blonde hair. She's wearing eyeglasses and she's related to him.

"Tyson? I'm Grey. Greyson Blackwood. Fourth alpha. I just got back, just heard, and wanted to come by and meet you."

"Fourth?" I inquire as I nod to her.

She smiles and wiggles her fingers beside her face.

"Yes. Born fourth that year," he says. "This is Bailey Blackwood, my sister."

"I remember seeing you," I say, still unsure of why the fact he was born fourth on some year is relevant, but I don't ask questions.

The young woman speaks up. "I told him you wouldn't welcome an unannounced visitor, but he insisted, so I came along so that you'd recognize one of the two scents coming to your house in the middle of the night. You recognize my scent from the clinic?"

"I do," I confirm.

"My sister wanted to show respect. I hope you don't consider my visit disrespectful. I know you've met Riley, Jason, Joel and Linc. I wasn't around, but just got back, so…"

"Who's missing?" I ask.

"Missing?"

"I was told there are supposed to be seven and what you've said adds up to six."

"Mason. He just got back, too. He's not ready to approach."

I notch a brow.

"I shouldn't have said anything," Grey says quickly. "He's not at his best. He'll meet you soon. When he's feeling 100%."

"Your sister is right; an uninvited approach was a bad idea."

"Riley needs us," he interrupts. "He needs you. We all do."

I wait for him to expand on that.

"He's lost. He's been excellent as second alpha sitting at the top and though we have always felt your absence..." He stops speaking and stares deep, as if to add emphasis to what he's just said, before continuing - "I know he's coming to see you tomorrow. Watch for it, you'll sense it if you pay attention. He needs you in the first alpha position so he knows he can take time to fix what's wrong in his life. He's very wrong inside. His wolf. Himself. The sooner you're with us, the better."

I already sense this thing he talks about. I don't reveal that though.

Bailey speaks up. "Grey's the one with the strength of insight. They all have it, but Grey has it in spades."

I don't know what she means so I stare at her.

She squats, her back against a tree and sits cross-legged. "I can fill in some gaps about things if you want information. I don't know how much you know about our way of life."

"Assume I know nothing."

"Do you know anything?" Bailey asks. "I'm the walking Wikipedia of the pack, but I don't want to come across as a know-it-all."

"Do you know it all?"

"Well...no, but more than most."

"Then tell me what you know. What I know might or might not be truth. My source of information about this pack was Cornelius Savage." For some reason, I feel at ease talking to Bailey Blackwood. "I don't know what was truth and what wasn't. But I also don't know if I trust any of you – so bear that in mind with whatever you say to me."

"I can understand that," she says, nodding slowly. "Trust is a rare commodity for many lone wolf shifters who don't have a pack at their back. But, you should know, your instinct about people will be right. It's one of your strengths. Maybe you have or haven't quite learned how to tap into that instinct but it's there. I mean, unless you already know this about yourself."

I say nothing. I wait and she looks quizzically at me for a beat before she continues.

"In our community structure, the pack protects the territory, leads the youth, protects the secrets, and shares our history. We live together as a community and we support one another. Our pack has a great reputation as a group that's happy to lend a helping hand. Having a diverse community with a whole lot of alphas in it means we've got a lot of strength and smarts. Our pack is unique. Because of our location and because of the presence of a lot of magic in this region, it grew from shifters settling here from elsewhere. Shifters from different packs moved here because it was a shifter haven for a time. The way it grew, how big it got quickly, instead of choosing just one alpha, a group of alphas decided to work together as a team. As time went on, it became a birthright for some, though not everyone. Sometimes leaders had sons who became leaders. Sometimes leaders would emerge from other families within the pack. With so many in close proximity, the community grew. We have several hundred people in our pack. And every alpha on our leadership council has some inherent qualities or certain heightened senses or skills that add up with the other alphas to form a well-rounded team. Some characteristics are essential for a pack council member. But to be our top alpha, our first alpha, you'll have all of the core qualities, so you know. For the past three generations, it's somehow worked out that each generation of pack alphas emerge in the same calendar year and the eldest tends to take top spot. What began as a measured decision transitioned to watching the youth to determine which age group had those inherent qualities. Three rounds of councils had the top alpha come from the same family, yours, and also have had the rest of the pack fall into place in birth order. The eldest born in a particular year has held all the vital traits and become the lead alpha on the council. In your birth year, you're first, Mason is second, Riley is third, Grey is fourth, then Jason, Linc, and Joel in that order."

I was told I had a strong sense of smell, was good with my hands, saw well, had strong ears, but are my senses stronger than theirs? I only knew they were stronger than Uncle's. My intuition? I don't know that it's been strong. Then again, I have only known what I've known. My world has been very small until now. And with Uncle Cornelius being all I knew, maybe I tried to ignore my intuition with him because he was all I had. I know I did on certain issues. He was like a father to me. The thought makes me angry.

She keeps talking. "If you have questions about the past alphas in your position or other positions on the council, I can share that too. But it doesn't all fall on you. You've got a team. You've got Linc who has a keener sense of smell than anyone. Greyson reads everyone very well and is wise beyond his years. Riley is strong, very strong, and extremely wise with a sense of hearing like nobody's. Mason and Joel are also very smart with strong strategy skills and above average intelligence. Jason is so good with his hands. *So* good with them. We have several alphas who aren't as involved as the top six as well as pack betas who are inherently alpha and could easily be alphas of their own pack because of their strengths, but we have a mutual respect so our alphas and the betas that lean toward alpha tendencies respect their place in the pack because every one of us provides value and every one of us feels appreciated. We love our pack. It's a community. A big family. We're a big pack and in demand as a group others wanna join."

"Can anyone just join?" I ask.

"People apply. As you can imagine, we only have so much room in our village. And we don't want it to get so big it's difficult to take care of everyone."

"That makes sense."

"Where we get a bad rep from others is mostly more primitive groups who have trouble understanding the way we operate. Some packs have alphas that are more like dictators and would never want to share what they consider to be 'power'. But instead of looking at it as sharing power, we look at it like sharing responsibility. One man shouldn't have all that burden and if he has a strong pack, it's not a burden. Our alphas take recommendations from all members of the pack. Occasionally someone who doesn't qualify to be on the alpha's council team has gone off and started their own pack or whatever, too. Some packs will try to chase down a wayward pack member, but we don't do that. We believe everyone should choose their path."

Greyson speaks up. "Except in the case where someone is just shrugging off their destiny. Like rejecting a mate or trying to be lone when we know it's not healthy. We will intervene if we all feel it's a good idea. There's very specific criteria, including a vote. We all voted to intervene with you, for example."

My brow notches.

He smiles and shrugs. "We're trying. And it's not entirely altruistic because you had your birthright stolen from you, it's also because we want that completeness that only comes with a full team. And in a pack with a lead alpha in the council, like I said, we all work together, but he'd have veto power. You would have the power to overrule a decision. That said, though, if your pack had a major problem with a decision you make, it could be problematic. We don't want a dictatorship. In a nutshell a group was formed and outlined the ideal structure for a leadership team. Over time it's become a birthright in your family, but nobody got the chance to see if you'd be what your father was because you were taken too young. But we believed it should've been you by the loss we felt without you, and then when we saw you six years ago, we knew you were our missing piece. We've all agreed we feel it in your presence now that we've all come in contact. Well, five of us, anyway. Mason, that remains to be seen."

"He's right. And we have a great team. We want you to be a part of it but not just for us, for you," Bailey says. "Everyone does their own thing. A few of our guys work together in construction. One of them has a technology company. Two others are into real estate development. We've got a lot of expertise in our community, too. We're often called upon by other packs to help with problems, to sit on councils and bring objectivity. Our alphas are smart and want challenges, so if that sounds like you, we could bring you plenty of that. We get approached from other packs and a few of our guys are on councils that are offered bounties to help other packs with problems. Some don't take on those roles, are busy enough with local stuff as well as their own livelihoods."

"What sorts of problems?" I ask.

"Rogue wolves, mate rejections, other threats to our way of life. Grey has solid diplomacy skills. He's got witch blood in his family line on his mom's side, so he's got pretty strong persuasion powers. He and a few other alphas just worked with a pack in the Northwest Territories. Their alpha refused to step down and let the new voted alpha take over despite dementia setting in. These guys helped negotiate his stepping down without any bloodshed, which was a worry. Mason was off last week with two alphas from another pack and a beta in our pack who were working with a mountain pack doing damage control over rumors flying around their local area after a couple got caught shift-fucking. An out-of-town hunter threatened to expose them."

"Shift-fucking?" My eyebrows rise.

"Shifting while having sex," she explains. "They were caught in a whirlwind. It was their mating night and she went into spontaneous heat and they lost control, weren't careful about their surroundings, they were so caught up in one another. They both shifted repeatedly during copulation and they were seen."

I can see how this would be a problem. Uncle told me from as young as I have memories that our nature had to be kept secret. At least he did that right.

Grey shuffles uncomfortably and then leans in. "We need you to take your place as alpha as soon as possible so we wanna help you get acclimated. Then Rye can heal and also the rest of us can start getting ready to mate."

"Explain."

"He's told us to hold back with you, to give you time. But you should know that beyond me being here worrying Rye is taking on too much, you should also know that none of us have found our mates. Except Rye, likely because he took the leadership role, but she died, so he's in pain. He's taken on too many responsibilities and hasn't taken the time to grieve properly. We all believe once our team is complete we'll all begin to sense our mates out there. We're hoping he gets a second chance."

"Well fuck. If that wasn't emotional blackmail, right?" Bailey laughs.

I don't respond. I'm just taking everything in. As if I care if other wolf shifters find their mate.

Though, if I'm honest with myself, I do. I barely know these people, but the emotion I feel after having found Ivy? I can't imagine how good it'll feel when she's fully settled with me. And if I'm honest, I do feel a strange connection with them so maybe I do care for that reason.

"What happens when someone loses their mate is ugly," Bailey adds. "But, Riley hasn't gone through that grieving process. He lost her and he jumped straight into taking care of the pack."

"He's not second in birth order. Why not Mason as leader?"

Bailey answers. "They all agreed it would be Riley. Mason's entirely capable, too, any of them are. Riley's combination of strengths and blood relations to you and your father made him the most logical choice. Believe me, they all participate. Anyway, it's important for him to do his grieving and once he doesn't feel so many burdens, it could allow for that. It'll allow the rest of your team to be open to finding their mates, too. And maybe Riley can find love again. The past few years have been difficult for him. The happiest we've seen him in that time has been since he first spoke to you. He's hopeful. He needs you. The team is incomplete without you. Once functioning as a complete unit, it'll help everybody."

"How does the team get ... constructed?" I ask.

Grey speaks up. "The elders take notice of a group born within a year and it's known they'll eventually step up. Key alphas in the pack often stand out before they mature, but we always know for certain once they do mature."

"At maturation, do you all shift uncontrollably for a week?" I ask.

He leans back. "No."

"No," I repeat. I guess that doesn't solve the mystery of why it happened to me.

"That happened to you, Tyson?" Bailey asks.

"Yes."

"What age?" Grey inquires.

I think on it. "I don't know. Maybe fourteen, fifteen years."

"That's when the year was identified. In my fifteenth year," Grey says. "Our birth year was identified, though it'd been talked about since your birth, and eleven alphas were born in our pack that year. From there, eyes were on all of us to see who would make up the team."

"Maybe something instinctive happened to Tyson," Bailey muses. "Can I ask you more about that another time, Tyson? I document pack happenings for the global shifter archives. I know your life has been difficult and I know it's extremely personal, but if I could interview you..."

I say nothing. I don't know how to feel about this.

"Table that for now, Bailey," Grey orders and continues speaking. "More about the process… there's a vote and the selection happens. Except for the top alpha. That's been carried down through generations the past three times via your family line. One of your sons will likely be next, though it's not guaranteed, and it might not be your firstborn. The rest of the team retired a year ago, five years to the day after you approached the village. They knew it was time. Their successors stepped in then and worked with our fathers or uncles to learn. We wanted to try to find a way to reach you. The elders told us to wait, that you'd be called home eventually. They felt it. Your mother believed you'd find a mate soon and that'd make you open to our approach or that you'd approach again. We knew that there was a reason you were drawn here. Now we know it was after Cornelius's death, and now that you've mated, we're hoping you'll spend time with us and wanna take your place with us."

"The retired team, where are they?" I ask.

"They're all alive," Bailey says. "All six."

"Six? I thought it was supposed to be seven."

They're both quiet a beat.

"Your father…died," Bailey tells me a second after I realize who the seventh is.

Right.

"Tell me about that."

I sit down on the ground in front of her. Grey sits down as well, off to the side, and the three of us are in a sort of circle.

I sense nothing but the truth from her as well as Grey, who adds bits to the conversation as they explain that my father was a triplet. One brother: Riley's father, Atticus. The other: Cornelius. Riley's father is a beta even though Riley is an alpha. Cornelius wasn't just omega; he was a disabled omega of the trio.

"What exactly happened to my father?" I repeat as she goes off on a tangent telling me about how the alpha council will listen to opinions of anyone in the pack, not treat omegas like they're bottom of the ladder.

Grey cuts her off, telling her she's off topic. "The way it's told, they all grew up together and Cornelius was in love with your mother, swore she was his mate. Your father disagreed and claimed her. Cornelius descended into madness. She walked in after being away collecting some herbs and found him standing over your father's body. He told Cat he hooked up with a witch who gave him poison that he used on your father. He tried to take her, too, but she escaped with the bassinet. It was just a bundle filled with your clothing and a doll. He'd already moved you. Must have already disguised your scent with the herb Cat says you used to take. The pack looked for you but couldn't find a trace. He later surfaced and caught her off guard, tried to take her again. He said you were gone, dead, and promised to show her the grave so she could say goodbye. She fought him off, stabbed him. He left and she didn't know if he'd survive the gut wounds. He turned up again, many years later but during the time in between there was no trace of either of your scents."

I grind my teeth, remembering those gut wounds, remembering that he lied by saying he took them as an unjust punishment.

"If he was so deranged, why was he allowed to be with the pack? Why wasn't he put out of his misery?"

"Triplets are rare," Bailey says. "Twins usually work out fine and we get an alpha and a beta, two betas, sometimes a strong council-level alpha and an omega. Single births don't always turn out alpha. Beta is the most common. A triplet pregnancy with our pack's lead council alpha, your grandfather being the father, Cornelius had to have been half-starved in the womb during development, didn't get enough of anything because his brothers took it all, so he had underdeveloped senses, and it was a hard life for him growing up. He was a very sickly child. Our pack takes care of those who are disabled; we don't just destroy those that are weak or physically challenged. He couldn't accept his life and the blessings in it. He was treated as eccentric and looked after. He was a talented artist, there's a storage area in the library basement dedicated to his paintings. If he hadn't committed those crimes, they'd be displayed. He would've been loved and had a happy life. He just couldn't let it go... his obsession with your mother drove him to murder his brother. I guess he kept you when she wouldn't give in and be with him."

He taught me to paint. And he was mad. I always thought so. He would shout obscenities out of nowhere, just go off on tangents, nonsensical ones.

We're all quiet for a moment.

Poisoned. He poisoned my father. Fuck. And stole me. And hurt Catrina. She's lived with the fallout of his evil madness every day for all this time.

If I could kill him... if I could take back all the times I saved his hide, all the times it was down to me that he got to eat, down to me that he had a garage filled with money to buy his whiskey for the times he was man.

"How's it going with your mate?" Greyson asks.

"Meaning?"

"I know it's new. Brand new. Cat didn't say much, but I get the impression your mate is reluctant."

I bristle.

"Bring her into the fold with us," he says. "We'll help get her acclimated."

"We can't have you without your mate. Anything we can do to help..." Bailey adds.

"I won't be without her. I need no help."

Grey raises his hand defensively. "No disrespect meant, Tyson. I just get the impression issues are there, and community often helps with non-shifters who have no ties to our way of life. We're here to help. Show her what our lifestyle is and how fulfilling it is to be in our community."

"I need no help," I snap.

He looks down and says nothing.

I'm irritated.

"You've given me a lot to think about. I'd like you to go so I can do that. Think about everything."

"Sorry we disturbed you," Bailey says. "And I only meant –"

"Cat comes tomorrow. Please come with her," I request. "I'd like you to befriend Ivy."

She brightens with a smile. "I was hoping you'd say that."

Grey extends his hand and I take it. And I feel with him what I felt with the others as he pulls me toward him and slaps my back and bumps his right shoulder to my left.

"You're our brother. We want you to be part of our family, Tyson. I know it seems like a lot. Give it a chance. Just spend time seeing if we feel like your pack. We've got no heavy expectations. It'll come naturally over time, bro."

He lets go of my hand and steps back.

I swallow and look into his eyes. I say nothing. I know I don't need to because he sees. We see things in each other. This guy is genuine. I feel the strange, new sense of camaraderie with him, just like with Riley.

"Goodnight," Bailey says and hugs me awkwardly.

I pat the top of her head rather than embracing her and step back as soon as she lets go.

I CLIMB INTO BED WITH Ivy. She's exhausted and taken the pain medication so she doesn't even stir. I caress her face and stare at her features in the moonlight.

I'm glad Greyson and Bailey came to see me.

I hate some of what they told me. Hate it with a fever that makes me want to rip things apart. If I could run and feast right now, I would. I can't leave her yet.

So many thoughts flood my mind.

Catrina has suffered so much loss.

They're worried about Riley. They want me to be a part of their pack.

Most alphas, I'd have expected they'd see me as a threat. I was taught that they would, and it made sense at the time. Why would anyone want to willingly give up their power? But these shifters don't seem to think that way. They seem to feel there's strength in numbers and that makes more sense.

I'm awake until nearly dawn and I know it's because not only have I thought a lot about everything I learned tonight, all I've seen so far from them, I'm also thinking about them going for a run together every dawn. Running together as people, maybe, but especially as wolves. Together. Running and maybe hunting together. Maybe feasting together. Possibly sharing stories and laughing together afterwards as men with that elevated and euphoric feeling that comes after a long run and a feast.

I want that.

I want it fiercely.

I WAKE TO THE SMELL of bacon, to music, and to singing. Terrible singing from my Ivy and it makes me smile.

Like I think her silly purple bits in her hair are cute, I also think her bad singing is cute.

I'm alone in the bed and I like that it smells like her, but I find that my back is a bit stiff. Time for a new bed.

If not for the bacon smell and the sound of her singing, I'd wake up frantic.

I rise and pull my black stretchy pants on, then stop in the doorway and lean against the frame. Ivy is at the stove, singing a song off-key while she tends the bacon.

Music plays from her computer tablet where a female singer chants about being a bad guy.

I sneak up and slip my arms around her waist.

She startles. My skin stings as the sizzling bacon spits at my forearm. I pull her back a step to protect her and then spin her.

She looks up at me with shock all over her face. Her hair is pulled up into a ball on top of her head and she's wearing one of my long-sleeved shirts. It comes to her knees. She has those pink rubber shoes on again.

"Good morning," she greets. "You snuck up on me!"

"Good morning," I kiss her and take her ass cheeks into both hands. She's not wearing panties.

I suck on my mark on her and she giggles.

"Ooh. Can you do that after we eat? I don't wanna burn breakfast."

"You're putting weight on your ankle, Ivy. You're not supposed to do that." I lift her and set her bottom on the table, which is set with two cups of honey tea and a bowl of diced fruit between the two plates.

"I'm making us BLTs. It doesn't hurt too much today. Cat said give it a day and see how I feel." She hops down and tries to hide a wince as she lands on her foot.

"Ivy," I growl, "she's coming soon so don't walk on it until she looks at it."

"Are you gonna finish cooking breakfast then?" she asks, putting her hand to her hip and shifting her weight to her non injured foot. She has a haughty look on her face.

"Yes," I say, scoop her up, and set her on a chair. "Stay there."

"You're lucky you've got no shirt on or I might argue with you."

She lifts a piece of strawberry from the bowl and pops it in her mouth. "Go for it." She gestures, looking at me with a smug look on her face.

She likes it when I have no shirt on? Good information for me to know.

"Instruct me."

"The bacon is done." Her neck is stretched so she can see from her seat. "Use the fork and put it on that plate lined with paper towel. I already sliced tomatoes and got lettuce ready so all you gotta do, big guy, is make the toast. You don't have a toaster so the oven will do." She jerks her chin toward the bread. "I preheated the oven already."

I burn myself twice with the bacon. I like this meat, but I don't like the burn of how it spits at me.

I toast the bread inside the oven, checking constantly by opening and closing the door because the light inside it doesn't work, and burn my hand removing it. She gets up to try to help me and I growl in response, startling her.

"Sit."

"I was just gonna help you…" She looks like her feelings are hurt.

I put the pan with the toasted bread on the counter and crouch in front of her.

"I wanna make you breakfast. I don't want you on that foot. Tell me how to make it." I kiss her kneecap and caress her calf near the sore ankle. "Don't be cross with me Ivy, look at my muscles." I flex my biceps and she giggles.

"Better? I can get away with bossy when I do this?" I flex my chest and then turn and flex so she can see muscles in my back.

"Alright, studly, bring everything to the table and we can assemble the BLTs together," she says softly.

I lean over, kiss her temple, and then I do that.

We eat the sandwiches and what she's told me is called fruit salad and then I carry her to the bed so I can fuck her, but she informs me that she needs to shower and dress for my mother's visit.

"But I haven't fucked you since last night," I protest.

"You'll survive a few more hours," she says, patting my chest soothingly with playfulness in her eyes.

"I don't wanna wait a few more hours," I complain, suckling her neck where my mark is. She shivers and thrusts her fingers into my hair. I put a knee to the bed and take her to her back, then grind my erection against her. This gets me what I want, a whimper, and her legs spreading wide.

"I won't wait a few more hours. I want you now."

"Ty, they're gonna be here soon," she says, breathily, but despite her protest, she's now rocking against my cock.

"I'll fuck you fast, Ivy," I say, hauling my hardened cock out of my pants, finding her sopping wet pussy with the tip and then I shove in, fast, deep.

"It's been too long since I've been inside you," I inform as I hear her cry out.

"Mm. Way too lo-onnggg," she sings out.

I purr and this makes her eyelashes flutter.

My fingers go to her clit while the inside of her body strokes my cock and I feel like a king, seeing her lie beneath me with her beautiful hair spread out over the pillow, her teeth embedded in her bottom lip as she lets out these sexy little sounds, responding to what I'm doing to her. Her inner walls go extra-tight around me as she comes, beautifully crying out "baby," to me while she digs her fingernails into my shoulders.

The bite of it feels fantastic. My mouth finds hers and I groan into her as I knot. Her cries get louder.

"Oh wow. Ty, Ty, baby..." she cries loudly as my knot vibrates and that's when I hear a car, two cars, and catch the faint scent of Cat, Riley, and Bailey. They're on the property.

I spill into Ivy and she's oblivious to the approach of the three of them.

By the time there's a knock on the door, I've just finished emptying into her.

"Oh fuzz," she says. "Shit. She's here. I'm a mess. Go. Stall them." Her face is red, and her hair is a mess. A beautiful mess.

"What? Stall them?"

"Let me get myself presentable. Talk to her for a minute so I can get a fast shower. She's a werewolf, too, right? I don't want her to smell the sex on me. Go!"

I laugh and pull jeans on as well as a shirt and then lift her out of bed and take her to the bathroom so I can set her on the toilet. I do this despite her protesting that she can walk and that I should hurry.

"They know we're here; they'll smell us. I'm sure they can wait one minute, Ivy."

"Bring my bags in here, please." She looks red in the face and panicked. "All of them."

"Okay, okay."

I answer the door to Cat, Bailey, and Riley. They've all come with things. Riley is standing back, off the porch. Bailey carries food and Cat has a large box filled with things.

I open the door wide. "Come in." I jerk my chin at Riley. "Come."

They come inside.

"Ivy's just getting ready."

"I smell food," Bailey says. "We're starving."

"I smell more than food," Riley says low with a smirk, pulling a box on wheels with a handle.

My lip curls instinctively.

He waves his hand. "Sorry, cuz. Just taking a shot at you. It's just brotherly teasing." He punches my shoulder playfully and I realize he means no harm. Our eyes meet and something sinks in, deep. In that moment, I know without question that he respects my bond with Ivy, that he's even happy for it. That my bond with her is what he feels will bring me into their pack.

I don't know how I know all this, but I do.

A pack doesn't try to steal your female from you. They think of you as part of their family and by extension, her. As it should be. Not as Cornelius told it to me.

These men helped me when Ivy got bit by the venomous snake. If not for them... I hate to think of it.

"Ivy told me yesterday that you didn't have a coffee machine, so I brought my old one for you. We brought coffee and lunch, too, though you two have already eaten so I guess—-"

"I can eat again," I say.

Cat squeezes my hand with a big smile on her face and I have the urge to drop a kiss on her forehead. I don't. I just stare as she begins to unpack the things she's brought.

I remember Ivy needs her bags.

"Burned off some calories, did you?" Riley jokes.

"Would've burned off more if you people weren't on time," I joke back on my way into the bedroom.

I feel a strange and foreign lightness in my chest as he laughs good naturedly.

I open the bathroom door just enough to set the bags inside. Ivy is in the tub with her leg hanging over.

"Thanks, baby," she says, smiling as she lathers up her soapy hair and scrubs it.

My eyes flash with heat at her nudity. She's beautiful.

"Call me when you need help out. Be careful," I order.

She waves at me with a dismissive look on her face that I don't like. I don't want her falling and injuring herself.

I shut the door and return to the living area.

Riley is still looking amused. He's now sitting on the sofa and looking around. "This place is a hovel, Ty."

"It is. I want to make it better for her."

"Don't," Riley says. "There's a beautiful house for you in Arcana Falls."

I say nothing, because it's not something I can even think about right now.

It's as if he reads my mind.

"I get it. You're learning how to live with your mate. You want privacy first, to find a rhythm in your life with her before you get bogged down with the pack and pack responsibilities. The pack is going to be all about bringing the two of you into the fold and it'll be overwhelming after your upbringing. So, you don't have to jump immediately, but Tyson... we're there. Don't spend energy on this place. Use it for now as you and your mate get closer, and then when you're ready, it's there."

"We have the strawberry moon party this weekend, Tyson," Bailey says. "You and Ivy should come. Spend time with us for an evening. You can either stay at your house and at least see it, feel the energy there, or come here after."

She is setting the coffee maker up on the counter. Cat is washing my and Ivy's breakfast dishes.

"I agree," Riley says.

Cat keeps washing.

I stretch to catch a look at her face, and I can't read it. I do read emotion from her though. Or more, feel it.

"The car is all fixed," Riley tells me. "Here." He passes me the keys. There's a long silver square on the keychain that says "Drama Queen" with sparkled purple stones. I flip it over and it says Ivy on it. I tuck the keys in my pocket. "Who do I pay? You?"

"Naw, no worries. It's our pleasure."

"Thanks," I say.

Bailey smiles at me. "Worried she's gonna run off again?"

Cat makes a *tsk* sound and gives Bailey a look.

"Oops, sorry. I have no filter. Whatever I'm thinking just comes straight out of my mouth. It's sometimes a problem."

"At least with a personality like that, there's no deception to worry about," I say.

She smiles nervously and shrugs. I see Cat's eyes on me.

"Yeah, I told her and Grey to give you time, but they came here last night anyway," Riley says with disapproval in his voice.

I say nothing. I'm not about to encourage these people to barge in on my life but I'm also not quite ready to discourage it either. Truthfully, I've got mixed feelings about all of it but more than anything, I'm intrigued by the prospect of everything they have to offer. I don't know if it's me, don't know if I'm built that way after my whole life being as it has been. It might be too late.

A few moments later, Ivy is emerging from the bathroom. Her hair is damp and in a braid and she's wearing black tight pants and a black top with a hood. She has her thumbs through hoops on the long sleeves of the top. She's wearing pink socks and she has her face painted.

"Hi everybody," she waves shyly.

I move quickly to her and lift her up into my arms.

"On your feet, I see," Cat says, and dries her hands on a towel before moving away from the sink.

"Trying," Ivy says at the same time as I mutter, "Against my wishes."

"Is that coffee I smell?" Ivy gasps. "Ooh, coffeecoffeecoffee!" She claps her hands.

I smile at her excitement. She certainly likes coffee, it seems.

"Is coffee *that* good, my only?"

"It's better!"

"I brought my old coffeemaker," Cat replies. "And some coffee, sugar, French vanilla creamer like you said you liked, and we brought lunch."

"God bless you!" Ivy says enthusiastically.

I sit on the couch on the opposite end of where Riley sits and keep Ivy on my lap.

Riley rises and moves to the table and sits in the chair opposite Bailey.

Ivy moves off my lap, but stays beside me.

I grab her and haul her back up where I'd put her.

"Ty," she grumbles. "He's all about PDA," she tells them with a pretty pink hue to her cheeks.

"PDA?"

"Public displays of affection," she says.

Cat sits on the edge of the sofa in the place Riley vacated and lifts Ivy's calf, putting her foot on her lap.

"I left the dressing off because I knew you were here," she says. "I kept it dry. Just took a quick bath and left my foot out. It was trickier this time getting out without Ty helping me. I nearly wiped out." She laughs.

"Why didn't you call me?" I demand.

The idea she struggled and could have been hurt bothers me deeply.

"I managed," she says. "You were entertaining guests."

A growl comes up from my chest.

"It's okay, big guy. I'm fine." She pats my thigh.

I grab her hand and give her a look that shows my disapproval, but I also like her hand there, so I squeeze it affectionately and keep it there under mine.

"This is Riley, my nephew, and that's Bailey, a good friend and part of our pack," Cat says.

"Hi!" Bailey greets. "I run the library and maintain the pack archives. It's great to meet you."

"Hi," Ivy gives Bailey a big smile. "Hello. Thanks for your help, Riley," she says, giving Riley a nod.

"I'm glad we were able to get you to Aunt Cat quickly," Riley says softly.

The coffee machine beeps three times and Bailey jumps up. "How does everyone take their coffee, other than Ivy? I've already got those orders."

"I've never had it," I say.

"Make Ty's black first and see if he likes it," Riley suggests. "That's how I take it. These girls tend to take it like it's dessert." He makes a face of disgust.

"I like the sound of that," I tell him. "Make mine like dessert, Bailey Blackwood."

Bailey smirks and pulls cups down out of the cabinet.

Riley snickers.

"You might want to wash those. I've only gotten half his dishes washed and nothing up on that top shelf," Ivy calls over.

31

IVY

The coffee is amazing, and Ty is taking it all in. He was in a great mood before they got here, being all playful and sweet with his usual can't-keep-his-hands-off-me edge. He's listening to everything they say, and I could swear he's cataloguing everything about them. Paying extra-close attention. I can only imagine that this is all strange for him, but I do think it'd be really good if he built a relationship with them.

Part of me thinks this because I know that it'll be easier on him if I'm gone for him to have people. I don't want to think of him simply going into the woods and a lonely wolf forever because there's nothing else for him. When I let myself think that, it hurts. I don't know how I've gotten so attached so quickly.

Maybe because he has. It's hard not to respond to this kind of devoted 24/7 attention from someone.

I like Bailey so far. Cat is fantastic. And I'm sure there are many more of them in the pack. It's a small village but they've got hundreds of people, apparently. Cat mentioned in passing yesterday at her clinic before Ty rushed us out of there that she took care of everyone as the town healer and that she had a couple hundred patients of all ages from newborns to the village's oldest resident who is 102 years old.

Am I thinking about having them in my life long-term, too? Am I thinking about staying? It's crazy. I don't love the idea of being out here in no man's land with barely any creature comforts, but I really am getting kinda lost in Tyson. He's dreamy. Like, six foot four, probably, and with all those muscles and that sexy jaw line, those expressive eyes. There's also those full lips that are strong, but yet pillowy-soft when he kisses me. Massive hands that know what they're doing when they touch me. Abs for days and a body I can curl up and sleep on. And then there's the sex. The supernatural vibrating locking-himself-inside of me sex. And the protectiveness. And the treating me like he worships me.

A girl could get used to that. Most guys that are this attractive certainly don't act this way because they know they have the upper hand with women. No vulnerability, and usually so much ego.

Thinking like this is not real practical. I have a job, a life, a family. But then, people move away for love all the time, don't they?

This guy thinks I'm his soulmate.

I don't have a boyfriend and I always figured I'd want to be married and having kids before I hit thirty.

But I hadn't met any contenders before. This kind of relationship is hard to come by.

Understatement, because of who he is, because of *what* he is.

Why me? What about me is so special that he's sure we're meant to be?

It's crazy to be thinking this stuff over after just a couple days together. I need to just cool it and enjoy this. When these guys leave, I'll turn my phone on, talk to my mom, check in about the boutique and go from there.

Yep: reality; it's out there and I probably need to connect with it.

"Everything okay?" Bailey asks.

"Hm?"

"You look as if your mind is a million miles away," Cat whispers.

Riley and Tyson are in conversation by the window, and they excuse themselves to go outside so Ty can show him the truck Riley asked about, obviously having seen it when I drove it almost to him, Cat, and the others that day. Tyson kisses me goodbye as if he's going on a long journey and will miss me. My foot dressing has been changed and Cat tells me she wants another look on Friday. If anything changes, I'm to let her know right away.

They're setting out containers of food that they brought in insulated bags and emptying a cooler.

"Oh, I'm good," I say, waving my hand dismissively. "Lots of craziness in the past few days, that's all. I had no idea your...kind... even existed."

"It's not easy getting claimed by a wolf shifter. They get pretty adamant and sort of all *Me Tarzan, you Jane. You my woman now*." She says this in a deep voice and both Cat and I laugh. "When a shifter alpha claims you it can be pretty intense."

"I'd say," I agree.

"I knew what was happening when it happened to me and it was still so intense," Cat agrees. "Alpha men are very strong-willed and stubborn, but you've got a voice and you don't have to lose it. You just have to learn how to deal with them. They're territorial over you and protective. But if you find a good one, they'll give you everything." She says this with nothing but love in her eyes and I feel a pang of sorrow for her because of the loss she's endured.

She must read my expression because her smile slips. "After all this time, I've found a way to just think back and remember the good times. Not that there weren't hard ones, bad ones. It's not easy being with an alpha, never mind one with so much testosterone in him that he's destined to be the protector of a whole village."

"Holy," I groan.

"I'm just so happy that I've got Tyson back in my life again, it's a dream come true. Until six years ago I thought he was gone. You can't imagine the feeling of..." she trails off and stares for a second into space.

I swallow down a lump of emotion. Bailey grabs her hand and squeezes and Cat shakes it off and continues. "Cornelius came to me three separate times since he killed my husband and each time, he lied about Tyson. Told me he was gone and wouldn't tell me how. Spouted off all sorts of accusations about others in the pack. Now I know how he masked his smell and snuck up on me before he forced himself on me all those times. I had no idea my boy was alive all this time, thought I'd never find out what happened to him until six years ago when Tyson approached our village and I caught the scent. From there, I could only guess what he'd been through. Cornelius was barking mad. I went into a deep depression after that day six years ago, worrying about him. Wondering what he'd endured, but something inside told me he'd be back again."

"I'm so very sorry," I say, tears pricking my eyes.

"I don't want to look back," she shakes her head. "I'm excited about looking forward. About getting to know him. And you. And about grandchildren." She smiles brightly with wet in her eyes.

"Oh, hold up," I raise my hand. "I've known him a couple days. The only reason I can even be here is because my workplace caught fire and it means I have a bit of extra time off. I have no idea what the future holds."

They both look at one another and I see concern on their faces.

"Sorry to burst your bubble, but like... all of this came about out of nowhere. I was here only by chance, and –"

"I find there are very few things that are just by chance," Cat says quietly.

I keep talking. "I'm driving along and outta nowhere, bam – I've hit him with my car and went down that hill and he was a wolf lookin' in my window and then he was a naked guy and he broke through a car to steal me and bring me here talking about how he's gonna mount me and make me his. It was all pretty scary. Biting me and doing that... supernatural knotting thing. Sorry. TMI."

She shrugs while she gives her head a shake like it's really not TMI. Bailey is leaned forward now, looking like she wants more TMI.

"Anyway," I continue, "I've learned there's a lot to him in a couple days but that doesn't mean I'm ... you know... staying and stuff. I'm super-happy that you guys are here because if I have to go back to my regular life he'll have you. He's obviously ready to not be alone anymore. He's had it really rough. I'm not gonna say anything because that's his story to tell, but I'm tellin' ya, really rough, you guys. Sorry, Cat. I'm sure that's not easy to hear."

Cat gets a faraway look in her eyes.

I feel remorse for even saying what I just said.

Bailey gives me a kind smile and gently rests her hand on my arm.

"He's your mate, Ivy. It's meant to be, or it wouldn't be. You might think you're just here hanging out and enjoying the great sex, and devoted attention, but this is *it* for you, girlfriend. He's your husband in his eyes and he's not gonna be okay with you just saying, 'It's been a slice.' For some reason, fate decided you were his and you and Tyson met that night by design. It might take some time for you to come to terms, but you will." She pats my hand.

I go tense.

"You're not just enjoying a romp with him while you make sure he's good with us so that you can go off with a clear conscience," she adds.

"You got mind-reading powers or something?"

"Well, not exactly, but it's been suggested. For me, you're kind of easy to read."

"Bailey has strong intuition," Cat puts in. "So do I. It's clear you're already developing feelings for him, so we just want you to know that you're not alone. If things get confusing or if you need to figure out how to cope with being a mate to an alpha that's as alpha as Tyson, you've got us. And the rest of the pack. None of this generation's council alphas have mates, but there are plenty of us around with experience who can help you navigate your new world."

I shake my head in denial but realize it's pointless to argue with them. I haven't made a decision about anything. My head swims with confusion when I try.

"You're about to become a very important part of our pack being his mate."

"You know I'm not a shifter so..."

"Doesn't matter. I can't shift. I'm an important part of the community. My mom isn't even half shifter and she's definitely an important part of the community. We're all here for one another. Just know that if things ever get confusing or you don't know how to handle that very alpha man you've got."

I say nothing. I sip my delicious coffee.

"Gimme your phone. I'll program my number and Cat's number."

"Oh; I'll give you my digits and you can text me and I'll save you. My phone's not on right now."

I ramble off my phone number and she puts it into her phone.

I'll turn my phone on and face reality after they leave.

"We're having a party Friday night," Bailey says. "We're hoping you and Tyson'll come. It'd be a great way to meet everyone. Maybe you can work on him if he's reluctant."

"It'd be good for him to meet everyone," I say.

"And for you, too," Cat adds.

"She's a little shell-shocked," Bailey says.

"She is," Cat agrees.

"I am," I concur.

They laugh.

"We don't know him well yet so don't know exactly what you're dealing with, but –" Cat starts.

I blurt, "He's accidentally hurt me twice when he's angry, not knowing his own strength. He's really sorry about it afterwards."

I get looks of empathy from both of them.

I continue, "He's still sifting through all his memories," I add, "and he said not shifting for so long made it all foggy. He could drive a car but didn't know how to peel a banana. But he's not dumb. It's just like… he's recovering from basic skills amnesia or something. And I think he's also figuring out who he really is. He's probably struggling with the truth that was kept from him and there's other stuff he's realizing about his upbringing and about his uncle. And I think whatever you guys have been doing is a good thing. If he gets to know you, it'll be good – whether he chooses to live with you and be part of the community you have or simply to know you're there and that he doesn't have to be lonely."

"He needs to be with us. It's where he belongs," Cat says. "And you don't need to help us convince him of that because I can see in his eyes that he knows deep inside who he is. He'll come to the right decisions. He doesn't have a clue yet how wise he is, how much he'll accomplish in his life. He'll be a great leader because of what he's endured, not in spite of it. Anyway, I'm gonna go call them in for lunch. Be right back. We'll talk more later." She touches my cheek affectionately. "Whatever you're doing with him, honey, just keep doing it and he'll find his way." She smiles and leaves.

"I have so many questions about the sex stuff," I whisper to Bailey the second the door closes behind Cat.

"I know all the mechanics," she replies.

My head jerks in surprise. Is she saying what I think she's saying? "Pardon?"

"I'm single. Unmated. And… drumroll… untouched."

"Untouched? Bailey! You're a—-"

"A virgin. Yeah. I'm omega so there's a good chance I'll be mated to an alpha. It's the most common match for omegas. I don't shift but I do know my fate."

"Oh." I'm a little lost for words.

"Some of the girls in our pack have sex before they mate, but I've decided to wait. Besides, overprotective big brother." She laughs. "That makes it tricky."

"I bet. How old are you?"

"Twenty-five. Greyson's one of the alphas of the pack, so... yeah. Tricky."

"You have your eye on someone," I say, knowingly.

I recognize lovesick when I see it.

"Yeah, but he doesn't see me. I doubt he ever will. Hopefully, I get to be with someone local. And ... right for me. Not all love matches are easy ones. And I don't wanna leave the area. Anyway, I understand all the mechanics so if you have a question, ask away."

"The men identify their soulmate. What about the women?"

"We don't always know. Sometimes we think we know but don't know until we really know. It's confusing. I've known girls who thought it was one guy but then another set his sights on her and bam, different story. She'd be like - *oh! That's* the one. The other one was just a crush."

"So you don't know if the one you have your eye on is your destiny?" I ask.

She shrugs. "Time will tell. Maybe. What's your question?"

"Knotting," I say, "That's what Ty called it. Is it true they can only do that with their soulmate? He said he'd done it to nobody before me, but he's been with a lot of women."

"Yep," she says definitively.

"Oh."

"Was it amazing?" she asks, looking starry-eyed.

"Yeah. Um, to put it mildly. But he's really aggressive sometimes. And relentless. Most guys can go after ten or twenty minutes for round two if they're really randy, but Ty can just go 'n go. Beyond round two."

"Dreamy," she whispers.

I giggle but then I sober. "It's not all fun and games, though. He uh, held me down with his teeth once when he was mad, and it really scared me. He wasn't sorry that time. He didn't hurt me but he... used sex to try to punish me. Which is weird, because he was mad, but it felt so good. But then he wouldn't stop. He just kept making me orgasm over and over and..."

Bailey is biting her lip and looking at me with huge eyes.

"You get the picture," I say and cover my eyes.

"Yeah, but keep talkin.'" She laughs. "Typical alpha. Sounds awesome."

My face is hot. I can talk about sex, but this level of explicit isn't something I'd typically talk to a perfect stranger about.

She wiggles her eyebrows. "If you're gonna be punished, might as well be with sex. Why was he punishing you?"

"Because I tried to leave him."

"Ah. Punishment with orgasms so you'll submit. Classic alpha shifter move."

"I've lost count of how many times we've had sex since I've been here, Bailey. So many orgasms," I breathe out, "Best ones of my life!"

And that's when the door opens, and Ty comes in.

We both go quiet.

Too bad Bailey doesn't have extra-sharp hearing. Cat is fighting a smirk. Riley is smiling huge. Tyson's eyes are on me.

"So, Ivy wants to come to our Strawberry Moon party, Tyson," Bailey says to break the tension that is evident because it's obvious that Tyson, Riley, and Cat, who all filed in together heard me say the 'o' word.

"Does she?" Tyson replies, his mouth twitching with amusement. He scoops me off the couch, into his arms and kisses me hot and heavy.

"That's rude in front of guests," I whisper.

"Don't care," he replies against my lips. "What's for lunch, women?"

"He shouldn't be starving. We ate less than an hour ago," I inform. "But he's had very little experience with people food and he likes it."

Everyone laughs.

32

TYSON

Not only does my Ivy make food that I like, but so does Catrina.

She served us a dish called lasagna with some salad and bread with herbs and tomatoes and cheese on it. I ate all of mine and half of Ivy's.

It was strange sitting at a table with these people. My table was only big enough for four and we were five so an armchair from the bedroom was pulled up and I had Ivy sit there because it was most comfortable.

After the food was finished, Cat offered dessert, but no one was hungry, so she told us to eat it later, saying it is her famous cinnamon streusel coffee cake.

Ivy again thanked her for bringing the coffee maker and that prompted Cat to make more coffee.

"All this food, I need a run," Riley says, rubbing his stomach. "Wanna run this off?"

He's looking at me. Just me.

The world stops making noise as all eyes are also aimed in my direction.

"You should," Cat breaks the silence with an encouraging tone. "Nothing like a good run."

"Do you mean as wolves?" Ivy asks. "You guys don't just become wolves when the moon is full, I notice. And not just at night."

"Nope," Bailey says. "Shifters in our pack generally shift whenever they want a good run. It's one of the benefits of living where we do. Those who integrate with mainstream society don't get that flexibility."

"Shifters live in regular cities, too?" Ivy asks.

"Plenty, yeah. Some of them have clubs where they meet and can be themselves. Others belong to a pack remotely and do meetups at times to be able to spend time in wolf form. Our pack is a much tighter-knit community than some. We spend most of our time as people. Some more than others. And some, like me, don't shift. Some get the urge to run, crave it, particularly alphas."

I know what she means.

"Do you crave a run, Ty?" Ivy asks. "If so, you should go. Run with someone who might be able to keep up with you. He runs pretty fast," she says with pride, talking about me.

I find this funny, because she hasn't really seen me run as a wolf, just when I chased her the night we met, and it was just a short distance.

"I'd keep up with him no problems," Riley says with a big smile. "Could probably run faster than you," he adds, a sparkle in his eye.

"I'd like to see you try," I return.

"Put your money where your mouth is, cuz." He kicks his shoes off and throws his shirt off.

My eyes move to Ivy.

Riley has big muscles and she likes muscles. Her eyes move over him for just a brief instant and then they're on me with a smile in them.

It's like she knows I'd wanna do this and is encouraging me. She isn't staring at his muscles.

But do I want this? More importantly, do I leave her with them?

What if something happens? Will she try to leave?

I look to Catrina.

"It'll be fine. We'll take great care of her. Just go. Thirty minutes. Probably do you guys a world of good. Give us a chance for more girl talk." Catrina winks at me.

I don't know if I should. But my heart is racing with excitement.

"Go ahead," Catrina adds.

"No pressure, Ty," Riley says, the humor no longer on his face.

"Oh, you're backin' out?" I tease. "Guess you don't like to lose."

He bites his lip and shakes his head, then he's shifting, jeans dropping at his feet.

"No shifting in the house!" Catrina exclaims and heads to the door, opening it. "Bloody alphas. Go!" She gestures out the door and Riley, now his large brown wolf looks back at me and winks and then he's off.

Running.

Shit.

"Be good," I warn Ivy. "Stay here. Listen to Cat. I love you." I kiss her. She startles.

I peel my shirt off and then I'm shifting, and I'm gone to catch up with Riley.

I RUN DOWN THE LONG road that goes right and leads to nothing but forest, the road Ivy drove down the other day. It's a good straight run lined both sides by trees before hitting a fence that was there before Cornelius bought this property. Beyond the fence is deeper woods. In no time, I'm running alongside Riley.

My paws pound the pavement, which is cool today. It's breezy and the wind in my thick coat of fur feels good. We're keeping pace and then I'm outrunning him. And then he's outrunning me, by just a shoulder for a minute and getting cocky about it not realizing I'm allowing it. I overtake him again by two lengths. We go on that way for the few miles of straightaway until we're coming up toward the fence line and we both jump over the four feet high fence without catching on it, and head deeper into the bush.

The smell of loam, the cold and crisp air in my nose as I move? It feels incredible. I've missed this. I've missed it a lot.

And I don't just feel the wind, the smells, the earth, I hear his paws hit, I hear his breathing, and even hear that his heart beats at the same pace as mine.

It's strange to feel this level of physical compatibility with another male.

I have a fleeting thought that I hope Ivy's safe. I hope she won't run. I hope no one will harm her.

He barks at me and picks up pace, so I pick up mine and then we're fast coming down an embankment that I know ends with a shallow creek that will eventually wind and deepen, becoming the river that leads to Arcana Falls many miles away. I've never swam that far, as it's always been 'the forbidden village', and while Uncle lived, I ignored the draw to go there alone because of his rules. Before long, we're both galloping through the stream, water splashing high.

The energy I feel invigorates me. This feels incredible. And I feel drawn to go there, to finally see those falls.

Cornelius kept up when I was a kid but once I matured he never could, and I longed to run, really run at full speed with someone. I craved it with a fierceness that invaded my dreams.

Those dreams run through my mind now, for the first time in years. I dreamt of running with others like me. I dreamt of playing as pups, then running as older wolves. I painted based on those dreams, so many of them. Cornelius put the paintings away in the rafters of the garage. Except the one over my mantle in the bedroom. I put that one up when I took over that room. Of pups playing together. He never said a word about it but now that I think on it, he reacted to it and tried to hide how it made him feel.

So much makes sense now.

As a lone wolf I ran alone many times at full speed, but having someone to experience it with like this made it different.

The water deepens and we're both swimming until he gestures to a set of rocks with his nose and climbs up. I follow.

He shifts first, and then I follow, and he's got a wide smile on his face.

"Great run. Short one, but great."

"Yeah," I say, pushing my hair out of my eyes, then lean over to cup water to drink from the stream. I can't quench my thirst so after giving it a second of thought, I shift halfway and lower my head.

I know that behind me he's startled. I feel his stare on my back while I drink, able to get the water into my mouth faster with my larger mouth, my larger tongue.

I go back to man form completely and our gazes meet. He's shocked.

"I've never seen that," he says. "I've heard of it but never seen it."

"Cornelius told me to never let anyone see it."

I don't know why I let Riley see it. Maybe because I feel like I should never have listened to a fucking word out of Uncle's mouth.

"It's at will. Just easy like that to stop the shift part way?"

"I guess it is. I push, but slow it down and stop it from finishing. It lasts a little bit of time. Unless I'm overcome with immense anger, which has happened a few times, then I can stay like that longer."

"Your father could do it, too. My father told me about it. Does it happen when you lose it? It did to Uncle Tiberius."

Memories try to rush to the surface, of the murders Uncle had me commit. I push them back.

"Yes. Sometimes. What's going on with you?" I ask.

"Meaning?"

I need to deflect away from that other subject matter.

"Meaning you're doing your best at a courtship here with me, and I want to know how that works in your head. You want to give up the power you have to me?"

I know what Greyson said, but I wanna hear what Riley thinks.

He shakes his head. "We've spent our lives, all of us in the pack, thinking we had a missing piece of us. And your lack of presence is just... felt. Maybe that's how we should've known you weren't dead. If you were, we would've either filled the gap or not missed it, maybe. But we did feel it. We discussed it often. Things weren't right for us because you weren't gone. You were out there without us. Needing us, too. And I feel something from you, letting me know you're right for our team. Like I've gotten back a limb that I lost. Or, more like grown another sense that I didn't have. We don't expect you to jump in and be the person you would've been groomed to be all your life. You could be part of things and take your own pace. We have a collaboration here, not a hierarchy. You're like a king but you've got a government in place, if that makes sense. You don't have to delegate. It can be reverse of that. You step in when and where you're comfortable while you learn our ways."

I nod. It does make sense.

"Strength in numbers, Tyson. And for your mate and when you have children. Do you want your kids to grow up the way you did?"

I lean forward. "My kids will never face abuse like that."

He rears back.

"I've got no idea what you endured."

"That's right. You don't. But I know that even if I choose to live alone it doesn't mean my children will want for anything."

"Understood. I meant grow up alone. Did you miss not having a pack? Did your way of life feel natural to you?"

I stare into his eyes. And he has my answer because my eyes go completely unguarded. I bare it all to him without words.

And the returning look he gives me bares it all to me, too.

We understand one another.

He's honest. He means what he says. He wants me to be part of the pack.

I'm lonely. My whole life has had missing pieces. I've never felt whole. The closest has been since Ivy. I'm hesitant to embrace this. I don't know why. I do know that I don't want to fail at this role they think I should fit into.

And Riley... the man has been strong for a long time and he's barely holding it together. I see it. He hides it well but now that I'm looking, I do see it.

"What's your story?" I ask.

He stares for a minute and then lets out an agitated huff. "Grey? Fuckin' big mouth."

I nod. "He told me I'm needed. That you haven't taken the time to do what you need to do."

He shakes his head. "I'm fine. It's... fine."

"Greyson says you haven't allowed yourself to heal from a great loss."

"The greatest loss. And yeah, well ..." His eyes take on a faraway look. "It doesn't do much good to wallow, does it?" He lifts a rock from beside his knee and tosses it into the water.

"No, it doesn't," I agree.

"If I stop and let myself think about it, I don't know what it'll do to me. I just keep truckin', Ty. That's the only thing I know I can do. If I stop movin' forward, I don't know what'll happen to my mind."

I reach for his shoulder and squeeze briefly before I let go. I see the look in his eyes; he suddenly looks grief-stricken. The pain in his form hits me with a sensation in my chest like I've never felt. A strange sort of grief and loss. I wonder if Grey feels this from him and that's how he knows to worry about Riley.

I've never shown affection to a man. This feels natural, rather than strange.

"I can't even think about how she died, or I won't swim back." He wipes the expression away and rises. "I won't touch water again."

Obviously, he lost her in water.

He stares out at the creek for a minute and then his body shudders just briefly before he turns to me.

"Come to the party. Meet everyone. Let them all set eyes on you. Even if you two stay for an hour. It'll be good for you both and it'll be good for us. Really good for us."

"Fine," I say. "By the way, thank you. You and Lincoln for helping with Ivy the other day. I didn't know if I should trust you, but I *did* know. It was… confusing."

"You're welcome. She's yours and you're ours, which means she is, too. We would, any of us, go to great lengths to keep your mate safe. Come Friday. See your house. Meet your pack."

"Fine. And no promises from me but I'm keeping an open mind. And if you need—-"

"All I need is your open mind. No rush. Don't listen to Grey being a worrying old woman. I'm fine as long as you leave the door open for us to see if you feel like you belong."

"I can do that."

"Good. That's more than we could've hoped for," he says and slaps my back. "Now, that said? I got one thing left to say to you right now."

"What?"

The expression on his face has me bracing. And then he smiles wide. "Eat my dust."

He shifts while diving into the water and swims back the way we came.

I WIN THE RACE AND get home first, but win only by the skin of my nose.

We're in the door and Ivy is averting her gaze with a hand over her eye.

Ah. She sees Riley naked.

I laugh. Bailey tosses a bundle of clothing in his direction.

"Tyson, you need pants," Ivy says, still looking away.

Everyone looks at me with surprise. At my laughter maybe? I don't know.

I erase the space between me and my woman, hauling her from the couch up into my arms. I kiss her and then speak against her lips.

"Not right now I don't. It's been a good visit Catrina, Bailey, and Riley. Thank you for the food, and for visiting with Ivy while I got a much-needed run. Thank you, my mother, for taking care of Ivy's ankle." I glance up and my eyes meet Catrina's. Hers are filled with shock. "Truly, thank you for saving my Ivy." My voice goes gruff and I look back to Ivy's face as the emotion on my mother's face physically hurts. I can't let that penetrate any further or I'll go into an angry haze and spin out of control. I don't want that. It's felt like a good day. "That said," I continue, "Everyone, it's time to go. Unless you want to watch me mount my mate."

Nobody moves.

"You have to the count of five," I add.

"Tyson!" Ivy gasps.

They laugh and gather things up. "Give us to ten, please. We brought a lot of gear," Cat asks, her voice wobbly.

"Bye," I say and take my woman toward the bedroom in my arms.

"Tyson Savage put me down!" she orders.

I laugh and kick the door shut behind me.

"Not a chance, Ivy Savage. Your ankle is good, we're all fed, and plans have been made, I'm assuming, for that strawberry party?"

"Um, yeah…"

"Good," I say. I hear the front door open. "Will there be strawberries? I like that fruit."

"Probably," Ivy says with a smile on her mouth and in her eyes.

I set her down on the bed and put my knee to the mattress as I hear the door shut and then the receding footsteps of all three of them.

33

IVY

I'm on the couch, staring at my phone, and biting my lip.

My screen is lit up with notifications. My voicemail box is full. My mother is flipping out. Amelia is flipping out. Dad even texted me and called me and my father hates "those fuckin' things" (aka, smartphones).

My parents are recently separated so for him to message me – he has a clue as to what's going on and that means they've all got to be afraid. This makes me feel awful.

I've even heard from Bucket-List Megan. I scroll by that one with an eye roll, the preview screen showing she knows I got bit by a snake because she starts off with OMG and o-faces as well as snake emojis. Screw her. Who does that?

I scan through the rest of the notification previews and open the latest one from Becks, my boss, and it has a link to our local newspaper with information about the fire. The electrical fire set the whole block up in flames. It started in our store and the damage was extensive. We're talking months, at least. I'm getting paid for the next month and from there, we'll be updated on the status. I could be laid off or transferred to another store.

Well.

Okay then.

No rush to get back to civilization.

Hm.

Except for my freaking out family.

Mom is losing her ever-loving mind on my voicemail and all-capsing me in texts. Amelia, too, with four texts that all say

IVY! CALL ME

I knew this was how I'd feel when I turned on my phone – overwhelmed – which is why I've avoided it.

Ty is sleeping, catching an afternoon nap after a lot of eating, his run, and a whole lot of sexing. I figure now is probably the best time for this, so I've crept out of the bedroom in one of his shirts. All my panties are dirty. I officially need to do laundry.

I call Mom first.

Amelia answers.

"OhmygodwhathefuckIvywhatthefuck!"

"Oh. Ames?"

"Thank fuck!"

"Uh, hi."

Shit. I did not want to talk to Amelia. I wanted to talk to Mom and then let her talk to Amelia for me. Fuzz.

"Are you okay? Are you okay? What the fuck?"

"I'm okay."

"Shit. Shit. Okay, breathe, Amelia. Breathe."

My sister often talks to herself. She's hyperventilating.

"Breathe, Amelia," I tell her even though that's what she just told herself.

"Thank God. Thank God! Tell me what happened."

"Ugh. Okay, so I went away for a weekend with a girl from work, Megan, and the wicked wench screwed me over, so I decided to head home."

"You left her there, she said. How could you do that?"

"Believe me, it was warranted. When did you talk to her?"

"Mom and me have been losing our minds trying to track you down since your voicemail on Sunday about the snake bite. Mom's even been talking to *him* on the phone."

She means Dad. She always calls him 'Him'. Well, she has since he broke Mom's heart a few months ago.

"How could you not call us back, Ivy? None of the hospitals had a record of you, so I called your work and tracked down your manager who got me Megan's number, saying that she talked to you and knew you'd gone away for the weekend with Megan but that you'd gotten separated somehow and you were bit by a snake during that time and she didn't have any more info so I wanted to ask Megan questions and give her info to the cops in case it'd help with the search and where have you been since you called Mom?"

Ugh. So much for her stopping to breathe. My sister was nothing if not resourceful.

"It's a long story, Amelia, and frankly, I'm exhausted, so can we talk about it later? I just wanted to tell you guys I'm good, and –"

"Uh, no. We can't talk about it later. She said you left and that she hadn't heard anything. I told her you said something went wrong with your car on Mom's voicemail and that you got bit by a snake and were in a hospital but that we hadn't heard from you. She felt so bad about it but said it was you that left. Why on earth did you leave?"

"She was bangin' two guys and left me alone with three others. It was sketch-ville there, Ames. I told her I didn't wanna stay and she pretty much told me to take a flying leap. So I did."

Into the clutches of a werewolf.

A sexy, dominating, fuckable werewolf. I feel flutters in between my legs, in my nipples, and a sensation trills up my spine as the mark he made on my neck gets all tingly, too.

Just like Amelia, though, to assume that I made the mistake, not Megan who she never met. Grr.

"That was Sunday. This is Tuesday here, Ivy. We put in a missing persons' report last night. Where are you? Shit: we better call the cops and cancel it."

"Well..." I swallow, "I um... hit something with my car and wound up in a ditch and met this guy who brought me back to his place. Then, fast forward, I tried to leg it back to my car and tripped over snakes mating."

"Are you serious? You're joking!"

"No. Nope. Nuh uh." I'm biting my thumbnail now.

"You met a guy Friday night. In the woods..."

Shit. Here we go. Amelia has a really good bullshit detector and she's gonna try to add things together.

She continues, "And then you didn't leave his place until Sunday? You just yada yada'd me through all of Saturday. Hey Mom. Yeah, it's Ivy; she's in one piece."

Shit. Mom's there. Of course she is. I called Mom's phone, not Amelia's. Why didn't I think this through better? I'm pacing now. I look out the front drapes and see my car outside. Oh. What?

I unlock and open the door, then step outside and head toward it while Amelia is talking to Mom in my ear. Everything has been fixed. It's like it didn't even happen. This feels bizarre.

I hear Mom in the background, Amelia mumbling to my mother about me being fine and my mom is asking about a bazillion questions.

"Don't rat me out to Mom, Ames. Tell her I'm safe and sound. There's way more to the story but I can't get into it right now," I tell her, urgently.

"Hang on, Mom. So you're good, Ivy? Recovered from the bite?"

I hear my mom sounding like she's having a fit in the background.

"Much better."

"Where's your car? Do you need me to pick you up? Mom, wait..."

"It's fine. I'm good. I'm gonna stay here for a bit and..."

"Where's here?" That's Mom.

"Put her on speaker," Amelia says.

"One sec, Ivy. Don't you hang up, young lady."

Fuzz.

"Ivy Adeline Brennan!" Mom exclaims.

And in my head I think *Savage.* Ivy Adeline Savage. *Whoa.* Why was that the first thought that popped into my head?

And I'm on speaker phone now.

"Amelia!" I whine.

"She wrestled the phone off me," she defends herself.

"Ivy? What's going on? We've been worried sick!" Mom sounds frantic.

"I'm okay, Mom. I got bit by a rattlesnake and I'm recovering."

"What hospital are you at? We called everywhere! Why haven't you called me back sooner? It's been 48 hours!"

"I told you not to worry."

"Not to worry? Of course I'm worried. Have you met me? My daughter leaves me a message that she's in the hospital and has been bit by a snake and then she doesn't call me for two days. I thought you might be dead. Or worse."

"Worse?"

What's worse than dead?

"Kidnapped or something. Don't give me attitude, young lady. I've been worried out of my mind."

"She met some guy and she's at his place."

"Amelia!" I shout. Rat fink.

"Ivy!" Mom shouts.

Argh.

"What guy?" Mom asks when I don't immediately respond.

"He met her in the woods when her car broke down," Amelia says with a total tattletale tone.

"Where? Where are you?"

"Just outside Drowsy Hollow," I say.

"What? What?"

"Drow–"

"I heard you." My mother's voice has taken on a funny tone.

"Why do you sound weird?" I ask.

There's a beat of silence. A long one.

"Hello?" I check.

Did the call drop?

"Maybe I sound weird because my daughter has been missing. Maybe because she was bit by a venomous snake and didn't call for two days leading me to search every hospital in a four-hour radius."

"Okay, okay. I'm sorry. Things've been real weird," I say.

"How weird?" Mom asks.

"Drowsy Hollow. That's not far from our old house," Amelia says.

"I know," Mom says snarkily. "I lived there."

"Why does your voice sound funny, Mom?" I ask.

"Yeah. You're pale. She's pale, Ivy," Amelia says. "You've stressed her out like crazy. And me! I've got two stress zits and they better be gone by my bridal shower. We have a professional photographer coming."

I roll my eyes. "Then the pro can Photoshop the zits out," I say.

"But people will also see me, Ives..."

"So you're fine?" Mom interrupts.

"I'm fine," I confirm.

"When are you coming home? Do you need me to come get you?" Mom asks.

"I'm good. I'm just spending some time with Ty, the guy who... um... rescued me. Honest, I'm good."

"He rescued you and then you legged it and got bit by a snake so that suggests something wasn't good. Why were you legging it?" Amelia asks.

"It's a long story," I say.

"I bet," she retorts snarkily. "I need you here this weekend for your last fitting. You'll be here Saturday, four o'clock, right?"

"Of course."

"You coming back before that?" she asks. "Are you gonna have a scar? Where were you bit? Not on your face? Shit, not on your face, Ivy!"

"My ankle, Amelia, jeez. Worried I'll muck up your wedding pictures?"

"No. I'm worried your face got all mucked up, bitch."

"Girls," Mom cuts in. "Enough."

There's silence.

"I'm not sure when I'll be back," I say. "But I have my phone. It was lost but I got it back and if you guys need me, text or call. Don't worry. I'm fine. Can you call Dad and Leo?"

"I'll call our brother," Amelia offers, "but if you wanna get a message to *him*, either Mom can do it, or you can call him yourself. Better yet, you do it, Ives. Mom doesn't need his bullshit."

"Who is this man you're with, Ivy?" Mom asks.

"Tyson. Tyson Savage. He's a nice guy. We're having fun. We hit it off." I shrug. I can feel a smile stretching my face.

I do like him. A lot.

"How nice?" Amelia asks.

"Very, *very* nice," I reply cheekily.

She laughs. Well... that's kind of a surprise. She's been so high-strung lately.

"Who is he?" Mom huffs. "You're with a strange man, Ivy, and your loved ones need to know where you are in case he's..."

"A serial killer, Mom? He rescued me from what could've been a lethal snake bite. If he was set on offing me, that woulda made his life easy."

"But, what if he doesn't like it easy? What if he wants to be the one to do the killing?" That's Amelia. And now she sounds venomous. Or scared. I don't know.

"Oh God," Mom whispers.

"Listen guys, I'm good. I'm great. I'm really enjoying myself and after bein' bit by a snake and worrying for a minute there that I was gonna die after a sketchy trip to the country, I'm happy to be enjoying myself. And I've got a hot guy here who is determined to show me a really, *really* good time so I'm gonna go wake him up from his nap for some more naked time before we probably have a campfire and eat s'mores off each other's naked bodies so...the biggest risk I've got is hot marshmallow burns on my skin."

Amelia's laughing.

Mom says nothing.

I finish up with, "Text me later. I'll answer you after naked s'mores. Don't stress."

"I'm not amused. Check in tomorrow," Mom finally says.

"I will, Mom. " I smile. "Sorry I made you worry. It's been a strange few days. More on that later. Too much to get into on the phone."

I hear my mom's breath hitch.

"I'm good, Mom. Can you text Dad and tell him I'm fine?"

"Yes. I can. But... you're sure? Is everything okay there? I mean... really okay?"

"Absolutely," I say. "Just text Dad. You don't need to talk to him all emotional. He might try to come over."

"Yeah, he is not welcome here," Amelia adds.

"I think I can decide who's welcome in my house, girls."

Neither me nor Amelia reply. We're both worried she'll take him back. He's been trying to sweet talk her.

"Call me tomorrow," Mom demands. "Early."

"Why?"

"I just need to hear your voice and talk to you so I can know you're alive unlike the past forty-eight hours, that's why!"

"Okay," I say softly.

The line is quiet. "I'll text early, guys. Love you, Mom. Love you too, Bridezilla."

"Love you!" Amelia sings out. "No glove, no love, Ives!"

"Be careful. Love you," Mom says. "And I'm still upset about 48 hours with no contact."

"It'll make more sense when I tell you the whole crazy story," I say.

I have no idea how I'll explain all this. Can I even explain it? Shit.

"That's what I'm afraid of," Mom grumbles.

Huh?

"Bye," I say and hang up before the conversation drags on further. I turn and there's Ty. Directly behind me.

I startle with a little bit of a scream.

He hefts me over his shoulder.

"Whoa. Holy crap. What're you doing?"

"Taking you back to bed. For some more naked or naked some mores."

I giggle.

"What's funny?"

"S'mores. Do you know what that is?"

"No, but it involves you naked, so it sounds good."

"S'mores. It's a treat. It's marshmallow and graham cracker and chocolate and it's all melted."

"Sounds like a hot version of that ice cream. Make it for us later."

"We'll need a trip to town," I say.

"Then tomorrow. Right now, I need inside you, Ivy."

"Oh. It's been a whole forty minutes since last time, so by all means." I throw my arms up, though he can't see me obviously, because I'm over his shoulder.

And a minute later, I'm on my back in his bed and he's going down. He's going down *real* good.

34

TYSON

Ivy's asleep and I'm in the garage. I've pulled all the paintings down from the rafters. There are a lot of them. Paintings of mine. Paintings of his. And the paintings of his have had me ready to return to his bones again and pound what's left of them to dust.

Why?

Because there are paintings of her. The woman he ached for. My mother. There are paintings of her, looking beautiful, looking breathtaking at a very young age, barely a woman. And there's a painting of her in sorrow, covered in blood. And it physically hurts to look at it. His paintings are almost like photographs, they're done so vividly. Even her eyelashes look real in the pictures. My uncle was skilled with the paintbrush. Skilled with weaving lies through my brain my whole life, too.

She wouldn't let him have her, so he took everything from her. Her husband. Her child. Her happiness.

I'm in awe of her after having met her. Of her resilience. You see the pain in the lines around her eyes, but she's not bitter. She's looking forward. She's spent her life serving her pack. And she's found happiness again.

Beyond all his paintings, some of which were landscapes and some of which were abstract and manic looking, are paintings I've done.

I've found the one of the sprite. She has yellow hair and she's very small and as I painted it as a child there's not enough detail for me to know if it's a premonition of Ivy, but I think it is.

She's smiling and happy and she's floating over my pup wolf form beside a small blue butterfly that sits on my nose. I don't know why I drew that butterfly like that.

After going through all the paintings, many of which include me playing with six other pups, I leave them against the walls, then walk out of there with my head down, feeling sick about Cornelius.

Those six shifters felt my absence and clearly I felt theirs, too, even if I didn't know how to name it other than drawing about it.

I crawl back into bed with her and pull her warm and soft body close. Just the scent of her brings me comfort. This is calm and comfort I never thought I'd have. I didn't know I was missing it. Now that I have it, I know I won't ever give it up. Not for anything. And I won't ever let her be taken from me the way my father was taken from my mother. No one can hurt Ivy the way Catrina Savage has been hurt. I won't let it happen.

Despite feeling the comfort of my mate, I clench my teeth until I fall asleep.

35

IVY

Three Days Later...

It's Friday morning, and we're driving to town. I have my arms crossed and I'm pouting. He's acting like he's ignoring it, like he seems to do when I don't like something, but I know he knows I'm pouting.

What's the problem? Well, for starters he wouldn't let me go shopping by myself for a dress for the strawberry moon party.

Clearly, he thinks I'll take off on him. He's not saying that, but I know it's what he thinks.

And second, he's not giving me my car keys.

He also informed me this morning that after we're done dress-shopping, we're going to a furniture store and I should pick out a new bed and new furniture.

And then he wants me to tell him what else we need. He's talking about painting the place, too. He's trying to make it clear that I'm here to stay. He's never asked me to stay, he's only told me. And that's annoying as heck.

"What about what Riley said? About the house you have in Arcana Falls?" I asked.

"We have," he corrected.

I didn't reply and he got fidgety. And then he lifted me up onto the kitchen counter and tried to have sex with me.

"We need to go out." I tried to make him stop. His mouth was making its way down my throat into the opening of my shirt. "Tyson! Stop."

"We can go soon," he said against my skin and then he purred against that spot on my throat.

My hands landed on his shoulders and instead of pushing him, like I planned to, I wound up with my head rolled back and my hands in his hair while he nibbled, licked, and scraped his delicious stubble along my skin, pulling me tight against his body so that my legs were around him. I was a bit too high to be pelvis to pelvis, so he carried me to the couch and kept me straddling him as his hand lowered, about to free himself from his jeans.

"Wait. Before you get carried away, there, I have to buy a dress and shoes and accessories and—"

"And we need time to go to the furniture store. I know. They're close to each other. It's fine."

"I may need more than one store before I find a dress I like, so..."

He froze and stared at me.

I continued. "It may take five or ten stores and trying on half a dozen dresses in each of those places before I find something I like."

He frowned at me and his mouth went tight.

"This is why we should've gone yesterday instead of spending the afternoon in bed." I poked him in the chest.

He smiled. "It was a very nice afternoon in bed."

It was.

It's been a great couple days living in this little bubble...this little werewolf sex bubble. For real. I truly don't know how my vagina hasn't just fallen off. My inner thighs are a little sore, though, almost like I've been horseback riding. A girl could give up her gym membership with a guy like this who'd undoubtedly keep her physically fit, that was for damn sure.

Tyson liked the s'mores and we then spent that night cuddled up while he talked about books he liked.

He showed me all sorts of paintings in his garage painted by his uncle and that made me really sad for him. If the paintings were put on exhibit you could line them up, all thirty or forty of them and call them, "Bi-polar. Illustrations of the highs and the lows."

I also saw a stack of other paintings, but Ty stopped me from looking at those. He said they were more graphic ones of his mother, that they were too upsetting to look at as well as some of the ones he'd painted when he was young, and that he didn't want me to see them.

I didn't push. Something in his eyes told me not to.

In the past few days, I've spent 24/7 with him and it's been bliss. We spent time cleaning up together. I bought a mop when we got s'mores stuff and he acted like mopping was fun. It was adorable. We also cleaned up the other bedroom. Everything smelled like Pine-Sol when we were done, and he kept breathing it in as if it was the best smell ever.

Thursday, we did some more organizing and hung out outside weeding the garden beds and cutting the grass. He had one of those ancient manual push mowers and the place was already looking a lot better. It was also pretty warm that day and he cut the grass with no shirt on. That was fun to watch.

I showed him some nice pictures online of pretty landscaping ideas and suggested he get some flowers sometime, and then he immediately took me in his truck to the nearest garden center ten miles away and bought all sorts of flowers as well as some patio furniture for the porch. And a bunch of vegetable seeds.

He was trying to make this place a home for me. He was trying to encourage me to settle in here. Grow herbs. Vegetables.

Root me.

He started a compost pile back away from the house, too, and made a point of taking our organic waste from the kitchen scraps to it after each meal, like it was something important, because he was doing it for me.

God, he was sweet.

And affectionate. Normally, I got annoyed when a guy was too demonstrative with me, found it clingy and unattractive. But not so with Tyson. I couldn't get enough of how cuddly he was. He was always touching me, making eye contact with me, looking at me like he found me fascinating.

But that he was talking about painting the house, going to the furniture store; it was freaking me out.

Because I could stay here with him.

I could.

It was tempting.

So very tempting.

Things were hot and heavy, but we both knew I wasn't ready to declare that I'd stay and it created tension at times that resulted in marathon sex sessions where it was like he was convinced I was just a few orgasms away from agreeing to spend my life with him. Though, like I said, he never asked. He told me I was staying with his actions, with his plans that included me picking the furnishings and tending a garden.

I sent twice daily check-in texts to Mom and Amelia to prove to them I was alive. I rejected phone calls and hadn't listened to any more voicemails. All that and being vague in my texts despite Mom pushing to get more information about where I was and her digging for more information on Tyson.

She was being peculiar about it, really. Aunt Nelle always said mom was a little psychic, had great intuition. Did she sense something was off kilter here?

I got a text from Amelia an hour ago asking me whether I was meeting her at the dress shop or at her apartment.

I tucked my phone away before Ty saw the message. I still had to tell Tyson that tomorrow, I have to go home.

I need to go home, check on the apartment, which has been empty since my roommate Tamara is in Jamaica with her boyfriend, and I need to go for my final fitting for Amelia's wedding. All the bridesmaids and both my mom and Rick's mom are going for dinner afterwards.

I've got the feeling, after his behavior so far, that he'd take issue with this. Not only would he take issue with this, he'd try to stop me.

I was thinking I'd buy him a cell phone today. I'd do that while dress shopping and then sit him down very calmly after the party and tell him that I had to leave but that this didn't mean it was the end for us.

I wasn't saying goodbye, just going home and we could talk and make plans to get together again soon. I didn't have to worry about work for a while, but I needed to go home for the fitting and to check on the apartment and get my flippin' head together (not that I'd say that) and then I could come back again. For a visit. See where things went from there.

Maybe while I was gone, he'd do some more bonding with Cat and the others.

Maybe we'd just see what happened from there.

Or maybe I'd go home for a few days, get my head straight without all the sex and attention from him and decide to pack a bag and move here. Or not.

Or maybe something more realistic, like date him for a bit before I moved here. Or not.

I really hadn't thought it all out, but I had been thinking about it.

Or trying.

Every time I tried to get in my head too much, he was there, doting on me. Being affectionate. Being sexual. Making me coffee or tea. Bringing me a snack. Wanting to talk to me. Purring in that sexy/sweet way that managed to just melt me into warm Ivy goo.

The guy was really getting to me and I needed a bit of space to sort my head out.

He wouldn't let me go to the store alone. And he wouldn't give me my keys, so right now I was kind of pissed.

"YOU'LL LOOK GOOD IN anything," he says randomly as we're coming into the town.

"You mean dress shopping? Flattery is nice, Tyson, but I need to feel good, too. And that might not happen with the first store we go into."

I managed to fend him off sex earlier, bribing with the offer of a quickie when we got back if we got back in time for me to shower and do my hair without too much stress.

"In other words, the sooner we go, the sooner we're back and the more chances of a quickie," I had said.

"A quickie? What's a quickie?" He had no idea what that meant.

"Quick sex."

He blinked then barked out a laugh.

I loved it when he did that, especially after he'd admitted to me in bed the night his family left that he loved to smile and laugh. He had never been around it; his uncle never laughed, and it felt foreign to him, but he liked how it felt. So, I started telling him stupid jokes. And he didn't get some of them, but when he got a joke, the way he laughed felt like an accomplishment to me.

"What do you call a werewolf with no back legs and metal balls?" I'd asked.

"Huh?"

"No hind legs and metal testicles...you know... balls?"

"No. I don't know about metal testicles. There's metal balls? What on Earth for?"

"It's a joke! I'm telling you a joke."

He looked so confused.

"Just follow my lead. Okay?"

"Okay." He didn't look so sure.

"What do you call a werewolf with no hind legs and metal balls?"

"I don't–"

"Sparky!" I bumped his shoulder with mine.

He stared blankly.

"Sparky," I repeated with a big smile.

He didn't get it.

I tried to look up videos to show him how sparks would fly off the pavement if you dragged metal off it and it took some time and so the joke was ruined.

He didn't get it.

I then took that opportunity to show him a compilation of people slipping on banana peels. At first, he stared with unconcealed concern, and then a few slips in, he was laughing uproariously, finally understanding why I laughed at him that first day here.

This took us to Reddit, where I read him a bunch of Dad jokes and typical *knock knock* jokes.

There were jokes he didn't get, but he laughed at quite a few of them. And then later, while I was cooking dinner, I found him laughing in the chair with my phone in his hand, reading more jokes from the same page.

This was so adorable I just crawled up into his lap and snuggled him.

He read me three dumb jokes. I laughed at all of them. More than because they were funny, because *he* found them funny and his whole face was lit up with excitement while he told them to me.

But then my phone made a sound and his face changed.

"What?" I asked.

He read the screen, "Ben. Are you all right? I heard about what happened at the tux fitting today. Call me. I'd love to talk. Miss you, Ivy."

Oh shit.

I took the phone from him and tossed it aside.

"I don't miss him."

Tyson's face was red, his nostrils were flaring, and he looked like he was about to go find Ben and rip his face off.

"Ty, don't worry about a text message from Ben. Trust me." I put my lips to his. He let out a stuttered breath, like he was trying to calm himself down.

"Did you love him, Ivy?"

"Nope. Really, baby. It wasn't even serious."

"But he fucked you."

"Pff. Trust me. Not remotely serious. Ben is old news, Ty."

I tugged on his earlobe with my teeth and he shivered. I liked that so I did it again and made a little growl sound.

He whispered, "Your growl is cute."

"Is it?" I looked into his eyes.

And his mind was no longer on Ben.

But now here we were, in a tiff because on our way out the door, glancing at my car I asked, "Oh yeah, where are the keys?"

The look on his face said it all. "Why do you need your keys?"

I had my answer without him speaking another word. He didn't want to give me my keys back. He didn't want me to go anywhere.

He didn't say this.

We stared for a minute at one another in what felt like a stand-off.

I didn't say I knew that this was his thinking and now it had been fifteen or twenty minutes of silent brooding in the car on the way to town.

HE STOPS IN FRONT OF a discount department store. A lower-end one that would sell hardware, greeting cards, cigarettes, cleaning supplies, and maybe have a few racks of discount clothing options.

I stare at the sign.

"This is the store," he says and turns the truck off.

"Um, no," I say. "I'm not buying a dress from here."

He looks confused.

"A dress for around the house, a dress for traipsing to town or the beach, sure. Not a dress for a party where I get to meet the rest of your loved ones. And I need shoes. And not flipflops, either. I need something with a heel, something cute."

"I don't love them. I don't even know them yet, Ivy."

"Doesn't matter. First impressions and all. I need something a little more upscale." I pull my phone out and search for the closest dress shop.

"We'll go to the furniture store first. It's three doors that way," he says, reaching for the door handle.

"No, Ty," I inform. "The dress and shoes are the priority. Let's do that first and then we can shop for furniture if there's time. If. Furniture isn't required in less than eight hours. A dress and shoes are. And I have to have time to get back and shower, do my hair and makeup. And what are you wearing anyway? We should get you some nice slacks and a new button-down. I wonder if they have a tall guy store around here." I keep scrolling the options on my phone.

"I have plenty of clothes at home."

"Ty, you have four shirts, three t-shirts, two pairs of jeans and, what, two pairs of lounge pants? That's not enough of a wardrobe for anyone."

"It's worked fine for me."

"For supernatural hermit reasons, yes, but you need clothes for tonight. Maybe some new shoes. You have a pair of hiking boots and a pair of sneakers. You need something a little better."

I knew the extent of the wardrobe because I'd reorganized his armoire yesterday and done the laundry the day before that.

"Okay, twenty-five minutes from here is a bigger town with more shopping. Take this road to the end and then it'll take you in that direction." I point.

"You don't want to at least look?" he tries.

"Do you want to waste time?" I retort.

He shoots me a look of annoyance, but starts up the truck.

We have to buy gas a few stores later and at the third store we go to, an hour and a half from his place, I find a great dress, a fabulous pair of shoes, and I find him dark slacks and a gorgeous navy, nearly black dress shirt with green stripes the exact same color as his eyes. I also get him great new shoes.

Getting him to try clothes on is like pulling teeth. And he insists on paying, waving around a fat stack of cash, which I find annoying, but also sweet.

"This was not a werewolf issue, this is a guy issue," I told him. "I could've shopped alone, but you insisted on coming and holding my keys hostage, so this is your reality, big guy."

"We're done? Can we go home?"

WE DON'T GET BACK UNTIL four thirty, so I announce, "Okay, I'm taking a shower and then working on my hair before we have to head out. No sexy time!"

"No sexy time?" He frowns.

"Nope. There's no time for sexy time."

"There's always time for sexy time," he says, stalking in my direction.

I take off running with a giggle.

He smiles, realizing I'm teasing, and he catches me by hooking an arm around my waist. "Since you have a dress, sexy time is the new priority."

"We have to get ready for the party."

"Fuck the party," he growls against the mark on my neck and yep, full-body shiver from me.

"No way. They're expecting us. And I wanna show off my pretty dress and fantastic shoes."

"To who?" His eyes take on a dangerous glint.

"Everyone. It's the whole point of a new dress, silly."

He hauls me closer by grabbing my ass, directly against his crotch and I feel the hardness poking my belly.

"Explain. And do it now."

Uh oh. What?

He looks angry.

"You think I want men's attention? Uh no." I make a passable imitation of a buzzer sound. "Wrong. I just wanna feel good on a hot guy's arm about looking half decent. Looking my best will make me feel less stressed out, though only marginally less, about meeting a whole bunch of new people."

"I'm a hot guy?" he asks.

I laugh. Hysterically.

He frowns.

"You're definitely a hot guy."

"The dress isn't just for me?"

"It's for me first, for you second. Mostly for me though so I feel confident that you can feel proud of having me on your arm."

"I would be proud to have you on my arm if you were covered in dirt, Ivy."

"That's sweet. And it ain't gonna happen because I wanna look my best. Now ... let me go so I can go shower."

"I'll come with you."

"We both know what'll happen if you do, Ty. It'll be all naked and soapy and me having two orgasms before I get the shampoo in. That'll delay us."

"Three or four orgasms," he corrects.

"How about just one big one?" I counter.

"Deal," he says and then he's pulling me by the hand toward the bathroom while pulling his t-shirt over the back of his neck.

MY DRESS IS AWESOME. I feel great.

I'm having a great hair day and my werewolf looks so handsome it should be a crime.

I've tamed his hair in a low ponytail at his nape, which he says he likes, and he is clean shaven and smells awesome. His eye is also healed, even though I haven't been able to get eyedrops in for over 24 hours because he's been a big baby about it each time.

Not only did I buy him a razor and shaving cream, I also bought decent hair products when we were out today, too, instead of the budget 2-in-1 shampoo we'd been using, and my hair is thanking me for it with a great hair day. I've used my ceramic curling iron and given myself ringlets and

Tyson likes it. He really likes my strawberry colored taffeta dress. It hits above the knee with a flare to the skirt, cap sleeves, and a keyhole neckline with a hint of cleavage.

Tyson can barely take his eyes off me. My shoes are red, too, with a series of laces and a cute scalloped strap across the top of my ankle. My ankle feels mostly fine, but I bought wedges instead of stilettos for extra safety. He keeps staring at my legs and it's taking a lot of effort to ward him off from sexing me again. If he had his way, we wouldn't get out the door.

"Are those shoes a good idea, Ivy?" he asks, as I climb up into the truck, with his assistance.

"My ankle is fine." I've still got it bandaged, which takes away from the overall look, but I can walk on them, no problem.

"Don't you hurt yourself," he warns me, as if he'll punish me if I do.

I frown at him. His face softens and then he kisses me sweetly before shutting the door and rounding the truck.

36

IVY

We've pulled in behind a massive barn across the road from a general store and gas station. Someone gestures to an empty spot beside the door with a big smile. I see lots of big smiles in the parking lot, too, in fact.

Are all these people shifters? There are people of all ages and not only are they all aware of our arrival and paying attention, but I also note that they're a healthy-looking bunch. We walk hand-in-hand through the open barn doors, seeing twinkle lights and hearing music. Plenty of people are behind us in that parking lot, and while they keep their distance, I note with a glance over my shoulder that there are a lot of happy faces behind us.

Bailey runs toward us, dressed in a pretty black party dress with her hair in a fancy updo and she's in heels, doing so quite awkwardly, looking like she's about to break an ankle. She embraces me. "You're here! You're gorgeous. Both of you. Come on!"

We move further inside and the place is festive. And impressive. It's a big, open converted barn that's been clearly altered to accommodate all sorts of events. I see a long saloon style bar slash kitchen area, lined with barrels that have taps on the front, dozens of extra-large brightly colored picnic tables, comfy-looking seating and tables bordering the space, creatively made with wood pallets and wicker designed to look like haybales. There's also a big dancefloor. White twinkle lights are strung from one end to the other along rafters and I also see plenty of dangling red lights, obviously added for the strawberry theme. Each picnic table has a weighted set of red balloons with white curled ribbon as a table arrangement. In one corner, a stage sits a few levels up with a DJ. Behind the bar area is a set of stairs leading up to the loft that has twinkle lights wound around the railings. I can see people up there, chatting, drinking beers.

Music is on low, playing P!nk's *Get this Party Started*. There are dozens of people and it feels like every one of those sets of eyeballs points in our direction.

"See? Effort was important," I say to Tyson softly. He's taking it all in. He doesn't look spooked. He doesn't even look concerned. He's looking around and there's a calmness coming from him, I think, unless I'm misreading him.

For someone who has spent most of his life with just one other person and the last few years alone, I'm surprised he's not radiating a vibe of fish-out-of-water.

I see his eyes move to a taller pub-style table by the bar with several guys. A few sitting, a few standing. Riley's there. The sitting ones all stand up as eyes swing to us.

Holy crap. That table is full of sexy, hot men. All of them look like they've put effort into their appearances. I'm glad I forced Tyson to buy new clothes for himself. My eyes bulge.

Cat, dressed in a flattering polka dot maxi dress and gladiator sandals, her long and curly hair up in a twist, emerges from a cluster of ladies by a long table that's loaded with food platters. She and Riley are coming to us from opposite ends of the room. They arrive at the same time. More people are moving our way, including a group of other men, men who are a bit older.

And then people are making introductions and names and handshakes are shared rapid-fire. I do a lot of smiling and nodding, Tyson's holding my hand and seeming not only receptive, but also at ease. More people flood the space around us and form an orderly line. Suddenly, we've got a receiving line that goes out the door with absolutely everyone here. My hands are getting shook dozens upon dozens of times. Some people shake his hand. A few older ladies grab and hug him. He seems completely at ease.

And then two little old ladies and a tall, older man approach and despite being advanced in years, they're also fit-looking.

Riley whistles and people take notice of the three elderly people, move out of the way to let them cut the line, and Cat makes introductions.

"Ivy, Tyson, my mother, your grandmother, Aria, known to her grandchildren as Nan. My father Lawrence. Your father's mother, Grandmama Carolyn."

It feels emotional, but I hold myself together, not letting myself cry and ruin my makeup or make myself look stupid, until I catch the eyes of Cat who is openly weeping with joy as she watches her son greet and get welcomed by his grandparents, who are all looking emotional, even his grandfather who whispers something in his ear as he shakes Tyson's hand. Ty has kissed both the older ladies on the cheeks and they're both beaming with happiness. Another lady, close to Cat's age, bounds over to greet Tyson with a hug.

She hugs me next.

"I'm Aunt Lucy," she says, "Riley, Brody, and Trina's mom. I'm Cat's sister, too. We married brothers." She smiles and gestures over her shoulder. A man with long, dark hair and a salt and pepper beard steps up behind her and holds his hand out to Tyson. "Atticus Savage. I'm your uncle."

And he looks like he is, too. The resemblance is uncanny.

Tyson stares for a second and then takes the man's hand and pulls him into a hug.

Whoa.

My chin wobbles as my eyes meet Cat's and I try to blink the tears back, for her, for Tyson, for my own self composure, but it's really, really difficult and the tears come anyway. I manage to stop myself just short of sobbing, but this takes a lot of effort.

I don't know if Ty even knew he had family beyond Cat and Riley.

We spend a few minutes talking with the grandparents and someone snaps pictures of Tyson with them, Tyson with his mom, me and Tyson. My face hurts from all the smiling.

Five large, strong-looking, and ridiculously handsome men are with Riley and I know by looking at them that these have to be the other alphas of the pack. I recognize one, I think, that helped the day I was bit by the snake.

They all shake his hand and nod at me. Until the very last one of the group stops in front of Tyson and his eyes bounce between Ty and me. He's a big, built, handsome guy with dark blond hair and dark eyes.

Riley steps up and gets between him and us. "This is Mason. Mason isn't feeling his best. Mase? Hold it together, brother."

He shakes Tyson's hand and Tyson immediately growls. The guy releases Tyson's hand and takes a step back. A big one.

I have no idea what the problem is here.

"Good to meet you," Mason says. "And you." He means me but he doesn't look at me. He backs away, staring at his feet, and leaves, looking rattled.

Riley and another huge guy exchange looks. Another one goes out behind Mason after excusing himself.

I have no idea what that's about.

My eyes move to Bailey and Cat, who are whispering. In fact, there's suddenly a whole lot of whispering. Tyson looks pissed. Riley whispers something to him and Tyson calms, though just marginally.

"What?" I ask, resting my hand on his arm. He pulls me tight to his side as the reception line continues and the rest of the line of people move up, taking the time to greet us. Several more are related to Tyson, too. More cousins on his mother's side, second and third cousins on both sides of his family, relations by marriage, and every single person acts happy to see him. Everyone except that Mason guy.

Bailey and Cat steer us to the buffet after the seemingly endless line finally ends, and plates of food are loaded up and handed to us before we're ushered to one of the bigger pub-style sets ahead of the picnic tables. We sit with Riley, his parents, Cat and Bailey. The table of alphas is next to ours and the guy, Mason, isn't there. I see three other tables that are clearly designed for the elderly people of the village as they're comfy high-back cushioned chairs rather than picnic tables.

Riley says something else low in Tyson's ear and he speaks back with his finger in Riley's face. It's loud with the big crowd, the music, and the noises of people serving food, so I have no idea what is happening here.

Bailey leans in from the seat beside me. "I'm your wolf shifter pack life guide. I'll stay close."

"Good. What's wrong with that Mason guy?"

"Not a clue," she says with a shrug. "I haven't seen him since he got back from a project he's been gone on. It's weird. I think he got back Sunday and it's odd to not have seen him. I love your dress and your shoes. Dig in." She gestures to the food.

She's trying to act all nonchalant with me, but her expression and body language aren't remotely relaxed.

Tyson is already eating while in discussion with his uncle Atticus and with Riley. Men from the neighboring table are leaned in to participate in the conversation.

I catch that they're talking about a run in the morning. All of them. I know how much that run with just Riley meant to Ty; he talked about it, about how it felt, how he used to dream about running with other wolves. I'm excited for him.

He's taking everything in. He's been reserved but also warm with most everyone who approached. People had said sweet things. Men talked about what a wonderful man his father was. Women talked about being so happy for Cat that he was back. People said things like, "Welcome home."

"This is great," I whispered, forking up some creamy dill potato salad.

I wasn't just talking about the food. I was talking about all of it.

Bailey tells me there will be dancing and music all night long but that before that happens, there's a presentation for their youth in the pack. She chats happily while eating, telling me that after that's over, anyone under drinking age will go home. She tells me many of the alphas get into wrestling matches and wiggles her eyebrows while telling me that those are fun to watch.

"After dinner, if you want, during some of the community stuff, we can go show you the house. Are you guys staying tonight?"

"I have no idea," I say.

"We are." Ty leans in to tell her. His eyes then bounce to mine. "Oh. If that's fine with you, Ivy."

"I don't have anything with me," I say, "But if you want to, baby, that's fine."

"I do. Baby," he says and smiles. He dropped his voice an octave with that 'baby' and my insides are all tingly now.

"Taste this potato salad," I say. "It's so good!"

He leans over and tastes it off my fork as I'm about to put it in my mouth.

"You've got your own," I admonish and then I lean over and fork up a bite off his plate. He steals that before I'm able to get the fork to my own mouth.

There are amused faces around us.

"It's good," Tyson says.

"I can give you the recipe," Tyson's Aunt Lucy calls over.

"Oh. Great," I say. "It's delicious."

"Try the breaded pork cutlet," Bailey suggests. "And the stuffed tomatoes."

"I'd complain there's way too much food on my plate, but it won't go to waste, knowing Tyson."

"There's loads of food at these things. It's potluck, my favorite," Bailey says. "I'm an awful cook, so I get to bring soft drinks or paper plates." She rolls her eyes.

"Don't sweat it," I reassure her. "Saves you some work."

"Saves us some food poisoning," one of the guys at the next table says.

She pokes her tongue out at him, but her face goes bright red.

"Who's that again?" I ask.

"Jase," she whispers.

"Jason Creed." He holds his hand out.

I shake it.

Jason Creed is a tall drink of water with light brown hair and light brown eyes. He's wearing a brown button-down with dark jeans and that button down is only half buttoned, showing he's tattooed from his neck down to his wrists.

No wonder she's flushed. He oozes sexuality.

He smiles at her with dimples. *Lordy.*

A gorgeous woman in a miniskirt and cowboy boots signals to him from by the door and he says, "Excuse me ladies."

"He's a tall drink of water," I whisper, watching him walk away.

"Mm." Bailey stares at her plate and starts forking food in faster.

"Does he have a girlfriend? Was that her by the door?"

"Jase has plenty of girlfriends," she mumbles.

"He's not... uh... mated, though," I ask.

"Nope," she replies, staring at her plate.

Tyson's hand sifts through my hair and he puts his nose to the spot on my neck. I shiver.

"What are you doing, Ivy?" he growls in my ear, low.

His tone feels... dangerous.

I look into his eyes. "I may be doing some matchmaking."

His eyes flash with humor.

"Not mated? Hm," I say.

Bailey's eyes are on me and I think she heard what I said to Ty.

"Nobody's mated from our alpha council. It happens in birth order, usually, or it has in the past, but with our pack things went a bit wonky with Tyson being gone. Hopefully with Ty in the mix things will run their usual course and these guys'll all be taken off the market. Stop their whoring ways." She rolls her eyes and I look over to the door where Jason Creed is whispering into that girl's ear.

Is this Jase guy the one she's got her big crush on?

By her reaction, I would bet money on it.

The rest of the meal is spent on chitchat. Lucy and Cat ask me questions about my life, and I fill them in and talk about my job, my family, and tell them about my mom, sister, and brother.

Lucy is a teacher at the school here, telling me they teach via a Montessori-like method and she has students ranging in age from kindergarten to high-school age.

"Do shifter people go on to a special college?" I ask her.

"We have people that integrate with mainstream society because they want to for school, but we also have a university in Scotland that many choose to go to because it's easier. There's a wide range of programs there. My daughter Trina's there now, studying. My son, Brody, chose a mainstream school. He graduates in a few weeks."

"Oh, that's great."

"Being in mainstream society is complicated," Bailey adds. "My cousin fell in love with a guy and had to end it because she didn't think he'd integrate with our pack. In order to bring a mainstream person in, the pack has to agree first. Sometimes people leave the pack and give up their community for love with a mainstream person, but more often, that person integrates with us."

"The pack has to agree?" I ask.

"Unless it's an alpha mating," Bailey says. "In which case that stuff usually happens after because alphas have no self-control and aren't about to ask anyone for permission to be with somebody."

I look at Tyson. "Yeah, I can see that."

He smirks.

Laughter comes from the neighboring table and it's clear that some of those alphas agree with that statement.

"It's tricky with friendships, too," Bailey adds, "because if you become close with someone they'll eventually wanna meet your family and we have to keep a distance. If some outsider shows up there's an alert sent out so that everyone knows to be extra cautious. As you can imagine, we don't want mainstreamers to know about us."

"Is that something that's ever been considered? Telling the world about who you really are?" I ask.

The mood goes strange.

"Sorry, if that's offensive. I just don't see why it couldn't eventually be accepted."

"You're idealistic," Riley says.

Obviously at some stage of the conversation, all the guys at that table began tuning into what we were talking about.

"But the reality - it's safer the way it is. Supernaturals may be stronger, but there are more of the mainstreamers and history has taught us that it'd go wrong. Any time in history that anyone with differences has tried, it's gone wrong. They outnumber us and it's been shown time and again that mainstreamers can't handle the truth about anybody considered supernatural."

"That's sad," I say, "To live in secret."

"We're fine with it. It's our way of life," Riley tells me. "Believe me, we don't lose out. Each major pack has a voice in a larger council, like a United Nations of sorts. Any major decisions would be brought there. They interface with councils of other supernaturals."

"Others? You mean, non-shifters? What other sorts of supernatural beings exist?" I ask. "Or can you tell me?"

"You ready for this?" Bailey checks. "And you do realize, once we tell you this, you're deeper into a non-verbal but very binding contract to say nothing about anything to anybody. Anyone that finds out our secrets joins into a pact that's punishable by death if it's broken."

I gasp. "I'd never..."

Tyson leans toward Bailey threateningly. She squeaks.

"I'm not... I know, we know you wouldn't. You're Tyson's soulmate. Tyson, chill," she requests. "I'm being cheeky."

Tyson leans back but still looks tweaked at the perceived threat.

Aunt Lucy speaks up. "You wouldn't be his person if it weren't meant to be. We know that. He wouldn't have come back to us if he wasn't meant to be here, with us, leading us. We're all comfortable with you, Ivy. Shifters are taught from a young age how important it is to keep our lives secret. This all comes natural to us. People like you are outsiders, not of much consequence to us unless you link up with someone we care for. Believe me, we aren't here living in shame. People are just a nuisance we ignore, for the most part."

"Maybe you guys shouldn't tell me stuff," I change my mind.

"Tell her," Tyson orders. "And me."

My eyes meet his and my heart skips a beat at the intensity coming from him. Of course he wants me further entrenched, so entrenched I'd have no hope of ever extricating myself. I almost feel angry about that, but really, I'm more freaked out than anything. And what the heck... if I tell my family when I get home about what's happened here, I'm risking my life? Their lives?

"Just to say," I announce, knowing that not everyone here is listening but those in our immediate vicinity are. "I'd never, no matter what, do anything to put anyone here at risk."

"We know," Cat says, looking at me with a gentle expression.

"So, beyond us, do you believe in vampires, witches, aliens?"

"Not really. Or I never did before..." I say.

She nods.

Wow.

"Other shapeshifters. Fae. The list goes on..." Aunt Lucy adds. "Narrow minded people are abundant. There are lots of things that exist that they either don't see or that we simply choose not to let them see."

"Holy crap," I breathe.

Vampires? Witches? Fae?

"What about fortune tellers?" I ask, again thinking about Aunt Nelle.

"Fortune tellers are usually witches," Cat says. "Occasionally they're not, though, and in many of those cases it's because they're charlatans. Though some are descendants of witches and don't truly know it."

"Ah."

Whoa.

I focus on my food.

"Oh. You guys haven't got drinks. What to drink, guys?" Bailey asks.

"Something sparkly and clear. Like Sprite or 7-up if you have it?"

"Water for me," Ty says, and Bailey nods and slips away from the table.

Ty then leans over. "Sprite," he whispers and then kisses the mark on my neck. I shiver. "One of my first thoughts of you was that you looked like a sprite."

I snicker. "My Auntie Nelle used to tell me she thought I was switched at birth and came from fairies."

I see smiles on Cat's and Lucy's faces.

"Do fairies and werewolves pair up often?"

"They do," his mother chimes in. "And if they pair up with people, it's usually a calamity. Often, other supernaturals need to wade in to untangle the messes. I think Mason got back from one such mission a few months ago."

Wow.

"So, maybe I'm descendent of a sprite," I say. "Maybe way back."

"I painted a sprite when I was a kid and have that painting. I checked it the other night to see if she looked like you. Did I predict my future?"

I smile. "Did she look like me?"

He nods. "Yellow hair. No silly purple bits, though."

"Silly?" I lean back. "My purple highlights are silly?" I pout.

"They're cute," he says, "But a little silly. You should know I didn't ever find things cute before you."

I beam at him. "Aw shucks." I twirl a lock of blonde and purple.

He kisses the tip of my nose and steals another bite of my potato salad. "Hey! Eat your own!"

"EVERYONE, I NEED YOUR attention?" Riley is on the stage with a microphone in his hand.

He's smiling as the room hushes.

"You guys love any excuse for a party, so we agreed to come for the strawberry moon tonight, but turned out it was serendipitous timing because we had no idea when this got planned, that Tyson was about to come home."

Applause erupts in the place and Tyson looks caught off guard by it. His eyes sweep the room as Riley continues.

"Tyson, cousin, *brother*, we are beyond thrilled that you decided to come tonight. On behalf of all of us, I just wanna say *welcome home*. We hoped the day would come. We're thrilled it has. Congratulations on finding Ivy, and thank you Ivy for being here, too. We know it's down to you that he's here. And maybe also a pissed off rattler."

Everyone laughs. Except Tyson.

"It's a joke, baby," I tell him.

He doesn't find it funny. He stares stone-cold at Riley as if to admonish him for the joke.

Riley doesn't waver. He winks at Tyson with a big smile.

I didn't do anything good to get given thanks in a room filled to the brim with people. What did I do, other than plan a weekend getaway and have it go wrong? I smile anyway. I like these people so far.

"Now," Riley continues, "I know how much you guys love to cut up the dance floor, so now that we're all stuffed with all that delicious food, we've got some formalities to get out of the way and then DJ, our awesome DJ, is gonna get the fun started. Ty and Ivy, I know you two have plans right now but I hope you'll be back after that. Tyson, I bet I'm a better dancer than you are... Care to prove me wrong?"

Ty snickers.

"Back in ten minutes, everyone. Can our youth club get ready for your presentation?" He waves, getting a response of claps, woo-woo dog-pounds style hoots, and wolf-whistles.

Riley steps off the stage and people disperse, including those at our table. It's suddenly just us two.

"Have you ever danced?" I ask, turning my attention to Ty.

"Not really," he replies under his breath. "Some women have tried, but you don't wanna hear about that."

I chuckle. "You're right, I don't."

"Do you?" he asks me. "Dance?"

"Yeah. I love dancing," I say. "I took ballet, hip hop, tap. Started dancing at the age of three. Me and Amelia. She quit at about eleven, but I danced right up until I was eighteen. Love it. I wanted to teach dancing, actually, but I never did get that chance. Haven't given up the dream though. I got a job after school at a clothing store and just sort of wound up in the fashion industry from there." I shrug.

"Hm." He plays with my hair and then leans over and eats a strawberry off the lone remaining tart on my dessert plate.

"Do you wanna dance later?" I ask him.

"Maybe," he says with a smile.

I bite my lip. "Dancing can be very sensual," I say.

His eyebrows wiggle.

"I've met so many people. I'll never remember their names," I add.

"Why not?" he asks.

"Because we were introduced to so many people," I reason.

He tilts his head, looking at me quizzically.

"What?" I ask. "You'll remember every single name of every person we were introduced to tonight?"

"Yeah," he says, casually, then drains his water bottle.

"But, Tyson, there were a lot."

"Yeah," he says, as if it's no big deal.

"What's her name?" I point to an older lady walking by our table with her dessert plate.

"Fran Callahan," he says.

Oh. Okay.

I gesture to a child who is climbing up on the stage, looking up to no good. "What's that little boy's name?"

"Declan. He's Shepherd and Lorraine Creed's son. He's three. And he likes Paw Patrol."

I do a double-take. That little boy did try to tell Tyson his life story when he was introduced.

"What about her?" I gesture to another lady.

"Bailey's mother, Carrie Blackwood."

"Holy shit," I say.

He looks at me like he doesn't understand.

"You remember every single name of every single person here, Tyson?"

"Of course I do. I just met them."

I give my head an astonished shake. Wow.

Bailey comes back.

"What's your mom's name again?" I ask.

"Carrie," says Bailey as she sits down.

"And that little boy up there?" I see that little boy's father fetching him. The boy is throwing a temper tantrum.

"That's Declan."

Holy crap.

"You didn't believe me?" Tyson sounds affronted.

"It's astonishing. He remembers all of your names. All of them. Is that a shifter thing?"

Bailey shakes her head. "It's a Tyson thing. His father was the same. So was his father. These guys are stewards for their pack. They look after us like a shepherd tends his flock." She shrugs.

"So, no one else knows all their names?" I ask.

"Well, yeah. We all do but we've grown up together. So there's a difference."

Tyson is definitely their leader. She looks at him with a knowing expression. He stares at her a second and then at me and I can tell he knows this. Maybe he's coming to grips with it, too.

Maybe this guy isn't just supernatural in his ability to transform from man to wolf to man again. Maybe he's figuring out who he is. The intended shepherd of this flock of wolf shifters.

"Wanna go see your house and skip the next part of the party?" Bailey asks. "It's about to get started and you'll likely find it boring."

"Yes!" I exclaim.

Ty looks at me and he looks a little unsure.

"Can we?" I ask.

He sucks on his teeth for a second and then puts his hand on mine.

I put my free hand on top. "Sorry. If it's gonna be too much emotionally..."

"No. Let's go," he says and gets up. "I was interested in the next part, but don't worry."

"Oh. Sorry. We should stay."

"Don't worry," he says.

"Are you sure?"

He nods. "I am. Let's go."

Bailey leans over to speak to Cat and then we all rise.

"I'll run us over," Cat says, and we head out together to approach her SUV.

"How far is it?" I ask.

"Down the street from my clinic. Close."

Bailey calls out, "Shotgun!" and gets to the front door.

"Where?" Ty pulls me tight to him.

"That's Bailey claiming the front seat," I tell him.

"Oh," he says quietly, loosening his grip.

"Are you okay with this? I mean, you said you wanted to stay tonight, so..."

He nods but he doesn't look so sure.

"I'm sorry if my reaction made you feel on the spot. Or if you want to watch the presentation thing, we can do that. Just come after. Or we can just go back to the cabin."

He shakes his head. "No. It's fine. If I didn't want to, I'd say no. I wanted to spend the night to continue..." He trails off, looking like he's searching for the right words.

"Taking things in?" I offer.

He nods, opening the door for me so I climb in. He makes a grunt sound and then gets in.

"You okay?" I ask.

He leans over. "Your sweet ass was just about in my face for a second and it's been too long since I was inside of you."

"Tyson!" I gasp. "Your mother!"

"Understands alphas," Cat finishes.

Oh God.

"Especially a freshly mated one, right?" Bailey prompts.

"Not just that. Tyson's father was always like that. Your Grandma Carolyn told me that so was her husband. Get ready for a lifetime of insatiable husband," Cat says as she starts up her SUV.

I try to swallow and don't. I almost want to ask if they have weddings here or if there's just the whole knotting thing, but I don't want to ask these questions in front of Tyson. I'll ask Bailey later, maybe.

"Tyson's paternal grandmother and grandfather were at it like bunnies until the day he died," Cat says.

"How old was he?" I ask.

"Eighty-four."

"Holy crap," I say.

"Yep. Tyson, by the way, how would you feel about a breakfast tomorrow with me and your grandparents?"

"That sounds fine," Tyson says.

"Good. They'll be happy about that after having to share your attention tonight."

I get my seatbelt on and we're only in the car for about five minutes before we're stopping at a riverfront castle-like home.

"Oh wow," I say.

Gates are opening and this is where we're stopping.

"Behind the house is the Arcana Falls themselves, come." Bailey says.

She and Cat lead us across what looks, despite the dimness, like a beautifully manicured, lush front lawn.

We walk around back, and I see the set of waterfalls to the right of the banks. We're not talking Niagara Falls or anything so grandiose, but the river forks behind the house and to the right there is a set of small waterfalls probably about fifty feet up. The water trickles and trails down multiple levels of rocks. It's so pretty. There's also a stone set of stairs winding up to a giant rock ledge on the side. It's very pretty. It's also lit from behind.

"I present the Arcana Falls. Behind there is a beautiful hidden cave," Bailey says. "There's a lot of magic here. The spot is considered sacred to our pack. Witches have even come here over time to cast important spells, though not in several years, am I right, Cat?"

"That's right."

"Wow. It's so beautiful," I say.

"Tyson was most likely conceived back there," Cat whispers. "It's got a magical level of romantic ambience."

I giggle. I bet it does.

"And I think it's particularly a good spot for making shifter babies with extreme alpha tendencies," she adds.

It's dark out, but I can see the whites of his teeth as he smiles big at his mother.

"Hint, hint," she says, elbowing me gently with a huge smile on her face.

I laugh nervously.

"Come back and see it again during the day," Cat suggests. "See how special it is during the daylight."

"Maybe me and Ivy will go first. You can all visit some other time," Tyson says, cheekily, with laughter in his voice.

"Tyson!" I gasp.

Cat laughs heartily. Bailey is smiling.

We head toward the large house, featuring turrets at either side. We head to a set of French doors under a pergola-covered patio that Cat opens.

She turns a lamp on. Wow. We're in a beautiful space. It's big, open, and furnished with antiques. It smells like citrus furniture polish. My guess is that someone was here today cleaning, hoping we'd visit.

The main floor has a vast kitchen with a perfect blend of old country and modern touches. It's been upgraded in recent years, for certain, but has been done in a way that blends the old and new. There's a greenhouse attached at the side of the kitchen.

"A beautiful place to grow vegetables," Cat says. "Best tomatoes and peppers I've ever tasted have come from this kitchen. Herbs, too."

Tyson is looking at me. Intently.

I know what he's thinking. That this is perfect for me.

She shows us a massive dining room with a dining suite that seats eighteen. I don't think I've ever seen a formal dining suite this large. Through the library is a sitting room that leads to an office and library combination filled to the brim with old books.

The basement is the most alpha man-cave space I've ever seen complete with billiards tables and a bar that's big enough for a restaurant.

Upstairs are six bedrooms, including the master suite, which is not only a beautiful space with a massive spa-like bathroom, but this place is clearly a family-oriented home. The master has an attached nursery.

The whole place probably hasn't had a thing changed in thirty years other than that kitchen. Everything is classic rich antiques with neutral colors and warm tones, and the place is clean and tidy. Not a speck of dust. It's as if it has been preserved or has been recently cleaned to perfection in anticipation of Ty's arrival.

We're standing in the nursery and Tyson's got his eyes on a rocking chair.

Cat caresses the chair and there's a weighty silence.

"Your cradle is in the attic," she says softly. "I couldn't look at it day after day."

"He died in this room, didn't he?" Tyson says.

Cat's back goes straight. "He did. You feel it?"

"I do," Tyson says.

I do, too, oddly. But I say nothing.

I watch Ty wrap his arm around her and kiss the top of her head.

The silence in the room is loaded with pain. I want to give them privacy, so my eyes move to Bailey at the same time as her gaze moves to me. We're of the same mind.

"Come see." She grabs my hand and we leave Ty and his mother alone.

She shows me that attached to two other large bedrooms is what I'd imagine as an intended playroom. It's lined with bookshelves. They're empty. There are small rocking chairs big enough for children on either side. There's also a big toy chest, though it's also empty.

"Tyson loves books," I whisper, feeling a chill run up my back.

"He should've read them here," she says softly. "With brothers and sisters that he never got to have. So sad. But it doesn't have to keep being sad. You and Tyson could fill this place with kids. Fill this room with toys and books. Cat can sit in that rocker in the nursery and hold a grandchild in each arm and build new memories instead of feeling sad about the things that were taken from her."

I swallow down a lump.

Tyson and his mother come in then and they both have expressions that tell me they had words about the past.

I wrap my arm around his waist and snuggle in. I get a kiss dropped on my head and a squeeze from him.

"Well, it's yours if you want it," Cat says, her eyes bright with moisture. "No rush. You just tell me when you're ready. And it won't bother me a bit if you redecorate. If you want the furnishings, they're yours. If you don't, there are a few things I'd like and a few things I know my sister and Riley or his siblings might like."

Tyson says nothing but his eyes are on me.

I smile, noncommittally.

"Are we going back to the party?" I ask.

"What do you want to do?" he replies, fingertips caressing my face along the hairline.

"It could be fun to go back for a bit. Have a dance or two."

He smiles. "Okay, baby."

I smile.

"I had the bedsheets changed and put some basics in the fridge for a breakfast for the morning," Cat says. "But if we can eat here with your grandparents, I'll bring more food over and cook for everyone. There are extra toothbrushes and other toiletries in the cabinets in the master bathroom, too."

"That's very thoughtful," I say.

"Sounds good," Tyson says softly. "You can make more of that coffee cake?"

"I absolutely can."

"He ate three quarters of it!" I tell her. "It was delicious."

"I'm happy to make one whenever you like," Cat says, beaming with joy. "Bailey? Let's meet them in the car in case they want to look at anything else alone."

"Right," Bailey says.

They slip out.

Tyson puts his other arm around me and pulls me to his chest.

"This would've been where you read your books. Maybe with some brothers and sisters," I say and then I burst into tears and bury my face in his shirt.

His arms come around me tight. "Don't cry, my Ivy." His voice has softness in it.

I look up at him.

"If your uncle wasn't dead, I'd maybe kill him myself."

He smiles and puts his lips to my forehead. "You'd probably have to get in line."

"All the stuff that you were robbed of. These people are awesome, Ty."

"Yeah," he whispers, his eyes roving my face.

"If they know any witches, maybe we should ask them to bring him back over and over so we can take turns killing him in the most torturous way possible."

He scoffs while using his thumbs to dash the tears away from my cheeks. "It's crossed my mind. He spoke of witches often. I know he knew some. He took me with him when he went to see an old witch sometimes. I waited outside always. I don't know what he talked to her about."

"Hm."

"Her eyes were very strange on me. Like she knew me." He shivers. "Anyway, you sure you feel like going back to this party?" he asks.

"Yeah. If you do. It'd be nice."

"Okay. Let's go."

We step outside and it's dark now, and the moon is up high. And it's pinkish red.

I'm almost about to tell him about me having to go tomorrow, feeling like it might be a good time to bring it up, but I chicken out.

I'll talk to him about it when we get back.

37

TYSON

It's been an enlightening evening in some ways and a baffling one in others.

I didn't think about having other family before, beyond Cornelius. I had no idea my uncle Atticus existed before Bailey told me about him and no clue I would feel an immediate connection with him. He looks like Cornelius, but stronger. Bigger. And his eyes are different. It's only now I realize how manic Cornelius's eyes were. And the kindness in Atticus's eyes when our eyes met had an immediate effect.

Having all of these people around me with my Ivy here too instantly brought me a feeling of peace and completeness that I've never had before.

Until Mason Quinn.

The sensations I got from him immediately put me on alert. I did not fucking like what I felt from him as he approached my woman. It's as if his mind is wrong. His thoughts about her are wrong. The way his eyes touch her is fucking wrong.

Riley asked me to let it go and told me he'd talk to me later to explain. I need to have that conversation with him now, because my immediate instinct tells me that Mason wants Ivy. *My* Ivy.

Just the barest notion of anyone wanting her makes me want to let the angry red haze wash over me so that I can erase them. Rip them to shreds. This wasn't a bare notion. At all.

"Talk to me now," I ordered.

Riley asked me to trust him. Looked into my eyes when he did, and I read truth. He told me he'd talk to me later and said that something wasn't right with Mason, they knew this for a few days and based on that reaction and what all the alphas in the pack felt from him, he was going to be seen to by healers and elders to figure out what was going on with his mind. That's all he told me. I need to know more.

The reason I have had the life I've had is because nobody stopped the man whose mind was wrong in time to prevent him from killing my father, from hurting my mother, from ripping me from my life.

Ivy giggles at something one of the women has said and my focus moves to her. Seeing my woman happy in this space, interacting with these people who are my people, who feel like they're my people? I like it. Where I thought just days ago that I'd like nothing more than to have her all to myself and that I'd be content to live with only her and any children we made alone... now I feel vastly different. I feel like I want to care for all of them and give everything to them, and especially give them to her, so that she has a community around her.

Catrina Savage, Lucy Savage, Riley, the grandparents, Riley's father Atticus Savage – these people feel like they're mine, too, even more than the pack is mine.

They. Feel. Like. Mine.

This feels right.

And that house? The waterfall? The smell in the air around there? It also feels right.

Is everything in my life about to come together? Do I have a pack, a family, a mate? Am I where I'll belong? With purpose?

I look at her as we head inside the barn to rejoin the party and she's smiling and chatting happily with Bailey Blackwood, looking completely at ease.

We step across the threshold and drinks are put into hers and Bailey's hands by a younger woman who looks me over from head to toe and then lazily sizes me back up from toe to head again.

I recognize her type. The same as those female predators at the bar I used to go to. They were on the hunt. They wanted their drinks bought. They wanted men to lust after them. They wanted cock. She's a shifter woman, full-blooded shifter, and she was introduced to me earlier as Sherry Creed.

I smell arousal on her as she looks at me. Another girl steps up and smiles. Leona. She wasn't in the receiving line, but she was at the clinic the day Ivy was bitten by the snake.

I nod at Leona and then my eyes meet Sherry's. I look through her, showing her that I'm not interested.

Another woman, similarly aged, and dressed demurely and giving off a shy aura catches up to them. Audrey King. Half-shifter.

Ivy kisses me and tells me to go have some 'alpha talk' as she trots with her drink along behind those girls.

I want to warn her about Sherry's. I don't get the chance. Riley is coming toward me.

"Bailey," I call out.

Bailey spins around and comes back.

"One sec, Riley; I don't like that," I tell him.

"Sherry is an unmated alpha female," Riley tells me, clearly seeing what I saw. "She knows you're mated. She won't likely be dumb enough to make a play. If she does, we'll deal with her. Don't worry. Look. Aunt Cat's heading in that direction to warn her. She just likes what she sees when she sees you. Don't stress about it."

"Alpha females," I repeat.

"Most of our females are beta or omega by nature. There are a few alpha females," Bailey says.

And I think I've smelled this one before. I think I might even have encountered her scent as wolf. In my years living only as a wolf, I encountered other wolves, mostly ordinary, non-shifting, who all ran at the sight of me, but once, I caught the scent of a female shifter. I didn't let her get close. I'm pretty sure it was this woman.

"Take care of Ivy around her," I order. "I don't like the feeling in my gut right now."

She slices her hand up in the air and stops at her right brow, nods at me and then catches up with Ivy, Audrey, Leona, and Sherry.

"Drink?" Riley asks and leads me toward the bar.

I don't typically drink alcohol. I hated the way it smelled on my uncle. I hated, even more, the way it made him behave.

"I'll have a beer." I don't mind beer too much.

Riley grabs a mug and opens the tap on a barrel that's on its side, pouring me some.

"More about Mason Quinn, Riley. What the fuck was that?"

"I know it tweaked you, but Mase is solid, man. He's rock-solid in his loyalty. He got back Monday morning, right after you two went home from the clinic. He was disappointed he didn't get a chance to meet you. But then, man, he said he didn't feel right. And he went around in circles all day around the village. He shifted and went in more circles."

"Who's his mate?"

"He doesn't have one. He said he caught a scent of the woman who might be his mate and couldn't find her to make sure. He knew a trail led to your place and wouldn't take it."

"He doesn't think my Ivy is his."

Riley winces.

Does he?

I feel my blood heat up, my fists clench. What the fuck?

I repeat myself.

"He doesn't think she's his, Riley."

"Not exactly, he says. He's confused, though. He's having trouble figuring it out. I told him, there's nothing confusing about it. When he smells her, he'll know it. He knows she's not his or he would've followed that trail straight to Ivy."

He's right. He will know it. I had not a doubt. No confusion that Ivy was the woman for me.

I see my woman dancing in a group with Bailey, Sherry, Audrey, Leona, and three other women the range in age from Ivy's to likely the age of my mother. They all look to be having fun.

My woman moves gracefully, her hair moving, her hips swaying, as she drinks from a clear bottle containing a red liquid.

She catches my eyes and smiles at me, then one of the women, Carrie Blackwood, Bailey's mother, touches her arm and speaks to her while they continue to all move together to the music.

I like watching my woman dance.

She's gorgeous. She's graceful. She's having fun and looking at me like she loves me.

Does she realize she looks at me that way? She's done it a lot today. The past few days, really. I catch her watching me. When I'm chopping wood, cutting grass. I've seen her watching me when I wake up and get the impression she's been doing it a while. It feels good to open my eyes to her gazing at me with love written all over her face, her hair all messy, and my fluids leaking from her sore cunt.

I love her more than any man has loved any woman; I'm sure of this.

I won't let anyone take her from me.

Another song starts and Ivy looks excited as she begins dancing with more confidence, with more of a sway to her hips, with a look on her face like no one is here, just her and the song that she sings the words to.

Something makes the hairs rise on the back of my neck.

I follow the sensation with my eyes and catch sight of Mason Quinn on the opposite end of the barn and he has a glass to his lips and his eyes are on Ivy. My Ivy. He's drinking whisky by a doorway. I smell it from here. Whisky. Fucking *fuck*. My back straightens.

He's watching her and she's dancing with allure. Her ass is moving to the beat. Her dress shows so much leg. Even her ankles look appealing with all those straps crisscrossing over her feet.

"Wait." Riley touches my arm, obviously picking up on my mood shift.

I bare my teeth and a growl moves up from my gut, getting caught in my throat.

Riley's eyes flash with worry. "Let's talk to him. I'm sure he wouldn't be here if –"

I swallow it down but I'm already on the move, so Riley doesn't get a chance to finish.

I see Jason move in on one side of Mason and Joel on the other. As they get there, all eyes are pointed at mine except for Mason's. He's still watching Ivy. He's not even aware I'm coming for him until I get in front of him and stare.

I feel Lincoln and Grey move in step with Riley, flanking me.

"Why are your eyes on what's mine?"

His eyes meet mine and I see what I can only construe as a flash of challenge in them. His mouth twitches as if he's about to say something sarcastic.

And something strange occurs to me. It's almost as if he's got a right here. That something strange washes straight through me. I can't label it. I don't know what the fuck it is.

This guy feels like she's his. And his feelings are... what... real? Legitimate? I can't label it. It's hurting my head. My head is swimming with confusion because in his head, he has a right to look at her and right now he doesn't fear me. When he met me earlier, he was filled with other emotions. Remorse. Confusion. Conflict. Right now, he doesn't feel conflict or remorse. Confusion? Yes. But something in addition to that. Entitlement.

The music changes to a new song with a slower tempo and Ivy's scent is suddenly upon me as she's right here, reaching for me.

"Hey, handsome. Wanna dance with me?"

He can reach her if he reaches out. She's between him and I. All he has to do is reach and he could touch her hair, her arm, he could reach out and snatch her.

I watch, as if in slow motion, as he inhales and his eyes change. His pupils grow as he takes in her scent. He's breathing Ivy into his lungs, into himself. He's confused about why he's doing it, but that doesn't change the fact that he is doing it.

My Ivy.

Blood rushes through my ears and heat shunts through my body as I launch myself at him. He flies backwards with the force of my palms.

I hear gasps as he crashes into a table filled with drinks.

I see red. Only red. Lightning thrusts sharply up my spine, and I haul him off a table he's landed on and he's up off the floor in my grasp. I roar in his face with a deafening force that I've never had. It's even more powerful than the day at Cornelius's corpse.

I want to rip his heart out. His throat. But, first, his eyes. His eyes that touched her. His lungs that are full of her scent. I want to crush it all.

Something is stopping me. Something halts me from crushing his bones to dust.

He submits, curling into himself, showing me his throat.

I roar again, and I half-shift while the noise is still blaring from my mouth.

The floor shakes beneath us with the force of my anger and my teeth have extended. My jaw is inches from his throat.

Something inside prevents me from closing my teeth around it and ending his life. Something. What?

And there she is. At my feet, cowering, eyes wild with fear.

She's mine.

Only mine.

I drop him and rip the shirt from my body before I go for my fly.

I need her.

I need to fill myself with her. I need the warmth of her skin against my heart. She'll smell like me and he'll see. He'll watch me take her, knot her, he'll know that she's mine. Mine only.

Mine. Fucking. Only.

I stare into his eyes, which are filled with pain as he watches me, immobile. I push her to her belly on the floor and line up, rip her panties sideways, and haul her back by them because she tries to move away. I then spear into her from behind. My cock has never been harder. Her cunt has never felt better.

She's trying to claw the floor, trying to get away. I sink my teeth into the back of her neck and hold her there until she stops squirming. And then I release my hold at her throat as I stare at him while I fuck her. I throw my head back and roar as I thrust my cock inside my mate, over and over, grunting as I feel her body around me. She's mine. This beautiful little sprite is only mine. I feel her tightness around my cock as I ram up inside her with a slow and rhythmic pace. I show Mason Quinn that she belongs to me. Only me.

His eyes are bleeding. He stares at me with blood trickling down his face, regret washed across his features.

I roar, blowing his hair back with the force of it.

He needs to see that she comes beautifully for me. That she loves what I do to her. That I will be the only one to do these things to her.

I flip her to her back and thrust back inside.

"Mine!" I shout at him in a guttural tone that comes from the pit of my being. The very center of me. It's not just me as man, it's also my wolf telling him she belongs only to me.

I would kill him now, while I continue to fuck her, if I could. Slam my cock in her while my teeth tears his flesh apart, devouring him so that he's part of me every time I fuck her from now on. Why can't I reach out and rip him apart? It doesn't make sense. Is it because he's in a submissive pose? Something is physically preventing me from ending him.

He needs to know.

So, I knot.

I knot because I know he has never knotted. He's not expanding inside her; I am. He has no idea how good this feels.

I do.

I knot so he can watch how beautifully my mate comes for me.

She won't ever come for him. He won't ever know what this feels like.

She's crying out and I laugh. I laugh and then I halfway shift again to show him who I am. I'm man. I'm wolf. I'm both. I'm his alpha. His superior. And she's mine. *Fucking* mine.

When I finish knotting her, I'll kill him.

I roar out as I come inside her.

She's on the floor under me, coming for me. Her beautiful pussy spasms around my knot and her entire body is wracked with tremors from the force of it.

I grunt as I continue to spill into her. It feels incredible to know he sees. He sees how she comes for me; he sees that she's mine only.

I reach for her hair to make sure he can also see my mark on her. So all of them can see. For the past moments, it's been no one in this room for me but me, my mate, and Mason Quinn. But they're all still here. I feel their presence. I'll show them her mark so that if any of them get any inkling of fantasy about my Ivy, about being me, they'll know that she's mine. Even that alpha woman will know. Ivy Adeline Savage is mine and I am hers.

My eyes catch sight of my hand and I realize I'm still half-shifted. I pull it back and everything recedes.

My knot releases and my fluids spill from her.

I exhale and it feels like the first exhale since I saw his eyes on her. My eyes move to the floor.

To my Ivy.

My Ivy who is beneath me, leaking my fluid from between her beautiful legs in her pretty dress. She's bleeding. Blood on her knees. Blood on her hands. Blood between her beautiful legs.

Her face. It's wrong. It's so very wrong.

Horror washes over me.

38

IVY

He's Tyson again. He's looking at me like I'm actually here, like he actually sees me and it's dawning on him, what he's just done.

I need out. I need away. There are so many eyes on me. So many saw him fuck me, saw him turn into that monster and fuck me while he was a monster. He wasn't a wolf. He was wolf-like, but not.

I know he's torn me. Torn me between my legs and my blood is mixed with his semen coating my inner thighs.

There are so many sets of eyes on me. And they're all sad.

Sad, *sad* eyes. Except his. His irises were red, and his eyes are filled with rage. Or they were. Now, I don't know.

I can't look.

I see sadness now but saw horror in the other eyes all around me. Vertigo makes them all sway, makes them look like they come closer, grow larger, and then move farther away and shrink.

Bailey is crying. Cat has her arms around her, and Cat's eyes are haunted. His mother. His mother saw all of that.

I cover my face with my hands, which are bleeding, from when I was trying to crawl away. He threw me aside when he went after that guy and I have splinters in my hands from the rough wood floor. And my knees, too, from when he dragged me back by my thong. I can't even feel that pain yet because I'm just... I can't look at their eyes anymore.

A sliver from my palm pokes my cheek. I pull my bleeding hands away and blink at them.

I'm up and moving. He has me; he's carrying me out of there. Voices fill my ears, but I don't know what they're saying.

It's bedlam all around me.

There's shouting. Tyson is shouting over his shoulder at the guy that's on the floor, the guy with the bloody streaks on his face. The guy Tyson threw. The guy I thought Tyson was going to kill.

There are other men crowding us, trying to calm Tyson down.

I curl into myself and squeeze my eyes tight, trying to block it all out. I can't comprehend this. I can't.

I SMELL CITRUS FURNITURE polish and I hear low voices talking.

I'm under blankets, in a soft cloud.

My eyes open. I guess I fainted.

And then I woke while Cat tended to the bleeding and splinters. She also rewrapped my ankle, telling me in a soft and motherly voice that I can ditch the ankle bandage the next day, ditch all the bandages the next day. And then I fainted again, I think. I don't even know...

And everything slams into me with the force of a brick wall that I've driven straight into.

One second I'm asking him to dance, the next, he's throwing me behind him, and I fall as he attacks someone he threw about ten feet away, then he roared so loud that it deafened me, it felt like an earthquake shook the room. Before the noise and shaking stopped, he was undressing and turning me to my belly.

I thought for a second before I got spun around that he was taking his clothes off to shift, to fight as a wolf against that guy he'd roared at, but then he's on me, spearing into me from behind. In front of dozens upon dozens of people in a crowded barn dance.

Bailey told me that after those awards ceremonies the younger ones were leaving and thank God for that because that meant no small kids or younger teens would've seen that.

Seen me.

Me.

Getting screwed in public.

Seen me fighting to crawl away, only to get dragged back by my red lace thong, in front of everybody. Pain sliced through me as I was dragged. I had splinters from the wood floor in my palms, in my knees.

And the thing he became when he flipped me, and that knot filled me and began vibrating inside me?

He was Tyson, but also the black wolf. At the same time. Like the definition of a two-legged wolf man instead of a wolf down on all fours. Hair everywhere, though not as thick. His nose halfway between man and animal.

And his hands were like his normal hands, but larger.

And his body heat? Like I was inside of an oven with him while he did that to me.

And it was like I wasn't there. He was losing it. He was growling and snapping his teeth at the other guy while he thrust into me over and over.

And it was horrible. Every second of it.

Especially when my body turned on me and without a choice because of that vibrating and pulsing thing inside me I was climaxing.

Climaxing!

Climaxing in front of everyone while on the floor. I climaxed so hard beneath that monster who fucked me hard while holding me down with his giant hands. In front of everyone. I cried out an orgasm with my eyes tight shut because I didn't want to look at them. Didn't want to look at Bailey, his mother, his fucking grandparents who were probably still there, too.

My neck hurts, too; I think he broke skin when he held me down with his teeth to it.

I whimpered and writhed under him, crying out as his hot cum filled me, spilled from me. And while he was still coming, he began licking at that spot on my neck, laughing while I was writhing like a come-drunk slut under him.

I'm mortified. Horrified.

And my heart is absolutely shattered.

A sob tears out of me.

"Ivy?" Tyson's leaning over me, trying to talk to me.

Tyson. Tyson who did *that* to me.

My eyes open and I scream. I scream at the sight of him and then I'm running.

I'm running and others are moving sideways to let me go.

He chases me and catches me in the hallway, hooking an arm around my waist from behind, lifting me high and scooping under my knees with his other arm so he can pull me high and tight against his chest. He's carrying me back, making 'shh' sounds.

"Purr for her, Tyson," an older man's voice orders.

Tyson starts doing that as he approaches the bed and I go from struggling to lax. I'm bawling into the hard chest that I'm plastered against and can't break free from as he gets into the big sleigh bed in his parents' bedroom in that beautiful castle-house, keeping me tight in his arms. Rocking me. Rocking me and his chest vibrating that soothing sound straight through me.

I'm trembling so hard. And I can't stop. My body aches from how much. It's like convulsions.

"Harder, Ty," the male voice urges, and the sound gets louder. The sensation in my chest gets heavier along with my limbs.

My eyes drift shut as I feel like a warm blanket wraps tight around me. That blanket is Tyson.

39

TYSON

I fucked up. I fucked up huge.

She's broken.

I broke my beautiful Ivy. And I don't know how to fix her.

I'm in the bedroom in the house I was born in, holding her in my arms in my parents' bed and she's asleep, but one look at her and I know she's broken.

"Why? Why did I do that?" I ask Riley.

Ivy stares at the wall, like she's not even seeing it. Her lower lip quivers and she's breathing hard, but she's exhausted from crying so much. She cried so fucking much. And I did that. I made her cry like that.

Riley, Atticus, and Cat are with me. So is an older alpha called Lorenzo who I was told was on the previous alpha council with my father.

They're all here for moral support. And the other alphas who aren't with Mason Quinn are on the property with other retired alphas from the last council.

They're all here. For who though? Me or her? Or Mason Quinn?

"Tyson," Atticus says, "Something's wrong with Mason. He would never intentionally go after your mate. He wasn't even acting as if she was his mate. We have no explanation for his behavior. It wasn't right."

"He's here," Bailey says from the hallway. "Outside with Linc and Jase. He wants to talk to Tyson."

"Hear him out," Riley urges.

Lorenzo nods at me with meaning.

"A man whose mind is gone needs to be taken out," I tell them. "Or things like Cornelius happen." I give my mother a meaningful look.

She looks at the floor.

"We all felt it," Riley assures. "The alpha council and our elder alpha council all have a connection and every one of us felt exactly what happened in that moment before you reacted. Something is wrong with him. That's the only explanation. We have to get to the bottom of that. For him as much as for you. We need to know why so that we can fix it. Let's talk to him."

"I won't leave Ivy."

"I'll care for her, Tyson," my mother says.

"No! I'm not fucking leaving her."

Ivy's trembling harder in my arms. And then she's trying to squirm out of them.

I rock her, holding her tighter to me, even though she's struggling to try to get away from me.

"Purr for her," Lorenzo tells me. "A female finds comfort from their mate's purr, even if she's angry with you. It's a good tool to have in your arsenal."

I purr and she settles. She's always changed behavior since the first time I purred for her. But though she's settling, she's again weeping. She's weeping in my arms. And I fucking hate it.

"Most women, even shifters, want their pairings to be private," Lorenzo says. "But non-shifters, particularly. You've got a long road of groveling ahead of you. I'll go speak with Mason and be back."

He pats my back and leaves. I continue to rock her.

"I'm sorry, Ivy. So sorry, baby, please forgive me," I whisper against her hair while I rock her. I called her baby because I like when she calls me baby. And because she gave me soft eyes when I did it earlier.

She's weeping and curled into herself. I can't see her pretty purple eyes. Fuck. This hurts.

This hurts more than any pain I've felt. Ever.

When the red haze comes over me, I do bad things. I never thought I'd do something that would upset her so much. The despair I feel from her is crushing my lungs. It's hard to breathe for me. My heart beats too fast. My heart hurts.

I'm no better than Cornelius who took my mother against her will. I howl and don't even realize I've half-shifted with her in my arms until I hear "Pull back, son." Uncle Atticus is talking to me. "Pull back now, Tyson. You'll frighten her more."

I shake it off.

Ivy's mine, but clearly I've broken something in her by doing this. And doing it, I've also broken myself, I think.

I've never stayed half-shifted for more than a brief time. Or I don't think I have. Except for when… I shake it off. I can't think about the times Cornelius taunted me to get me to do bad things. That's why I call it the red haze. I see blood afterwards because I rip things apart.

I've never felt such anger before. And such despair now.

"Why couldn't I kill him? I wanted to fucking kill him."

"You knew," he says, "Deep down, you knew, Tyson. We all knew something wasn't right. You don't know Mase like we do, but you didn't kill him because though he straddled a line, he didn't cross it."

"And you know him better than you know me. Of course you'd take his side." I glare at Riley.

"No. This wasn't about picking sides. We're all tethered, cuz. If we weren't, you'd have been able to go through with ripping his throat out."

"Why the fuck didn't you protect my mate?" I shout.

They should've put me down.

No. Then she'd be free for Mason to take her.

Fuck. The urge to shift is overwhelming right now. To shift and tear apart everything in my field of vision.

"That's something beyond us, Ty," Riley says softly. "She's yours. And she's your responsibility."

Fuck. And I failed at that spectacularly. I slump.

"Here. This'll help." Cat hands me a glass of water.

I drink it down.

"What was it?" I ask as I pass her back the empty glass. It wasn't just water. Something bitter sits on my tongue.

"Just a mild sedative. It might not do much, but it should help you sleep. Your heart rate is too high. You won't let me take your stats, but I can see by your skin tone, can hear that it's too high. And you'll need rest. What you've been through tonight? You and Ivy both need rest."

"You drugged me," I accuse. "Don't give me shit without telling me," I hiss.

She jerks back, face falling. "I'm sorry. I'm trying to help."

"Fuck," I snap. "I don't take pills."

"Talk to Mason," Lorenzo says, coming back in. "He's confused. If she were his, he wouldn't be confused."

"He won't be anywhere near her," I state, pointing at them all.

"He doesn't wanna be near her, Tyson," Lorenzo raises his voice. "He wants you outside. Talk to him. You'll see. He regrets–"

I shake my head. "I can't worry about Mason Quinn right now."

I have to fix her.

I know that every individual in this pack is my responsibility. I know this deep in my gut. I can't deal with him right now.

She comes first.

But I'm failing.

I'm failing at being a mate.

I'm failing at being part of this pack. There's no way in the world I can think about leading this pack.

I fucked up huge.

I'm not worthy of their adoration, their loyalty, or their *welcome home*. *I don't belong here.*

"I'm taking Ivy home." I rise with her in my arms.

"Stay," Cat says. "Rest. Deal with all of it in the morning."

I glare at her, but she doesn't back off this time. She puts her hand on my arm. "Tyson. This isn't a typical situation. Please don't go. Please stay while we try to sort it out. I'm heading to go examine Mason now. I've already been in touch with specialists in Scotland at the university for some advice on what this could be. I hope to hear back in a few hours from them. Please, don't go. Stay here while we figure this out. Let's try to figure this out together. We're all stronger together than we are apart. That's what a pack is, my son. We're here for one another."

"I just want peace and quiet. To take her home and–"

Atticus touches my shoulder and gives me an expression steeped in emotion. "Stay, Tyson. Please. Let us help you both through this. We're here for you."

"We'll go. We'll leave you two in peace," Riley adds. "Me and your mom will be downstairs. We'll sleep in the family room and be here if you need us."

I sit on the bed with a sigh.

"We'll figure this out," Cat says and leans over to touch my temple with a kiss and then she drops a kiss on the top of Ivy's head. "I promise we will not stop until we figure it out."

Ivy's cradled close to my chest, but I can't see her face. I listen for her breathing. She's not sleeping.

Riley, Lorenzo, and Atticus have gone.

"Did he ever do this to you?" I ask my mother.

She shakes her head.

"And Cornelius wanted you? He showed that to him? With no confusion?"

She nods. "He was terrible at hiding it. Most times he didn't even try."

"Why? Why could my father control himself and I can't? Mason Quinn didn't... his mind isn't..." I stop speaking.

I can't describe what I felt from him. I can't describe that he wasn't crossing a line but that it felt, to me, like Ivy belonged with him, not me. With him. As if she was supposed to be his. I felt like an imposter. I felt like I had no right to the pack, to the family, to her. And I wasn't fucking having it, not the Ivy part.

Cat kisses my head again. "Tiberius wasn't perfect. Not even close. You're not perfect, either. You've had a very different journey from his and this is all part of your journey with her. It's gonna be work to fix it, but you can fix it. The thing with Mason... I don't know what it is, but it's not like with Cornelius. He's not an unstable person, but he hasn't been well since Monday."

Monday, when he got back to me and Ivy in their village.

I put my mouth to Ivy's forehead.

She's shivering in my arms. Saying nothing. I know she's not sleeping; she's just shivering in my arms. She's afraid. Of me.

Maybe with them gone, she'll listen to my apology. Maybe she'll melt against me instead of being stiff and trembling.

I bring my body temperature up a little to help with her shivering.

"I'll see you in the morning. I'm just downstairs if you need anything," my mother says, then leaves, shutting the door.

There's a pitcher of water and ice cubes on the bedside table with two tall glasses.

I pour a glass, still cradling Ivy to my chest with my free hand. She squirms away from me as I bring it to my lips, hoping to get that bitter taste off my tongue. Our eyes meet.

I pass her the glass before I drink any.

Her eyes are filled with hate.

Is that hate I see? Is it truly hate?

She looks away, as if she could barely stand to look at me long enough to show me that hate.

"Ivy, please. I'm sorry. I made a terrible mistake."

She shakes her head, looking the other way, cradling herself with both arms.

"Ivy?"

She won't even look at me. Her feet dangle from the side of the bed but her face is turned away.

I put the glass down, then drop to the floor, putting my forehead to her knees.

"He – you're mine. And I didn't... I don't know what –"

My words aren't adequate. I swallow and try again.

"Ivy, the haze. The haze came over me and I wasn't me ... I was me but that other me. I didn't realize the effect of what I was doing. I had a single-minded focus. Stop him. Show him. And I'm sorry. I'm so sorry."

She says nothing.

"I'll do anything, Ivy. Anything to show you I'm sorry."

"Do you mean that?" she whispers hoarsely, still not looking at me.

I'm so relieved she's talked to me. I breathe out my relief, and hope it pushes any of that toxic haze that's left out of me.

"I mean that. I swear I mean that, Ivy."

"Then go. That's what I want. Leave me alone."

"Why?" My throat hurts.

"I need space," she says.

"Ivy..."

"I… need…"

It sounds like the words are being torn from her.

"Space!"

Her voice breaks at the end and it feels like a boulder drops, landing on top of my chest and just staying there. Her body is wracked with sobs again. Even her curls in her hair jiggle with it as she weeps, cradling herself, her beautiful eyes hidden from me.

"I'll send Bailey in. To stay with you?"

"Fine," she bites off.

I rise and lean over, taking her chin into my hand so that she looks at me.

I immediately release her chin when I see the expression on her face. I can't look at her looking at me like that.

I put my lips to her forehead.

"Please forgive me."

"Never," she vows softly and with what feels like blades dripping from her words. Jagged steel coated in blood she wishes was mine.

She hates me.

I try to summon up a purr for her, to comfort her, but I can't seem to do it. My throat feels like it's lined with broken glass.

"I'll come back in the morning. I'll give you space," I croak out.

No response.

I almost had everything. A family. A pack. Brothers to run with.

A perfect soulmate.

Almost.

But right now it feels like I have less than the nothing I had when I spent all those years in the woods alone.

Was I better off there?

More important, was Ivy better off with me there?

40

IVY

Someone thankfully brought my purse, so I put it over my shoulder and slowly open the door.

I creep past him and he doesn't wake. He's asleep on the floor directly outside the bedroom door.

I've waited for hours, it feels like, and I'm glad Bailey never came in. Finally, I'm ready to try this. I'm going to escape or maybe die trying, because that's all I can think to do. Get as far away as I can.

I catch a glimpse of his sleeping face and the pain that cleaves through me at the sight of his profile is excruciating. It hurts just too much to look at him, so I won't. I tear my eyes away and don't allow myself to look as I step over his sleeping body.

While tiptoeing down the stairs I hear voices, so I peer carefully around a corner and see it's just the television.

Cat's sleeping on a sofa and Riley sleeps on a chair.

A silver and black wolf sleeps on the floor by Cat. I don't know who that is. He's snoring a little. He's massive.

They're all obviously tuckered out.

And good. Because maybe I'll get out of here in one piece.

I get outside and see Bailey standing there against the wall, smoking a cigarette. This surprises me.

"Oh, hi," she says.

Her eyes show me that she knows what I've been through.

Actually, it dawns that she was there while Cat was pulling the splinters out of my hands and knees with tweezers, disinfecting them, crying – no, sobbing – as she passed supplies to Cat and I just sat there bawling while Tyson paced the room and Riley tried to calm him. Cat and Bailey both cried with me during that thing that happened.

Bailey left while Cat bandaged me up, and others came into the room and that was when Tyson insisted on holding me again. He made me stay with him while he purred and I slipped under, in and out of some weird dream-like state.

I look around, feeling panicked that I'm about to be stopped.

"Are you taking off?" she asks, a plume of smoke floating out of her mouth.

She says this so calmly. Like she won't stop me.

"Are you gonna stop me? Or tell him?"

She shakes her head. "I don't blame you a bit. You need a ride?"

I'm shocked. I stand there and stare, jaw slack.

"You look wrecked, Ivy. Like that totally, completely shattered all your hopes and dreams."

I shiver and my chin trembles. I didn't have those hopes and dreams, because I hadn't let them surface, but maybe they had been bubbling just below the surface.

Bailey pushes off the wall and steps forward before she reaches out and squeezes my hand.

"I'm so sorry, Ivy. I've... I've never seen something like that happen. I – come on."

She puts her cigarette out in the terra cotta flowerpot beside the door and gestures toward the driveway.

We get into a black SUV near the gate; the keys are still in the ignition.

She presses something on her cell phone, making the gate open, then hauls ass outta there.

"Where to?" she asks as we pull out of the still open gates.

"To his place, so I can look for my car keys and grab my stuff. Thank you, Bailey." I've cried so much; my dry eyes burn. I stare ahead at the dark road and wonder if I'll ever be the same person I was a week ago.

I really doubt it.

BAILEY CLIMBED IN THE open window in the bedroom and let me in through the front door. And now it's not even five minutes later and she's already found my keys. She found them as if she sniffed them out after she walked around my car for a minute and then she went back inside. A few minutes later, while I packed up all my stuff, she produced them.

I was astounded.

"I'm part shifter even if I can't shift," she says. "I have a lot of the same senses, otherwise." She taps the side of her nose.

"Lucky me," I say, looking at my keys, which she found inside of a box of crackers that I didn't like. Tyson knew I didn't like them when we had a big bed buffet spread the other day.

"I have to tell you, though, Ivy," she says, biting her thumb nail. "He's gonna chase you down and bring you back."

I shake my head.

She keeps talking. "He's fucked up from stuff. And he's so full of hormones, girl. He's here taking it all in and feeling all sorts of emotions and all that? Something's definitely wrong with Mason. Mason is a good guy. The best. He and I are very close friends and he told me that he doesn't think you're his mate but that you've got something in your scent that's fucking him up. Making him spin."

"That doesn't make sense," I say. "Not that I can make sense out of any of this. A week ago I didn't know this even existed."

"I know. I'm sorry for what you went through. You should know that when you two make up, no one in this pack will look negatively at you. That was all a thing with two pack council alphas, and you were caught in that crossfire as Tyson's mate. Nobody but nobody will hold it against you or judge you for that. If anything, it'll endear you to them more. We're very protective of the non-shifters in our pack and any woman or man who has earned her way into the pack after pairing up or mating with one of us has become loved and protected by us. A few have had bad things happen that brought them here, and we're protective and nurturing, and – at times couples have gone into a frenzy and fucked in front of the pack before. Heat or hate sex or whatever, and… it's usually consensual, and I know it wasn't normal for you, but it isn't completely out there in terms of what many of them have seen, especially shifters who joined from other less functional packs."

"Thanks, Bailey, but it doesn't matter. They saw that happen. They saw my naked-"

"Naked isn't a big deal around these parts."

"I'm not a shifter and it's a big deal to me. And there's no way I'm coming back. That was more than nudity, Bailey. And you know it wasn't consensual."

She looks at her feet briefly and then looks me right in the eyes.

"I just want you to know, Ivy, that when you get back here, no matter what, you've got me. You and me are gonna be good friends."

I would believe that if I were staying. I really would. I like her a lot.

"I'm not coming back," I say. I give her a hug. "I better get out of here before... you know."

"Before he wakes up."

I nod.

"Mated pairs are destined, Ivy. And forever. You guys will figure this out."

She's not getting it. There's no coming back from this.

"Thanks for helping me, Bailey."

She nods with a sad look in her eyes.

I get my stuff and get into my car and I leave.

This time, I don't leave a note.

I have no idea what to say to him. No, it's not that I don't know what to say, it's that I have nothing to say. Nothing at all. Big difference. All I know is I need to go. I can't fathom what I've endured tonight.

41

TYSON

I wake disoriented, looking at red and gold carpeting when I wake. I'm on the floor in the hallway. I'm on the other side of the door. Separated from Ivy.

I sit up and scrub at my eyes with the heels of my hands. I feel… strange. Foggy.

"Run?" I hear.

I look up.

It's Greyson. He's nude and standing over me.

"What?"

"Come for a run with me and Rye. We have an hour until sunup. We'll catch up with Linc, Joel, and Jase. The six of us will talk."

"Where's Mason?"

"Mason's at his place. He's there with his father, some elders."

I scrub my eyes some more. I detest this foggy feeling. What is it?

Cat approaches. "Are you going for a run with the boys?"

I look over my shoulder at the closed bedroom door.

My vision blurs a little. I blink it off.

"Don't worry. Bailey will keep her company. We'll talk to her. It might soften things if we talk things over with her. And if you get a good run in, you might find it clears your head, too."

I nod and rise.

"I'll check on her first."

"You should run," Cat corrects. "I'll go in and check on them. I'm guessing Bailey slept in there with her as she's not here and her bag is downstairs." Cat sniffs the air and her face goes confused.

"I think Bailey went home. My truck isn't here," Greyson says. "She likes waking up in her own bed."

"I don't smell her in there," Cat says.

I strain to hear Ivy's breathing, her heartbeat. I should hear it if I listen. "Shh," I tell them.

I don't hear it. Her scent is vague, but it feels too vague.

I push the bedroom door open and find the room empty.

I frantically check the bathroom, the closet, and adjoining empty room with the rocking chair. It's all empty. No sign of Ivy or Bailey.

My eyes meet my mother's and I don't hide that I'm furious.

"That drug you gave me. If I hadn't had that, she'd never have gotten past me."

She jerks back, remorse spreading across her face.

42

IVY

I held it together, all the way home, knowing I just had to. I had to just drive. I had no radio on, made no stops, just followed the road home with a single-minded focus to stay alert and get myself there in one piece.

And now, five minutes after I'm at my apartment, seeing that life here looks just the same as how I left it, I'm in my bed, huddled into a ball, staring off into space with burning eyes, a dry throat, and feeling like my chest has caved in.

I'm not just staring into space, though. I'm being assaulted by scents and scenes. I'm smelling Irish Spring bar soap and that rustic cabin smell. Smelling him. Reaching for the feeling, the warmth that used to wrap around me. None of those smells or sensations exist here. They're all in my head. I guess I'm mourning that touch I'll never feel again.

On the heels of all the sentimentality, I'm seeing flashes of the rage on that monster's face. Watching the blood vessels pop in the other guy's eyes as they stared one another down. Watching him bare his throat in some weirdly somewhat submissive pose as Tyson roared while thrusting into me, though the guy's face didn't say he wanted Tyson to bite him. Though the guy bared his throat sort of submissively, the look on his face told me he wanted to fight. His bleeding eyes met mine for a brief instant where I saw defiance.

I squeeze my neck and my fingers land there. Where the sensation of Tyson Savage lingers. I pull my hand away, recoiling. I thought my eyes were dry, my tear ducts all tapped out, but I'm crying again.

I can't sleep. I can't settle down.

And now I see him eating a banana like it's the best thing he's tasted. I see him and I curled up on that chair, me on his lap and him reading knock-knock and Dad jokes.

I see him guarding me from the cold water in the shower, which was cold because of my flushing the toilet. I see him, standing over me, then lifting me up to rescue me when I got bit by a snake. I see him carefully walking a too-full cup of steaming tea to me, being so careful not to spill it that he seemed boyish.

I choke on a sob and decide I can't just lie here anymore.

I can't. So, I drive to my sister's place.

AMELIA MOVED IN WITH Rick when they got engaged last year. They live in a swanky townhouse in a nice gated community. It's four floors, brownstone style, and everything inside it is white. It's annoying how white everything is. Amelia's colorful so it isn't her. She said she'll redecorate after they get married.

Rick, her fiancé, comes out just as I'm about to knock on the door, in sweats and carrying a gym bag.

"Ivy. Hey. Are you all right?" His hand lands on my arm.

I recoil. "Uh, Is Amelia home?"

"Yeah." He pulls the door wide, looking concerned, and gestures for me to go ahead of him.

"Amelia?" he calls out.

I'm not Rick's biggest fan. I think he'd be the type to cheat just to prove he can still get some tail. I don't like the way he looks at me, and I said it to my sister one night over drinks when I'd had too much heavily alcoholic punch, when a few of us were trying to stage a relationship intervention with her, but she just shrugged it off.

"It's just because you look like me, but twenty pounds lighter and you're a blonde. He wouldn't cheat. It's just like imagined role play."

"He ever ask you to put on a wig? A blonde one? If he does, don't walk, run," I advised and laughed.

She didn't laugh. She went uncharacteristically quiet. I got the impression I struck a nerve.

I never brought it up again; neither did she.

Today, I'm pretty sure that's genuine concern on his face, but I'm also guessing Amelia has been chewing his head off while she worried about me. I spot her over on the big white couch with nail polish in hand, her foot up on the arm of the sofa, and a phone to her ear. The minute she sees me she says, "Gotta go, Mom. Ivy's here. I think you better come over." She drops the phone and runs to me.

I fall into her embrace bawling.

"What did he do?" Amelia demands. "Do we call the cops? Want Rick to go beat the shit out of him? What?"

I look at Rick, standing there in his muscle shirt and sweatpants and I laugh, but it's a bitter and weird laugh. Rick couldn't land a punch on Tyson.

Rick frowns at my reaction.

I shake my head and wave my hand at Rick. It's not that my sister's guy isn't strong looking. He's average height, but he works out and has a six pack and some guns. He's one of those guys that puffs his chest out when he talks about his workout regimen. Truthfully, though, Rick is a bit of a dick and he's a mouthpiece that I get the impression wouldn't deliver on a promise to beat someone up. None of us in the family or our friend group are crazy about him, calling him Rick the Dick behind Amelia's back, but Amelia loves his fat wallet, his fancy cars, and the fact that he proposed in a ridiculously romantic yet cliché (to me) way, during a baseball game on the Jumbotron.

I know she loves being engaged, loves planning a wedding, and she jokes that he's her 'starter' husband.

That's the problem. We're all sure that the day after her big, fancy wedding, she's going to deflate and be ridiculously bummed out with her new reality.

"What happened?" she repeats.

"I just – I…"

I can't talk about what happened. I can't.

And I can't talk about who and what Tyson is.

Not just because of that thing about not telling outsiders, because I liked all those people, too, and I know they were concerned about what happened to me. It isn't their fault. I know that he had some supernatural reaction there that maybe he had no control over, but I also know I'm not okay with it. That said, I don't want to hurt any of them. And that's besides the fact that I could get put on a kill list if I said a word, putting myself and anyone I told at risk.

And also, I'm just not ready to talk about it. I don't know if I can even tell anybody what happened. It's bad enough it happened. Having people I love, people who love me know about it, too?

"We had a – um... fight." Massive understatement. "I had to go. I'm just... I'm..." I bawl some more.

"Devastated?" Amelia asks, pulling me into a tight hug.

I nod. She rocks me while she rubs my back with her palm.

"Oh, no, baby sis. Cry it out. I'm here."

"Hey Ivy?" Rick pipes up. "Ben wasn't happy you moved on. He wants you back. Said he wants to take his relationship with you more seriously. Want me to call him?" Rick asks.

"Go away," Amelia snaps. "Have you got an ounce of sensitivity, you meat head? Go to the gym. Leave us be."

"Want me to bring Benny back? He's meeting me at the club for a sesh."

"God, you're dense." Amelia says.

"Sorry you're upset, Ivy. If you girls want me to bring back ice cream, just text me," Rick says.

"Thanks, Rick," I say, "I appreciate that. But it's okay." Ice cream isn't going to heal me from this.

I hear the door shut..

"He's such a doofus," she grumbles.

I look up at her face and shrug. He tried. I guess.

She flinches.

"Your eyes are so... I mean you're crying, but your eyes...it's like they're purple."

"Oh. I know. It's weird."

I thought it was the lighting in Tyson's bathroom at first, but then saw them in the mirror in his truck and had no idea what to make of them. My eye color has changed. Amelia's eyes are the blue that I used to have. Her eyes look like mine did a week ago. Only a week ago? Why does it feel like I've been gone so much longer?

How has my life so drastically changed in a week?

And how come I feel like I will never, ever be okay?

"I didn't sleep much last night and I left at like three thirty in the a.m. Can I sleep in your guest room for a little? I didn't wanna oversleep and miss the fitting, so I just figured I'd come here because you'd wake me."

"Did he hurt you?" she asks. "What happened to you?"

I examine my bandaged ankle, my bandaged-up knees. My hands are even wrapped. I'm crying and bandaged all over the place. Of course she's worried about that.

"It's a long story. I just wanna sleep."

"Do we call the police? Were you hurt like that?" She pushes my hair out of my face sweetly.

I love my sister. Even if she's been a bridezilla lately and despite that she's always been such a type-A personality. Amelia is also fiercely protective over the people she cares about. If she thinks someone hurt you, she won't care how big and bad they are. She'll go head-to-head with them.

"No, Amie. Nothing like ... um... that."

She looks at me like she knows I'm lying.

"I just wanna close my eyes. Okay? And sleep on your comfy guest bed. You know it's more comfy than my own bed at home."

But not comfier than sleeping on Tyson...

"Go in. I'll get you something to sleep in. Pretty dress, Ives."

"Thanks," I say, looking down at the dirty skirt of my pretty strawberry moon dress. I didn't realize I hadn't changed. My lower lip quivers and I trudge off to her guest room.

By the time the flipflops I threw on at home are off my feet, she's coming in with a pale purple designer track suit and a bottle of Sprite along with a foil packet of makeup wipes in her hand. My sister always keeps a bottle of my favorite fizzy drink in the back of her fridge for when I come over.

I accept it gratefully and take a long pull.

"Do you need anything?" she asks, sitting on the end of the bed and starting to work on the remnants of last night's eye makeup with one of her wipes.

It's so my sister to take care of me like this. I'm glad I came here. I feel bad for all the angry thoughts I've had about her recently.

I sit and let her wipe my face. She has another wipe in her hand and she then uses that one.

"Can you keep Mom out until I get a few hours?"

"I'll wake you up as late as possible before we have to go for the fitting. If you need anything, you tell me," she says.

I nod and cap the bottle. I wait for her to go before I start changing my clothes.

Normally, I would change right in front of my sister. But I have bruises. I don't want her to see them.

The bruises between my legs are ugly and very telling.

And, looking down I can see there are bloody streaks on my inner thighs.

Shit.

I call out, "Ames? Can I have a pair of panties?"

"Sure, Ives."

She brings me in a fresh package of white silky panties that say 'bride' on the bum in gold script.

"I can't take these," I say.

She makes me take them. "I bought three pairs. It's okay."

I go to her bathroom and use bathroom wipes to clean the dry blood from between my thighs, then change and head back to the guest room to sleep. I almost want to take a shower, wash last night off me, but for some reason I can't fathom, I don't.

I HEAR VOICES. ANGRY ones.

The little alarm clock on the bedside table tells me I've slept two and a half hours. Not nearly enough.

My mom and Amelia are outside the door and my sister is trying to keep her out.

"She can go back to sleep after I talk to her," Mom says, and the doorknob turns.

I sit up.

Mom rushes to me, panic in her eyes. She's got my blonde hair, though hers barely grazes her shoulders. Me and Amelia got our eyes from her, too. Mom wraps her arms around me and hugs me tight.

"I tried," Amelia defends. "I managed a couple hours at least…"

I blow her a kiss.

"Ivy, talk to me. Talk to me, sweetie." Mom gives the best hugs.

Well, second best.

I shake that thought off.

"I don't wanna talk about it."

"Ivy." Mom gives me a stern look. "Tell me about meeting him. Tell me about him. Tell me everything. Tell me about those bandages."

I wave my hand. "It doesn't matter, Mom; it's over."

She stares at me, eyes working, giving me the math question face that Tyson gives me.

God, my heart hurts.

I bury my face into the pillow and bawl. I'm full-on ugly-crying. I feel my sister behind me, sort of spooning me and stroking my head.

"It's gotta be pretty bad for you to be like this. I've never seen you like this," Amelia's voice is soft.

I turn and look at her. "It's never been like this. I'm never *ever* falling in love again."

Wait, what? Love? My whole body feels weird at that phrase coming from my mouth.

I've never used it about a guy. Not a real one, anyway. Fantasy hall pass guys, sure, but never about a real person.

Never.

I thought I was maybe malfunctional as a woman because all my friends, my sister, everyone I was close to felt love for guys. Deep love. They got heartbroken at breakups. I never did. I just moved on. Even when I got dumped.

Until now. How hard is it going to be to move on from this?

> *"I've never felt this way about anybody before, Ivy. My only. It's because you're the only one for me. We're meant to be together."*

I shake Tyson's words off.

Because if I love him, if I finally love someone then it just figures, right? It just figures I'd fall in love with a guy that would so completely obliterate me.

"You love him?" Amelia asks.

"It's been a week," Mom says, face radiating disbelief and maybe a bit of disgust.

I turn away from her penetrating gaze.

"What's wrong with your eyes?" she asks.

I empty my lungs loudly.

"Ivy, you gotta tell me everything. Now. It's really important."

"No, Mom. I can't. I'm sorry. I just... can't."

Mom doesn't understand. Of course she doesn't.

"Are you wearing colored contact lenses?"

I shake my head.

"What the hell, Ivy?" Mom shrieks.

"I can't tell you. It's too..." Dangerous? Painful? Absolutely unbelievable? We never talked about my eyes, I should've asked Cat and Bailey, but it's obvious that it has something to do with Tyson.

"I can't talk about it. Please just cut me some slack, okay?"

"You're scaring me," Mom says, clutching her throat, eyes horror-stricken.

"Don't be scared, Mom, I'm just being a drama queen."

"That's my job," Amelia says, her voice sounding funny. She looks scared, too.

And that's why it's so funny that she bought me a drama queen keychain. Because everyone knows my sister is the one who blows up, who has meltdowns, who has the temper.

> "No, I'm not a drama queen, you're a drama queen."
> "You're such a drama queen, you need a warning label," I'd argued back.

She bought me the keychain for a joke when I was sixteen, her seventeen. And I still use it.

"I bet Ivy wants some pancakes?" Mom looks to Amelia. "Do you have the stuff for pancakes?"

"I don't, but I can go get it," Amelia offers. "You want pancakes, Ives?"

I nod. "I really do."

I don't. But, if they have something to do, this conversation can be over.

"Okay, I'll be back." Amelia snaps to it and heads out, leaving me and Mom in the guest room.

My mom's eyes hit mine and now I know she got rid of Amelia on purpose.

Fuzz.

"Wanna go watch TV on Rick the Dick's ridiculous eighty-six inch?" I try, faking a smile.

She shakes her head. "Wait until she goes." Mom flicks between the white horizontal blinds to peek through.

I feel the groan of the automatic garage door opening under my feet. The guest room is directly over it.

"Now, young lady, talk to me," Mom demands, turning around and folding her arms across her chest.

"I can't, Mom. I'm too..."

"Broken-hearted?" she asks.

Yes. But more. So much more. Just broken, mostly.

"I guess."

"I'm gonna tell you a story. If it doesn't make sense, it's just a story. But, if it makes sense... you'll talk to me. Okay?"

I nod and shrug at the same time.

She sits on the bed and gets comfortable.

I put my head in her lap and she strokes my hair.

"Aunt Nelle believed in a lot of things that most people think aren't real," Mom says. "She was more than a conspiracy theorist in her beliefs. You know this."

My body goes stiff. Holy shit. Where the heck is this going?

"And I know a lot of people never took her seriously, but she was serious. She believed everything she told us. And she didn't talk about the things she believed with just anyone, Ivy. She did it with you. She did it with me. With your brother a little. Never your sister for some reason. At least not that I know of."

This was true. And odd.

"Never your dad. She never liked your dad. The way you feel about Rick? That's how Nellie felt about your father." Mom takes a deep breath. "Nelle was ten years older than me and before she came to live with us when you guys were little, she lived like a bit of a gypsy. She traveled a lot. Always on the hunt for answers, my sister. She was like Fox Mulder of the X-Files, kind of. Believing the truth was out there for her to find. But in BoHo gypsy form. We all know she was quirky, but also, she was incredibly lucky."

Aunt Nelle was lucky in a lot of ways, for sure. Except that she got cancer and died in her fifties.

Mom continues. "She won the lottery, as you know. She won it twice. And yet she traveled and splurged on airfare, but other than that, lived on next to nothing. She'd go off on her adventures. She'd go tree planting way up north and be gone for six months. She'd join a mission with her latest church and be gone a year before coming back and joining another church or cult or whatever. Yeah, some of them were definitely cults. She always came back with crazy stories and on the rare occasion your dad caught wind of something out of her mouth, he'd tell me she did drugs." Mom laughs. "He used to call it that Nellie peyote or some shit. My sister didn't touch drugs. She wouldn't even drink alcohol. She was just one of those naturally happy and adventurous people."

Mom's right. I remember when she came to live with us and started telling me all the crazy stories of the places she'd been, the people she met, the mysteries out there that she'd heard or crazy things she'd seen. She'd talk about seances. Ghosts. Listening to her stories was like sitting around a campfire for ghost stories, but she wasn't trying to scare me with them. She was trying to convince me that magic was real. That I could find it, too, like she had, only find more of it because I was so young.

More than once, she asked,

"When are you gonna look for magic, Ivy? It's out there, you know."

"All the time you girls were growing up when she lived with us, she didn't spend much. She helped us by paying off the house when she died, but put a caveat that the deed went in just my name. And she put away enough money for Leo's education. Your father balked. Why have his name taken off the house? Why only Leo and not you girls in the will? No wonder." Mom goes quiet. "It's like Nellie had a hunch about him. Anyway... she didn't have much else left. I wondered what she did with it. All her winnings. I knew she should have in the seven figures stashed away but figured she gave most of it away. Besides paying off our mortgage and putting a tidy sum into a special account for me for when I retire, she left me a letter when she died. A really crazy letter."

I sit up and cross my legs, then reach for and take a sip of my Sprite. I offer it to Mom.

"No thanks. I'll make some coffee in a minute. Anyway, she told me when you were born, sitting there with Amelia on her lap, that she spent the majority of her savings not on an education fund for you kids or anything practical like that. She said she spent the lion's share of it on securing you and your sister a happily ever after. I thought maybe she meant stocks, bonds, something like that at first, but she acted like I was way off base. I let it go; my sister would just talk in riddles a lot, especially once the cancer went to her brain. But then I got that letter when she died. In it, she told me she went to her fortune teller and paid for you two to have the best fortune possible. True love. She told me, in the letter, to keep my eyes open on the anniversary of her death. That it would begin. And then you went missing." Mom's voice hitches. "On the anniversary of her death."

I'm trembling.

"She said some other stuff too, but the important part here is about you and Amelia. I find out from your sister that you're gone away for the weekend and then I look at the calendar and it hits me. The anniversary of Nelle's death. It hit me like a ton of bricks. And I called your phone a hundred times and you didn't answer. And then you finally call and tell me you've been bit by a snake and you disappear again and, well... you can imagine what I'm thinking..."

I can imagine. And she has no idea.

"Especially with you being in Drowsy Hollow. They still never caught that guy that went on the killing spree in town last Fall. Still never found his wife. They both just vanished."

I shiver. I heard that story before. It was all over the news. Talk about chilling.

"My sister's letter hinted at something that would convince you girls that magic is real."

"Rick isn't real magical," I mutter.

Mom laughs loud. "No, he's not. Maybe my sister knew something I don't."

My laughter dies in my throat and my chin wobbles.

"What about you?" Mom asks. "What about this man who's made you cry?"

I shiver. She grabs my hand and her voice takes on a strange tone. "We grew up around that area and there were some rumors," Mom whispers. "About shapeshifters, witches, vampires..."

I shiver some more. No, more than a shiver. More like a full-body shudder. She grips me tight. She felt that.

"Crazy stories we'd tell around the fire. It was like a rite of passage for teenagers to go looking for them. I've heard stories about nosy kids getting too close to the truth and bad things happening to make them back off, to make them unwilling to talk about it."

I gulp.

"A guy Aunt Nelle dated in high school said he'd seen a man change into a wolf in the woods one night. He told everyone who would listen. And then that boyfriend of hers... he disappeared. Weeks later, his parents told her, when she was so distraught she was pleading for them to answer the door... they said he joined the army. She asked for an address. They said they didn't have one. She knocked at their door again a few weeks later again asking for an address to send him letters. They told her he died in a military accident and slammed the door on her. But... he would never have joined. It was completely out of character for him."

I blow out a breath. "Holy crap."

"And then she saw him, in a crowded marketplace sixteen years later in Eastern Europe. I have a feeling she went on a quest for him. But anyway, he pretended he didn't know her. She was sure it was him. She said he hadn't aged."

"God, Mom." All the hairs on my arms are standing on end.

"Yep. Anyway, you go missing and you tell us about a snake bite, and then you come back distraught after having said you met somebody, and you're all bandaged, and your eyes are different. Not just the color, Ivy. Your eyes are different."

I blow out another breath.

"Do you have anything you want to tell me?"

"I can't," I whisper. "I'm sorry, Mom."

"I see." She goes quite for a long moment. "Sweetie..." She lets that hang.

"It's over with him," I say.

"Do you believe in magic, Ivy?" Mom asks in a whisper.

"Yeah, Mom. I do." My voice breaks on the 'do' and I burst into tears again and bury my face into Mom's chest. She holds me tight.

"Then, maybe it shouldn't be over with him. Your Aunt Nelle wanted you to be happy."

I can't do this. I can't tell her. I can't. I shake my head vigorously to make her stop saying those things.

"But, how bad of a fight?" she pushes.

"Please drop it, Mom? Please, please please?" I look up at her.

She looks like she's aged ten years suddenly. There's so much concern on her face. She nods.

"You talk when you're ready. I'll go make some coffee."

I'll never be ready to talk. I nod anyway.

AMELIA IS BACK THIRTY minutes later, so Mom makes us chocolate chip and banana pancakes and bacon. We say nothing about any of that stuff to my sister, but I only get two bites into me before I've lost my appetite. I stare at the plate thinking about how much Tyson loves bananas. And bacon.

Amelia looked between us upon getting back. We were sitting at the breakfast bar, drinking coffee, not talking.

Her eyes bounced between us and her mouth opened, as if she was about to speak. I pretended not to see Mom give her a sharp shake of her head, clearly discouraging her from bringing anything up that would upset me. Then we pretended like nothing happened. Amelia didn't typically let things go.

Thank God she did this time.

43

TYSON

After lecturing me on not doing anything in public to call attention to myself, Riley and Greyson insisted on coming with me to bring Ivy home.

"You can't let yourself shift let alone half-shift, Ty. You have to hold it together in public. If she made it to a town, you'll have to be careful about getting her into your car without anybody alerting the cops."

"Cornelius did something right, he taught me at least all that."

I argued with them against coming and they told me they'd just follow me.

"We're your reinforcements. Let us help," Grey offered.

"I don't need help."

First, I thought they might be doing their duty to make sure I didn't reveal my true nature where I shouldn't but before long, I listened to what they said, to how they said it, and watched their body language. They were relentless in their pursuit to show their support, to help me.

"We're here for you, brother," Grey says. "Let us help. She lives in a bigger city. If she gets that far before you catch up to her, we know bigger cities."

"Hate 'em," Riley mutters.

"Yeah, we hate 'em but we know 'em," Grey pressed. "You can drive if you want. Or we can. But, let's all go together. You've got backup. Want my help looking her up or you gonna hunt?"

"Of course I'm gonna hunt," I say.

She couldn't have gotten too far.

I knew I'd find her just as easily as I'd find my own home.

"You're discombobulated, Ty," Riley touches my arm.

I glare at my mother. I'm still discombobulated because she drugged me.

Her face is remorseful. "Please eat something before you go. Have breakfast with us," Cat says. "Your grandparents are here, and..."

"Not now."

"Then, let me pack food for the road. In case she's deep in the woods."

"I'm not waiting."

"Don't you think giving her time to catch her breath, time to cool off might help, Tyson?" Cat suggests.

"Yeah," Greyson says. "Maybe one of us can find her, bring her to you, talk to her first, and –"

"I don't..." I thrust my hand through my hair.

I didn't know if I was coming or going. I was filled with a combination of frustration, panic, remorse, a bunch of emotions.

I shift, not thinking about the closed door, and am about to shift back halfway so I can open the door when Bailey steps inside.

I shift back to man.

"Did you see her?" I demand, backing her up against the door.

Bailey's chin quivers and she shows me her throat but then she chokes out. "You asshole. You fucking broke her."

"Bailey!" Greyson warns.

I growl.

"I don't give a shit. He needs to know. Lead council alpha or not, able to rip my throat out without trying or not, and whether you choose to join us or not... you need to know that it's fucking *not* okay to do that to a woman. Never *ever*."

I back up. Fuck.

Bailey advances and pokes me in the chest. Her face is red.

"She's gutted, Tyson. Just gutted."

I bare my teeth.

"Tell me everything. Now."

"I drove her to your place, and I gave her the key."

My eyes narrow. "The key? The car key?"

"Yep," she says defiantly.

"She took her car and left?"

"Yes." She folds her arms across her chest.

"She's gone?" I try to confirm. Shit. The heels of my hands fly to my temples. "When?"

"Three, three thirty, I guess." Bailey shrugs defiantly.

She's clearly very angry with me.

I'm also very fucking angry with me.

Cat touches my forearm. And then she's shaking me to get my attention. "Go home, shower and change and see if she left a note and I'll meet you at your house."

A note.

She left me a note before. Where's that note with her telephone number? At the cabin. I'll look for it. I need a telephone.

"I'll come with you," Cat says. "Wait for me."

"I'm not waiting. Stay here, mother."

"We'll come," Greyson says.

"No," I say. "Stay here, all of you."

"Ty..." Riley says. "You running? You walking, driving? If you're shifting you need clothes. If you're driving, you need a car 'n your truck is at the community center. We came here in Aunt Cat's Jeep, remember?"

Shit.

"Where are my keys?"

"Maybe in your jeans. We got you to put them back on when we got here."

I reach for the jeans on the floor and dig into my pocket. They're there.

"I'll drive you to your truck," Riley offers.

"Fine. Hurry."

"We'll be here," Bailey says. "Grovel good. Grovel real good. It might take a year for her to forgive you. If you're lucky."

Pain shunts through me.

"Out of my way," I tell Bailey.

"I hope she makes you work for it," Bailey snaps as she moves aside.

"If you need us," my mother says, "We're here."

"Did I mistake her as omega?" I ask Grey, jerking my thumb toward his sister.

He shakes his head. "No, but she's pretty ticked. Women get ticked on each other's behalf; it can be hell."

"YOU HAVE A PHONE?" I demand, seeing there's no note in the cabin, but finding the note that Ivy wrote me last time. I find it tucked into the little monkey book on the shelf of my old room. I wanted to save it for some reason and that seemed like a good place.

Grey passes me his phone.

It's different from Ivy's and I get confused with the navigation to find how to make a phone call.

I only used the apps on Ivy's phone to look at her photographs, to go into the one app with the funny jokes.

"Here," Grey says and shows me how to make a call.

It makes a noise for a minute and then I hear Ivy talking.

"Hi, this is Ivy."

"Ivy!"

"I can't take your call right now so you can either leave a message or you can hang up and text me. Hint. It's better if you hang up and text me. I hate voicemails."

The phone makes a beep.

I don't want to text message her. I can barely use the phone as it is, nevermind try to fiddle with it to send a word message. I want her here with me so I can hold her, so I can fix this.

"Ivy!" I say. "It's Tyson. Please. I need you. I need to show you I'm sorry. I'm coming. Call me at this phone if you can. Grey, how can she call this phone from her phone?"

"She'll see the number, Tyson." Grey says.

"Call. Or come home. I love you. I'm sorry, Ivy. I'll find you. I'm on my way."

I pass the phone to him and shove Ivy's note in my pocket.

"Let's go."

Riley gets into the passenger side of my truck as I start it up. Grey follows in his truck because my truck hasn't got room for three men and Ivy for us to bring her back.

I don't want Riley Savage's company right now and tell him as much.

"You should ride with Grey," I say.

"Respectfully, Ty, I'd prefer to be with you until we get there. We can talk."

"Don't feel like talking, man."

"Okay well, I get that. But I have a few things to say. And if you feel like talking, talk. If you don't, just listen."

I growl in his face. "I'm not in the fucking mood for listening, either."

"I know you're not. Believe me, I know. We'll get some road behind us first; I'll give you time."

"I'm not interested in talking. I'm interested in getting my girl back. You can talk to me after that."

"Fine. Then I'll just be a passenger. Let's go." He gestures ahead of us.

I follow my senses, which take me on a three-hour journey to a city that smells disgusting, that's filled with cars and people, that's ten times more crowded than the grocery store when it's full.

I do not like cities. I don't like that Ivy's here either. It doesn't feel safe. The smell of it, even the sky... they're not right. There are hardly even any trees. The other smells are sour in my nose, but her scent is there. And it doesn't *fucking* belong.

44

IVY

"Stay over," Amelia pleads with me.

I shake my head. "I'm just gonna go home, I think. I'll be fine."

She pouts. "Are you sure?"

I nod and she hugs me.

We're in her driveway and we've done the whole fitting and dinner thing. I'm here to get my car after riding with her. Me, her, our mom, her other bridesmaids and Rick's mom spent the past six hours together and I've felt like I've been in a daze, like I've been walking around with weights on my body. I've really tried to not be a bummer but kept getting long looks from my sister and mother. They knew I wasn't having fun. They know my heart is broken.

All the times I didn't feel heartbreak over a guy... it's like I'm getting it all at once. Instead of being like most girls my age who've had it at least half a dozen times I'm getting it all piled on me at once because a) he's the only guy that I've had this depth of feeling for and b) I'm so absolutely, completely crushed by what he did.

I don't know where things would've gone. I don't know anything right now, except that it hurts. This hurts just so much.

I get out of Amelia's driveway before Mom gets back. I don't need to deal with her, too, right now.

I GET INSIDE MY APARTMENT, sit down, and turn my phone on for the first time since yesterday.

There's a missed call from a number I don't recognize. And a voicemail.

I start listening.

I hang up as soon as I hear his voice. I squeeze my eyes shut tight, as if it'll ward off the pain that's coming at me, but I can't. It engulfs me and I crumble to the floor and melt into myself.

There's a knock on my door. I gasp and then my hand claps over my mouth.

I can't deal with anybody right now.

I just can't.

There's another knock.

"Ivy?"

Whose voice is that?

I get to my feet and use the sleeves of my sister's hoodie to wipe my eyes, then I look out the peep hole.

Ben.

Shit.

Shit.

I hold my breath and remain frozen.

"I heard you in there, Ivy. Can I please talk to you for a minute?"

Damn it.

I open the door just a little.

"It's not a good time, Ben."

"I heard you crying. Are you okay?"

"I'm..." Not okay. Not even remotely okay. I'm so not okay that I'm not sure if okay is even on the horizon. "Fine. Just having a moment. But it's really not a good time for a visit."

"I heard you were hurt and I..." He thrusts his hand through his dirty blonde hair. I used to find his polished and clean-cut look appealing. Now he looks too... refined to me. Almost feminine in contrast to Ty. Ben isn't feminine. He's fit but just so metrosexual. So coiffed. I can't imagine he even knows how to growl.

"I'm okay," I interrupt.

"I realized how I felt, Ivy. I know things with us were fairly casual, but I... was catching feelings. I'd like to explore things further. See if we're ready for things to... deepen." He motions to move closer and not only do I back up, I feel almost queasy at the thought of his hands on me.

"I'm sorry, but it's not a good time for me for anything, Ben. Not even a conversation. And thanks, that's um-sweet, but I don't think I want anything deeper. I don't–"

I stop talking because my thoughts are cut off with the sight of headlights pointing at us in the doorway.

My and Tamara's apartment is the bottom of a triplex and our door is at the very bottom of the deeply sloped driveway. A truck has pulled in behind my car and the door on the driver's side of a pickup truck flies open and here he comes. *Oh fuck.* It's Tyson.

I quickly spin Ben around and stand in front of him.

Shit. Shit!

"What are you doing?' Ben asks.

Protecting you from the big bad wolf.

Tyson is closing the distance between us and I'm blocking Ben.

I point at Tyson, my eyes blinded by the headlights pointing at my face, but still making out that his chest rises and falls with intensity as he prowls toward us, I know this means bad things. Very bad things.

"Do not come any closer!" I shout.

I hear another slam. And then another.

Two of the alphas from Arcana Falls are here, too.

"If you lay one hand on him, Ty... I will make. You. Sorry." Pain shoots through me.

"Who is this, Ivy?" Ben asks from behind me and tries to step around me. I physically back up so he's squished against the bricks beside my apartment door.

"Riley!" I shout. "Don't let Ty put his hands on him!"

Riley's in front of us quickly. "I got him, Ivy. Follow me, man."

"What? What's happening here?" Ben protests. "Ivy?"

Instead of marching Ty away, Riley has grabbed Ben by the elbow and he's marching *him* away.

"Has he touched you?" Ty demands, towering over me suddenly, his chest still rising and falling fast. Thank God he has clothes on. He's wearing that white and blue soft flannel I've slept in. He's in jeans and his hiking boots. The scent of him assaults my senses. I can't hack this. I'm about to crumble again.

He takes my face into both hands.

"Ivy, look at me," Ty's voice has gone soft.

I refuse to look up. I look down at my feet instead.

"Not that I have to answer to you," I say. "But he heard I was back and came to see me, to check to make sure I'm all right since I got bit by a snake, and no he hasn't touched me. Though it's not your business who touches me."

"Wanna bet?" Ty growls. "She's mine now, fucker. Go home while you still have legs."

"Yours?" Ben asks, sounding stunned. He's trying to shrug Riley off, his head turned back toward us.

"Yes. She's mine," Tyson growls.

"Buddy..." Ben says. "You wanna quit the Neanderthal behavior for a sec and—-"

"Leave!" I demand at Ty. "Ben, please go. I'm fine here. I'll call you later." No way do I want Ben trying to be a hero.

"She won't be fucking calling you, asshole," Ty snarls. "Look at me, Ivy."

"No. Leave!" I point at the headlights that are still pointed at me.

"Ivy, what's happening here? Should I call the cops? Is this clown harassing you?" Ben asks ignoring my efforts to protect him.

I step in front of him again.

Tyson grabs my hand and pulls me closer.

"Don't touch me!" I snap. "Touch me and I will fucking scream my head off."

Tyson lets go and holds his hands up.

Riley and Greyson are now crowding Ben and leading him up the driveway, not touching him but sort of herding him; all sorts of animosity rolling off them. It's like they're Tyson's enforcers or something. Bile rises in my throat.

"Yo, Ivy!" I hear. It's my upstairs neighbor, Julio.

"You're causing a scene in front of my neighbors. Go."

"Man! Your high beams are blinding me through my window," Julio calls out.

"Sorry, Julio," I call up. "He's just leaving. I apologize."

Greyson moves to Ty's truck and the lights are shut off. Riley is talking to Ben by his car. Ben is now getting in his car. And, Ben is leaving.

I breathe out relief.

Whatever Riley said to him obviously got rid of him. I don't know what it was, but all I know is I don't want Tyson hurting Ben, turning into that monster and fucking me in my driveway.

I hear Julio slam his door. Of course. He wouldn't dream of coming to anyone's aid. Asswipe.

I head for my own door.

"Ivy?"

"No! Get out of here. We're done." I slash my hand across my throat. "Done!" I glare at his chest. "Forget we ever met. Forget you bit me, forget you ever got a kind word from me. I'll do my best to do the same, despite what you did to me." I spin around to go inside, but he reaches out and hauls my back against his body. I see his corded forearm across my stomach, and it causes a physical reaction that makes my heart feel like it's breaking all over again.

"No! Don't!" I struggle. He doesn't budge. "Riley, Greyson? Please get him out of here before I call the police. I can't do this. You're his family, teach him to be a civilized person and to leave a woman alone who doesn't want anything to do with him."

"Ty," Grey says, " Chill."

"Remember what we talked about, Ty?" Riley says in a gentle voice, looking Tyson in the eyes.

Tyson growls at him.

"Ty," Riley urges.

"Let go!" I demand.

"I won't let go," Tyson says into the top of my hair. He inhales it.

My shoulders crouch and I try to shrink away. He's not letting go of me.

"Make him let go, Riley, please," I plead.

Riley looks at me with what looks like sympathy.

Tyson's mouth is now an inch from that mark on my neck.

Oh hell no.

"Don't you dare, don't you dare, don't you dare..."

"Wait," Tyson grunts, to them, I guess, because then he lifts me into his arms and he carries me inside my apartment. He slams the door, puts his back against it and slides down to the floor with me in his arms, burying his nose in that spot. My hands are over my face and I'm crying so hard it feels like I can't catch a breath.

"I'm sorry, I'm sorry, Ivy. I'm so fucking sorry."

My breath hitches and an ugly sound breaks free of me. A horribly ugly sound.

"Ivy?" Ty whispers.

I shake my head frantically.

He starts to purr.

No. Not that.

I go from hyperventilating to being able to catch a breath.

"I'm so sorry, baby," he says.

"I can't. I can't, Tyson. Please go."

"Ivy. Come home. We'll—-"

"No. No no no no. I'm begging you, please go. Please leave me alone. I can't do this. I won't do this."

His purring gets louder and I try to struggle but it's feeble at best. He fights so god damn dirty.

His mouth is against that spot on my neck and then he's kissing it.

"Don't you dare do this. I swear, Tyson, if you try to fuck me right now, I...You already broke me, I swear if you-"

He twists me so that I'm facing him in a squat. I pull back and fall on my ass.

"I'm sorry, Ivy. I'm sorry." His eyes bore into me.

They cut straight through me. So green, so expressive.

"This isn't gonna work. I can't just get over that. What you did to me...it will haunt me for the rest of my life."

He closes his eyes and his face is just stricken with pain. He reaches for me again.

"No!" I backwards crab-crawl away from him. "Go. Please leave me the fuck alone."

"No," he says. "I'm not leaving you. You come with me or... or I stay here."

I bark out bitter laughter.

"You'll stay here. With me here? In my apartment that I share with a roommate, in a big city? Right."

His lip curls. "It stinks here. It's crowded and smells bad and there aren't enough trees, but I would. I will. Until you agree to come home."

"This is home," I say, pointing at my cheap linoleum floor in my rented apartment.

"Then this will be my home, too." He folds his arms across his chest.

"You have a family now, Tyson. You don't need me. There are people there like you that –"

"You're mine," he declares.

"Only because Aunt Nelle made some deal with a witch."

"What?"

"Go see a witch. Have them undo it."

"What?"

I get to my feet and he does too.

"Ivy, explain..." He approaches me so I dash around him and pull the door open. Riley and Greyson are right outside still, talking. Their eyes bounce to me.

"Come take him, please? Take him home. I'm done with this guy." I look over my shoulder at Ty, who's directly behind me. "Get out." I don't look at his face, just sort of point my gaze over his head. "Now."

"Tyson, let's talk a minute," Grey says. "Riley will talk to Ivy, you come sit with me in the truck."

"No," Tyson says. "No. You're coming home." He turns around and grabs my overnight bag from the floor where I dropped it that morning and grabs my purse from the table by the door. The table falls over, knocking a plant over. "Come on." He reaches for my hand.

"No!" I snap and back away. "You guys, go find a witch and get her to undo what Aunt Nelle did."

"Yes!" he shouts, and I stumble backwards with the force of the growly sounds.

There's pounding over my head. Julio. Julio and Sasha have a baby. We're being too loud. They're not the types to call the cops or get involved but they won't hesitate to give us shit, or call the landlord and complain.

Any time we make a bit of noise they stomp on the floor. Tamara always retaliates by pounding the broomstick on the ceiling.

Tyson comes at me.

"No!" I sprint toward the kitchen island, but he crouches as he comes at me and catches me over his shoulder. He's up and grabbing my car keys from the counter and knocking stuff over as he hefts me up higher.

"Tyson, stop! Put me down!"

He's heading for the door with me.

Shit.

"Put me down," I demand. He ignores me.

"Here. You drive Ivy's car," Tyson says.

"Go ahead. I'll lock the door," I hear Riley say. I'm busy squirming and trying to find my way off his shoulder but he's not budging. He grips me tighter, taking me back to his truck and putting me inside.

I see through the windshield that Riley is locking my apartment. He gets into my car.

Tyson grabs my hand and jerks me toward him.

"You wanna give me more bruises?" I cry out. "I've already got splinter wounds in my hands and knees from when you *fucking* dragged me across the floor in that bar."

Tyson lets go of me and his face shows that I got my point across. Because of that, I strike again with the only thing I've got – words.

"Let's not talk about how you made me bleed between my legs because you were so rough."

He wears an expression like he's just been slapped in the face.

Riley's knocking on the window. Tyson rolls it.

"If she's gonna fight you, better we drive in Grey's car and send someone for your truck later. You can keep control of her in the back seat."

My jaw drops. "You're on board with this? You're as bad as he is!"

"You're his, Ivy. He's not giving up no matter what anyone says or does. We're his support here and we'll do what we have to do to help him get you back home."

I blink in shock.

"It'd be easier on all of us if you cooperate," he adds.

"Why should I make it easy on all of you? Just go find the witch and she'll undo it."

"What do you mean by that?" Riley asks.

"My mom just told me my aunt made some deal with a witch and I think that's why Tyson thinks I'm his mate. Get it undone and we can all get on with our lives."

"A witch? What witch?"

"I don't know. It was twenty-seven years ago. My aunt died so I can't ask her."

Riley stares at Grey. Grey's eyebrows are up high.

"This guy fucked up. Huge. He loves you. You love him. Go home and figure it out. You're mated for life, Ivy. Don't cause yourself or him more pain than you have to. Let him fix what he broke."

I stare in shock.

"He's not walking away," Grey tells me. "Witch or no witch, this is unbreakable."

Riley's right. Tyson isn't giving up here. And they're here to help him.

Tyson straightens up and starts the truck. "We'll be fine."

"You want, I'll drive, you hold her and purr to keep her settled," Riley offers.

Oh. My. God.

"Unfuckingbelievable," I mutter.

I feel like a piece of chattel right now.

"I don't need to be held and purred at," I say with as much venom as I can muster, folding my arms across my chest and staring straight ahead.

I have no choice but to go because there are three giant men determined to take me and I'd rather he not hold me and make me feel things. Things that hurt just too much.

I'll figure out how to get away from him later. I'll find a witch myself if I have to.

"Okay, let's go," Greyson says, and he and Riley move away from the truck.

Tyson reaches over and I recoil as he puts my seatbelt on me.

I stare out the windshield as we leave. I refuse to look at him.

45

TYSON

After a long drive back where the cab of the truck feels like it's filled with hatred, I park and shut the truck off.

Riley and Grey have followed me here to the cabin.

I step out and Riley hands me Ivy's keys.

Grey says, "So, the things she said about a witch..."

"I don't care if a witch was involved. She's still mine," I tell him.

"Of course. We need more information, if possible. It might be connected to Mason's behavior."

"I give no fucks about Mason Quinn right now, Greyson," I inform, getting in his face.

Grey raises his hands defensively. "We'll talk later then. What about bringing her back home. We –"

"This is her home. Not some underground place in a city!"

"Arcana Falls, bro. Bring her there. Safer within those gates and the girls can come by and help. Your mom. Bailey. If they talk to her..."

"Not tonight." I say. "Thanks for the help."

"Good luck, cuz," Riley slaps my arm and glances into the truck where Ivy sits with her arms folded across her chest.

We all look in that direction and she glares in our direction and then undoes her seatbelt, leans over and pushes the lock down on the driver's door.

Fuck. Not this again.

"Don't you dare, Ivy. Don't fucking dare try to leave!" I order, rage clawing through my blood, electricity arcing at the base of my spine.

"Luck. Yeah, you're gonna need it," Grey says.

I jump over into the bed of the pickup realizing I made the mistake of leaving the keys in the truck again.

"Shit. You want some help?" Riley offers.

"Grab me the spare set of keys from on top of the fridge? You're gonna have to either break down my door or climb in my bedroom window around the side."

She hasn't started the truck. That's something at least.

Riley smiles. "Got yourself a little spitfire, man. I envy that."

His eyes go funny and for a split second I see his longing. I don't feel threatened. I know it's not about Ivy, it's about the mate he lost. He heads to the house. Grey follows.

I don't want my Ivy to be a spitfire. I don't want her to be angry. I want her to forgive me.

"Riley and Grey are getting the other keys. You should just open the door now, Ivy," I say to the back of her head from my spot perched behind her in the bed of the truck.

She says nothing. She puts her forehead to my steering wheel and her shoulders tremble.

She's crying. I hate it when she cries. Hate isn't a strong enough word. I want to inflict pain on whatever it is making her cry, which means I want to rip myself apart. It's torture straddling the line between avenging her and self-preservation.

Hopelessness claws through my body. My wolf wants to wail his anguish at the sky.

RILEY AND GREY HAVE gone, and I have the spare keys in my hand.

I unlock the door and lift her out of the driver's seat, snatching the second set of keys from the ignition and gathering up her bags that sit on the seat beside her.

She doesn't struggle. She doesn't do anything.

Her eyes close and her lip and chin quiver.

I carry her inside, dropping her bags to the floor, then stride to the bedroom, kick my boots off and climb into the bed pulling her closer to me, holding the back of her head to my chest, throwing a leg over her, trying to cocoon her. I purr to her. I purr loud. Her hands are balled into fists between her breasts and my chest. Her whole body is tense and then it loosens until she melts into me and weeps loudly into my chest. Very loudly. She's crying so hard that it's physically crushing my will. I feel my eyes moisten and I debate ending myself so that I can end the source of her pain.

"Ivy, please tell me how to fix this?" I plead. "I didn't think. I just reacted. I can't undo it. I don't know what to do."

She continues crying.

I purr some more, and she falls asleep against the wet spot on my shirt from her tears.

Her fists don't loosen.

I don't sleep. I simply, with all my might, try to absorb her pain, try to take it all away through sheer will. I want her to give it all to me so that I can feel it instead of her. I don't want her to hurt anymore because of me. I'd take all the hurt instead if I could.

"I'm so sorry, my only," I tell her.

46

AMELIA BRENNAN

I pull into the gas station and turn my car off. A woman somewhere in her early thirties, I think, with clear blue eyes and great skin steps outside, eyes on me, filled with suspicion.

I smile in the hopes of putting her at ease. "Hi," I greet.

"Need directions?" she asks.

It's probably obvious that I don't need gas since I haven't stopped at the pump. It's strange that she greets me outside though, as if assuming I don't want to come in and buy something from the store or use their restroom or something like that. Very strange.

"Actually, I'm looking for Savage Construction. I'm told it's somewhere around these parts."

Her head tilts sideways and she wrinkles her nose. Like she's sniffing the air. She's a suspicious one. Her eyes move from my face to my feet and back up.

"You related to Ivy Savage?"

"Ivy what?" I gasp.

I'M HERE BECAUSE MY sister is gone. Again.

She wasn't answering her phone and she told me in a phone call right after her snake bite incident that the guy she met up here was named Tyson Savage. After what I found at her place last night, I stayed the night with Mom and at dawn, snuck out to drive to Drowsy Hollow.

Someone in a little diner, where I dropped the Tyson Savage name mentioned there was a company not far away called Savage Construction. A bunch of big, strong men who built homes and commercial buildings.

No one knew where it was. I was directed to a website. I called the phone number.

"Is Tyson there please?"

"Tyson?" The man's voice went strange. "Did you say Tyson?"

"I'm looking for Tyson Savage," I said. "Is he there?"

"Who are you?" the husky male voice asked.

Something didn't feel right. Something felt *very* not right.

"Is Tyson Savage affiliated with this company? I'm trying to find my sister and have reason to believe she's with him."

"Your sister?"

"Do you know a Tyson Savage or don't you?" I demanded.

"What's your name?"

"Amelia," I answered.

"Amelia." His voice was strange. Or stranger.

Way weird. I hung up, feeling odd. Feeling panic, I think. A minute later, the phone was ringing with 'private caller'.

I rejected the call for some reason.

And then I regretted it. I don't know why all the hairs on my body were standing on end from that phone call. I should've answered the phone, I was sure it was that same guy. I should've answered and demanded more information.

I searched the phone number I dialed with a map search and it came up with Savage Construction listing with a PO Box address. I went to the map to pinpoint the zip code and it brought me to this corner, to the Arcana Falls General Store and gas bar, which has a post office kiosk.

Ivy was a mess yesterday and I hated letting her go back to her place. I got home after dinner and my fiancé was just like sandpaper on my nerves for some reason, so I packed an overnight bag and told him I was going to stay with Ivy until Tamara got back from Jamaica next week. He wasn't happy about it, but I told him I'd call him later, that I was too worried about my sister to not be there for her. I loaded up my car and went to Ivy's. But Ivy wasn't there. Neither was her car. Her upstairs neighbor came down and started spouting off to me about the commotion a while earlier, about three giant men being there and making all sorts of racket and pissing him off. This guy went on about complaining to the landlord and not so that he could alert me that my sister might be in trouble, because he didn't like that my lights shined in his window when I pulled in.

"My sister was here in an altercation with three men and you complain and threaten to call the landlord and don't offer to help or at least call the police in case my sister is in trouble?" I was flabbergasted.

"I mind my own business," the guy said, putting his hands up in the air.

What. An. Asshole.

"You're a fucking tool," I told him. "Maybe you should get some blackout shades instead of putting sheer curtains on a window overlooking a driveway."

"Fuck you, bitch," he replied and slammed his door.

Moron.

I have a spare key for Ivy's, so I went inside, and the kitchen was a mess. There was a plant and table toppled, a pile of mail scattered, too, and a really unusual cologne-like scent in the air.

My body broke out in goosebumps and I immediately dialed Ivy's number. No answer.

I text-messaged my mother.

"Did Ivy come to your place?"

My mom phoned me instead of replying. "She's not here. Why? Why?" Mom sounded panicked.

"I just got to her place and she's not here. There's a mess and her upstairs neighbor said something about three big guys being here and there being some sort of commotion."

"Oh God. Oh God. Did you call her?"

"No answer."

"Oh Jesus! I'm coming over. Wait there."

Mom came over and while we cleaned up the mess in Ivy's and Tamara's place, Mom told me what she said she'd told my sister that morning while I was at the supermarket. That she thinks Aunt Nelle set some strange supernatural shit in motion and she doesn't know what sort of crap is going on but thinks my sister got stolen by either a vampire or maybe a shapeshifter who wants to keep her.

Shapeshifters? Vampires?

My mom is not crazy and despite how batshit crazy that sounded, she seemed like she was totally serious. Like she believes every word she's said to me. I'm not sure what the fuck is happening but all I know is that I need to find my sister.

Mom made me go home with her and spend the night. I called the cops from her place and they were no help. I couldn't rest. I was just freaking out. At dawn, I snuck out, deciding to drive to Drowsy Hollow to see what I can find out. Ivy still isn't answering her phone. I left before Mom got up because she was just hysterical until the wee hours when she finally conked out on the couch telling me that Aunt Nelle had plans for all of us, Mom included, and how crazy it is that this all happened right after she and Dad split up.

I know how nuts people think Aunt Nelle was. I also know she wasn't nuts. Not at all. She saw things in her life. Wild things. We had our secret chats and she told me stuff I've never repeated to a soul. She never told me, though, that she'd done some crazy thing with a fortune teller.

"I pulled my sister's letter and all the cryptic stuff she said lines up with your dad and I splitting up too."

"God, Mom, you think you're about to be whisked away by a were bear?" I laughed.

My mom's face went stone serious. "You didn't grow up where I did, Amie, hearing the stories, talking to people who said they saw things. Did you see how purple your sister's eyes were?"

The eye thing was definitely very freaky.

She gave me Aunt Nelle's letter and I read it.

And then I made Mom crack open the bottle of vodka in the freezer and read it a second time.

I tried to call the cops but after calling off the search last time when they'd begun putting resources into looking for Ivy they suggested, grouchily I might add, that we wait until Ivy's been gone 24 hours to see if she isn't just off on another adventure.

No, I didn't mention anything about supernatural stuff or witches or my aunt who's been dead a year. I tried to reason with them that my sister was keeping something from us about why she went missing last time and that I thought maybe they should go interview her upstairs neighbor about what he told me.

They told me they still wanted me to wait 24 hours.

I was pissed and went up the food chain two levels and got nowhere.

So, since I don't want to wait until tonight to make another report and it's been six hours since I had a drink and I definitely didn't get drunk, I've thrown my overnight bag into my SUV, armed myself with bear mace from the garage (Dad hasn't cleaned his stuff out yet), and headed the three hour drive to Drowsy Hollow to find Tyson Savage and see what the fuck is going on.

"COME IN AND SIT DOWN. I'll call somebody to talk to you," the lady at the gas station says.

"I'll be right in," I tell her.

I go back into my car to grab my purse and put it on cross body. I have my hand inside it, gripping the can of bear mace inside because something is definitely weird about all this, her attitude included.

I step into the store and she's on the phone with a strange look in her eyes as she tracks me coming inside.

"Almost her double. Brunette though," she mutters into the phone.

I meet her eyes with challenge.

"Who's that? And where's my fucking sister?"

47

IVY

I wake up to Tyson letting go of me. He's getting up and leaving the room. We're both still dressed in what we were wearing yesterday.

He got me in his cabin, dropped my bags on the floor, carried me to bed and wouldn't let go, wouldn't stop purring until I guess I passed out.

I feel wrung out right now. Completely, absolutely wrung dry.

He's leaving the room, so I haven't had to look at his face yet but even the sight of his back hurts.

I close my eyes. He's outside and I hear voices.

I stare off into space for a few minutes until there's a knock on the door that's not even closed. I look over and see Bailey and Cat standing there together. Both of them have doleful expressions. Cat has a travel mug in her hand.

"I brought your favorite coffee," she says.

"Thank you," I mouth. I clear my throat and sit up. "I have to use the bathroom. Excuse me."

They both move away from the doorway and I slip out. Pain hits me square in the chest as I spot him, in the kitchen, emptying a cooler of food containers into the fridge. There are also two boxes on the floor that I'm guessing are also filled with supplies. Cat is so maternal, even if she only got to be a mom to him for a short time when he was a baby.

When I'm back out, I reach for my purse and take it back into the bathroom, ignoring that his eyes are on me. I feel them, like the gaze contains heat.

I quickly wash my face, brush my teeth, and take my birth control pill.

I breeze back, ignoring him, and find Cat and Bailey in the bedroom. The bed is made. Cat is sitting on the end of it. Bailey is sitting in the chair.

"Thank you," I say and reach for the coffee and take a sip.

It's still hot and it's French vanilla. Cat is so thoughtful.

She's looking at me with agony on her face. "You're still not okay," she says.

I shake my head. "How can I be? After everything he did, he kidnaps me and brings me back here?" My chin trembles.

I try hard to stop the tears from coming again. I've cried so much in the past two days, I'm just sick of it. I feel like all my energy got used up to go to the bathroom and come back so I plop onto the bed beside her.

"I appreciate that you both came over to check on things," I muster up all I can to get loud so I'm certain he hears, "but things aren't okay and they're not gonna be. I don't want to be here, but he decided to take my choices away. Again. And I really don't feel like talking. I'm sorry, but if you can just—-"

"What happened was awful, Ivy. Just awful," Cat says. She's fingering the quilt on the bed.

Bailey is staring at her feet. Her face says it all; she still agrees with my decision to go.

I want them to leave. I can't take their kindness right now.

"I think I know that. I was there. It happened to me."

Cat's face falls.

"I don't wanna hurt your feelings, guys, but nothing you can say right now will erase what he did to me. In front of everyone. You said yourself that your husband, a man in the same position never did that to you. I can tell by Bailey's reaction that she never saw something like that. And she's the self-proclaimed walking werewolf encyclopedia."

"I never claimed to know everything," Bailey says. "But I do know that he didn't do that intentionally. He's a wreck. I'm pissed, too, Ivy, on your behalf, but your mate is shredded over what happened."

I swallow. That doesn't bring me joy. That doesn't feel like sweet justice. All of this just hurts.

"Something is just very wrong with Mason," Bailey says, "And this was a chain reaction. Add to that, Tyson doesn't function like a typical alpha or a typical man for that matter. He's, for lack of a better term, a super alpha and super dysfunctional because he a) grew up outside the pack with a mental case for a guardian and his only company and b) he spent six years in the forest in wolf form. If he'd spent one more season as a wolf, he'd never have come back to us. Six years is sketchy enough. Seven is the absolute limit and he got awful close to that limit. I'm not saying those are valid excuses, but they're reasons that should be taken into account."

I shrug. "I'm not trying to be heartless, but none of this is an Ivy problem. It's a Tyson problem. I didn't ask to be here; I don't want to be here."

I'm trying to say all this with a calm and detached manner but of course I'm failing. I'm not calm. I'm broken. I wish I could be detached. But all of this feels very, *very* attached to every part of me.

"And no matter what, you guys, you don't have to worry about me telling anybody any of your secrets, so –"

"Ivy," Cat tries, reaching out and grabbing my hand. "Mason –"

"Regardless of what is or isn't wrong with Mason –" I hear Ty growling from the other room and get a full-body shudder "That was done to me. *Me*." I flatten my palm on my chest. My sore, empty chest.

Ty is suddenly in the room with us and he looks furious.

"I never want his name on your lips again, Ivy. Never!"

My mouth drops open. My stomach pitches. I don't like the look in his eyes. At all.

"Out, women. Now."

"Son…" Cat rises and puts her hand on his forearm. "You need to –"

"I tried to stay awake all night and absorb your pain, Ivy, so you wouldn't feel it. I tried. And I feel bad. I have never felt worse than this. It didn't work. But you know what? I think I'd do it again. If anyone thinks you're not mine –"

"Tyson!" Cat calls and I can feel the winces from both her and Bailey.

Ty ignores her.

"Deep down, I know – so I'm telling you I'd do it again, Ivy. I'd fuck you in front of him again if he put his eyes on you. This time, though, I'd kill him while I was doing it. You. Are mine. Mine, Ivy! I'm sorry I hurt you, I am very," he thumps his chest with a fist "*fucking* sorry I hurt you. But I won't lie and say I won't do it again because you're mine! Mine to love. Mine to fuck. Mine to protect, and –"

A lone tear trails down my cheek. "Protect? Really?" I ask, my voice steady, even, and by his reaction, it delivers a blow.

A phone rings. Bailey's.

"Go, women," Ty orders. "Your talking is doing nothing. It's time for me to fix this with Ivy."

Suddenly, I don't want them to go. I really don't.

Bailey's phone stops ringing and then starts to ring again. She looks at the screen and then slips by Tyson, answering it.

"Tyson," Cat tries.

"Mother, will you please purchase me a phone and put in everyone's numbers and drop it off to me?" He reaches into his pocket and hands her a wad of cash.

"Yes, okay."

"Do that, please."

"Okay. No problem. Son, can we talk for a quick moment?"

"Trust me," he looks into her eyes. "Trust me. I've got this."

She looks over her shoulder at me.

"Don't go. He's gonna use sex to try to get me to..." I shudder, "submit."

"Damn right I am," Tyson tells us.

"You're a fucking jerk," I shout.

His eyes blaze with anger.

"And you're mine! Even when you're angry at me. And I'm going to show you."

"Angry? This isn't angry, Tyson. This is destroyed."

His face falls.

"He loves you," Cat says. "You've got a beautiful gift here, Ivy. Forgiveness is going to be important in the years to come. Be sure you don't make it so that you can't ask for his forgiveness if you someday make a grave mistake. Trust me, you never know if you'll be able to apologize for something or if something or someone will suddenly take that ability away from you." Her eyes are haunted and that tells me right there that there were things unfinished between her and Tyson's father when he was killed. There are things she's haunted about.

"That sucks that something like that happened to you, Cat, but you were married."

"You're married, too, sweetheart," she says.

"I'm not," I insist.

"Well, you two fix things and then we'll have a wedding so that you'll be married in both of your minds." She blows me a kiss, gets on her tiptoes and he leans down so she can kiss him, though he doesn't take his eyes off me, and then she leaves.

"Tyson!" Bailey pokes her head in. "Here a minute."

"Later, Bailey."

"It's important," she insists.

His jaw flexes and he turns and disappears from the doorway.

I sit there a second, blankly, then cover my face with my hands, blowing out a breath... a sigh? I don't even know.

I get what Catrina said. That whole "Never go to bed angry" kind of thing, but that's for people in relationships. We're not in one, not one that I agreed to anyway. And if I had, even if I had, what he did to me wasn't okay. What he did was a dealbreaker. *If* we had a deal. We didn't.

I'm his captive right now. And that's not okay either.

48

TYSON

I follow Bailey and my mother outside onto the porch.

I don't know what the fuck to do. One second I want to kiss my Ivy's feet and beg for forgiveness and the next, I want to throw her to the floor and fuck her, join our bodies and show her how much we belong together.

Bailey's eyes are huge.

"Ivy's sister showed up in Arcana Falls looking for her."

I straighten. "What?"

"She pulled up at the four corners, Cicely called Riley's office, but Mason answered and went right over there and took Amelia Brennan. Cicely said he identified her as his mate."

I sit down on the step and catch my breath and try to make sense of this news.

"There was witchcraft at play, Tyson. That could explain everything. We need more information, but it could be why Mase reacted like that. Can I talk to Ivy a second?"

I gesture to the door, but then jump to my feet and stop Bailey before she gets over the threshold. "Wait," I say.

My mother speaks up. "She doesn't need this information. She doesn't need to worry about her sister before her and Tyson reconcile, Bailey."

My mother has taken the words from my mouth.

"I agree," Bailey says. "We're all on the same page. I just want to ask her one question. Don't worry, I won't make things worse."

She goes inside.

My mother has hope in her eyes. "This could be the answer."

"Is his sense of smell fucked up enough that he'd not recognize that she's not his, only has similar blood because of a sibling?" I ask. "My nose recognized Aunt Lucy as your sibling, Bailey as Grey's."

My mother shrugs. "I'm not quite sure what's what with Mason's senses, but I want to talk to our Scottish contacts to ask the questions. The fact that the guys say Ivy told them there's witchcraft at play is a big deal. I wanted to ask Ivy about that, but she wasn't very receptive. We're going to have to call the local coven and get some answers."

"Will there be answers?"

"There'd better be. They're required to document every single spell they cast. If they don't? It could cause a war. They'd have to answer to every supernatural being council in the country."

"How are mates chosen outside of scent? Should someone else have been mine?" I ask. "I don't care if that's the case, Ivy is mine, but I'm curious about this. Did the witch spell alter destiny?"

"It's a complicated matter, son. I have no answers. It wouldn't be the first time a coven interfered with what would normally happen with a myriad of factors outside our knowledge. Fate? Compatibility? Chemicals? We don't know what makes someone attracted to someone else. With alpha shifters, it's especially complex. It's sometimes been said that you're all at the mercy of past generations of witches who very carefully ensure the balance of things in nature. Is that true? I don't really know. Is it a matter of love at first sight? Sometimes. Sometimes a couple grows up together and realizes out of the blue that they're mates. Witches are very secretive and there's also nature at play so while we don't have all the answers, neither do the witches."

"Well, that's as clear as mud," I grumble.

"I know," she whispers.

"It doesn't matter. She's mine."

"But if there's a reasonable explanation, maybe it'll heal things with you and Mason."

I bare my teeth but say nothing.

"At least that's not a *no*," she says and taps my arm affectionately.

"I like you, Catrina Savage. I'm glad you're my mother."

She looks startled for a beat at my words, then she laughs.

I like the sound of her laugh, even if my expression doesn't show it right now.

"I need to work on my way with words," I add.

She smiles bigger and throws her arms around me. "I love you, my boy. I'm so glad you found your way back to me."

I squeeze her tight. I take in her scent and instead of reminding me of the pain I was feeling at knowing her scent was on Cornelius, I now have other feelings associated with her scent. Care. For who she is. For all she's shown me of herself so far.

"Go fix things with your girl. Please know, being gentle might be the key here, son. Rather than listening to your alpha instinct to take control of her. And I want you to know, I have all your father's diaries. He talked a bit about his approach to fighting off his temper. He got tips from his father, who also had temper issues."

I nod.

"You'll have to learn the ancient language to read them," she adds, "but Bailey learned from our elders. I'm sure she can help."

Bailey comes outside. "Amelia Brennan is the older sister," she says.

My mother looks alarmed. And then just as quickly, her face changes, like something makes sense to her.

"What's this?" I demand.

Bailey lowers her voice, presumably so that Ivy can't hear. "If a witch made some spell to match two sisters with two alphas from the same pack, really, it should've been the older sister with the older alpha. Our pack works chronologically with such things. Always has. Though it was strange that Riley mated before Mason. We figured that although he was third in birth order, it was because he took second alpha place instead of Mason. As for you and Mason... being in the council together, you being born first and him being born right after you, if you're destined to be mated to girls from the same family, logically you should be paired with Amelia and Mason should be paired with Ivy."

My blood heats on the verge of boiling at those words.

"Hear me out," Bailey pleads. "I know you don't like the sound of that, but I think something must have malfunctioned in that spell. We need to reach out to that coven and get them digging through all their grimoires."

"When was Mason born?" Cat asks Bailey.

"January 19," Bailey says.

"Only one day after Tyson," Cat says softly. "Maybe not even a full day. Tyson was born just before midnight. I don't know what time Mason was born, but... What about Ivy's sister?"

"Ivy said they're born a year apart, to the day."

Enough of this. "I don't know where all this is going and right now I don't much care. Can you go buy that phone, Mother? Leave it on the step here when you do, if you have time for that."

"I'll make time," she says. "I'll be back quickly."

"Good. Don't knock. I'm going to be busy."

"Tyson, be sweet. Be whatever sweet you were that had you winning her over," Bailey suggests.

"I can only be me."

"I respect that. It's just that she's very wounded in her heart, and – if you break a woman's heart – you can't always mend it."

"You're heard. Go, women. Please."

Bailey nods and heads to Cat's car. So does Cat.

I go inside and lock the door.

Ivy's not in the bedroom. I see the door to my old room is slightly open. I find her sitting there on the floor against the wall with the yellow book in her hand.

Her pretty eyes look dull, red-rimmed. And they look more blue than purple right now and I don't know why, but I find that alarming. Her lower lip protrudes in a pout when she looks up at me from the book.

"The guy wearing the yellow hat set a trap and stole the baby monkey from his life and took him away. He kept him. Maybe that monkey would've been better off in the jungle. Maybe the guy with the yellow hat was a monkey thief. How did I ever like this book?"

"Are you saying you think you're better off without me? Am I the man in the hat?"

"I don't know what I'm saying." She puts the book down. "It's like those old cartoons that we watched as kids, thinking nothing of it and now seeing how racist they were. It's disappointing. It's disappointing to think you feel some way about something and then realize you were stupid."

I sit on the floor in front of her.

"Mason Quinn has your sister," I say.

Her body jerks in shock and her eyes meet mine.

I swallow. "I could've kept that from you hoping to get you to forgive me instead of making you angrier, but I won't hide things from you. I don't know much, but she went to Arcana Falls to find you, she somehow knew to look there, and I've heard word that Mason left with her."

"My sister's wedding is in a couple weeks."

"Looks like she's getting married today, instead. Tell me about this witchcraft regarding us."

Ivy blinks rapidly at nothing, processing this news I just told her, I guess.

Finally, her eyes meet mine.

"My aunt went to a fortune teller, my mom said, when I was a baby and paid money to the witch for some special supernatural happily ever after for me and my sister. I didn't know about it until yesterday."

"Seems there's some mishap at play," I say. "My mother and Bailey are trying to track down the witches."

"To have it canceled?" she asks and the hope in her eyes feels like a blade sinking into my chest.

Her expression drops, realizing the effect her words have had, I think.

"To get information. According to typical pack pairings, the first alpha born in the calendar of a council mates first. They seemed to think if the spell was cast against my pack with your family that your sister should have been paired with me and you with..." I can't even fucking say it.

"Mason," she finishes for me.

The anger rises in me so quickly that it takes everything to tamp it down.

Her eyes flash with fear and I see my hands, see the fur receding. I half-shifted briefly.

I must learn to control that somehow. It's never been this out-of-control. Maybe my father's journals will have some answers. Maybe I can ask a witch what Cornelius would have injected me with so I can give that to Ivy.

"Ivy, I can't help what I am any more than you can," I say, using her words from not long after we first met.

Her eyes point to her hands.

She fiddles with her fingers in her lap.

"But I will do everything I can do to fix this between us. I fucked up. I'm sorry. But I'm me. I can't promise you it'll never happen again, or I'll be lying. And I do promise never to lie to you."

She continues staring at her hands.

"I wanted to come back here and fuck you until you submit to me. Make you come over and over until you know you're mine."

She cringes. Physically cringes. This hurts.

I keep talking. "But I'll give you space instead. I love you, Ivy. I'm very sorry to make you hurt like this. To make you recoil at the idea of me touching you." I swallow and let out a big breath. "I'll do my best to be a good mate to you. I changed my mind. I can't live in that city with the stench and the noise and so much pavement. We can live here, or we can live in Arcana Falls. It's up to you."

She says nothing.

"Now, I really need to run, and I also need to ... do wolf things. So, I'm gonna go do that. Please stay here. If you leave again, I'll just have to hunt for you and if I do, I can't promise I won't fuck you until you submit. I'm fighting all my instincts right now and believe me, it's not easy. Obey me, please. Do you know how to reach Catrina?"

"I have Bailey's number saved," she says softly. "She sent a text with a bunch of peoples' numbers."

"Give me your phone. I need to phone Catrina. I'll ask her to come sit with you while I'm gone. If she can, she'll be here soon. If she can't and can't send Bailey, don't leave."

"It's in my purse," she says softly, not looking at me.

I bring her the phone. She presses buttons and passes it to me, still not looking at me.

The phone makes a noise and then Cat says, "Ivy? It's Cat. Bailey's driving."

"It's me. I need to run. When will you be back here?"

"Um, half an hour, an hour maybe? I'm just about to the electronics store to get your new phone, honey."

"Can you wait with Ivy until I'm back? I need to –"

"Run? Of course you do. Yes. I'm glad you're taking your energy out on the forest. Giving her time to think is a good idea."

"See you soon." I pass the phone to Ivy, kiss the tip of her nose, then get up and leave.

I'm still not good with my words, but I think I got my message across.

And now, I need to run and rip things apart.

But I don't want to risk Ivy running and harming herself, so I shift to wolf, and I mark the property with my scent. It didn't help when she left and got bitten by the snake so I can't bring myself to leave.

Instead, I pace the property around the cabin until my mother's car pulls in. She nods at me and I run toward the road.

49

IVY

Amelia and Mason? My stubborn, alpha female sister and the wolf shifter that Tyson fucked me in front of? The guy Tyson wanted to kill?

This is crazy.

This is c-r-a-z-y!

All of it's crazy. I look at my phone. Missed calls from Amelia, from Ben, and from my mother.

I call Amelia's line.

No answer. I text her.

> "Please get ahold of me! 9-1-1! Are you with someone named Mason?"

I stare at the phone for the longest time, waiting for the read receipt. Waiting for her to reply. Nothing.

I call my mom.

She answers on the first ring.

"Ivy? Thank God!"

"Hi Mom, um –"

"Where are you? Where the hell are you?"

"I'm at Tyson's."

"Tyson's," Mom says.

"And Amie came looking for me and apparently some other werewolf got her and is claiming her the way Ty claimed me."

"Werewolf?" Mom repeats.

Oh shit. Shit. Shit. Fuck.

I bite my lip. "I wasn't supposed to say that."

"Never mind all that for now. Are you okay? Is she okay? Are you okay?"

"Um, I don't know about her. I'm ... not really okay, but that's mostly ... feelings." I wince.

I don't know how else to explain it. I can't possibly tell my mother what happened. She already knows too much.

"Does your instinct tell you your sister's okay? Do you know this werewolf that has her?"

I blink. I bite my lip. I let out a long breath.

"Ivy?"

"I think she is. All these people, Mom, they're good people, I think. They care about one another. The mating thing is really important to them. I don't know how Amelia's gonna feel about all this, but I don't think she's in danger. You can't tell anybody what they are, you can't, Mom. It'd be dangerous. For all of us."

At least I hope she isn't. My sister's mouth can get her in trouble. But with the way a werewolf deals with a mouthy mate...

My head spins at the notion of some guy trying to make Amelia Brennan submit.

My head spins in general because so much has happened in a week.

"What can I do? Do I come there?"

"I think maybe wait, Mom. I'll talk to Tyson's mom or Bailey, another girl here I've been talking to. I'll see what I can find out."

"How am I supposed to just sit here, Ivy?"

I shrug. "I don't know. I just... don't know. I'll call you back when I know more, okay?"

There's silence on the line. Loaded silence. Mom feels helpless and she doesn't do well when feeling that way. Who does, though?

"Don't you dare make me sit here for forty-eight hours again."

"I won't."

She sighs.

"To you, what's the best and worst case scenarios here?" I ask her. That's something she's always done with us when faced with what feels like an impossible scenario.

"Best case, your sister either falls in love or gets home without a hitch. Worst... someone hurts her or makes her upset."

"I think right now she's probably got a very horny wolf shifter pursuing a relationship with her. She's going to have her hands full with that, but I can tell you from experience, it's not unpleasant."

I can't believe I just said that. And of course I'm only talking about the beginning. I can't possibly tell my mother how things have turned for Tyson and me.

"And Mason? He's ... extraordinarily hot," I say.

My hand lands on my neck and I squeeze at some stiffness. It happens to be right there, right where he bit me. Images flash through my mind of my first time with Tyson. That first surprising knotting experience.

I feel a smile creep across my face.

Ames, you're gonna like that.

I hear noise, so I spin to look out the window.

The big black wolf walks by. He sees me in the window. He keeps walking.

I stare out at the trees ahead. A minute later he walks by again. He's doing circles around the house.

And my chest hurts at the sight.

There's a strangely potent scent of him all around me.

Can I forgive him? Is it possible?

Can I stay here and embrace a life with him?

Or in Arcana Falls where he's part of something bigger, something better for him, something he was supposed to have but got robbed of? What would that mean for me, though? Life here?

With Amelia?

Amelia is engaged to Rick the Dick. And she's probably getting dicked by the very good-looking, big, and strong Mason the werewolf right now.

Is it as simple as me and Amelia being from the same family that screwed with Mason's senses about me because of witchcraft?

So much has happened. It's a lot. It's overwhelming.

I finish the last of my coffee and decide I should go take a bath.

Baths are always therapeutic for me.

I've gotten clarity on a situation more times than I can count sitting in hot and bubbly water. I've even gone so far as to symbolically give my problem to the drain and let it wash down.

Can I wash all this hurt down the drain?

50

TYSON

I shift back to man form and lift my jeans from the dirt beside the porch. There's more than just my mother's SUV here. Riley's motorcycle is here, too.

I pull the jeans on and carry my boots up to the porch and drop them.

I step inside with my shirt in my hand.

My mother sits at the table with Riley. They both have mugs in their hands.

They watch me approach.

"How are you, cuz?" Riley greets. "Good run?"

It was a long run. And a long swim, all the way to Arcana Falls and back. Did it help? I don't know. I'm too tired right now to know.

I jerk my chin up in return greeting and ask my mother, "Where is she?"

"She's in bed. I got here while she was in the tub. She went right to bed after that. Not feeling too talkative. Want some coffee?"

I shake my head.

"You probably want us to go, but sit for a minute and talk with us before we do," Riley says.

I sigh and sit down in an empty chair.

Riley leans forward. "Mason has Ivy's sister at his house. He called me and we already knew, but he called to ask me to tell you that he got it wrong. He couldn't make the scent out with Ivy, but the second Amelia stepped into town, he knew. In fact, he said she called our office, we work together, and he happened to answer when she phoned trying to track down her sister and he was pretty sure he knew by her voice. The call to him and to his wolf was that strong. She's a little... resistant, though. He's got her at his house on Chariot Lake."

"Things are coming together, Tyson," my mother says. "We have word from Scotland on his bloodwork. I emailed the lab results from a local doctor who is a friend to our pack, and everything looks normal with Mason's labs. This definitely seems like witchcraft has come in to play."

"The night Ivy hit me with her car, the moon wasn't right. Neither was the road. We were pushed into the same place," I say. "I thought witchcraft was part of the night. Thought Ivy might even be a witch for a moment because of the way it all initially... felt."

"Hm," Riley says.

"Cornelius used to go to a witch. I didn't know why. He often went and made me wait outside."

"Where?" Riley asks.

"Drowsy Hollow. It used to be a fortune teller, now it's a dry-cleaner. I saw it when I was in town with Ivy when she went shopping for the strawberry moon party."

"We'll look into that immediately. It's probably a good idea to get the four of you in a room at some stage. See if you have any reaction to Amelia Brennan," Cat says.

"Probably Amelia Quinn by now," Riley says with a smirk. He drains his coffee. "Okay, we'll go."

"Here. Your new phone. The rest of your money. You gave me too much. We're all in there under contacts." Cat shows me the phone, pointing out how I turn it off and on and where the phone and message options are.

"I can figure it out," I say. "Thank you for staying with her."

Cat gives me a tight smile. "Call me tomorrow. Let me know how you're doing. How she's doing. Let me know if you need anything. Try to get her to eat something."

"I will. Love you," I say and kiss her forehead.

She looks about to weep. I look away, swallowing down a lump. "Call me tomorrow, Rye. Tell me what's what."

"I will. We'll see what we can find out before we get the four of you in a room. We'll have to have all sorts of reinforcements first. So we can protect you all. It might be a few days before Mase is willing to come up for air though." He smirks.

And suddenly, I'm smirking, too, not feeling so much hatred for Mason Quinn.

I close the door and lock it behind them.

I open my bedroom door. She's not there. I frown. The clothes she wore are on the end of the bed. I lift the shirt. It smells like her. And someone else. Her sister? On top of the pants are a pair of underwear with lettering on them. I look at them. They only smell like Ivy.

The word 'BRIDE' is on the ass of them in scrolled lettering.

I drop them and go to the other room, knowing that she's in there. I put my forehead to the door for a moment and fill my lungs with air before turning the knob.

She's made up the mattress where I slept as a kid, where Cornelius slept after I grew.

She doesn't want to sleep in my bed with me.

I bite my lip, also biting back the emotion I'm feeling. And then I scoop her up into my arms. She startles and lets out a little scream, eyes bolting wide open.

I carry her to my bed and set her down, then I leave her there and take myself to that bed instead. I lie there and stare at the ceiling for the next few hours.

I'M RUNNING. I'M RUNNING and being chased by barking wolves who are gaining on me. They catch up to me and begin ripping me apart.

I jackknife upright. A dream. I'm in the dark and it takes a split second to realize where I am. It's the wee hours of the night and I hear noise.

I rise and step out quietly. I see her sitting at the table eating from a tub of ice cream.

Her neck twists so she can look over her shoulder. She sees me in the doorway before she goes back to her food.

"That's quite a feast you've got there," I tell her. She's got more than ice cream.

She makes a grumble sound. Upon closer examination I see it's not a tub of ice cream. I should've trusted my nose instead of my eyes. It's that creamy cold potatoes with dill spice. My mother obviously brought some to her in an ice cream tub. The fridge is full to bursting with food.

Ivy's also eating cold meat with spice on it. Cheese. And grapes.

My stomach makes noise.

"Are you hungry too?" she asks in a small voice.

My heart warms. She still wants to take care of me.

"I am," I say and sit at the table.

"Then you can just put it all away when you're done." She pushes her chair back and stomps off to the bedroom. She slams the door, leaving me sitting there with all that food.

I'm not so hungry anymore.

I put the food back in the fridge and go outside. I find myself in the garage. Ten minutes later, I'm burning all Cornelius's paintings in a bonfire that's too high, that's as high and careless as the idiots at that house Ivy was at that night I met her.

When I watch the last of them turn to flakes of ash, I douse the fire with several buckets of water and go back inside.

I open the bedroom door. I see her eyes pointed at the ceiling. She closes them immediately, not likely realizing I can see her as perfectly in the dark as she can see in the light.

I shed my clothing and climb into bed. I climb over her body to the side near the wall and then I pull her to me.

She grunts a sound of disapproval. I turn her to her back and put my mouth to my mark on her.

"I love you," I say. "I wanna feel you. I *need* to feel you. Please, baby."

"Whatever," she mutters.

"Whatever?" I inquire.

"Yeah. Whatever. You're gonna do whatever you want whether I want it or not. Just get it over with so I can go back to sleep."

Repulsion crawls through me. I hate that she thinks this of me.

I despise it. I roll off her, roar out my anger, and then she's running.

No! She thinks I mean to hurt her. That's not what that sound was. I clench my teeth together, hear her running out the front door.

When I get outside, she's already to the willow tree, running as fast as she can. I hear her heart. I hear her bare feet pounding. She's winded. Her beautiful blonde and purple hair flies behind her.

I sprint and am upon her in just a handful of paces. I tackle her to the dirt, breaking her fall by rolling so she lands on me first. Then I roll and pin her to the ground.

"Don't run from a predator, Ivy Savage," I growl against the mark on her throat.

I smell her arousal instantly.

But she's denying it by writhing under me, scoring her fingernails across my face. "Get off me you filthy monster."

"That sound in bed was my agony, Ivy. That sound was turmoil at how you feel about me, at how I incinerated your love for me to ash. I hate that I did this. I hate that you think I'm a fucking jerk. That wasn't a noise to intimidate you. But I'm not about to tuck my tail between my legs and walk away. I won't do it. I'm going to fix this, even if it takes years. Even if you try to deny me."

Her chest heaves up and down as she gasps for breath.

I purr for her and her heartrate slows a little. She's not gasping so hard. I can't help myself, as her chest heaves up and down, her breasts touching my pecs, so I run my nose along the mark on her throat and grind my cock against her center. She's in shorts and a shirt with no sleeves, just strings over her shoulders, and the black top has the tops of her breasts spilling out.

Before I think better of it, I haul the top down on the right, exposing her creamy breast and her peaked nipple. I take it into my mouth and suckle hard.

She moans.

I suck again. Harder.

She cries out and grabs my hair. For a second I think she's trying to pull me off, but then she grinds against my cock.

Yes. Fucking yes.

I fumble down below and free myself from my pants. I pull her shorts to the side and she's sopping wet when I slam inside her. She groans as I push hard, to the root, feeling her hips beneath me. I feel like I can't get close enough. I put my lips to hers and our tongues twist up together.

Our teeth even clash, but I don't care. I plunder her sweet lips, taking everything I can get. Every fucking bit of it. I flip over, taking her out of the dirt; my beautiful girl doesn't belong in the dirt; I do. I bounce her on top of my cock as I lay back, taking a handful of her perfect breast in my hand as I continue making her move with the other. I cock my knees and she leans back against my thighs, mouth opening into an o-shape. She looks beautiful against the backdrop of the black sky with her angelic face and halo of wispy hair. She is an angel. My angel.

I grab the length of her hair and bounce her some more, growling with ferocity at the possessive feelings engulfing me.

She looks at me with panic. I've half-shifted again. *Shit*. The panic in her eyes! I quickly knot so she can't escape. And I push my wolf back. Or I try. But my wolf pushes forward, wanting to be seen, wanting her to know.

There's clarity for me right now. This is me. All of me. All of me loves her.

I hold her tight as my knot pulses inside her beautifully tight heat.

My wolf recedes as she's coming, coming beautifully with her eyes locked with mine, her entire body trembling on me. She collapses into me as it ebbs away from her and I feel a prickling sensation in my veins as the angry heat inside me cools.

I wrap my arms tight around her and lift her while standing, my cock still inside her. I kick the pants, which are still around one of my ankles, off and carry her back to bed. I lay down on my back with my cock still inside her.

"I love you, my Ivy. All of me loves you."

She makes a sweet little sound that sounds almost like a purr of her own as she falls asleep.

Something strange dawns on me.

I think my Ivy might be in heat.

51

IVY

I wake up on top of Ty. I lift my head from his chest and see his throat, his chiseled jawline. I blink a couple times. I'm naked.

My clothes are tangled up in the bed.

When I ran outside, that scent of his got stronger and it did something to me. It was like an aphrodisiac.

After we fucked outside, he fucked me again in this bed, this time ripping all my clothes off. And he didn't turn into the monster this time, but for some weird reason... I wanted him to.

And that's so fucking twisted, I can't believe it.

There was something about the way he fucked me outside, the way he roared out his orgasm in that partial Tyson, partial monster form was... I don't even know how to describe it.

I should be repulsed, like I was before, but I'm not. It's Tyson. Not a monster, just Tyson. That's who he is. Man. Wolf. Both.

I'm not over what happened, though, being taken like that in front of everyone.

So, why the heck am I so horny?

I squirm against his cock. It wakes. I slide over it a little and know I'm coating it with my juices. And with his juices, too, because I didn't get out of bed after the last time and so I fell asleep messy. Really messy.

His eyes open and he smiles.

I look away.

He catches my jaw with his hand. He cups it tenderly and kisses me.

"You're still so angry with me, aren't you, my only?"

My chin quivers.

"But you want my cock."

"And your eyes have gone purple again."

I squeeze my eyes shut tight.

This is humiliating.

He slides it inside, then turns me to my back.

"There's a leaf in your hair, beautiful Ivy," he softly tells me, plucking a green leaf from my hair and tossing it.

His hand grazes down my boob to my hip and then he reaches behind my knee and lifts my leg as he slides inside.

My mouth drops open. I absorb the sensation.

He moves down and then slams inside hard.

I whimper.

"You know why you want my cock so much?"

I say nothing.

"Even though you're angry?" he adds.

I gulp.

"Because you're mine." He slams in again and then there's the fullness increasing, there's the pulsing action, and yep... there are convulsions on my part as I splinter apart.

His eyes glow with heat as he bites his lip, rocking into me, enjoying the sensations he's getting.

"Because you're in heat, my little one. This cum that's filling you, it might be making children for us. What will we name them?" He caresses my face.

I keep crying out, realize I'm looking into his eyes instead of avoiding his gaze, and then I'm spent.

He finishes, then flips me so that he can gather me on top of him again.

I listen to his heart beating. I fall asleep to it.

And then I jolt awake, feeling like it's only been a minute, but I'm in the bed alone.

I sit up, pulling the blankets over my nakedness. I'm in a soggy mess of messed-up bedlinens. I need a shower.

I get up, wrapping the sheet around myself and head to the bathroom, remembering there's only one clean towel left.

We need to buy more towels.

He. Not we.

My face goes hot and I stomp to the bathroom, pissed off.

OUR EYES MEET.

He's there, at the kitchen table, talking on a phone that's not my phone in his lounge pants, barefoot and all his muscles on display. He's wearing a ponytail. It seems he's taken to the ponytail since I gave him one the night of the strawberry moon party.

I defiantly and snottily twist so that my nose is straight up in the air, so he knows all is definitely not forgiven, and I storm the rest of the short walk to the bathroom. I slam the door for emphasis. And lock it.

I drop the sheet and the towel and sit on the toilet with a harrumph.

Yep, I actually make that noise.

I know I'm being ridiculous, but I'm sort of pissed at myself. Why have I let him fuck me?

I'm not over what happened. How can I be?

Am I actually in heat? I reach over to my makeup bag by the sink and pull out my birth control pack, pop a pill out of the blister pack, and take it.

No way am I ovulating. The pill is over 99% effective when used correctly. I am always sure to use it correctly.

Even when my heart shattered the other day, I took my damn birth control pill at my usual time because it is programed into my brain to do so.

52

TYSON

"Every mated female, huh? Interesting."

Apparently, the pack's females go into heat on a similar cycle. Even the ones no longer in their childbearing years. It's something that can happen according to certain moon cycles and this post strawberry moon phase seems to have love in the air.

I marked the perimeter yesterday. When she got outside, it was as if my scent slammed into her and made her wet for me. That's exactly how it felt.

I'm on the phone with Greyson who called to check in on things. I've also had a cell phone words message from Bailey, from my mother, and from my Aunt Lucy, all telling me hello or that they hope all is well and offering to help, should me or Ivy need anything.

"We have word from the coven connected to Drowsy Hollow, Ty," Greyson tells me. "Riley, Mason, and I are meeting with them the day after tomorrow."

"Oh."

"Yep, we should have some news soon. Once we do, if it seems like a good move, we'd like to have a meeting with all council alphas in the community hall. You bring Ivy. Mase brings Amelia. We're all there to break things up if things go sideways."

"We'll see."

"Okay, man. I'll call you later."

"Where are you in the pack order again, Grey?"

"Fourth."

"So, when will your mate be revealed?"

"Hopefully soon, man. I'm fuckin' ready. You, Mase, Rye. Me, Joel and Linc are all keepin' eyes on Jase right now. He should be next. Then me."

I laugh. And then my laughter dies.

"What about Riley though? Will he find someone else or forever pine for his lost mate?"

Grey lets out a sigh. "He has to heal first, I think. And for him to heal, he has to start the process. He's avoidin' that."

"Shit."

"Yeah. You in the fold, I think it'll help."

"But I'm not entirely in the fold, am I?"

"Aren't you?" he asks.

I chew the inside of my cheek for a second.

"You're torn about it?" Grey asks.

"I'm torn about her. About what I did to her. I don't think she'll ever wanna show her face around you all again. And that's my fault so the least I can do is do my best to make sure she doesn't get daily reminders of how I hurt her. If she can't forgive and move forward, I have to remain…"

"A lone wolf," Grey finishes for me.

My eyes close briefly as that loss washes straight through my body.

I catch movement from the corner of my eye. Ivy's standing there. She's just heard all that.

"Yeah. Whatever it takes. She comes first. I understand. And gotta say, bro, I hope she finds a way to get past it. We need you. You need us."

"Yeah. But I need her more," I say, staring at her. Her eyes are locked by mine. I don't want to release them.

"I know," Grey says, "Or I don't. But hope to soon be able to relate entirely."

"I hope you can, too," I say, still staring at Ivy showered and fresh and I don't know how to read the look on her face. "Without this part, the pain part."

"Sometimes you gotta feel the pain, maybe come close to losing it all in order to make sure you always appreciate it," he says.

I hold the phone.

"Later, Ty. Keep the faith. Love conquers all, so they say."

"Bye." I look at the screen and touch the red 'end'.

"You'd give them up?" she asks, voice hoarse.

"Yes," I say without hesitation.

"They're your family. Cat's your mom. You..." she swallows and secures the towel around her breasts as she stares at me with her wet hair dripping down her throat, landing on her breasts.

She smells so alluring. I want to plant myself inside her again.

This conversation is important though.

"I would like to consider moving to Arcana Falls, to moving in my parents' house and becoming a member of my pack. But, if you can't face them after what I did to you in their presence, I won't do that. I'll pay that penance and remain a lone wolf here and I'll do it gladly because no matter what, my first priority is you. I'll build this into a bigger, better house for you and our children. I'll do my best to earn your forgiveness over time." I moisten my lips.

She frowns and sucks on her lower lip.

And then she turns and goes into the bedroom and closes the door.

She doesn't slam it this time. That's something. Maybe.

I slump forward in the chair and rub my forehead with my fingertips.

I'll make her breakfast. She needs food.

I get up and put water on to make honey tea.

I look through the fridge and find the eggs and begin to make her some French toast. And bacon.

I get bits of the eggshell into the French toast liquid and it's tricky to fish them all out.

The bacon is burning by the time I do that and then when I put the bread in the pan, it first tears, then sticks, and the egg looks fried all around it in white clumps. It didn't look like this when Ivy made it for me.

It's shit. Just shit.

I lift the pan, wishing to throw it, but then I *do* throw it because *fuck* is it hot! Bacon liquid singes my wrist and I've smashed the window with the pan I've thrown.

Ivy's behind me. I smell her, I feel her. I tamp down my rage and spin.

Her eyes grow larger at the sight of my arm. She grabs my elbow and steers me to the sink. "Here."

She turns the tap on and pulls my wrist under the cool water.

I grind my teeth, hating the burn.

"What were you doing?" she asks.

"Trying to make breakfast for you," I snap through clenched teeth. The cool water is helping but it still hurts.

"I'll get something from the first aid kit your mom brought over. Hang on. Keep that under the running water."

She disappears into the bathroom and comes back with the red bag with the cross symbol on it. She turns the water off and puts a towel to my arm to dry it, then applies clear salve to my wrist and then she's wrapping it in a bandage that goes around and around me.

"There." She pats my hand. "Sit down. I'll make something."

I watch her clean up my mess from the chair, but jump up when I see her dealing with shards of glass on the counter from the window that's over the sink.

"Don't cut yourself!" I order.

"I won't. Sit your bum down," she bosses me right back.

I feel a smile tug at my lips, but I halt it. I watch her carefully clean up and then she opens a drawer and finds a very old roll of sticky tape and tapes up the small apple-sized hole in the window.

She then cleans up more of my mess and begins making a new batch of French toast. We're out of bacon. She slices some fruit and sets both plates at the table.

She brings over the two cups. One of honey tea for me. The other, coffee that she made for herself.

She's wearing a pink t-shirt and her tight black pants with her pink rubber thong shoes. Her hair is in a rope that starts at the top of the back of her head and has the length of her hair weaved in a funny pattern. Little bits of purple are showing through it and a tendril of purple hair has come lose over her temple. The long rope of hair is fastened with a black circle at the bottom. I like her hair like that. I smell that she's still in heat and want to hold that rope while I fuck her.

I'll do that after she eats her breakfast.

She lifts her fork to her mouth with the French toast.

"I'm sorry I burnt breakfast," I say.

Her eyes meet mine and then she turns away.

"I'm sorry you're so angry with me. I'm sorry for making you angry."

"I'm not angry, Ty. I'm crushed. There's a big difference."

I swallow down a lump. "If you're so hurt that you punish me forever, I'll deserve it. But I'll be here. Trying to be better. Trying for you."

She pulls her lips tight and looks at me with tears in her eyes.

She swallows and it looks like she does so with difficulty.

I drop to the floor and kiss the top of her foot and then put my forehead to it. "I love you," I tell her.

She doesn't move.

"I'm sorry, Ivy. Please forgive me."

I eventually look up at her beautiful face because she's said nothing in reply.

"You should eat," she says, finally. "It's gonna get cold."

I get up and sit down across from her. Her French toast looks perfect. She's sliced bananas and strawberries for my plate. She knows I love them both and the sweet gesture makes my chest feel funny.

I stare at the plate. I'm selfish. I'm a fucking jerk, like she called me who has only thought about myself, my wants. What about what she wants? I've hurt her that badly and said sorry and forgive me at the same time as threatening to do it to her again.

She doesn't deserve that. She deserves better than me.

Should I let her go and just go back into the woods and stay wolf so that eventually, she can move on with her life? Eventually, maybe I'll forget. And if I don't, maybe I'll deserve the pain I feel every minute without her.

If I've really broken her, I shouldn't force her to be with me. Shouldn't force her to look into the face of the man that hurt her day after day.

I look in her eyes.

She looks in mine.

She looks deep into mine and the hurt from her eyes seeps into me. They're dull now. They've lost the vibrant lavender color. Is it because she hates me?

"Do you want me to go away?" I ask. "I said I wouldn't. I said I couldn't. But I hate that I hurt you so much."

Her hurt expression is now fear.

I don't want her to be afraid.

"What would you do?" she asks in a small voice.

"Go back into the woods as a wolf. Stay that way." I look down at my beautiful breakfast.

The silence is loud. Very loud.

I loathe it.

I look up at her face, despite the fear of what I'll see. That I'll see that she wants me gone from her life. I see tears streaming down her cheeks. Fuck, I've caused so many tears for her.

I get up.

I'm done making her cry.

"I love you," I say. "Again, I'm so sorry." I turn from her, which is the hardest thing I've ever had to do, and I head for the door.

I get to the porch and I throw my shirt off. I drop my pants. And I shift.

As soon as my paws hit the ground, I hear the door swing open.

"Wait!" she cries out. "Wait!"

I turn and stare at her.

She walks up to me and approaches slowly, carefully holding her hand out.

I stand tall and watch as she crouches and then she throws her arms around my neck and hugs me, hugs my wolf, burying her face into my fur.

My heart soars and I shift back to man and wrap my arms around her, too.

I stand, lifting her. She wraps her legs around my waist and I take her back inside.

I take her to the bed and lay down and hold her, burying my face into her neck, inhaling the scent of my Ivy. She's mine.

All mine.

She forgives me? Does she?

"Why did you stop me?"

"Don't go," she whispers and then her lips find mine. "Please don't go."

"I won't. Never." I kiss her with everything I have.

"I love you," I say.

She nods. "I love you, Tyson."

My wolf wants to leap into the air, feels like it can leap over the sun.

"I've never said that to any guy before, Ty," she tells me.

"Good," I say, breathing her in. "I love that."

I turn her to her back and caress her face. "I can't promise I won't ever fuck up again. I wish I could make that promise. I don't know social rules very well. I don't have control over that monster in me. But I'll do my very best to always put you first. To try to teach it to put you first. But, if I screw up again..."

"Shh. Make love to me." She pulls my head forward to kiss me.

"Because you forgive me or because you're in heat?"

"Because... fuck me," she orders.

I smile.

"Okay, little boss," I whisper, and I peel her pants down to her ankles and then throw her ankles over my shoulders. The pants are still attached to her and serve as an excellent handle. I find my way inside her. She feels like heaven. She feels like mine.

I'M DRIFTING OFF TO sleep, playing with the rope of hair at the back of her head. Her sweet voice rouses me.

"Ty?"

"Yes?"

"Everything in me is telling me it's you. For me. I've always had a bad habit of ignoring my instincts. I'm not gonna do that this time. That's why I stopped you from going."

I squeeze her. "Good."

53

IVY

I wake up and have the oddest, queasiest sensation. I think I'm going to puke.

Please don't tell me I'm pregnant.

Please don't tell me that his super alpha sperm made me drop an egg despite my birth control pills.

Oh God. Will our babies be puppies? Will they be born as people or wolves? I feel so hot and gross.

I roll off Ty and stagger toward the bathroom. I grip the doorframe for support and hear him call my name.

"I feel so sick," I tell him, but then abruptly ralph all over the floor by the doorway. And then my legs give out.

Tyson catches me.

54

TYSON

"Her skin is burning hot. Burning. I don't know why? She threw up. She's very sick. What do I do?"

"Bring her here, Tyson. Get her here as fast as you can to my clinic."

I wrap her in the quilt from my bed, though I don't know if that's a good idea, because she's so hot yet she told me she was cold, so I did what I could only think to do. Wrap her in a blanket. I drive like a maniac with her slumped against me, skin hot, face pale.

I don't know what the fuck is wrong with her.

She forgave me and then got sick.

Why?

Why?

THE CLINIC IS CRAWLING with people who are here to lend support, but I don't need that. I just want to know Ivy is going to be fine.

I yelled at my mother and I felt bad. She couldn't make Ivy's temperature go down. I didn't mean to yell, but I'm terrified that she's going to die. I know by Catrina Savage's face that Ivy's temperature should not be so high.

Riley, Grey, Joel, Jase, and Linc have all been here, all of them putting their hand on my shoulder or my back, all of them looking deep into my eyes and showing me that they feel my pain.

They don't. Maybe Riley does. The rest of them don't.

They haven't feared loss like this. And I hope they never fucking do.

Cat has put her body on ice, given her many medications to take the fever down, wiped her body down with another liquid, and set up a needle with fluids for Ivy since she threw up three more times since we got here.

IT'S LATER. I'M AWARE suddenly that it's only me, my mother, and Ivy here. I sit up and rub my eyes.

"Her fever is down a bit, Tyson," my mother says. "I've sent everyone home. We'll just keep an eye. If it spikes again, we'll have her airlifted to a city hospital."

"No!"

"Yes. If we can't control it, they'll have more tools at their disposal."

"Fuck."

She reads the machine she's pointed at Ivy's forehead. "Her temperature is down a bit, so it's possible it's getting better. I've sent her bloodwork with a rush."

"Is it my child that's hurting her? Did I get her preg –"

"She's in heat so it's possible that she is, too soon to tell, but I don't think it's that causing the fever. I don't think it's that at all, sweetie. She's meant to be yours; fate wouldn't be that cruel." She wraps an arm around my shoulder.

"Wouldn't it?" I ask.

She flinches.

We both know how fate has treated us thus far.

My forehead drops to Ivy's bed. Cat rubs my back rhythmically and it's soothing.

What is it, though?

I smell Mason Quinn.

I smell someone else. Ivy's sister.

They burst into the room.

My eyes meet hers.

Fuck, she looks like my Ivy. Dark hair but similar eyes. Similar face. Rounder face. Curvier. A little taller. I give my head a shake at the uncanny resemblance.

She runs to the bedside. "What's wrong with her? What the fuck did you do?" She glares at me and then the little vixen slaps me across the cheek.

Mason hooks an arm around her waist and hauls her back.

He says soft words into her ear and purrs for her and her eyes change before they drift closed. Her posture relaxes.

He kisses her throat. He's marked her there.

She jerks in reaction at that and lets out a whimper.

He spins her so that she's got her face buried in his throat. He holds her and caresses the back of her head.

His eyes move to mine and we lock gazes.

"Is Ivy okay?" He asks me.

I swallow.

My mother speaks before I get the chance. "Her fever is finally coming down a little. We're hopeful. If it spikes again, we'll have to evac her to St. Jude. Amelia? I'm Catrina Savage. Can I ask you some questions about Ivy's medical history?"

Amelia pulls away from Mason, moves to her sister, then leans over and kisses her head.

"Her face is so pale. She's so hot. What is it? I'm a nurse, so talk to me." Amelia looks at the bag that feeds medicine into Ivy's arm and then lifts the temperature-taking tool and points it at Ivy's head before reading the screen.

"It came on suddenly," Cat says. "She's weak, high fever, and vomiting, unable to keep even water down. I'm rotating ibuprofen and acetaminophen to try to tackle the fever. Tell me about any allergies, major illnesses. She was here when she got bit by a snake and said there was nothing, but are you aware of anything she might have forgotten to mention? Any allergic reactions, anything like that?"

"No, nothing I can think of. I'll call my mother and ask her. Do you have a phone I can use? Somebody took mine. She shoots an angry glare at Mason who is looking at Ivy.

I don't feel threatened by his eyes on her.

I look at Amelia Brennan. Now, Quinn, I guess. I know who my mate is so I feel nothing for her, but by her scent I can guess that perhaps I'd have been confused by it if I smelled it first, before mating.

"Man, I gotta say," Mason has moved in closer, "I don't blame you. I woulda done the same." He holds his hand out for me to shake. "I know that now. I'd have done the exact same."

I take his hand. I feel the same connection that I feel when shaking hands with Riley, Grey, Jason, Joel, Lincoln.

I get it. I get why they protected him, why they wanted to stop me from doing something I wouldn't be able to undo.

"Though, I mean, I couldn't do that cool half-shift thing, but other than that... yeah, I get it. I'm sorry for the trouble it caused, though, Tyson."

"Thank you for that. I get it. I don't feel anything for your woman, but that's probably because I already found mine. I can see, can guess how confusing it must have been."

"It's all instinct," Mason says. "All of it. Your reaction. Mine. I'm glad it makes sense now. Can't tell you how crazy it was drivin' me. Weird though, I've known couples with siblings. Your mother and father, their siblings were mated and there was nothing like this."

"Atticus is beta," my mother says. "Not alpha. And there wasn't witchcraft at play... that we know of. But we had that whole other issue with Cornelius. Sometimes shifter relationships are... complex."

"Point taken," Mason says.

"Things good with you and her?" I ask.

Amelia is pacing the waiting room with her hand on her neck, talking on the phone.

She stops in her tracks, pulling her hand away from her neck and I watch him as he watches her and a slow smile spreads across his face.

Her shoulders tremble and she says something else into the phone before her eyes meet his, narrow, and then she sticks her tongue out at him before pulling it back in and spinning to turn her back to him.

His shoulders shake with laughter.

"She's in denial about it, but it's better than good. Man, it's everything."

Three Hours Later

I'M ON THE COT WITH Ivy, my arms around her, my body temperature as high as I can get it because she's trembling. Hard. She's got a severe case of the chills and this is good because her temperature is down to normal but it's also bad because she's in a lot of discomfort.

Her teeth chatter. Her body trembles. Cat keeps rotating blankets through a dryer and piling them on us as I hold Ivy close under the quilt and three other blankets. Cat told me that this quilt I brought from my bed is the one that my grandmother made when I was a baby. Not only did Cornelius take me, but he took me in it.

"I never thought I'd see it again," she said.

"I've never used it until Ivy," I admitted. "I pulled it from the back of the cabinet and draped it over her when I mated her the first night. I'd never used it. Don't even remember it around over the years."

She smiled. "I'm glad it's still around. Grandma Carolyn will be happy if we show it to her. Though, it'll remind her of the sons she lost. She lost them both, your dad and Cornelius. It's been a source of deep pain for her."

I squeeze my mother's hand.

Her face brightens. "I look forward to making one for your first child."

I hear the door and catch the aroma of someone else in Ivy's family.

Ivy's mother. I know it as soon as I see her. Blonde hair, blue eyes. My mother's age or a bit younger. Panic in her eyes as she rushes to Amelia in the waiting room and embraces her. Riley and Linc are behind her. They've obviously escorted her to the clinic from the four corners of the village.

Her eyes meet mine as she hurries into the room I'm in. "What's happening?"

I brace, thinking I'm about to get trouble from her, too, but her eyes are simply filled with concern.

"I'm trying to raise her body temperature. She's got severe chills."

My mother speaks up. "I'm Catrina Savage, this is Tyson. Ivy's temperature is back to normal but her fever medication will wear off soon so that'll be telling."

"I'm Kathleen Brennan. What can I do?"

"All we can do is wait."

"Shouldn't we get her to a hospital?"

"If her fever spikes within the next hour, yes. If not, we keep watching closely. Her temperature has been normal for two hours." A phone rings. "Excuse me," my mother says as she leaves the room with the phone to her ear.

"I think we should get her to a hospital right now," Ivy's sister says.

"Let's give it a bit and see," Kathleen suggests.

"Even though her temperature is down, we don't know why it spiked. We don't know why this is happening. We need a hospital, you people!"

"Ames?" Ivy calls. "Ames?" Her teeth chatter and she burrows closer to me. I stroke her hair.

"Ivy, oh god. Hi Ivy. How do you feel? Amelia asks.

"You're being dramatic," Ivy says and then she shivers.

Her eyes flutter open. "Hi," she says, looking up at me, her chin planted in the center of my chest.

"Hi," I repeat, hoarsely. "Are you feeling okay?"

Her teeth chatter again, and she burrows some more.

"Amelia, are you here or am I hallucinating?" she asks.

"I'm here. Mom's here, too."

"Mom?" Ivy calls out.

"I'm here, baby girl." Kathleen leans over her daughter and kisses the apple of her cheek.

"Amie, did... did... you get claimed by a werewolf too?" Ivy asks.

Mason straightens up in the chair he's sitting in over in the waiting room. My eyes meet his and his brow quirks up as he listens.

"Looks like it," Amelia grumbles.

"Has he done that knot thing?" Ivy's teeth chatter. "Did he make a neck clit on you?" She laughs and trembles some more.

"She's delirious," Kathleen remarks. "Ivy?"

"Yeah, Ives, he did," Amelia says as if she's admitting something terrible. Mason smirks.

"A neck clit?" Kathleen whispers.

I can't help it; I smirk too.

Ivy giggles and burrows into me some more.

I catch Amelia smirk, but she tries to hide it.

Her eyes meet mine and I feel the barest twitch of my mouth and as Amelia tries to look away, I can't help the chuckle that escapes my lips.

My mother bursts into the room.

"Ivy, are you still taking that birth control pill every day? It just dawned on me while I was on the phone with the doctor in Scotland."

Ivy lifts her chin up and nods. "Yeah."

My mother breathes out a sigh. "And we have our culprit. I think. When did you last take it?"

"What's this?" I ask.

My mother lifts an index finger and continues talking to Ivy.

"Ivy?" she prompts.

"When I wake up every morning. What time is it?"

"It's almost seven in the morning. We'll see what happens over the next few hours. Let's take your temperature."

I'm confused.

I know my mother reads this from my eyes as she points her device at Ivy's forehead.

"Still up a little," she says, "but definitely better. How are your chills, Ivy?"

"I'm still c-cold."

I realize I've stopped focusing on giving her warmth, so I raise my body temperature again for her and wrap my arms tighter around her. I stare at my mother.

"Let's let Ivy rest for a bit, everyone. I think it's safe to be optimistic here that we've found the culprit. We'll wait a few hours. Once she's about thirty-six hours from her last pill, I'll do more bloodwork and send the results to my contact. Her hormone levels are totally out of whack here. You should all get some rest."

"I'm not leaving," Amelia announces. "Not until then."

Mason's jaw tenses and he folds his arms across his chest and tries to get more comfortable on the couch in the waiting room.

"I could use a couple hours," Kathleen says. "I feel like Ivy's in great hands."

"Mom?" Amelia says with a gasp.

"Aunt Nelle went to a lot of trouble to put all this together, apparently, and something tells me it's all gonna be okay," Kathleen tells her daughter.

"I have a guest room. Come on up and you can get some rest," my mother tells Ivy's mother. "Amelia?"

"Yeah, I'll go lay down with Mom," she says and follows.

Mason rolls his eyes. "Crash on your couch, Cat?"

"Absolutely, honey."

"Nice to meet you, Tyson," Kathleen says. "And you, Mason." She leans over and kisses Ivy's forehead.

"Love you, Mom," Ivy whispers.

"Love you, Ivy."

Kathleen moves over to Amelia and kisses her forehead, too.

Amelia doesn't look settled. Or pleased. She looks like she's still concerned about her sister. And she's not happy about this situation.

Mason puts his arm around her. She pushes his arm off.

"Mason, can you show them upstairs? I'll be right there."

My mother looks at me.

"What is this pill she's been taking?" I fucking knew pills were bad. Knew it.

"It's something a lot of mainstream women take to prevent getting pregnant. It's hormones that prevent heat, in essence. But you're an extremely alpha male and you've mated her and triggered a hormone surge in her, plus the moon is definitely pushing a super-heat cycle for all the fertile and mated females. And the pill seems to have counteracted with what's become a massive cocktail of hormones to make her ill. That's what I think, anyway. We'll know for sure by this afternoon if everything levels out if this was the culprit. It's a safe bet that it was. Rest. We'll see where we're at in a few hours. If her body gets hot again, call me." Cat puts a phone beside me. "Hit this button." She points to one that says "intercom".

I grunt in reply and she leaves.

"Fucking pills," I growl.

Ivy looks up at me.

"Why are you taking those stupid things?"

She blinks. "I've been taking them since I was eighteen. I…"

"They hurt you!"

"Um, they've never hurt me before, whatever affect you had on me hurt me because of them. They've never been a problem before."

A growl comes from me. "You're mated. You don't try to stop nature from taking its course."

She rolls her eyes. "Neither of us knew, obviously, and if I'm now allergic to birth control pills, you'll just have to use a condom. I have to turn over. My shoulder is falling asleep." She turns her back to me and then shivers some more.

"I will not fucking use a condom," I tell her. "I had women thrust them at me when I fucked them before, and there's no way a condom is being put on my cock with you. Never."

I'm falling off the small cot onto the floor. I land with a grunt.

She pushed me.

I blink rapidly in shock.

"Did you just push me out of bed?"

"Did you just talk about fucking some other woman?"

I stare a beat and then I bark out a laugh.

She's not smiling with her mouth or her eyes.

"Looks like I'm not the only one in this marriage with a jealous streak." I climb back in and wrap my arms around her and bury my nose in her neck. I laugh. She's still stiff.

"Sorry, baby," I tell her. "No more talk of fucking anybody. Except you."

She's still stiff.

I purr for her.

She shivers and kisses my forearm. "Okay."

"No more pills," I tell her.

"Obviously," she whispers.

"I want babies," I tell her.

"So do I," she whispers.

I chuckle. And then I drift off to sleep feeling complete. I have a pack with six brothers, family; I have Ivy. She has my family and her mother and sister are being brought into the fold. And very soon, we'll have a bigger family, because I intend on getting her pregnant as soon as possible.

55

IVY

So, birth control pills and heat cycles when you're mated to a super shifter do not blend. Good to know.

Cat didn't know this, feels terrible about it because she told me she meant to talk to me about my birth control after the snake bite, not because she thought it'd be dangerous, because she thought Tyson would lose his mind when he found out. Alpha shifters apparently don't take well to their 'mates' attempting to block their heat cycles.

Apparently, there are drugs that will do it and they're not looked upon favorably by alphas, particularly super alphas who have a lot more male hormones than the average male.

She wanted to talk to me about it but got caught up in everything.

And now, she's gaining information from contacts at the university in Scotland to help ensure there are no surprises with pregnancies for either me or my sister, since we're not shifters. Apparently there have been no human / council alpha matings for two generations in this pack so she wants to get up to speed on things to avoid unhappy surprises.

I'm anxious to get some alone time with Amelia. Not only to find out what she thinks, but to try to give her reassurance, too. I know this stuff is crazy, that it's wild and wacky that this stuff exists. And if Mason is anything like Tyson, she's in for a rude alpha awakening. And my sister is an alpha female, if that's really such a thing in the non-shifter world, so I'm sure my new potential brother-in-law will have his hands full.

Once the 36-hour mark passed and we knew I was out of the woods, knew that the birth control pill was definitely the culprit, Mason whisked her away back to his lake house. Against her wishes. Literally. She stomped her feet and demanded he fuck off and he carried her out of there over his shoulder.

My mom missed that, thankfully, and when she emerged shortly after that from taking her shower upstairs at Cat's, Cat simply said, "Mason and Amelia had to go. I'm sure she'll call you later."

Mom seemed fine.

Weirdly.

And then she kissed me goodbye, told me she was going home and putting her house up for sale. She was moving to Drowsy Hollow to be closer to us.

"There's an apartment for rent above the dry cleaners in that town. I passed it on my way here and I'm going to call about seeing it on my way home."

"What are we going to tell Leo and Dad?"

"We'll tell your brother you moved. You fell in love. So did Amie. I'm moving to be closer to you girls. He's busy anyway, at school. When he's finished, he can either move to Drowsy Hollow with me. Or not. It's time for me to live my life, too. I've spent too many years in your father's shadow. It's my time in the sun, I think." She smiles brightly. "I don't know what Nelle has in store for me, but she told me in her letter that my *happy* was coming. I'm feeling like this is all good, all right."

I hug her tight. "Talk later, then."

"He's very handsome. And he is very very smitten with you."

"I know. It's wild, isn't it? Crazy stuff."

She nods. "Crazy is right. And wonderful. And magical." She winks.

"Drive safe. Text me when you get home."

"I will."

Tyson walks in and she hugs him, startling him.

"Welcome to the family," she says.

"Welcome to mine, too," he replies and kisses the top of her head.

Mom looks at me with a big smile and approval on her face and then she waves.

Tyson gets to me and puts his lips to my forehead. "No fever?"

"I feel better," I tell him. "Let's go home."

"I'm going to order us a better bed. And better furniture."

"The bed seems pretty good at the house in Arcana Falls," I say.

His eyes flash with surprise.

"Let's make that our home."

"Are you sure?" he asks.

I nod. "I think so. It's what you want, isn't it?"

He lets out a big breath and then he pulls me to him. "You being happy is what I want most. But that you'd give that to me, despite everything? I don't deserve you."

"And don't you forget it," I joke.

He looks into my eyes and the glowing heat, the love there, they knock my socks off.

"I won't. I swear I won't."

I cup his jaw and kiss him.

"Let's have a wedding," he says. "You can wear the bride panties I saw at home."

Is he actually asking me something instead of telling me?

I jerk in surprise. "Are you asking me to marry you?"

"I already married you. I'm asking you to marry me back."

"Yes," I say. "I will."

He smiles big and kisses me.

56

TYSON

Something isn't right; I feel it in the air. I don't know what it is, so I'm walking around the house, checking out windows, pacing. I've been doing it an hour.

At first I thought it was just that it's our first night in this house together, but it's more. I just can't pinpoint it.

Ivy's asleep upstairs. We picked up our clothes and our food and moved into the Arcana Falls house this afternoon.

I also fucked her twice. At her request. I wanted to let her rest because of the ordeal she's just been through, but evidently, she's either still in heat or can't resist me. Either way, it was nice. It felt right being in that bedroom with her.

There's a knock on the door and the tension in me surges. I yank it open.

Mason and Grey are standing there. And I know, immediately, that something isn't right. I open the door wide and am asking "What happened?" as they cross the threshold.

They met with the coven tonight.

"They found the records," Grey says. "Sure enough, Nelle Jenkins paid a bucket load of money to have her two nieces matched up with two alphas from our council."

Mason's eyes and my eyes meet.

It matters to neither of us that witches are the reason Ivy is mine and Amelia is his. I know we're on the same page here.

"And?" I ask.

Grey takes in a big breath. "And they think that things went screwy because it usually follows birth order, but suggested if you were more suited to Ivy and Mason was more suited to Amelia, nature could take precedence over witchcraft. They say sometimes spells have flaws and things go awry. Or spells are perfect and nature simply intervenes. They think that's why Mason got confused. If you'd come across Amelia first, it might've gone the same way."

"Hm," I say.

Ivy is definitely suited to me.

Mason's eyebrows rise and I know he agrees.

"And Nelle Jenkins paid to have something interfere in the marriage of their parents. Basically, a chain of events that we're in the midst of now for the Brennan girls. They say they can only reveal what they must, they won't tell us any more than we need to know, so that's all fine. It's all good. Right?"

I shrug. "I'm good. You good, Mason?"

"More than good," he says. "That's not the problem."

"What is the problem?" I ask.

"The coven," Mason says. "And Riley. Riley caught scent there. Scent that drove him nuts. He went mental. Worse than I went when your woman's scent hit the village."

"What? Why?"

"He swears he smelled his mate. The two witches there, one old one, one younger one, they started asking him questions. They searched their ledgers and found his name."

"Riley's?"

"Yep," Grey says. "Riley's name. His mate... get this: she's not dead. She's is a witch. A witch who cast herself into the role of Riley's mate through a spell she wrote and then she faked her own death."

My eyes bulge.

"He's on a tear. He's unglued, Ty. We're glad you're here, glad you're with us, because we're gonna need you. Riley's gonna need us. All of us."

Epilogue

IVY

Two Weeks Later

We swim, Ty and me, underneath the waterfall, and he catches me by the waist as we look up at the cave we're now in. It's beautiful. The rocks are sparkly. Green. Like his eyes.

"Oh my goodness," I exclaim. "Beautiful isn't a strong enough word."

"I agree." But he's looking at me, not the cave we're in.

He's so fucking sweet.

He lifts me by my hips up onto the ledge. And then he pulls himself up beside me. I wring my hair out and then lean over and wring his out.

"Why do you squeeze water from my hair?" he asks.

"So you won't shake like a puppy at me."

He smiles and then kisses my nose.

"I can't believe this is right outside our back door. This is amazing, Ty."

He gazes into my eyes. "Tomorrow, we'll stand on those banks on the other side of the waterfall and get married."

"We will," I say and lean over and kiss him. "Can't wait."

"And then I want to swim in here in our wedding clothes and fuck you while they all have their party."

I laugh. "That sounds like a typical Tyson thing to say."

He smiles wide.

It's been fun planning the wedding. It's been a plan thrown together fast, but I know it'll be perfect. It'll be on the banks, like he said, and we're having a big party in our backyard. The ladies are doing potluck and Stan, Ty's mom's beau, is going to officiate. He and Ty get along quite well, actually.

I bought Ty a ring. He can wear it when he knows he doesn't have to shift. He told me he bought me one, too, and I can't wait to see it.

"Are you scared about seeing the whole pack at once again for the first time since..."

I shake my head. "No. I've seen a few people. None of them made me feel weird. I mean, I can't say I didn't feel a little weird, but not because of them, because of me. I'm working on it."

"I'm a lucky man," he whispers against my temple and drops a kiss there.

No way would I deny him his pack. That he was willing to give that up to give me what I need even though he has the brawn to force me to live with him, to face them whether I want to or not, it means a lot to me. It means everything to me that he was so sorry, so sincere in his remorse. I feel like a very lucky girl.

I just wish Aunt Nelle could be here tomorrow.

But maybe she, wherever she is, will be here in spirit.

"I guess I'm not going back to work at the boutique," I say.

I told Tamara that I was moving out. She was shocked that I'd moved in with a guy so fast. We've been friends since high school. But I can't exactly tell her everything. I'll figure out what I can tell her later. Her boyfriend is really touchy-feely with me and it's gonna be a while of prepping Ty before I can introduce them. She's going to ask him to move in with her, so she's okay about me leaving, as long as I promise to see her once a month for girls' night out.

I feel bad that I can't invite Dad or Leo to the wedding. Leo won't care much. He's twenty years old and busy with school out of town. Dad isn't our favorite person right now with all the crap he's put Mom through. He's in for a rude awakening when she leaves town. She's already sold the house. It sold after just two days on the market. She's filed for a divorce, too.

"Why don't you open a dance school? There are dozens of little girls in our pack who might like to be ballerinas," Ty suggests.

My eyes light up.

Whoa.

"That's an idea," I say.

Wow. I never thought my dream of having a dance studio would turn into anything. My mind is racing with the possibilities.

"Lots of time to figure all that out," he says and kisses my hand.

I haven't seen my sister, but I have talked to her on the phone twice. Once, when she called after I found out she took off from Mason and he brought her back. He made her phone me to tell me she was okay. She was so grumpy about it. I tried to reassure her that I'm happy, that she can be happy. She burst into tears on the phone and he took the phone off her.

"Are you being good to her?" I demanded.

"I am, Ivy," Mason said, sounding exhausted.

"I know Amelia is exhausting, Mason, and you've got your work cut out for you but once she falls for you, I bet you any money you'll be the happiest guy around."

Ty chuckled at that. "Second happiest," he corrected. "Say bye to Mason."

I smiled big. "Purr for her, Mason. Bye Mason!" I ended the call.

The second time, I called to check in and after we talked about all the wedding stuff, all she did was complain about Mason being bossy. It's kind of funny because she's the bossiest person around. I would love to be a fly on the wall. I tell her that and she complains that he ends arguments with orgasms. But the way she complains, I could swear she's not really against it.

And she will be here for me tomorrow. As my maid of honor.

I can't believe I'm getting "mainstream" married, as the pack calls it, before my bridezilla sister.

I don't know what happened or how it happened (but am looking forward to the gossip), but her engagement to Rick was broken. He obviously knows she won't be at the church tomorrow.

Yes. Tomorrow. I'm marrying Tyson on Amelia's planned wedding day. She worked with Mom to have all the flowers, church décor (tulle, ribbons, twinkle lights), and party favors sent here. Mom made the arrangements with Joel and Jase who drove a truck filled with the stuff here yesterday. Tonight, me, Bailey, Cat, Mom, and Amelia will go through it together.

Riley is not doing so well. Apparently he's off the rails with rage and is trying to hunt down his wayward mate. He can't seem to catch her scent. He thinks she's done something to disguise it. And he's hunting her down the non-shifter way. With the help of a private eye shifter.

The pack's minds are all blown over the whole thing.

I have no idea what'll happen when he finds her.

"YOUR MOM SAID YOU WERE most likely conceived here. Right here, likely," I smooth my hand over the rock.

It's gorgeous in here. Everything sparkles. There's light but privacy, and the wall of trickling water in front of us just adds to the appeal of the cavernous space.

"Mm hm," he says, his hand landing on mine. "Care to see if lightning strikes again? If we can make the next generation's super alpha right here on this rock?"

I bite my lip.

His lips meet mine. He lays me back and unties the side of my string bikini bottoms. His hips meet mine. Our hearts beat together against each other's bodies, and then he unties the tie behind my neck and my halter bikini top falls as he fills me. As he knots me. Our eyes are connected, then our lips, and I know for sure that so are our hearts.

Lots of people don't mate for life. But, I have. Lots of people are born skeptics. I'm no longer one of those. A butterfly floats above us and I smile. It's blue and purple.

Aunt Nelle had a big gawdy but awesome necklace with a turquoise and purple butterfly that looked just like it. Just exactly like it.

My heart leaps. Wow. Aunt Nelle.

I feel like the luckiest girl in the world as Tyson spills inside me and the butterfly hovers there for a moment, then flits through the wall of water.

I mouth, "Thank you, Aunt Nelle."

The End

(For now... YES... I have plans for books for Mason and for Riley. Maybe all of them. We shall see.

Join my reader group on Facebook[1] and subscribe to my free newsletter[2] to stay in touch! Following me on Amazon and BookBub[3] are another way to get notified of new releases.)

---

1. http://facebook.com/groups/ddprincefangroup

2. https://ddprince.com/newsletter-signup/

3. https://www.bookbub.com/authors/dd-prince

Playlist
Come to Me, Goo Goo Dolls
Forever Loving You, Tesla
Blinding Lights, The Weeknd
Break My Heart, Dua Lipa
A Million Reasons, Lady Gaga

Author notes:

Hope you enjoyed the DD Prince take on shifters. I have to say, I knew I'd eventually write a shifter romance. After all, shifters brought me back to reading back in 2011 (I think) when I bought my first iPhone, a 3GS and the first app I downloaded was iBooks. I looked for free books and a high ranking one was The Mating by Nicky Charles.

I didn't know at first what this was. One minute they sound like people, the next minute, they're...what? Dogs? I wasn't sure. It took me a minute to figure out that this was a shapeshifting series but once I did, I was enthralled. I read it, then the next two in that Law of the Lycans series and this was the kindling that re-ignited my reading addiction as well as began my education on the fact that authors existed without publishing contracts. Incidentally, that series is now a lot more than 3 books and I should go back and read the rest!

The next series I got really hooked on was The Submission Series by CD Reiss (Johnathan Drazen, UNFFFFF) and then, not long later, I read Fifty Shades of Grey. As soon as I finished FSOG, I immediately re-read it.

At this time, I was a fulltime 60-80 hour a week freelance writer with a toddler and grade schooler writing for clients around my kids' schedule. I was trading time for dollars and it was back-breaking and soul-sucking work at times. A few years later, I decided to take the plunge and see about finally writing some fiction. I figured I'd try it and see if it went anywhere. After all, that was my original dream job -—being a writer and being able to work from anywhere. I'd tried my hand at fiction many times in my teens and twenties but never got all that far.

That began The Nectar Trilogy, the idea came to me while in the tub, and my longtime readers know that I put that aside at 75% of book one and wrote and actually released The Dominator before going back and working more on The Nectar Trilogy.

Anyway, I digress... bottom line:

I knew I'd want to write a shifter story someday. I just hadn't had stories in that genre any hit me until sometime in 2017.

When Ty and Ivy first came to me, I thought it was going to be a bit of a Tarzan and Jane type story.

It took on a life of its own.

And now we've got a bunch of other characters that want their stories told.

I thought Riley's book might come second, after having met him when I wrote The Hollow Duet #2, Holden. That series is where I first met Erica Young and her sisters. And let me tell you, I didn't know if I'd write a witch story for Erica with a werewolf to kick off a witch series or add her story to my werewolf series so it looks like that story will come as book three of my shifter series and also may be the beginning of a witch series (but we'll see. I don't know yet for sure.)

But, based on how things crept up with Amelia Brennan which totally surprised me, you'll have to get Mason and Amelia's story before Riley's because of the whole birth order thing in the Arcana Falls shifter pack.

Yep: The only reason Riley jumped the birth order line was because of a little redheaded witch. Tee hee. I can't wait to see what sorts of sparks fly when Riley catches up with her. Ooh eee! I have a feeling some punishment knotting is in order...

When? When? When?

No idea when more shifter books will come because I have other stories and series on the go and I shall listen to my muse. <wink> as it knows best.

If you loved this story, I hope you'll leave a review. Even a short one.

As always, thanks to my ARC and beta readers, my street team and my amazing street team captain, Robin, for all you do to support my efforts. And for your friendship. My street team is a freaking dream team!

Huge thanks to my beta readers, too, with an extra big shoutout to Maria Williams-Howard who AGAIN rocked my world by getting back to me about 12 hours after getting her copy to tell me she loved this story. This isn't the first time you've done this and I appreciate it just as much as I did with Alessandro. Big hugs.

Lainey – your help was invaluable! Many thanks for the fresh perspective.

As always, thanks to Peggy for her eagle-eyes.

Thanks to ALL of you who read this early and put my mind at ease by telling me you loved it.

DD's Chickadees: I love you guys! Thank you for all that you do to fuel me. Thanks, too, for tolerating my kink – teasing you relentlessly about what's to come.

And again to my sister Kelly -—your support, your ideas, your willingness for shenanigans -—mean the world to me.

So, ... yes, I have plans for more shifter books. Mason. Riley. Maybe even all of them. I kinda need to know what'll happen with Bailey Blackwood, too. (Psst...I've already got some pretty good ideas)

If you enjoyed this book, I recommend my Beautiful Biker Series, a biker romance series that's got laughs, feels, a bit of darkness, and smokin' hot alpha biker book boyfriends.

I've also got more paranormal romance, including my Nectar Trilogy (dark and taboo) as well as my Hollow Duet where you'll meet Erica Young (Hint: Riley's wayward mate) and gain a little bit of insight about her. Erica isn't one of the main characters, but she's important to the story, and there is a Riley spotting, though he isn't named, you'll know it's him, but it takes place a few months after the end of this timeline, so you'll see them together but of course you won't know how they got that way.

Note: The Hollow Duet has a darker feel than this book. Book one is an erotic thriller. Book 2 is an erotic horror.

My most popular series so far is my dark mafia series, The Dominator Series and that one has trigger warnings for some dark subject matter. It's an arranged marriage story with an antihero. Non/dub-con triggers.

For something light and fun, there's also my Hot Alpha Alien Husbands books with a Mars Needs Women trope (my aliens look like regular guys, but they're seven feet tall and have SERIOUS stamina). I've also got Alphahole, a smokin' hot enemies-to-lovers roommate romance with sexual tension up the wazoo.

I'm on social media and interact almost daily in my Facebook reader group. I'd love for you to join:

http://facebook.com/groups/ddprincefangroup

Fun, teasers, book chats, giveaways, the insider scoop, ARC/Beta reading opportunities, and most of all... shenanigans!

I've also got a free newsletter that goes out with new release info, sales, and freebies and I've got plans to cook up some exclusive content so I hope you'll join- http://ddprince.com/newsletter-signup/

DD Prince's Books:

This list might have been updated since publishing so check my website ddprince.com for the latest information.

Alphahole, an enemies-to-lovers contemporary and roommates romance. Yes. It's all those things. And more. Aiden Carmichael is absolutely infuriating. You're going to fucking love him.

MC Romance: Romantic suspense with comedy, angst, steamy scenes, and a little bit of gritty darkness.

This alpha-male is not an alpha-hole. You're going to FLOVE Deacon Valentine.

Detour (Beautiful Biker 1) Deacon & Ella

Joyride (Beautiful Biker 2) Rider & Jenna

Rider starts out as a little bit of an alpha-hole. Jenna resists, but resistance is futile when a Valentine brother has you in his sights.

Scenic Route (Beautiful Biker 3) Spencer & Pippa

Crossroads (Beautiful Biker 4) Fork & Jojo.

LOTS more biker books coming.

Dark Mafia Romance: dark romance with a debt flesh payment plot.

This one DD's most popular book, but it is dark. Non-consensual / rough sex. Tommy Ferrano is an anti-hero you may love to hate and hate to love.

The Dominator

The Dominator 2. **Truth or Dare**

Sex slave rescue romance with dark themes. Dario Ferrano's story.

The Dominator 3. **Unbound**

More Tommy, More Dare; More Domination!

Saved

Spin off Dark Romance (maybe DD's darkest romance book yet). Lex isn't the hero in this story. Holly is.

TNT – 4th Anniversary Novella – Timeline is book 1.5 but best experienced after book 3.

Dark Paranormal Romance: Vampire dark romance / kidnapping. Capture romance with dark and taboo elements.

Nectar Trilogy (Includes Nectar, Ambrosia, and Essence)

Dirty / fun / instalove alien romance

Hot Alpha Alien Husbands: Book 1 – Daxx and Jetta
Hot Alpha Alien Husbands: Book 2 – Zane and Tanya
The Hollow Duet: (Hollow and Holden)
A dark and erotic fairytale retelling. Erotic thriller/horror.

There's a quick list of all currently available books with universal links at http://ddprince.com/about-dd_prince/quick-info-buy-links-for-all-dd-prince-books/ .

Please note: book retailers and subscription program participation may change without notice.

www.ingramcontent.com/pod-product-compliance
Ingram Content Group UK Ltd.
Pitfield, Milton Keynes, MK11 3LW, UK
UKHW011339050825
7244UKWH00004B/39